# A QUESTION OF IDENTITY

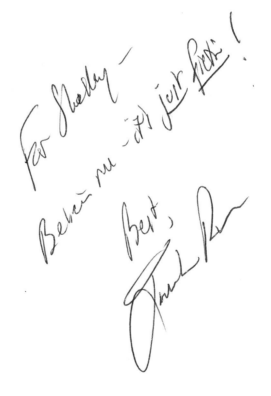

For Shelley —

Believe me — it's just fiction!

Best,

# A QUESTION

# OF IDENTITY

## JONATHAN ROWE

First Page Publications

First Page Publications
12103 Merriman Road
Livonia, MI 48150
Phone: 1-800-343-3034
Fax: 734-525-4420
www.firstpagepublications.com

Printed in the United States of America

Rowe, Jonathan, 1954–

Summary: A droll comedy about David Fisher, tabloid reporter, who uncovers the true identity of a fugitive radical from the Weather Underground activist group, and struggles with his own crisis of identity.

ISBN # 1-928623-74-3
I. Rowe, Jonathan. II. Title
Library of Congress Control Number: 2005907279

Cover design by Kimberly Franzen
Cover photo courtesy of Alissa Kendall

# READER ADVISORY

Some people go far in life. Others do not. I live a quarter mile from the house in Ann Arbor where I grew up. That tells you which kind of person I am.

Some people lead dangerous lives. Full of excitement and risk. Others just write about people like that. You can guess which kind I am.

Half the characters in *A Question of Identity* are criminals. Half are adulterers. They all lead dangerous lives. Full of excitement and risk. But it's *just fiction*. Hence the usual disclaimer applies: *Any resemblance between the characters and events in this book, and people or events in real life, is purely coincidental and unintentional.*

This disclaimer bears special emphasis here. Since the story is set in my hometown. Since the narrator talks a lot like me. And since his personal history resembles my own. So let me say it again. In plain English. This is *not* a self-portrait. So please. When you finish reading *A Question of Identity*, don't call my wife with condolences. Don't ask her how she can stand living with me. We get enough of those calls already.

The same applies to the other characters in *A Question of Identity*. If you think any character represents someone you know, *you're wrong*. All the characters here are fictional. To be sure, the characters in any novel are always *composites* of people the author has encountered. In life. And in reading. So if you see a *resemblance* between a character in this book and some real person you know, chalk it up to the normal artistic process. And understand. It's *just a coincidence*.

One last advisory. The narrator, a tabloid hack, often engages in illegal surveillance. Criminal trespass. Theft. And various other unsavory news-gathering practices. Far below normal journalistic standards. Again, this is just fiction. I'm not accusing the tabloids of such tactics. I'm sure they would never stoop so low.

**For Susan Kessler**
*and all the dreams that never die*

Let seed be grass, and grass turn into hay.
I'm martyr to a motion not my own.
What's freedom for? To know eternity.
I swear she cast a shadow white as stone.

But who would count eternity in days?
These old bones live to learn her wanton ways.
(I measure time by how a body sways.)

—Theodore Roethke,
*from* "I Knew A Woman"

# PROLOGUE
# DAYS OF RAGE

## Monday 27 October 1969

A warm, dry autumn evening in Ann Arbor, Michigan. 5:45 p.m. No more daylight savings this late in October. So dusk is gathering fast.

A beat-up blue van eases into a parking place on Monroe Street. The *perfect* parking place. Just thirty yards from the loading dock at the back of the University of Michigan Law School. With a tow-away zone in front. So no one can block the van from making a fast getaway.

Twenty witnesses see the van park. To the west are two law professors, gazing out their office windows. To the north are two law students, walking out the back door of the Law Library. To the east are four undergrads, smoking cigarettes on the Law Quad's lawn. And to the south, across the street, are twelve more witnesses: three in student houses, and another nine drinking beers on the front porch of an open-air campus café called Casa Dominick's.

All twenty witnesses see the van park. But none gives it a second look. The van seems as unremarkable as all the other details of the day. The fiery red ivy climbing the great gothic stones of the eight-story Law School. The background chatter of the crows high up in the eaves. The fall smell of dead leaves littering the Law Quad, mixing with the smell of pizza from Dominick's. The brilliant colors of the leaves on the trees—blazing ambers, burnt oranges, and flaming reds. The honking of horns from rush hour traffic on State Street. And the amplified voice at Dominick's, periodically announcing when a patron's pizza is ready.

The witnesses scarcely register any of these details. So of course they miss the one *important* detail, too. The mud. *Thick* mud, smeared across both the front and back license plates of the old van, rendering the letters and numbers on the license plates indecipherable. Mud which, on this dry October evening, cannot be an accident. Mud which an *attentive* observer—say, a policeman— would have seen as a sure sign that here, at the University of Michigan Law School, some kind of shit is about to go down.

The van with the muddy plates has solid blue side panels. Solid back doors, too. No windows, except the front windshield and the front side windows. Behind the front seat hangs a large paisley cloth, blocking anyone from looking into the back of the van.

The only visible occupant of the van is its driver. A young woman. Wearing a black motorcycle helmet, painted with a bright rainbow and a jagged red lightning bolt. The helmet's wide chin strap obscures most of her face. She exits the van. Empty-handed. Walks toward the Law School. Wearing hiking boots, blue jeans, a denim jacket—and that motorcycle helmet.

The two law students leaving the Law Library stop to gawk. For even half-concealed in her wide-strapped motorcycle helmet, the young woman is plainly very pretty. With long red hair flowing out from under that helmet. And an hourglass figure that even her jacket cannot conceal.

But she ignores her ogling fans. Does not break stride. Glances up at the Law School's leaded glass windows. Most are dark. But some spill yellow light out into the dusk. Including the third-floor office windows where Professor Pembroke Watkins can be seen, seated at his desk.

The red-haired woman walks thirty yards to the loading dock. Climbs seven concrete steps. Crosses the loading dock. Opens a gray metal door. And disappears into the Law School.

The beat-up blue van with the muddy license plates just sits there. Motionless. Silent.

Five minutes later, the gray metal door opens again. The red-haired woman emerges from the Law School. Still empty-handed. Still wearing her motorcycle helmet, with the rainbow and the lightning bolt. She crosses the loading dock. Descends the seven steps. Walks the thirty yards back to the van. Climbs in behind the steering wheel. And stares straight ahead. Helmet still on.

Thirty seconds later, the back doors of the van open. Two men step out into the gathering dusk. One tall and thin. The other short and stocky. Each wears a black motorcycle helmet, painted with a bright rainbow and a jagged red lightning bolt. Each wears a dark sweatshirt. And black gloves. Each carries a satchel.

The two men do not head for the loading dock. Instead they walk north up the sidewalk. But forty yards up the sidewalk, they stop—twenty yards short of the Law Library's back door. Directly beneath the third-floor windows where Professor Pembroke Watkins can be seen, seated at his desk.

The two men set their satchels down on the ground beside the sidewalk. Only the red-haired woman in the van sees what they are doing. The two law professors, who five minutes ago noticed the van, have since gone back to reading. The two law students, briefly besotted with the pretty redhead, have left the scene. The four undergrads, still smoking to the east, cannot see the satchels because of a three-foot-high stone retaining wall that runs along the east side of the library sidewalk. The twelve witnesses to the south—the nine beer drinkers on Dominick's front porch, and the three students in the adjacent houses—also cannot see the satchels because the parked cars and trees along Monroe Street block their view.

The two men move fast. Each pulls a brick from his satchel. Sets his brick down on the ground beside the stone wall. Each pulls four mason jars from his satchel. Sets the jars down on the ground beside the bricks. The jars, filled with gasoline, have rags stuffed in the top for wicks. Eight pre-prepared Molotov cocktails. Each man pulls a butane lighter from his satchel. Ready for radical action.

Busy with their tasks, the two radicals do not see Ann Arbor Police Patrolman Dale Hunter, age twenty-four. Alone. In uniform. In a squad car. Cruising slowly down Tappan Street. Less than eighty yards to the east. With no idea what kind of shit is about to go down.

The two radicals grab their bricks. And heave them up at the third-floor office windows where Professor Pembroke Watkins sits at his desk.

The bricks find their targets. Glass shatters. Professor Watkins yells.

Patrolman Hunter, less than half a block away, hits his siren. It emits a huge whoop.

The crows perched up in the Law School eaves shriek and take to the air with a hurried beating of wings. One second the dark, gray sky is black with crows. The next they are gone.

Patrolman Hunter hurtles west down Monroe Street, past the van with the muddy plates, where the red-haired woman still sits in her motorcycle helmet. Then Hunter swerves hard right, and drives halfway up onto the sidewalk, until a metal pylon at the base of the sidewalk forces him to slam on his brakes. He bounces to a stop directly in front of the van, pointing up the sidewalk—forty yards from the two radicals, still standing beneath Professor Watkins's windows.

Patrolman Hunter leaps out. *"Freeze!"* he yells at the two radicals in their helmets.

In one fluid motion, the short stocky radical pulls a revolver from beneath his sweatshirt and fires. Patrolman Hunter goes down in the street. From the pavement, Hunter returns the fire. With Hunter's first shot, the radical with the gun falls face down on the sidewalk. Hunter fires five more rounds. Somewhere in the hail of bullets, the tall thin radical goes down, too.

Then everything goes quiet. For what seems an eternity of seconds.

A piercing scream breaks the silence. From the van the red-haired woman in the motorcycle helmet bolts. Screaming. She runs up the sidewalk to the prostrate bodies of her fallen comrades. Hurls herself on top of the tall thin one, who lays on his back, twisted and contorted. She lifts his limp neck. It lolls lifelessly. Against his lips she presses her lips. No whisper of life.

She crawls three yards to the short stocky radical. Sees he's also dead. Looks forty yards down the sidewalk, at the young Ann Arbor cop lying in the street. He's not moving, either.

"*Hey, you!*" a voice yells from above. Professor Pembroke Watkins. Peering through his broken windows. Shouting into the gloaming. "*What the Sam Hill is going on down there?*"

The red-haired woman in the helmet ignores Professor Watkins.

On Monroe Street, people begin to materialize. From Dominick's. From the student houses. Inside the Law Library more people can be heard, heading out toward the scene.

The red-haired woman springs to her feet. Runs two steps back toward the van, then freezes in her tracks. The van is pinned by Patrolman Hunter's squad car. Extricating the van from its parking place now would require several time-consuming back-and-forths.

Nearby sirens can be heard. More police cars, on State Street, closing in.

She changes course. Whirls back to the tall thin radical and reaches beneath his sweatshirt. Grabs *his* revolver, still stuffed in his pants. Holding the gun in her hand, high above her head, she scrambles through the thick ivy at the base of the Law School. Clambers up onto a stone wall. And leaps off the wall onto the loading dock. Just as the back-up police cars arrive.

"Officer down!" a male voice cries.

"Halt!" another male voice commands.

The red-haired woman ignores the command. She skitters across the metal floor of the loading dock, holding the gun high. And lunges with her free hand for the gray metal door at the back of the Law School.

A shot rings out. Followed at once by a cracking sound, as the bullet glances off the red-haired woman's motorcycle helmet. Her head jerks back, and to the left. But she does not fall. The helmet saves her. Before another shot is fired, the woman slips into the Law School.

Six police officers follow her into the building. Less than fifteen seconds behind her. They fan out. Cover all the exits. Quiz the students, the faculty, the staff. All deny seeing anyone in a bullet-cracked motorcycle helmet. All deny seeing any red-haired woman at all.

The police seal the exits. Search the hallways, high and low. Search the Law School, room by room. The search takes hours. Yields nothing. The red-haired woman, in the bullet-cracked motorcycle helmet, vanishes into thin air. A legend in the making. The Fugitive Radical.

* * *

6:00 p.m. Ann Arbor Police Officer Greg Hunter, younger brother of Patrolman Dale Hunter, rides in the ambulance that rushes Dale toward the hospital. At the direction of the EMT beside him, Greg Hunter presses a gauze wrap against his older brother's blood-soaked stomach.

"Did we get her?" Dale Hunter murmurs.

"Shhh," Greg Hunter says. "Stay calm, buddy. You're losing a lot of blood."

"I'm okay, little bro'," Dale wheezes. "Tell me what happened out there."

"Bitch lucked out," Greg mutters. "Only time for one shot. But I was dead on. Without that damn helmet, she'd be dead."

Dale grunts.

"Why didn't *you* shoot her?" Greg asks. "Black out before you could reload?"

"Wasn't her who shot me," Dale mutters. "Short guy shot me. She was just sitting in the van."

"But *she* had a gun, too," Greg insists. "I saw it."

"She took it from the tall one. *Afterwards*. Lifted his sweatshirt and pulled it out from his pants." Dale pauses while the EMT checks the pulse in his throat. "Hey, you think these might be the same radicals that bombed them other campus buildings this year?"

"Doubt it," Greg says. "The CIA, the ROTC, the military research building—those were all bombed with dynamite. On timers. Here we got Molotov cocktails. No timers. Plus, those were all *military* targets. This is—fuck, it's just *law professors*."

"Why the hell would you want to bomb a law school anyway?" Dale mumbles.

"Symbolic, I bet. Tell you what, though. They mighta burnt it right down to the ground, buddy. If not for you. You're a hero. You know that? So you hang on now, you hear?"

Dale nods. The EMT hands Greg a fresh piece of gauze to swap out for the blood-soaked one he's been pressing against his brother's stomach.

"Hey, Dale," Greg says, "how'd you happen to be right there anyway—just the right place, at just the right time? Campus informant tip us off?"

"Luck," Dale wheezes through teeth clenched in pain. "Sheer . . . dumb . . . luck."

The color is leaving Dale's face. With each breath he labors. Harder. And harder.

Greg leans closer to his brother. Murmurs softly: *"So why didn't you shoot her?"*

The ambulance swerves and weaves through campus traffic. Dale gives no reply.

"You said she knew where to find the gun," Greg continues. "'*Lifted his sweatshirt,*' you said, '*and pulled it out from his pants.*' Proving she *had* to be part of their conspiracy."

Still Dale gives no reply.

"She was a *fleeing felon*," Greg persists. "By rights you coulda shot her."

"I almost did," Dale whispers. "Like I shot the tall guy. But then I thought, do I really know . . . *for sure* . . . she's with 'em? What if . . . she wasn't . . . nothin' . . . but a scared kid—"

At the emergency room of the University of Michigan Hospital, Ann Arbor Police Patrolman Dale Hunter is pronounced dead on arrival.

* * *

9:00 p.m. Greg Hunter exits his mother's home. After three heart-breaking hours consoling his mother and trying in vain to console Dale's young widow Jeannine.

Greg Hunter returns to the Law Quad. Where a large crowd pushes close to the barricades around the crime scene. The mood is electric. And ugly. Buzz-cut sheriff's deputies aim tear gas canisters, point-blank, at long-haired protestors chanting anti-police slogans. A bearded man stands on the wall at Dominick's, shouting, "Police brutality! That pig shot those kids down in cold blood! Don't let them fuck with the evidence back there! Storm the barricades!"

Greg Hunter clenches his fists in anger. But the bearded man's ranting incites no action. Warily the crowd eyes the police pepper-spray truck, parked in their midst. Many must recall how, four months before, the pepper-spray truck broke up the South U riots. So no one now heeds the bearded man's call to action. Hunter shoves through the crowd. Crosses the barricade. Walks forty yards up the sidewalk, to the chalk lines that mark where the two radicals died.

Officer Al Smith sidles up beside Hunter. "Man, I'm so sorry . . . 'bout your brother."

"Thanks." Hunter chokes back tears. "Did we find the hippie bitch? Or we still huntin' her in there?"

Smith shakes his head. "Search inside is done. She ain't there. Vanished into thin air."

"Then why the fuck don't we all just go home? Give these freaks no one to shout at."

"Sgt. Hensley's worried someone might claim your brother used excessive force."

"Excessive force?" Hunter spits. "Dale's *dead*, for Chrissake!"

"Yeah, he is. But the two radicals fired only one shot. Dale answered *with six*."

"He had a perfect *right* to shoot 'em. They were fleeing felons."

"He had a right to shoot the guy with the gun, sure. But the witnesses all say the tall guy never pulled a gun. Never started to run neither."

"This is such total bullshit!"

"It's *your family* Hensley's protecting. In case someone sues. But we need daylight. To show why six shots was righteous. 'Til then, gotta keep these freaks from tramplin' the scene."

"What a fucked-up world! Guy lays down his life. For eight grand a year. And this is the thanks he gets? After he's dead, they'll let someone sue him? For shooting *two firebombers?* Fact is, six shots wasn't enough. Only reason Dale's dead is, he didn't fire more. And faster."

Smith nods, silent. Greg Hunter glares at the crowd. Fists clenched. Teeth bared.

At last Hunter turns his back on the crowd. Looks up at the broken third-floor windows. Looks back down at the firebombs, still lined up beside the low stone wall.

"Why'd they bother with the bricks?" Hunter asks. "If they had the fire-bombs all ready?"

"To break the glass first. So their jars wouldn't just bounce off the windows. FBI figures they were about to throw these jars through the broken windows, when your brother— "

" —had the bad luck to pass by," Hunter says. "But—was it really *that* simple?"

"No," Smith says. "Because the FBI can't explain the girl."

"She was the getaway driver."

"Yeah. But she was up to somethin' more, too. Witnesses all say she went into the Law School five minutes *before* her boyfriends started throwin' bricks. Went in empty-handed. Came out empty-handed. With that red hair and that helmet, she had to stand out like a Negro at a Klan rally. But no one saw her. And no one can figure what the hell she was *doin'* in there."

"Any leads on who she is?"

"We *know* who she is," Smith says. "Rachel Clark, nineteen. Sophomore at the U. She was kind enough to leave her fingerprints on the steering wheel. And the van's door."

"She's got a record?"

"Two priors. Disorderly conduct. Centreville, Michigan. 1967. At a high school football game. And rioting. In Chicago. Two weeks ago. At the Days of Rage protest."

Hunter whistles. "Rachel Clark's with *The Weather Underground*?"

"FBI thinks so. Squad 47's here. But not everyone at Days of Rage was with the Weathermen."

"Yeah, but when the Chicago Police shot bullets over their heads, most of the little hippies shit their pants and ran. Only the hard core Weathermen kept marching and got busted." Hunter snaps his fingers. "And what did those hard core Weathermen *wear* that day?"

"Motorcycle helmets," Smith concedes.

"With *rainbows and lightning bolts*. Just like Rachel Clark today. And her boyfriends."

"That still don't *prove* they're Weathermen."

Hunter points at the chalk outlines of the two dead radicals. "We ID her boyfriends yet?"

"Cocksucker who shot Dale was Al Brown, twenty-eight. Tall one was Paul Zimmerman, twenty-nine."

"How'd we ID them so fast?" Hunter asks. "Looked like they had gloves on."

"Not inside the van they didn't. And they both got records. Original members of Students for a Democratic Society."

"Original members? Shit." Hunter snorts. "Then they shoulda known better. In the beginning, SDS was supposed to be peaceable peaceniks. All *opposed* to violence."

"Weatherman changed all that. And Zimmerman. He came back last fall all revved up. From the Chicago riots. He and Brown took over the SDS here. With their 'Jesse James gang.'"

"How long're their rap sheets?"

"Two arrests, no convictions. Both got busted at the U of M Admin Building takeover. And again at Days of Rage. With Zimmerman's girlfriend, Rachel Clark."

Greg Hunter looks up at the broken office windows. "If you want to fire-bomb a building, why aim for third-floor windows?" He points at the first-floor windows, ten feet away. "*These* windows here are a whole lot easier to hit. From here, you could just *roll* the damn bombs in."

"Up there is Pembroke Watkins's office. Zimmerman had a major jones for Watkins."

"So that must be what the girl was doin' inside then: making sure Watkins was in his office."

"No," Smith says. "The witnesses all say you could see from the outside Watkins was up there. So she musta been doin' somethin' else. But no one knows what."

Hunter shrugs. "Well, whatever she was doin', Watkins makes sense as their target. SDS hates him. For leading the charge to kick the damn radicals outta school."

"Still, if you wanna *kill* a man, there's lots better ways than firebombing his office."

"Not if you lack the guts to look him in the face," Hunter counters. "Watkins scares—"

Sounds of a scuffle at the barricade interrupt Hunter's conversation with Smith. A deputy drags a protestor by his long hair. Hauls him under the barricade, into the cordoned-off area. And handcuffs him—while several other deputies aim tear gas canisters at the heckling crowd.

The people's fury rises. But still they do not riot. Instead, those closest to the barricade link arms. Sway slowly back and forth. And sing, loud and off-key, "We Shall Overcome."

"Man, this crazy town is fifteen square miles surrounded by reality," Hunter sneers. "Look at that crowd. That's not just students. Chances are, you got half the damn *faculty* out there, too."

"C'mon, Greg." Smith shakes his head. "It ain't *that* bad."

"Yeah? See that old guy with the Father Christmas beard? That's the history prof, Bob Nelson. The one on City Council. From the Human Rights Party."

"So it is. But he's just one guy. Most people in this town are still sane. You know a local banker already put up a reward? *Twenty grand!* 'For information leading to Rachel Clark's arrest.'"

"No shit." The news calms Hunter. "Okay. So maybe *one person* here cares about protecting police officers. But this town is still basically a freak show."

"Well that much green oughta loosen some little hippie's tongue real fast, eh? Though I gotta say, I doubt we even need a reward to catch Rachel Clark."

"Why not?"

"She's only nineteen. Her whole world is her roommates, her friends, her family. She has no experience as a fugitive. No cash. No idea where to hide. How hard can she be to track down?"

"I don't know." Hunter shakes his head. "Three hours ago, Hensley swore she was trapped inside this building here. But she slipped away from Hensley, didn't she?"

"Squad 47'll find her. They've staked out all her hangouts. Put out an APB on her, too."

"But if she's with the Weathermen, she's already got a fake ID. Pre-prepared. Figuring someday the shit would hit the fan. And the Weathermen—those people know how to hide a fugitive." Hunter jabs Smith's arm. "Hey—is Squad 47 putting up 'Wanted' posters, too?"

"All over campus," Smith says. "With Rachel Clark's mug shot from Chicago."

Hunter's eyes narrow. "Do the posters say she's wanted for *murder*?"

"Naw. They just call her a 'fugitive radical.' Wanted for questioning. In connection with an attempted campus-bombing." Smith shoots a quick sideways glance at Hunter. "She wasn't the one that shot your brother, you know."

Hunter smacks his right fist hard into his left palm. "She's still guilty of murder, dammit!"

"How you figure?"

"She was the getaway driver. For an attempted bombing. That makes her guilty of conspiracy. To commit a felony. During the attempted commission of the felony, an officer was killed. That makes everybody in the conspiracy equally guilty. Of first-degree *felony* murder!"

Smith winces. "I guess—you're right. Good. So if we find her, she gets the chair."

"*When* we find her," Hunter insists. In a flat, hard voice. "If the reward money don't flush her out, I'll hunt the bitch down myself. Mark my words, Al—Rachel Clark is gonna pay. *With her life.* For what she and her piece-a-shit pals done to my brother Dale."

# FIRST WEEK

# CHAPTER ONE
# ENQUIRING MINDS

**Tuesday 12 October 2004**

Tabloid work is for the young. The critical skills—spying and lying—fade with age. In my day, I was the best reporter *The National Enquirer* ever saw. (Talk about damning myself with faint praise.) But at age forty-eight, I'm too old to wear disguises. Too old to hide in trees.

So why, on a gorgeous autumn afternoon, am I sprawled on my stomach on the hot gravel roof of an office building on Main Street in Ann Arbor, Michigan, peering down into a small law office forty feet below? With a long-lens camera at my eye? And a listening device in my ear?

Cuz I'm a hothead. A *prima donna*. And a damn fool.

At least, that's what my boss at the *Enquirer* called me last fall. When I refused to skip my daughter's state tennis finals. He wanted me to go cover a hearing in the Kobe Bryant case. After all, he reasoned, I'd missed dozens of family events over the years. Why stop now?

I told him to go to hell. So he fired me. Like he'd fired dozens of hacks before me. About once a month the *Enquirer* fires a reporter. I just lasted longer than most. Twelve years.

My name's David Fisher. If you've picked up the *Enquirer* anytime in the last twelve years—and don't bother pretending you haven't, because everyone at least leafs through it in the supermarket—then you've seen my work. You just didn't know it was by David Fisher. Because I write my tabloid articles under a pen name. Sandy Hill. First name: childhood pet. Last name: the street I grew up on. That's how porn stars pick their names. What's good enough for porn stars is good enough for me. Writing as "Sandy Hill" allows me to travel incognito as David Fisher. While I hunt celebrities. All across the globe.

It's a tough job. But someone's gotta do it.

Getting fired by the *Enquirer* was no big deal. I just went down the street. Conveniently all the major American tabloids are located in one tiny town.

Lantana, Florida. Ancestral home of the *Enquirer*. The knock-offs all set up shop there, too. Years ago. To hire the *Enquirer's* monthly rejects. Turned Lantana into the world's leading exporter of sheer, unadulterated crap.

I chose a start-up tabloid. *The National Spy*. The *Spy* couldn't match my *Enquirer* salary. But the *Spy* made me an editor. So I borrowed a page from the spin doctors. Instead of *getting fired* I said I was *receiving the promotion I'd long deserved*. Not that my wife Elaine cared. Or my mother. Or Elaine's mother. They're all mortified that I work for a tabloid at all.

Most of the time being an editor at the *Spy* is great. Much less time on the road, running the crazy risks a tabloid reporter must run. Much more easy time at my desk. Editing gossipy exposés about celebrities' illicit love affairs. Reporting on new drugs that "scientists" claim will keep you forever young. And writing those logic-defying classics your enquiring minds just can't resist. About aliens abducting Hillary Clinton. For sex. Or Elvis dancing on Grace Kelly's grave. In drag. (In this digital age, we can produce photos to "document" *anything* we make up.)

The only problem at the *Spy* is the tight budget. The *Enquirer* hires *squads* of reporters. To cover every star's every move. Just to be ready. Whenever and wherever scandal breaks. You have no idea. With two million weekly buyers, at three bucks a pop, the *Enquirer* can afford it.

But *The National Spy* is still a start-up. The budget is very tight. So everyone has to be a jack-of-all-trades. Which is why an otherwise dignified editor like me sometimes ends up looking like the lowest of paparazzi. Lying sprawled across a rooftop. Sweat trickling down my back. And gravel sticking to my chin. In the very town where I grew up, as it happens. Ann Arbor.

Rule #1 in the tabloid biz: *Get there early*. I did.

Yesterday we got a reliable and exclusive tip that Norma Lee was coming here today. To this dinky little Ann Arbor law firm, Davis & Nyman. For some extra-marital canoodling. With an old flame named Lane Davis. A left-wing lawyer—and a married man. A *mayoral candidate*, too.

In case you watch no TV, Norma Lee's a megastar. Looks like Dolly Parton. *On steroids*. Norma's a big story. Anywhere she goes. (Norma's *chest's* a big story. Anywhere *they* go.) But if Norma's truly coming here *with cheating on her mind*? Tabloid heaven! Because these days Norma is so sickeningly moral. Preaching marital fidelity. Unlike her wild youth, when she was always getting arrested at No Nukes rallies. And bedding various mangy-looking lefties—like Lane Davis, I gather. So if this works out, what an exclusive it will be! The big star. Caught cheating. With a left-wing *politician*, no less. And with any luck, I'll get the pix to prove it.

Obeying Rule #1, I flew up last night. Used my pick gun to break into Davis & Nyman. (It's in a charming old house. With easy old locks. And no alarms.) Once inside, I planted bugs. Tapped the phones. But hid no video cameras. Sure, videos are great. But law firms have lots of foot traffic. Too often video cameras get spotted. And in mid-October, with daylight savings still in effect, you can get great pix even in the evening with a telephoto lens from a nearby roof. The upper halves of the windows at Davis & Nyman have no blinds. So who needs video?

Today I got here early, too. Climbed out on this hot, flat roof at 4:00 this afternoon—even though Norma Lee's not expected 'til 5:30. Found to my chagrin that the sightlines up here aren't as good as I'd anticipated. I can only see halfway into the first-floor conference room. Though I can see all of Davis's second-floor office—the likeliest location for after-hours love.

Even worse, I found *tons* of people at Davis & Nyman. Some kind of fundraiser for Lane Davis's mayoral campaign. Parking lot was packed. But luckily, the party ended at 4:30. I counted fifty people trooping out. Most of the cars in the Davis & Nyman parking lot were gone by 4:45.

From listening to my bugs, I know all eight Davis & Nyman employees are still inside. And from the firm brochure I pinched last night, I know all their names. Plus the ages of the five with college degrees. Two partners: Lane Davis, fifty-eight; Sheila Nyman, fifty-four. Two associates: George Robertson, thirty-two; Emily Harris, twenty-seven. One paralegal: Naomi Williams, fifty-four. Plus office manager/legal assistant Sue Webber, legal assistant Janet Fickel, and receptionist Debbie Smith. The brochure has pix of the four lawyers. And the paralegal. No pix of the three staffers. But still, listing the staffers by name in the brochure is very egalitarian. Classic Ann Arbor. Long live the Revolution.

At precisely 5:00, three women exit. Head for their cars. I check the brochure pix. Not Sheila. Not Emily. Not Naomi. So these must be the three staffers. I only get a quick glimpse. From my rooftop perch. But one is quite the hot little minx. High heels. Stockings. Killer short skirt. Tight little butt. An absolutely *wicked* walk. More like a slow *prance*. I snap a few quick pix. For the, um, record. But then she's in her Chevy. And gone. In a flash. Like all my dreams.

At 5:15, George and Emily go home. Wholesome kids. Fresh out of law school. You know. Nerds. I waste no film on George and Emily. Now all we need is to get rid of Sheila and Naomi. And then the coast will be clear. For Norma Lee to come boogie with Lane Davis.

But at 5:20 my dreams of a tabloid spectacle are dashed. Two cars arrive in tandem in the Davis & Nyman parking lot. A Volvo and a Honda Civic. From each a woman emerges. But neither is Norma Lee. Worse, the woman in the Volvo is Lane Davis's *wife*. Camille Davis.

Now in Hollywood, group sex is not uncommon. But here in the heartland, I doubt I'm going to catch Norma Lee doing the nasty with Lane Davis *in front of his wife*. Not to mention the *other* woman who's just arrived. In the Honda Civic. Raven LaGrow. A feminist law professor at the Michigan Law School. Rush Limbaugh's favorite "Feminazi" target. Raven's very stern. No way Raven LaGrow's here for swinging sex with the Davises and Norma Lee. Clearly our normally reliable informant was misinformed about the true nature of today's activities.

I consider packing up and going home. But I'm no quitter. After all, if Norma Lee *does* show, I might still get some pix of her with Lane Davis. Then we could *crop out* Raven and Camille. And Sheila and Naomi. And *insinuate* that Norma Lee was getting cozy with a married pol.

Would we really stoop that low? You bet we would.

At 5:25, a taxi pulls up. Bingo. First the bodyguard. Looks like an ex-cop. Asian. Think Odd Job, from *Goldfinger*. Sport coat bursting at the seams. From the sheer pressure of his bulging biceps. Odd Job could plainly crush me like a bug. I feel a sudden need to pee.

Nevertheless, I hang tough. It's show time. I get five great pix of Norma Lee exiting the taxi. Really, *no one* looks good getting out of a car. It's especially awkward for a fifty-year-old woman in a skirt. I'm too high for one of those is-she-wearing-panties shots that tabloid readers know and love. But those shots work better with the *younger* celebs anyway. Norma Lee has a few too many miles on her for *that*. Yet I'm in the perfect spot for an ample sample of Norma Lee's tremendous cleavage. Which is deep. And long. Like the San Andreas fault. From a spot just two inches south of her super-sternum notch, Norma's cleavage runs—through mountains measureless to man—all the way down past her sternum. If Norma even *has* a sternum.

So. Just ninety minutes on a hot tin roof (well, gravel, actually), and I've got next week's cover. Without shelling out a small fortune to one of the independent photo agencies. Not bad. Not bad at all, for an aging has-been tabloid hack broomed by the *Enquirer*. Ha! Fuck 'em.

But it gets better. *Much* better. From the trunk, the cabbie hands Odd Job two suitcases. And hands Norma Lee an intriguing square box. The size of a hat box. But heavier. Too heavy to be a hat box. Norma cradles that square box like it's got the crown jewels inside.

Lane Davis comes outside. Wearing a rumpled suit. Athletic. Trim. Not bad-looking. For fifty-eight. Except he's wearing goofy, round, John Lennon glasses. And a ratty beard. But Norma's always had a thing for scruffy guys with beards. Davis whisks Norma and Odd Job inside.

Unfortunately, they go to the first-floor conference room. Where my sight line from the roof is poor. I can only see half the room. Though at least my bug allows me to hear everything.

I *see* the backs of Lane Davis, Odd Job and Norma Lee. I *hear* introductions for the other four people in the room. Davis's friend, Professor Raven LaGrow. His wife, Camille Davis. His law partner, Sheila Nyman. And his paralegal, Naomi Williams.

I won't have a problem distinguishing Lane Davis's voice from Odd Job's. If Odd Job even knows how to talk. I know Norma Lee's syrupy voice all too well from TV. Who doesn't? And I know Raven LaGrow's voice, too. Raven was an expert witness at the Yankee stripper trial I covered last year in New York. But there's no way to tell if an unfamiliar voice is Camille Davis or Sheila Nyman or Naomi Williams.

All seven people hover around the conference room table. Where, I gather, that heavy, square box sits. From all the breathless excitement down there, you'd think they were about to unseal King Tut's tomb. I can't actually see the box. But I can hear Davis opening it.

The opening of the box is followed by an awkward, heavy silence. Like someone farted.

"You know what it is?" Norma Lee gushes. In that cloying, cutesy voice she uses on TV.

"I can guess," Raven LaGrow says, coldly. "From that bullet crease on the back."

"The most famous bullet crease in the history of the Movement!" Norma enthuses.

"It's really poor judgment to bring this *here*, Norma," Raven counters.

"Why?" Norma sounds hurt. And flustered.

"Lane's already trailing in the polls," one of the unfamiliar women says. "Because people feel he's too far to the left."

"For Lane to win this election," a second unfamiliar woman adds, "we have to *play down* his radical past. But something like this only serves to . . . *remind* people of— "

"Well, it's only a private gift," Norma interrupts. She sounds defensive. "It's not like Lane has to stand up and tell the world about it at tomorrow morning's press conference."

"Yes," Lane Davis says. "That's right. And it's . . . very *thoughtful*, Norma. Thank you."

"Maybe one of you could get in touch with her?" Norma's voice is bubbly again. "See if she wants it back?"

Silence. I fiddle with my earpiece. But the bug's still working. I can still hear muffled sounds from the conference room. People breathing. Clothes rustling. Only no one's talking.

At last Raven LaGrow speaks. *Very* coldly. "No one here has any idea where she is."

"That's right," a third unfamiliar woman chimes in quickly.

A murmur of general agreement sweeps the room—no one here knows where "she" is.

"Well then you could display it here," Norma says brightly. "With all these other wonderful mementos from the Movement." Norma waves at the walls I can't see. But from my B&E last night, I know what's there. Photos of Malcolm and Martin. The Kennedys. Ralph Nader. And a collage of old bumper stickers: *Give Peace A Chance. Impeach LBJ. Impeach Nixon. Free Huey.*

"Because this is," Norma continues gushing, "genuine *history*."

"It's a lot *worse* than history," Raven says. "It's—*evidence*."

"Evidence that might be used against you, Lane," warns the first unfamiliar woman.

"Damn right," the second unfamiliar woman says. "You should *never* display it here, Lane. People see it, they may think you know where *she* is—or that you've been *hiding* her."

Heavy silence. I shift a little. To get an angle on the thing they're discussing. No luck.

"How'd you get this anyway?" Raven asks. "I take it *you're* not in contact with her?"

"Oh, no," Norma titters. "Heavens, no! My agent doesn't allow me to talk to people like *that* anymore. You, Raven, are about as far out on a limb as I'm allowed to go these days!"

This provokes a throaty lawnmower laugh from Odd Job. But no one else is laughing.

"So how do you know it's genuine?" Raven persists.

"My friends who found it assured me it's real. And it *does* have that bullet crease."

"And since it's thirty-five years old," Lane Davis says firmly, "it's not 'evidence' of anything. It's just history. So I'll keep it here in the office. With the rest of my collection. Thank you, Norma."

Davis gives Norma a hug. No easy feat—giving Norma a hug. You need some *awfully long arms* to get all the way around Norma Lee. But Davis manages. In front of his wife, no less. Since they're standing closest to the window, I get three nice pix of the bosomy hug.

"So c'mon, Norma." Davis speaks with exaggerated cheeriness. As if forcibly trying to lighten the mood. "Tell us where you got it! These *friends* who found it—do I know them?"

"Oh no," Norma Lee says mischievously. "My sources are"—she titters again—"secret."

Davis turns serious. "Does her *family* know you got this?"

"No," Norma admits. "That's why I thought if one of you could get a message to her— "

"We can't." Davis cuts Norma off. *Very* quickly. "Believe me. None of us has any idea where she is. But what if her parents hear about this helmet? And claim it's theirs?"

"They disowned her thirty-five years ago," Norma says.

"What about the little girl?" the second unfamiliar woman asks.

I miss the answer. Fiddle with my earpiece again. But the bug's still working.

Lane Davis is speaking. "Strange. You raise a kid. Send her off to college. She fucks up. Big time. But then you just turn your back on her? *Forever*? That doesn't seem right."

"But that's what happened," Raven says. "The FBI's been sitting on her parents since 1969. And it hasn't gotten them any closer to finding her than the day she went underground."

"Where do you think she is now?" Davis asks.

"Probably dead," the first unfamiliar woman says.

"No, I don't think so," Raven counters. "You'd have *heard* about it if she'd died. No reason for her to stay underground *in death*."

"Timbuktu would be my guess," says the second unfamiliar woman. "That's the only place you can hide out from the FBI for thirty-five years."

"No," Raven says. "I think she's very close. Maybe even here in Michigan."

"Why do you think that?" asks the third unfamiliar woman.

Maddeningly, Raven's reply is lost in static. I bang my earpiece on the roof. Which fixes it. But by the time I get clear reception again, the talk has moved on to Ann Arbor politics. Then they agree on a restaurant. The Gandy Dancer. And all seven file out of the conference room.

At last I have a clear sightline to the dingus in the middle of the table. But I *still* can't tell what the hell it is. Figuring I'm done here and I can reload in the car, I quickly shoot all the remaining pix on my roll. Thinking later I can blow the photos up. And maybe tell what the thing is.

The conference room lights go out. I flex my stiff legs. Pack my camera in its case. I'm halfway up from my prone position. When suddenly the conference room lights blaze on again.

Fearing I've been spotted, I drop back down on my belly. A dumb reaction. Because if someone had spotted me, they'd have left the lights off. Anyway, no one's looking out the window.

Yet someone *has* come back into the conference room. My earpiece registers the door closing. Then footsteps. Inside the room. Sounds like just one person. Too far from the window to see who it is. I fumble with my camera case. A real paparazzo would have a *second camera*, at the ready. A digital back-up— which never runs out of film. But not me.

This is what happens when an editor tries to be a jack-of-all-trades.

While I get my camera back out, I keep an eye on the room. The unknown person walks to the middle of the room. Lifts the artifact off the table. And in a single clean motion, puts the thing on his or her *head*. While at the same time pivoting. So I'm now looking at his or her back.

I've got my camera out and focused now. The unknown person is wearing a dark skirt. Light blouse. And flat shoes. Seems too tall to be Norma Lee. It's one of the other four women. Lane Davis's friend, Professor Raven LaGrow. His wife, Camille Davis. His law partner, Sheila Nyman. Or his paralegal, Naomi Williams.

I try to remember what Raven and Camille were wearing when they got out of their cars. Seems like they both had on dark skirts. Light blouses. And flat shoes. But I'm pretty sure one of 'em was wearing a cardigan sweater, too. And the other one wore an aviator-style jacket. I think.

This woman who's returned to the conference room wears no coat, no sweater. So chances are, she's Sheila or Naomi. Not Raven or Camille.

The thing she's put on her head, I now see, is a motorcycle helmet. Black, with a colorful design on the back. I push the camera button. Just in case I've got any film left. No luck. The button jams. I shot all the film thirty seconds ago, when I thought we were done here. No time to reload. I'm not fast enough. So I just study the woman—whoever she is—through the telephoto lens.

She stands very stiff. And perfectly still. Like she's in a trance. Or like she's looking in a mirror. That's it! I saw a mirror there last night. On the back of the conference room door.

The woman spreads her legs defiantly apart. Eiffel Tower style. Bows her head slightly. No hair is visible coming out the back of the helmet. Then she balls her left hand into a fist. And punches her fist high above her head. The old black power salute. A salute some white radicals used, too. Especially the *really* radical ones. The members of the Weather Underground.

A middle-aged white woman. Striking the classic revolutionary stance. The exact pose I saw on dozens of Weatherman recruiting posters. Plastered on kiosks all around Ann Arbor, back when I was a kid. *Bring The War Back Home. End Racism. Stop The Draft.* Etcetera.

I'm not sure why I remember those Weatherman posters so well. I was only thirteen in 1969. And it's not like I ever considered joining. But the casual defiance of those militants was very compelling. They always posed standing. Legs spread, fist raised. They seemed so free. From all the social bullshit confining the rest of us. And their slightly bowed heads made me feel they'd found peace. In their fierce commitment to a cause. Peace I imagined, even at thirteen, would always elude a self-conscious, wise-cracking little ironist like me.

So seeing through my telephoto lens this middle-aged woman strike the same revolutionary pose, thirty-five years later, rivets me. She holds the pose. For what seems an eternity. There's something almost *eerie* about the way she holds the Weatherman pose. Like she was *born* to hold this pose. Like this pose is her *whole life.*

Then from outside the conference room I hear a noise. She hears it, too. Abruptly she steps toward the door, at the same time ripping the helmet off her head. She's too far into the room now for me to see her head. Her veiny, middle-aged hand sets the helmet back on the table.

"Time to go," I hear Lane Davis say in my earpiece. I can't see him. But it sounds like he's poked his head in the conference room door.

The woman does not reply. So I still have no clue if this middle-aged radical poser is Sheila Nyman or Naomi Williams. Or even conceivably Raven LaGrow or Camille Davis. But whoever she is, she leaves. Because again the conference room lights go off. This time for good.

I race downstairs. Fast. Trying, as I take the stairs two at a time, to make sense of what I've just seen. But I really can't run and think at the same time. At least, that's what my high school basketball coach always used to say. And I'm afraid he was right.

The house next door to Davis & Nyman's parking lot has a nice tall hedge. I hide behind the hedge as all seven of them troop out. No suitcases in hand.

Raven LaGrow is wearing the aviator jacket I remembered. And Camille Davis has on the cardigan sweater I saw before. But Sheila Nyman also has on a sweater. And Naomi Williams wears a shawl. Which means, the woman who struck the Weathermen pose must have put on her wrap *after* she left the conference room. So I guess they're all four equally likely suspects.

I can see what's under their various wraps. Maddeningly, they're *all* wearing light blouses. And dark skirts with flat shoes. So it could be any one of the four who just struck that Weatherman pose.

Raven LaGrow. Or Camille Davis. Or Sheila Nyman. Or Naomi Williams. They're all four about the same height, too: 5'5", give or take an inch. (Norma Lee is shorter. More like 5'2".) And though they all have different hair color, they all wear their hair short enough that it wouldn't be visible out the back of a motorcycle helmet. What a pisser!

They *are* built differently. But not differently enough for me to say "that's her." Or even to eliminate one. None is really heavy; none is really skinny. Studying their backs, I see *nothing* to indicate which one was just wearing that motorcycle helmet and giving the Weatherman salute.

Raven LaGrow is the most striking. Short black hair. Razor-sharp cheekbones. Big sexy lips. Flashy makeup. Minimal wrinkles. Nice boobs, too. Raven's pretty hot—for a fifty-four-year-old.

Camille Davis is a looker, too. Short blonde hair. More wrinkles than Raven. Less makeup. And not as stacked. But Camille wears a raspberry beret at a rakish angle. Very sexy. Camille's face is a little strange, though. Her eyes seem asymmetrical. Plastic surgery? Doubtful. That's just me. Hang around celebrities long enough, you start thinking *everyone's* had work.

Sheila Nyman is plain. Short brown hair. No makeup. Not much chest. Large features. Weird nose. So—plastic surgery for Sheila, too? C'mon! This is the Midwest. I gotta get a grip.

Plainer still is Naomi Williams. Short gray hair. Sad, tired eyes. *Tons* of wrinkles. Hunched shoulders. Naomi is the classic wallflower. Blank and nondescript. The girl who never got asked to the dance.

They pile into Camille's Volvo and Raven's Honda Civic. I tail them, in my rental Sebring, to the Gandy Dancer. En route I reload my camera. But I really don't need more pix. I'm only tailing them to be sure no one else is on this story. In the tabloid biz, we *guard* our exclusives. Like jealous husbands guard their wives.

Luckily, I see no signs of my fellow paparazzi outside the Gandy Dancer. We all park.

As they walk to the restaurant door, I study my four suspects one more time.

Black-haired Raven LaGrow has a power walk. Fast. Purposeful. Her whole aura says, to any male who might be watching, "I know I look great, but don't even *think* about it, fuzznuts."

By contrast, blonde-haired Camille Davis, gliding beside Raven, projects serenity. The raspberry beret gives Camille a jaunty air. And she isn't battling the world like Raven.

Sheila Nyman and Naomi Williams walk more slowly. Brown-haired Sheila's shoulders slump. Like she's carrying very heavy burdens. Her walk is ponderous. And subdued. But frumpy Sheila seems downright perky compared with hunched Naomi Williams.

Gray-haired Naomi looks down at the sidewalk the whole time. Picks her way cautiously. Like she's afraid she'll step on an ant.

Once they're all safely ensconced inside the Gandy Dancer, I drive back to Davis & Nyman. Make sure the neighbors aren't watching. Pull on my latex gloves, again. Use my pick gun, again. Normally I'd retrieve my surveillance devices. But I'm intrigued by that little pantomime I saw with the helmet and the power salute. So I leave the bugs and taps in place.

I riffle through Norma Lee's suitcases. Debate stealing her 36-FF bra. What a trophy *that* would be! But she's only packed one. She'd miss it. Can't risk alerting them to my intrusion.

In the conference room, I don't touch the motorcycle helmet on the table. Just inspect it. And photograph it. It's an old-style helmet. With a very wide chin strap. And it has the bullet crease on the back they were talking about. Same spot on the skull where JFK was shot. Old cracks line the helmet's surface. Radiating out from the bullet crease. Like a spider's web. The cracking adds extra electricity to the design on the helmet. A jagged red lightning bolt, running across a bright hippie rainbow. The Weatherman insignia.

As I said before, I grew up in Ann Arbor. (Which, by the way, is the real reason I came up here myself to cover Norma Lee's visit, instead of sending one of our line reporters. My thirtieth high school reunion is this Saturday. I wasn't about to miss this chance to come back home *on the company tab*.) In the 1960s, I used to hang out on the University of Michigan campus. With my teeny-bopper pals. We'd sit on our Stingray bikes. With our handlebars turned backwards. To show how cool we were. Watching the Vietnam protests. The South U riots. The Hash Bash. The teach-ins. The love-ins. All the radical action.

I was thirteen when Rachel Clark and her Weathermen boyfriends tried to blow up the Law School. When they killed that cop. The FBI's Squad 47 was *everywhere* that fall. Searching for Rachel Clark. Man, they even rousted my *junior high school*, grilling every kid with long hair. We knew they were grasping at straws. Rachel Clark was from Centreville. Not Ann Arbor. But the hunt for her was all the buzz in the fall of '69. Especially with that big reward money.

We weren't specifically rooting for or against Rachel Clark. We were just fascinated by the spectacle of it all. Like watching a car wreck. And when Squad 47 couldn't catch her, Rachel Clark became a legend. *The Fugitive Radical*. Hiding deep underground. On the lam forever—for deeds so dark we could scarcely imagine. *Cop got shot, man. And she got away with it.*

I shoot more pix of Rachel Clark's motorcycle helmet. It's more than just the echoes of my childhood that draw me to it. There's a *story* in that helmet. I can *feel* it.

How about: "***Norma Lee's Mysterious Links To The Radical Underground***."

Naw, that's not it. Sure, it's weird as hell that someone as ditzy as Norma Lee has given Rachel Clark's helmet as a gift. To a politician, no less. But the story here isn't Norma Lee. It's in the Weatherman pose that *other* woman struck. *That's* what's haunting me.

Staring at Rachel Clark's helmet, I realize the chin strap is awful *complex*. If I were to put that helmet on, right now, I'd have to fumble around awhile to get it on right. Yet *she* picked that helmet up and put it on in one fell swoop. A single, effortless motion. Like she'd worn the thing before. Seemed like it fit her perfect, too. Like Cinderella's slipper. And then she struck that old Weatherman pose. Like that pose was all she ever lived for.

Let's be real. Bob Woodward I am not. There's no danger the Pulitzer Committee will call for me in this lifetime. I know my limits. I'm a tabloid hack. And my nose for news ain't what it used to be. Not after so many years of chasing senseless stories about celebrity cleavage.

But this old dog can still hunt. A little. And my newsman's nose tells me this might be a great story. Not a tabloid story. A *real* story. If one of those four women turned out to be, in truth, Rachel Clark. Hiding right here in Ann Arbor. Right under everyone's noses!

It's a long shot, I know. But what the hell. I gotta find out.

Placing my gloved hands carefully along the edges, so as not to disturb any fingerprints, I pick up the helmet. And walk out the back door of Davis & Nyman. Helmet in hand.

* * *

Law school is normally a three-year program. Took me *eight*. I kept dropping out. Backpacking in Europe. Bartending in Boston. Writing novels even less profound than the one you're reading now. Then one dark day in March 1986, just as I turned thirty, I got a nasty shock. Some killjoy in the dean's office had discovered I'd *inadvertently* accumulated the requisite credits to graduate. I pleaded for a second chance. Pointed out it was an *accident*. Begged them *not* to give me a degree. But they were determined to force me to grow up. Heartless bastards.

I passed the Bar. Worked five years as a federal prosecutor. Then I got disbarred. For failing to produce exculpatory evidence that would have helped a dirtbag cop I was prosecuting. It wasn't fair. Really. I was a scapegoat. And it was all political. But it's a long story. And who cares anymore, anyway? It's all ancient history. The point is, they took away my license. They said I could reapply in three years—but I had a family to feed. So I decided to give journalism a try. *The New York Times* wasn't hiring disbarred lawyers at the time. So I landed at the *Enquirer*. Sure, my family and friends all feel I'm a chronic underachiever. Even my dog feels I could do better. But I'm not apologizing. I make better money than most lawyers. And I have way more fun than any of 'em. If you think I'm a wastrel, you're entitled to your opinion. But you can bite me, too.

While at the Department of Justice, I learned how to conduct an investigation. Skills that came in handy, when I rose above mere lawyering to become a lofty tabloid hack.

Rule #1 at the DOJ: *Make the FBI run every conceivable lab test.*

Of course, we don't have a lab at *The National Spy*. But next to hotel concierges, cops are the best tipsters we tabloids have. Cops tip us off—and we tip cops back. Big *green* tips.

And as a former prosecutor, I know lots of cops. So when I need a lab test, I just call a cop. In Ann Arbor, it's easy. I call Cliff Bryant. Ann Arbor Police Department. My old high school basketball teammate.

Luckily, Cliff's working late. I don't tell Cliff it's *Rachel Clark's* old helmet. Don't tell Cliff *how* I got it. Or *where* I got it. I just ask if Cliff can have it dusted for fingerprints. And checked for stray hairs. Cliff says sure, no problem. I tell him I can't leave it with him. Gotta get it back ASAP. Cliff says sure, no problem. Bring it on over. They can't run the computer check 'til morning. But they can lift any prints tonight. Collect any stray hairs. And let me take it back.

I figure the police computers must have fingerprints *at least* for Lane Davis, Norma Lee, and Odd Job. The Davis & Nyman brochure says Davis is an ex-prosecutor like me. Norma was arrested at 1970s protests. And Odd Job looks like a former badge. So all their prints should be on file. Which will help eliminate any extraneous prints. And help AAPD narrow in on the prints of the woman who struck that Weatherman pose. To see if she's really Rachel Clark. What the hell. Won't cost much to get Cliff to check. And if they find any stray hairs, I'll know for sure which one it was. Since my four suspects all have different color hair.

At the Ann Arbor Police Department, the techie processes the helmet. While I endure Cliff telling two young cops about some of my more ignominious moments playing high school basketball. Like the time I got confused after a time-out. Picked up a loose ball. Dribbled the wrong way. And scored a basket—for the other team. "Wrong Way Fisher" they called me after that one.

And then there was the time Cliff got in early foul trouble. I'm spaced out at the end of the bench. Checking out the babes in the stands. Suddenly coach Banks yells, "Fisher! Get in there!" I leap up. Like a drunk shot out of a cannon. Yank off my warm-ups. Report to the scorer's table. The scorer, a local wit, stares at my chest. "You gonna be *number zero* today, Davey?" I look down. Find I've yanked off my *uniform* along with my warm-ups. With the whole school watching. And hooting. Bare-chested I scramble back down the bench. Peel my uniform out from inside my warm-up. Fumble to get it back on my torso. *Not* my finest moment.

Cliff has a good laugh at my expense. Recounting "Wrong Way Fisher" and "Number Zero." Ancient stories I've only heard about eight thousand times. But I smile along. Like the good sport I am. Finally slip Cliff a few Benjamins. When the other cops aren't looking.

The techie reports she found no stray hairs inside the helmet. But she did lift several fresh fingerprints. Cliff promises he'll call me right away if the computer matches any of them.

Next stop: Davis & Nyman. Make sure the neighbors aren't watching. Pull on my gloves. Use my pick gun. Put the helmet back on the table. And get the hell out of there.

It's only 8:00 p.m.—too early to go back to my hotel. And I'm way too excited about my theory that one of those four women might really be Rachel Clark. In my head I know it's a long shot. But in my heart it's the kind of story I've always longed to find.

I dig a Power Bar out of my pocket. Gnaw on it while driving down Fifth Avenue. And try to convince myself something good might really happen here, by reviewing my "case" against the unknown woman who struck the Weatherman pose in Rachel Clark's helmet.

First, the helmet fit her perfectly. Second, she put it on faster than I could get my camera out of its case. Like she'd done it before. Third, she sure knew the Weatherman *pose*. And last, there's Raven LaGrow's tantalizing comment, just before my listening device crapped out on me: "*I think she's very close. Maybe even here in Michigan.*"

Why did Raven say that? What if Raven's right? What if one of these lefty pinkos in Davis & Nyman's conference room *really is* Rachel Clark? What if some of the others are helping Rachel Clark hide out? They seemed awful *quick* to deny that they could get a message to her. And yet awful *worried* that her helmet might be used as "evidence" against them.

What a great story this would be. For any paper—but especially for my fledgling tabloid, *The National Spy*. Biggest tabloid story since the *Enquirer* outed Gary Hart with Donna Rice. I can almost see the headline. **"National Spy Catches The Fugitive Radical! Secret Ann Arbor Cabal Harbors Rachel Clark For 35 Years. But <u>No One</u> Hides From The National Spy!"** Man, a story like that could really put us on the map. Put *me* on the map, too. Finally.

You think I'm a dreamer? Remember Kathy Boudin? The most famous radical terrorist, except for Patty Hearst? Kathy Boudin was on the lam the entire 1970s, after the Weathermen blew up that Greenwich Village house. For *ten years* Squad 47 staked out Kathy's parents. Yet Kathy and her parents got together all the time. How? Friends ferried messages to and fro. Arranged for safe places to meet. Really that's the *only* way Rachel Clark could possibly have eluded the FBI for thirty-five years. With a little help from her friends.

Anyway, call me crazy. Call me a dreamer. I don't care. We underachievers cling to our dreams. Now I've convinced myself Rachel Clark is alive and well. And right here in Ann Arbor. I've convinced myself she's one of that small cabal of lefty pinkos gathered in Lane Davis's office. And since I can't just go to bed, I go to the Ann Arbor Public Library. Read everything I can find about Rachel Clark, both online and in hard copy. Mostly old news articles from the fall of '69.

The articles recount the attempted firebombing. Speculate about the bombers' plan. And raise a question I never heard before.

Call it Question #1: Were the bombers really trying to *murder* Pembroke Watkins in his office?

I can't tell you how bizarre it is to see Pembroke Watkins's name connected with Rachel Clark. I was only thirteen back then. At the time his name meant nothing to me. So I never registered it was Watkins's office they attacked. By the time I got to Michigan Law School, Rachel Clark was long gone. No one talked about her anymore. But Watkins was still there. Older than dirt. Yet still kicking. The only dinosaur still using the "Socratic Method." The tedious ritual where the law professor never answers a student's question—except by posing *another* question.

And it didn't matter how many times I dropped out. I kept drawing Watkins. For Civil Procedure. Conflicts. Class Actions. One time, in my fifth or sixth year of law school, Watkins called on me. He wanted to play Socratic torture games. But I wasn't in the mood. So when he said, "Mr. Fisher?" I whipped out my wallet. Held it close to my mouth. Like a *Star Trek* walkie-talkie. And said, "Beam me up, Scottie." The class was deeply amused. Watkins was not.

Anyway, I find a well-reasoned article from 1969. Arguing that the bombers could not possibly have been trying to murder Watkins. Because you couldn't depend on firebombs through a window to land right in Watkins's lap. And if the bombs were to land anywhere else, he'd have time to escape out his office door—long before the fire got him. But persuasive though this article is, it gets lost in a tidal wave of other articles lambasting the Weathermen for betraying the Peace Movement, by resorting to violence. In the end, most writers conclude, illogically, that the radical bombers were indeed attempting *both* to burn down the Law School *and* to murder Watkins.

The 1969 articles raise two other questions I never heard before:

Question #2: Since twenty witnesses saw Rachel Clark first go into the Law School five minutes *before* Paul Zimmerman and Al Brown started throwing bricks at Watkins's windows, what the heck did she *do* while she was inside the Law School?

Question #3: Since the cops were only fifteen seconds behind her, and had the Law School exits sealed within sixty seconds of her *second* entry, how the heck did Rachel Clark escape?

I read a lot of 1969 articles. But find no answers to any of these questions.

The old news articles do have some human interest stuff—which we tabloid hacks love. There's a candid of Rachel Clark from her high school yearbook. Quite the little hottie. *Very* sexy. Big, wild-child eyes. *Huge* boobs. Short skirt.

Everyman's wet dream! Rachel Clark also looks very hot in her Days of Rage mug shot. Surreptitiously I razor-blade both these pix out of the news articles in the Library archives. Put the pix in my briefcase. For, um, future use.

There's also a human interest interview with Rachel's parents in Centreville. Ray and Ruth Clark. Very rough stuff. Ray and Ruth pledge full cooperation with the FBI. *Disown* their daughter Rachel. And hope the FBI catches her soon. Tough love from the parental units.

But after 1969, the articles about Rachel Clark peter out. Like everything else in our sound-bite culture, she becomes old news in about three months. Fades to black. Like all of history.

As I drive to my hotel, the Campus Inn, I ponder the fact that Sheila Nyman and Naomi Williams are both fifty-four. Just like Rachel Clark. But how old are Raven LaGrow and Camille Davis?

At the Campus Inn, I requisition three small Scotches from my fridge. Then I Google Raven. Find her Michigan Law bio. Born 1950. Same as Rachel Clark. Next I Google Camille. Nothing. So I pay ten bucks with my credit card to an on-line background investigation site. They've got her. Camille Davis, formerly Camille Jensen, Martin Place, Ann Arbor. Born 1950. Same as all the others.

I'm tired. My three Scotches are gone. The whole idea of Rachel Clark hiding in Ann Arbor, masquerading as one of four fifty-four-year-old ladies, is beginning to feel surreal. And kinda stupid. But before collapsing on my pillow, I remember to phone home. For once in my life.

* * *

"I hope you're not *misbehaving* up there in Ann Arbor," Elaine teases over the phone.

"*Sweetie!*" I protest with mock indignation. "How could you even *think* such a thing?"

"Oh, I remember you and Barry used to get pretty wild on the road. In the old days."

"Exactly!" I counter. "The *old* days. At the DOJ. Before Barry and I both got *married*. Now Barry's not even *here* anymore. And we're both way too *old* to misbehave."

"Good," Elaine says.

"But I'll have to cut this call short. Inga and Frieda are coming up in five minutes."

"*Inga and Frieda?*" Elaine echoes.

"Very nice girls. You'd like them. Twenty-year-old Swedes. Twins. Imagine. What are the odds? Said they could help me 'stretch my back.' Just the thing. After a long day's work."

"Oh?" Elaine knows I'm joking but plays along. "And what do 'Inga and Frieda' look like?"

"Don't worry. Not my type at all. Huge boobs. Short skirts. I hate even *lookin'* at 'em."

"Oh, *sure*," Elaine says. "Not your type. Not at all."

We both laugh. Joking on this subject is easy. Elaine herself has great boobs. And she knows no reason to doubt my fidelity. In truth, in eighteen years of marriage, I've only strayed twice. Both times at office parties. With twenty-four-year-old receptionists whose short skirts and stockings I couldn't resist. Each of these "flings" was over an hour after it started. By now you've gathered, as Stevie Forbert put it, '*I ain't no saint and I don't pretend to be.*' But if you're fair, Virtuous Reader, you'll admit: *two hours* of misconduct in an eighteen-year marriage really ain't all *that* bad.

Elaine never discovered either of these two one-hour flings. And she *has* heard about me turning down enticing overtures from beautiful women elsewhere. So Elaine trusts me. Hell, I trust myself. Not because I'm Mr. Moral. Far from it. As you already know, I'm a disbarred lawyer. And a total scofflaw when it comes to invasion of privacy, B&E and theft. I'm also a scofflaw when it comes to marital vows. Thirteen years in the tabloid biz would convince anyone you might as well cheat on your spouse whenever you can. Because everyone else seems to.

So why do I trust myself? Because having a real affair would require so much more energy and commitment than I would ever want to give it. Living that whole *secret life* kind of thing. It would tire me out. Like being Rachel Clark, on the lam. Exhausting. I'd probably end up sending flowers for the mistress to Elaine. Or vice-versa. Something dumb like that.

Plus, I love Elaine. In a middle-aged way. And Elaine's a terrific person. We have so much shared history. We have two great kids, too. Whom I would never want to disappoint. Even at forty-eight, Elaine still looks great. And—if you'll pardon my French—Elaine's still a great lay. So why would I ever want to start a messy affair, replete with all the lying and cheating that comes with that territory? I get all the lying and cheating I need *at work*. Each and every day.

"Before you go frolic with Inga and Frieda," Elaine says, "Sara has a homework question."

Our sixteen-year-old gets on the phone. Sara. A live wire, if ever there was one. Sara's the one who had the state tennis finals that got me fired from the *Enquirer* last year.

"Hey, Dad," Sara says.

"Hey," I reply.

"I need your help."

"What a nightmare for you."

"You're not kidding. Feel my pain, Dad."

"I'm trying, Sara. But they have these great little bottles in the refrigerator here in my hotel. Just sitting there. Three of these, and it's hard to feel *any* pain."

"Don't tell me you've been *drinking* again, Dad!" Sara was born a hundred years too late. She would have been an *outstanding* member of the Temperance Movement.

"Am I allowed to lie?"

"Not to me, Dad," Sara scolds. "Dad? Have you been drinking?"

"No comment?" I venture.

"I'm shocked, Dad. *Shocked*!"

"Me, too," I confide. "Well, do you still need my help? Or can I go pass out with the other winos here in this hotel?"

"I'm not happy with you, Dad." Sara doesn't like to let me off easy.

"I know." I try to sound contrite.

"But I *do* need your help," Sara admits. "Even if you *are* drunk as usual. It's for school."

"What class?"

"Law. *You* used to be a lawyer, Dad. Remember?"

"Don't rub it in. You sound like your grandmother."

"Which one?"

"Exactly, you little wise-ass. What's your question?"

"I need an example of how someone's *state of mind* affects The Law," Sara says. A second passes by. If that.

"Dad?" Sara continues. "Dad? Are you still there? Hell-*lo*? Dad?"

"I'm thinking."

"I don't have *all week*," Sara presses. "This is due tomorrow. I've got to get to bed."

"You mean, you've got to go watch *Real World*." Even when drinking, I'm not stupid. Claims that Sara is going to bed anytime before midnight never fool me. "Okay, you little TV addict, I've got one. My friend, Carol Jones, was a public defender. In DC. The nation's capitol."

"I *know* what 'DC' is, Dad," Sara says dryly.

"Carol's client was a nice little old lady charged with third-time possession of heroin. Not a dealer. Not a lot of heroin. But in DC back then, it was three strikes and you're out. She was facing twenty years in jail. Think about that, Sara. That's longer than you've been *alive*."

"I know how long twenty years is, Dad."

Actually, I'm pretty sure no kid has any idea how long twenty years is. But I let it pass.

"So her lawyer Carol pleads a mental defense," I say. "A *state of mind* defense. 'Inadequate personality.' Basically, it meant the nice little old lady had so little self-esteem, so little sense of herself—such an *'inadequate personality'*— that she shouldn't be held responsible for her actions. I know it might sound like bullshit to a hardened little cynic like you, Sara—"

"Don't swear, Dad," Sara interjects.

"But the jury *acquitted* that little old lady. Based on the 'inadequate person-ality' defense. And when she got the news of the acquittal, right there in the court-room, the little old lady *proved* she really did have an inadequate personality. Here she is. She's just found out she will *not* have to spend the next twenty years of her life in jail. And what do you think is the first thing the little old lady says to her lawyer, Carol Jones?"

"'I'm so happy *for you*.'" Sara beats me to my own punch line. "*Proving* that the little old lady really did have no sense of her own self."

I'm astounded. "You've heard this before?" Showing my usual keen grasp of the obvious.

"I've heard them *all* before, Dad," Sara says. "Don't you ever get any *new* stories?"

# CHAPTER TWO
# MONKEY BUSINESS

## Wednesday 13 October 2004

Best sentence ever written by a journalist? Some droll bloke in the *London Times*, describing Dame Barbara Courtland, all dolled up for the 1981 wedding of Lady Di and Prince Charlie: "Her eyes, twin miracles of mascara, looked like two black crows that had dashed themselves to death on the white cliffs of Dover." Great stuff. If only *I* could write like that.

The line comes to mind at the Lane Davis breakfast press conference, which turns out to be right here at the Campus Inn. Norma Lee's eyes look just like two black crows. Dashed to death on the white cliffs of Dover. But her chest looks great. With each breathless remark it *heaves* like Mount Vesuvius. And she follows a nice little script. How she's known Lane Davis *forever*. How she doesn't want to be a distraction. How she knows Lane's is a campaign of *ideas*. Of *substance*. And (big dramatic pause here, while Norma bats her twin miracles of mascara) a campaign of *truth*. So Norma just wants to lend her *support*. And blah-blah-blah.

The good news is, I see no evidence of any tabloid rivals. We have them totally scooped on this nice little story about Norma Lee dropping in on Ann Arbor to help out her old radical pal, Lane Davis. The *dailies* are here, of course. The mainstream press. They'll beat us easily, because we tabloids are all weekly. We all go to press on Monday (all slavishly printing the same day as the *Enquirer*), which is still five days away. But getting beat by the dailies doesn't matter. The dailies don't cover celebs like we do. We'll show our readers a side of Norma Lee's visit to Ann Arbor they'll *never* see in the dailies.

For one thing, I have those great cleavage pix of Norma getting out of her taxi. And the bosomy shots of Davis hugging her. Plus, no one else knows about Rachel Clark's Weatherman helmet. I'm still not sure exactly where that goes. But it's definitely *a story*. And better still—it's *exclusive*.

Someone grabs my elbow.

"David?" It's Cliff Bryant, looking very tense.

"Hey, Cliff." I turn to greet him. "How you doin'? Any luck with my helmet?"

"Yeah." But Cliff doesn't sound happy. Doesn't *look* happy, either. Cliff is normally a cheerful fellow—for a cop. We used to call Cliff "Meathead" in high school. Not a compliment. Even in his youth Cliff's face looked like a slice of uncooked meat loaf. So Cliff has always compensated for his ugliness. By being just about the nicest guy you'd ever want to meet. But today, Cliff looks hard and unforgiving—the way most cops look all the time.

As I turn further around, I see that Cliff is not alone. Another plainclothes badge is with him. Uglier than Cliff. Tenser, too. Even harder and more unforgiving.

"Dave," Cliff says, "this is Detective Greg Hunter."

Hunter does not extend his hand. He's a scary-looking dude, like an old bulldog. Loose skin. Big jowls. Paunchy. With small, hard eyes. The eyes of an assassin. A *dyspeptic* assassin.

"We need to talk," Hunter growls.

Abruptly Hunter spins and walks out of the press conference. Cliff gestures "you first" with his arm, and we follow Hunter out the door. Hunter steers us into a small room off the main lobby at the Campus Inn. Ominously, Hunter closes the door. I feel distinctly like a *detainee*.

"Don't you ever answer your phone?" Hunter barks.

I apologize for having disconnected it when I went to sleep, per my usual practice.

"Don't you ever check your messages?" Cliff chimes in.

I apologize for having slept late (also my usual practice), and then having gone straight to the press conference downstairs.

"Where'd you get that helmet?" Hunter demands.

I'm not sure where this is going, so I shake my head. "That's privileged."

"Like hell it is," Hunter growls. "It's *evidence*. In a murder investigation."

"Hold on there, hoss!" I say. "Who got *murdered?*"

"*My brother,*" Hunter says. "Now for the last time—*where'd you get that fuckin' helmet?*"

His brother? Murdered? This is bad. But I can't tell a cop, whom I don't know, that I broke into the law offices of a mayoral candidate. Just to take a motorcycle helmet for a joy ride.

"Whose fingerprints did you find on that helmet?" I ask, going on the offensive.

"Lane Davis's," Cliff answers. He pauses to raise his eyebrows. "*And—Rachel Clark's.*"

Shit! No wonder the cops are on the muscle! Even though I convinced my *heart* last night that the woman striking the pose might be Rachel Clark, my *head* never believed it. I figured this was just another in a long line of foolish fantasies that have distracted me over the years.

"Your brother was— " I start to ask.

"—the police officer Rachel Clark and her hippie boyfriends murdered." Hunter pronounces each syllable very slowly. Like a death sentence. "By the Law School. Thirty-five years I've been hunting that bitch. And now *you* show up. With a helmet. Bullet crease from my gun. And *Rachel Clark's* fingerprints on it. When everyone thought she was in Timbuktu."

It seems odd for Hunter to say Timbuktu. Because someone else said Timbuktu—just last night, when Hunter wasn't there. But I can't ask a cop if he bugged the same room I did.

"Probably *old* fingerprints," I say, trying to buy some time.

"No," Hunter says. "Rachel Clark's fingerprints on the helmet are fresh."

"Davis's prints are fresh, too," Cliff adds. "We're here to arrest him, David."

"Arrest *Lane Davis*? For what?"

"Aiding and abetting a fugitive," Hunter replies.

Arrest a mayoral candidate? Three weeks before Election Day? This is way too deep for me. I can see I'll end up having to tell them where I got that helmet. But not 'til I talk to my boss, Graham Hancock, publisher of *The National Spy*. And maybe talk to a lawyer, too.

"So where'd you get that helmet, Dave?" Cliff slaps me on the back. My old teammate.

I shake my head a third time. "No way. Reporter's privilege, fellas."

"*Reporter's privilege?*" Hunter explodes. "You're sitting on *material evidence*. In a *murder* investigation. What the hell kind of *bullshit* is 'reporter's privilege?'"

"The First Amendment to the United States Constitution," I say, very pompously, "gives journalists the right to shield our sources. We cannot be compelled to identify our sources."

I omit to inform Hunter that the shield laws based on the reporter's privilege all carve out an exception for *criminal investigations*. I also don't mention that the reporter's privilege doesn't even apply here, because my only "source" is myself. But I see no reason to give these gumshoes that much detail. Let 'em go to law school, if they want. At night.

"Actually, Dave," Cliff says, "you're wrong. I know you went to law school and all. But the Michigan shield law for journalists has an exception. For felonies. Murder is a felony."

I hate it when cops go out and attend seminars and learn stuff.

"The statutory exceptions never stand up in court," I lie, to buy time. "A mere Michigan *statute* can't trump the United States *Constitution*." Pembroke Watkins would have been so proud of me for *that* one. It sounds so right. Even though, in this case, it's dead wrong. Because *the Constitution* has exceptions, too. Including one for murder investigations.

Hunter looks ready to burst. Apparently arcane legal argument does not float his boat. "Look," Hunter says, "we were hoping to do this the easy way. Since you're Cliff's old buddy."

"Yeah, Dave," Cliff chimes in, giving me the whole Meathead hang-dog look again. Like he can't believe his old *teammate* is letting him down on this. Making him look bad.

"But if you won't cooperate," Hunter continues, "we'll just *subpoena* you. Then you can either talk to the grand jury, or you can go to jail. There's no third way."

"Then I'll go to jail. But I'll *never* give up my source."

That, by the way, is bullshit. No way would I go to jail. (At least, not over a mere *principle*. Someday I may get busted for B&E. Or illegal surveillance. *Then* I may have no choice.)

But to buy time, I decide to play the bluff out. Remember that Humphrey Bogart riff at the end of *The Maltese Falcon*? About how a detective can't stand by and let his partner get killed? Because it's bad for business. Bad for detectives everywhere. I adapt the riff for reporters.

"See, fellas, it's like this. If a reporter gives up his source, he's outta work. Won't no one *talk* to him no more. Everyone will think he's just a tool for the cops. A snitch. That's bad for business. Bad for reporters everywhere. The whole idea of a free press goes out the window. And if you don't have a free press, you don't have a free *country* anymore. Fellas."

I try to gauge the impact I'm having on these hard-ass cops. But they wear poker faces.

"Would I like to help you fellas out?" I continue. "Of course. But don't you see? I *can't*."

"Let's arrest this asshole now, Cliff," Hunter snarls.

"On what charge?" I demand.

"Material witness in a murder investigation." Hunter turns to Cliff, as if I'm invisible. "Don't let him out of your sight 'til I come back with a grand jury subpoena."

"Not smart, Greg," I admonish. "Not smart at all."

"Why not, asshole?" Hunter turns back to me.

"Because newspapers fight grand jury subpoenas in public," I say. "Material witness warrants, too. Newspapers *always* fight in public. You don't want that, do you?" I meet Hunter's hard, ugly stare. To show him I mean business. "Think about it," I continue. "Right now, no one knows you have Rachel Clark's fingerprints. Right? Or have you already blabbed it all over town?"

"Right now the three of us are the only ones who know," Hunter says in a guarded tone. "Along with the officer who ran the computer fingerprint search. Who won't tell a soul. Not unless I tell her to." Hunter anticipates my asking how he can be so sure. "She's my girlfriend."

"Good. So then Rachel Clark has no reason to run. But pinch me with a subpoena, and this thing'll be on the seven o'clock news. There's no story the media likes better than a newsman heroically going to jail to protect a source. And after that, how long do you think she'll stay in town?"

"Rachel Clark's here?" Hunter demands. "In Ann Arbor?"

"I don't know." I open my hands. Palms up. The universal gesture of innocence. Even though I'm not innocent at all. Since I just let that remark about Rachel Clark being 'in town' slip out on purpose. I look at Cliff. "I haven't seen her. God's truth, Cliff." As if I know anything about God. *Or* truth.

Cliff nods. But still looks like he'd just as soon slam a basketball in my face.

"But as near as I can tell," I continue, "Rachel Clark must be *somewhere near* Ann Arbor. That's where I got that helmet with her fingerprints. Right here in Ann Arbor."

"In Lane Davis's office?" Hunter asks.

"C'mon, Detective," I say. "This isn't 21 Questions. But I'll tell you what. I *will* play ball with you. If you'll play ball with *me*."

"Go ahead," Hunter growls.

"You want Rachel Clark. And I want an exclusive story. I got no problem with you getting Rachel Clark. You got any problem with me getting an exclusive story?"

"No problem," Hunter agrees without hesitation.

"Then we can be *teammates*! My paper goes to press on Mondays. So hold off pinching me with that subpoena a few days. If I find Rachel Clark, believe me, you'll be the first to know. Just let me interview her first. That way I'll get my story. And you'll get your fugitive."

Hunter shakes his head no. "I don't know you, Fisher. But you sound like you're just blowing smoke out your ass. The stakes here are too high. This isn't some *game*, you know."

"What have you got to lose?" I counter.

"*What have I got to lose?*" Hunter sounds incredulous. "*Thirty-five years* I've been kicking myself for letting Dale's murderer go free. And you ask—" Hunter pounds his right fist into his left palm. *Hard.* "Tell you what," Hunter says, his voice suddenly quiet. *Spooky* quiet. "Since you want to be *teammates.* Go interview Dale's kid. Boyce Hunter."

"Where would I find Boyce?" I have no intention of interviewing Boyce Hunter. But I find it best to play along with large men with guns who look like they're about to slug me.

"At the bus station, maybe," Greg Hunter says. "Or maybe the homeless shelter. Sometimes Boyce's down at drug detox. But mostly he's just on the streets. A pathetic little loser."

Hunter smacks his right fist into his left palm again. This time he *rotates* his fist into the meaty palm of his left hand. Rotates it *over and over.* Like a pestle grinding into a mortar.

"After Dale died," he continues, "Boyce's mommy took the money a policeman's widow gets. Which ain't much. Blew it all on booze and pills. Little Boyce grew up with nothin' but mommy's bad example—no Dale to keep him straight. Dropped outta school. Ended up lookin' like the punks who killed his daddy. *Still* ain't never held a job more than six weeks in his life."

I wonder if Uncle Greg here feels a little guilty about all this, too. Since presumably *he* failed to keep his brother's kid out of trouble, too. But this seems like a very poor time to ask.

Hunter pulls his right hand out of his left palm. So he can jab a thick, gnarled forefinger in my face. "You asshole reporters at the *National Enquirer*," he continues with a sneer.

"*National Spy,*" I correct. Call us what you will. But please. Get the *name* right.

"Whatever. *You* could never understand Boyce's pain. But it's real. There's people *dyin'* out there, Mr. Hollywood Reporter. Every goddamn day. Boyce is *still* dyin' out there, because of what Rachel Clark and her little shit pals did to his daddy. *That's* what I have to lose. *That's* why I ain't gonna play games with you. *That's* why we can't be '*teammates.*'"

Well. There are very few things in life as painful as having someone tell you to your face you're an asshole. Especially when you know they're right.

But that's what makes tabloid hacks special. We know no guilt. We have no shame.

So I just keep plugging away. "No matter what you think of me, Detective, it would still be dumb for you to go public now. Yanking me into a grand jury. Or arresting Davis. All you'd be doing is hassling *small fry*. And splashing so much water in the process, you'd scare the big fish away."

Greg Hunter exchanges a long glance with Cliff Bryant.

"What else can we do, Dave?" Cliff asks at last, sounding like he really does want to find a compromise. "We can't just *ignore* the evidence you brought us. We have to do *something*. Or we'll be up on charges ourselves. Dereliction of duty."

"So stake out Davis. Stake out Rachel Clark's parents. Hell, *you're* the cops. You don't need *me* to tell you what to do. Do whatever it is you do *whenever* you're investigating a group of crooks. You don't always just run out and arrest the first guy who moves, do you?"

"Give us a minute," Hunter says. He and Cliff step out in the hall to confer.

Which gives me a minute, too. Maybe I *should* just tell them where I got the damn helmet. And tell them those fingerprints came from one of the four fifty-four-year-old women in that room last night. But do I know that *for sure*? Fingerprints don't lie. Yet Rachel Clark could have touched that helmet sometime *before* Norma Lee brought it to Ann Arbor. The woman I saw striking the Weatherman pose might be an innocent bystander. But if so, why didn't Cliff say they found fingerprints on the helmet for Lane Davis, Rachel Clark *and someone else*?

Yet as fast as I think of this, I realize there *had* to be other fingerprints on the helmet that Cliff didn't mention. *Norma Lee's*. Norma must have fondled that thing a few times before boxing it up for Davis. Yet they didn't mention Norma's fingerprints. Which means they might have found *other*, unidentified fingerprints on the helmet, too. Fingerprints they didn't bother telling me about. But then why mention Davis, and *not* Norma Lee? Why wouldn't they suspect *Norma Lee* of aiding and abetting Rachel Clark, too? Why didn't they come here to arrest *both of them*?

I feel dizzy. In the tabloid biz, we rarely think this much. But one thing I see clearly. If I tell these guys where I got the helmet, they'll just haul *all four* of my suspects into custody. Fingerprint the lot of 'em. Until they find which one is Rachel Clark. And I'll lose my shot at the greatest tabloid exclusive since Gary Hart and Donna Rice.

So I decide to hold off cooperating awhile. Investigate some more on my own. Get a little closer to Monday's press run.

The cops return. "Okay," Hunter says. "Here's the deal. We won't haul you into the grand jury. *For now*. But we might change our minds any minute. No warning. Got it?"

"Got it," I say.

"We won't arrest Lane Davis right away, either," Hunter says. "But we might change our minds any minute about *that*, too. No warning. Got it?"

"Got it." I wonder if Hunter is Catholic. We have a nice little catechism going here.

"You don't leave town without giving us four hours notice. Got it?"

"Got it." (No way *that* order is legally enforceable. So I see no harm in agreeing.)

"If you find Rachel Clark, you tell us right away. Got it?"

"Do I get to interview her first?" I counter.

"You can interview her right after we do," Hunter says.

"*Right* after?" I ask. "Or will you suddenly get bogged down in red tape?"

"*Right* after. *If* you find her, you get first and only crack at her. Right after us."

"Deal." I offer Hunter my hand.

He looks at my hand like it belongs to a leper. But shakes it, all the same. Cliff, too.

"Hell," Hunter mutters, "you find her, you can even keep the reward money."

"*Reward money*? You mean that money the banker put up back in '69 is still just—"

"—sitting there? You bet it is, boy-o. With all the interest, it's worth close to two hundred thousand dollars now. And I'm still the guy who says who gets it. You *sure* you don't want to just tell me where you got that helmet?"

"No thanks." Sure, two hundred large is a lot of jack. But I'm sure Graham would just claim the whole reward for the *Spy*.

I start to go. Then turn back. Like Colombo used to do. "Say. One more thing. Were there any *other* fingerprints on that helmet? *Besides* Lane Davis's and Rachel Clark's?"

Hunter exchanges a quick guilty-looking glance with Cliff. "No. Why?"

"Oh, nothing." I start to go again.

"One last thing, Fisher." Apparently Hunter's seen Colombo, too. "I have a very long memory. If Rachel Clark gets away because of you, well, *I wouldn't want to be you*."

A completely unnecessary remark. *Most of my life* I've felt like I didn't want to be me.

\* \* \*

By the time my Ann Arbor police buddies finish rattling my cage, the press conference is done and gone. Norma Lee is on her way back to La-La land. And Lane Davis is back in his office. So I do the mature thing. I go upstairs to my hotel room. And flop face down on my bed.

What the hell am I doing? (Besides biting off way more than I can chew.) What kind of shit will hit the fan if Rachel Clark escapes—again—and people decide it's *my fault*? We tabloid hacks know no guilt. Have no shame. But helping the Fugitive Radical escape—again—might be *criminal*. The boys in blue are already unhappy with me. They won't cut me any slack.

The only good news is, Hunter *ordered* me to stay in town. Probably not legally enforceable. But still. I'll tell Graham Hancock I can't disobey *a cop's order*. Which solves one little problem I had, namely how to drag this little trip out to Saturday—so I can attend my thirtieth high school reunion.

I debate calling Graham now and asking him to hire a lawyer. But Graham might order me to cooperate with the cops. I don't like orders. Not when they conflict with what I want to do.

Then again, maybe I *should* just cooperate. They can round up the four suspects now. Identify Rachel Clark by noon. I'll get my interview tomorrow. Friday at the latest. Plus, I'll be the hero. The guy who fingered the Fugitive Radical. What more do I want? What more do I need?

Unfortunately, the answer to these questions does not cover me with glory. But by now, Worthy Reader, you've figured out that I'm not the nicest guy in the world. Which means, if you're still reading, you must have decided to *overlook* my multiple character defects, right? So why not be honest?

The truth is, I'm a forty-eight-year-old disbarred lawyer working as a tabloid hack. At a *third-rate* tabloid, no less. Like Rodney Dangerfield, I get no respect. Not from my family. Not from my old classmates. Not from my journalism peers. Not even from *myself*. And now I have the chance of a lifetime. The fingerprints of the legendary Rachel Clark. The Fugitive Radical. And I'm the only person in the world who knows that, unless she touched that helmet sometime *before* Norma gave it to Davis, she has to be one of four Ann Arbor women.

This is my chance for glory. For respect. And for something more, too.

Call it ego. Call it mid-life crisis. Whatever. But I don't want to be *just* the casual hero who fingers a fugitive. The fifteen minutes of fame thing. I want to be the one who *tells Rachel Clark's whole life story*. Who finds her. Interviews her. Gets to know her. *Nails* her story. And then writes it all up, too—*before* outing her. I know this is egotistical. Self-aggrandizing. Showboating. All those things my boss at the *Enquirer* called me when he fired me.

But hey, life is short. If you don't *go for it*, at least once in a while, what's the point?

So I develop a simple plan. I'll interview the four suspects. Get each of them to touch something. A drinking glass. A piece of paper. Whatever. Then I'll take away the object with their fingerprints. Without them knowing I've taken it. Turn all the objects in to Cliff Bryant. One by one. For testing. To see which one is Rachel Clark.

This plan needs fine-tuning. I know that. But I feel better, just *having* a plan.

I get up. Fire up my laptop. Print out yesterday's pix. They turn out great. The Norma Lee cleavage shots are awesome. And Davis hugging Norma will be easy to crop, so it looks like they were all alone.

But the best pix? The shots of that hot little minx of a staffer from Davis & Nyman. I almost forgot about her.

\* \* \*

Rule #2 at the DOJ: *Visit the scene of the crime.*

So at 11:30 I walk over to Davis & Nyman. To sniff around. Where two of my four suspects work. (Not to mention the hot little minx of my dreams.) On the way I hatch a plan.

The receptionist, Debbie Smith, is *not* the little minx. I tell Debbie I'm a prospective new client. No, I don't have an appointment. But it's *urgent* that I speak with Mr. Davis. ASAP. Debbie looks dubious. Worse, she seems impervious to my (admittedly fading) charms. (In my youth I was tall, blonde, and good-looking. Now I'm just tall.)

Debbie buzzes upstairs. Speaks with "Janet." Whom I know from the brochure is Janet Fickel. 50/50 chance. The little minx has to be either Janet Fickel or Sue Webber.

One good thing about working for a tabloid: we see lots of beautiful women. True, it's mostly when they're slamming doors in our faces. Or giving us the finger. But still, they're lookers. So I'm not easily impressed. Besides, I'm a *professional*. I never let a hot babe distract me from doing my job. I'm here at Davis & Nyman on *business*.

Nevertheless, I'm impressed. Janet Fickel looks even better from ground level than she did from up on that roof. She is one *very* hot babe. And she knows it. In her high heels and her cinnamon stockings and her short tight skirt, she walks down Davis & Nyman's stairs slower than a Victoria's Secret model on the runway. "Her Strut" mesmerizes me. (Remember that Bob Seger song? *"O they do respect her but—they <u>love</u> to watch her strut."*)

Janet is only about 5'2". But with the heels she looks 5'5". And most of her height is in her impossibly long, slender legs. Her loose-fitting business jacket thwarts my Pavlovian desire to check out her chest. But her hips sashay back and forth as she approaches. And there is a faint rustling of elusive undergarments just beneath that short, tight skirt. The whole ensemble definitely provokes my, um, curiosity.

With what little remains of my forty-eight-year-old peripheral vision, I dimly see dubious Debbie watching me as I watch Janet Fickel. Which reminds me to close my mouth. With a quick swipe of my sleeve, I mop most of the drool off my chin. Then I introduce myself. And stick out my hand.

Janet Fickel cocks her head sideways. Looks amused. But shakes my hand anyway. Janet's hand is older than the rest of her looks. Before the hand, I was guessing mid-twenties. Now I'm thinking early thirties. While shaking my hand, Janet looks me up and down. In a stupefying, sexy way. As if she were actually *interested* in me. For purposes I can only dream of.

"Can I tell Mr. Davis the nature of your business?" Janet enquires.

"It's personal," I confide. "And *urgent*." I smile my nicest smile.

Janet gazes at me. Not only is she sexy as hell, she's also very *pretty*. Round face. High cheekbones. Uses makeup well. Light auburn hair, worn pageboy style. With bangs. Heavy eyebrows framing mischievous eyes. Eyes with a very *knowing* sexuality. Janet Fickel has definitely been around the block a few times. And she doesn't mind letting me know it.

"Well, I have to tell Mr. Davis *something*," Janet teases.

"Tell him I'm starting a non-profit progressive magazine," I say, following the plan I cooked up on the way over. How can Davis resist *that*?

"I'll see what I can do." Janet walks back up the stairs. *Her Strut* is even more provocative from the back. Ignoring Debbie, I ogle shamelessly the lovely flare in Janet's rump. The slow sashay of those hips. In Jimmy Carter's immortal words, I sin in my heart. And elsewhere.

To my huge disappointment, instead of a return visit from Janet Fickel, Lane Davis himself comes downstairs next. His gray beard and lean, wiry body confirm what I already know from his firm brochure and from the internet. Davis is fifty-eight, but still a serious long-distance runner. A West Point grad who served in Vietnam. Returned deeply disillusioned. Embraced left-wing politics. Worked five years as a local prosecutor in Ann Arbor, until he got fired in '78—for lending his car to Ralph Nader, so Ralph wouldn't be late for a sit-in at a General Motors plant. After that, Davis went into private practice. In the '80s his legal opponents "misunderestimated" him (as George Dubya would say) because he looked like such a flake. But by the '90s Ann Arbor lawyers had learned Lane Davis was one dangerous adversary, because juries loved his common sense approach. In 2002, Davis won a landslide election to City Council—*voters*, like jurors, loved Davis's common sense approach. In 2004 he decided to run for mayor as a third-party candidate. For the Human Rights Party—a long-moribund political party, last heard from in the '60s.

Lane Davis motions me into the conference room. Where I feign interest in all the left-wing decorations—as if I'm seeing the room for the first time. The photos of Malcolm and Martin, the Kennedys and Nader. The collage of old radical bumper stickers. And the Rachel Clark Weatherman helmet. Now displayed, per Davis's promise to Norma Lee last night, on the credenza.

"What can I do for you, Mr. Fisher?" Davis sits down. "My assistant said it's *urgent*." Behind his round John Lennon specs, Davis's shiny eyes bug out. Like a curious frog.

"Well, *to me* it's urgent." I also sit down. "But if you're too busy today . . . "

"No, no," Davis assures me. "You caught me at a good time. My assistant says you're starting a non-profit magazine? With a progressive focus? Here in Ann Arbor?"

"One of the few towns left in America that still *has* progressives in residence." Davis laughs sympathetically. Good start.

"Do you have litigation issues?" Davis asks. "Or do you just need business advice?"

"Both."

"Well, I handle the litigation myself. And my partner Sheila Nyman handles the business side. Sheila advises dozens of non-profits. She's *very* good."

"Is Sheila here now?"

"Yes. But she's in an all-day board meeting, I'm afraid."

"Will Sheila be able to see me *soon*? To me, it's important to get started right away."

"Oh yes," Davis says. "Her assistant, Sue Webber, can get you an appointment."

"Will Sheila work on my business matters alone? Or does she have support?"

"Sheila gets all the support she needs. We have two associates. And a paralegal."

"The paralegal—has he been with you long?" (I pretend I haven't seen the brochure.)

"Fifteen years," Davis replies. "*She's* very capable. Naomi Williams."

"College degree?"

"University of Michigan. All of us here are U of M grads."

"Is Naomi Williams here now?"

"Yes. But she's in the all-day board meeting with Sheila. I'm sorry . . . "

"It's okay. What did Naomi Williams do before she came to work here?"

"Humanitarian work in Central America."

"This *is* a progressive law firm, isn't it?"

"We try to be. Everyone here is committed to social justice for all people." Davis removes his John Lennon specs and cleans them with his rumpled, tweedy tie. "But you said you need some *litigation* advice, in addition to the business advice?"

"*May* need litigation advice," I say.

"What's the problem?"

"There's a cop hassling me. Detective Greg Hunter."

"I know Hunter. He's been in Ann Arbor forever."

"Are you friends? Would you have a *conflict* representing me against Hunter?"

"Oh, no," Davis assures me. "Fact is, Hunter hates my politics. Hated me even when I was an assistant prosecutor."

"Well, I suppose you weren't a straight-arrow kind of prosecutor, were you?"

"What do you mean by that?" Davis bristles.

"Well, you lent your car to Ralph Nader and all . . . "

"That was a little more complicated than what you might read on the internet," Davis says tersely. "What exactly is going on between you and Detective Hunter?"

"Hunter is threatening to search my offices," I lie, fronting mild paranoia. "As a journalist, I have First Amendment rights, don't I?"

"Absolutely. What's Hunter looking for?"

"He's got this crazy idea I know where Rachel Clark is."

Davis doesn't bat an eye. Betrays no emotion at the name Rachel Clark. Or at the idea that someone might know where the hell Rachel Clark is in 2004.

"You do know who Rachel Clark is, don't you?" I ask.

"Oh, yes." Davis points at the credenza. "That's her Days of Rage helmet over there."

"No kidding! Where'd you get that?"

"Gift. A memento. From the Revolution that never was."

I inspect it. "Wow! It's even got the bullet crease. Is this the bullet crease from—?"

"—Greg Hunter's gun," Davis says. "Yes. The day his brother got killed."

"Does *Hunter* know you have this?"

"No."

"Good thing. Or he'd search *your* offices. The man's *obsessed* with Rachel Clark."

"She's the only reason Hunter hasn't retired," Davis agrees. "Back in '69 he vowed to bring Rachel Clark to justice. Can't bring himself to admit she's long gone."

"Any idea where Rachel Clark is today?" I ask. Blandly.

Davis looks shocked. "Of course not," he protests. "How should *I* know?"

"You must know some of the same people Rachel Clark knew. To get that helmet."

Davis relaxes a little at this explanation. "No one I know has seen Rachel Clark since 1969. She disappeared thirty-five years ago, through that Law School steam tunnel. After that, everything you hear about Rachel Clark is just urban legends. Underground myths." Davis loosens the knot in his tie. "And you? Why does Hunter think *you* know where she is?"

"I've done research on social protestors, for 'where are they now?' articles," I say, while wondering how Davis knows she escaped through a steam tunnel. "Including some research on Rachel Clark. Probably Hunter heard I was asking around about her."

"Well, if you want me to," Davis says, "I could call Hunter and back him off. Review for him your First Amendment rights. Or I could write him a letter—"

"Naw. I'd prefer you not contact him—yet. But I'd like to retain you. To be ready. In case Hunter hits me with a warrant. Or a subpoena. And I'd like to meet with Sheila, too."

Davis buzzes upstairs. Asks Janet Fickel to prepare a retainer letter.

I decide there's no point asking Davis how he knows Rachel Clark escaped through a steam tunnel. He's not going to admit anything incriminating. And the question may just piss him off.

Next Davis buzzes Sue Webber. Gets me the earliest available appointment with Sheila Nyman. Next Tuesday at ten. Six days off. Not quite as "early" as I'd hoped, but I seem to have no choice.

I notice a small bronze *moving van* among Davis's left-wing mementos. "What's this?"

"Gift from my wife, Camille. In 1989 I drove a moving van full of medical supplies to Nicaragua. That's where I met Camille. She got this made for me to commemorate the trip."

"I've read a lot about Camille's work for the homeless. I'd like to meet her sometime."

"She'll be at City Hall tonight, giving a presentation on the new homeless shelter."

"My college roommate was very active in getting that new homeless shelter built," I say. "Saul Schwartz. I think Sauly works a lot with Camille."

Davis brightens immediately at Saul Schwartz's name. "Saul's a great guy."

"Is Sauly working on your campaign?"

"Sadly, no. I'm the *third-party* candidate, you know. The old Human Rights party. That's hard for Democrats like Saul. The Nader problem. They don't want to cross party lines."

"But *The Ann Arbor News* has given you great press. And they're pretty mainstream."

"The *News* hates me. They only give me good press because they hope I'll draw lots of Democrats away from the Mayor, and open the door for the Republican they'd like to win."

"*Could* the Republican win?"

"Not in this town. Republicans in Ann Arbor are just a noisy minority. No votes. If the students turn out big, I'll win. Otherwise, the incumbent Democrat will hang on."

Janet Fickel comes in. Hands Davis the retainer letter. Smiles at me. Then leaves.

I sign the retainer letter. Promise a five-hundred-dollar check by next Tuesday. Of course, a Florida check could raise questions. But if need be, I'll get *my mom* to write the check. My mom still lives here in Ann Arbor.

We get up. Shake hands.

"Say, do you know Raven LaGrow?" I ask. "The progressive Michigan Law Professor?"

"Sure," Davis says.

"I'd like to interview her. For my new magazine. But I hear she doesn't like the media."

"Oh, she'll like you fine. It's the *tabloids* Raven fights with. And Rush Limbaugh."

"Well, if I have any trouble getting an interview with her, would you be able to, er— "

"Put in a good word for you? Sure. I'm seeing Raven tonight. I'll mention your name."

So. All four suspects are still in Ann Arbor. Present and accounted for. That's good news.

* * *

Since I don't pray, my prayers are seldom answered. But as I leave Lane Davis's office, there she is. Just fifty yards ahead. Moving at a languorous pace, like a sleepy lioness. *Her Strut.* Janet Fickel. Sashaying down Main Street. Alone. In those stockings and high heels.

Why am I such a sucker for stockings and heels? It goes back to my formative years. In seventh grade, all the girls of my wet dreams wore stockings and heels. But by the time I found the gumption to actually *talk* to any of them (*eleventh* grade), they'd all moved on to overalls and hiking boots. That's Ann Arbor for you. In college and law school it was even worse: no self-respecting U of M woman would be caught dead in a skirt or a dress. So I didn't actually get to *speak* to a woman in stockings and heels until I joined the workaday world in my thirties. By which time I was married to Elaine. Who *never* wears stockings. So in my whole life, except for my two one-hour flings, I've never actually gotten my hands on a woman in stockings.

But I'm a professional. So it can't be those cinnamon stockings driving me to double-time it down the sidewalk. Not *me*. It's just that Janet Fickel could be a great *source*. Of information, that is. On Sheila Nyman. And Naomi Williams. But chasing Janet down the sidewalk is hard. Gotta move fast enough to catch her, before she gets wherever she's going. Yet can't arrive all sweaty and breathless. And can't make so much noise she might catch me sneaking up on her.

"Fancy meeting you here," I say, sidling up to her. "Would you like to have lunch with me?" I try to sound nonchalant. But fail miserably. Can't be done when you're out of breath.

Janet Fickel doesn't stop walking. Doesn't answer right away, either. But then, with a what-the-hell tone, she says, "Sure." To seem like a real local, I suggest Zingerman's.

"Where's Zingerman's?" Janet asks.

"Where's Zingerman's?" I repeat, like an incredulous parrot. "*Everyone* knows where Zingerman's is. An Ann Arbor *landmark*. *USA Today* wrote 'em up."

"Never heard of it," Janet says. In a level, non-confrontational, just-the-facts tone.

"It's just two blocks up Kingsley," I say. "C'mon, I'll show you."

"Is that the pricey deli that's always packed? I don't have time for standing in lines."

"No problem. I have a friend there who can sneak us in," I boast. "If he's there."

Luckily we've only got two blocks to cover. Because small talk, while walking side by side with a perfectly gorgeous stranger, is hard. Even for a naturally gabby guy like me.

Fortunately, Ann Arbor's streets provide distractions galore.

First we encounter a fully mobile homeless woman. A wizened lady with a round face, of indeterminate age. Anywhere from thirty to seventy. Wearing a big straw hat. And riding an old Schwinn bike. Which she's loaded up like General Patton's tank. The front basket's crammed with fifty pounds of food and drink. The two rear baskets are stuffed with fifty pounds each of clothing and junk. Her bedding is piled across the back baskets, three feet high. She herself is built like a tank—nearly as wide as she is tall, with stubby legs that barely reach her pedals.

A Cadillac emerging from a parking lot cuts her off. She's forced to dismount. Mutters dark obscenities. Because re-mounting is hard. With those stubby legs. And re-*starting* is even harder. With two hundred pounds in tow. She wobbles as she pushes off, listing badly to port.

So I catch her elbow and give her a gentle forward push.

"Hey, fuck you!" The homeless woman snarls at me as she rides off.

I jump back in dismay.

Janet Fickel laughs. "That's what you get for being a Good Samaritan."

"You're the first person ever to accuse me of being a Good Samaritan," I say. "Usually I get chastised for being a bad boy."

Janet laughs again. She's got a nice laugh. Throaty. Hearty. Totally real.

We cut through the Farmer's Market. Where we're engulfed in a tight crowd of people. And immersed in smells of cider and fresh-cut chrysanthemums. But Janet seems to like it. So I stop and buy her a small arrangement of mums. Then arrange to pick them up on our way back.

We cross Detroit Street. At Community High School, several teenage boys playing football stop dead in their tracks. To ogle Janet. She pretends not to notice their attentive stares. But I catch her smiling to herself.

Zingerman's is packed with people. Long ropes of thick sausages hang from the ceiling. We're awash in smells of body odor. Strong cheeses. Warm bread. And spicy sausages.

Luckily, my friend Saul Schwartz *is* there. And yes, he was my U of M roommate, just like I told Davis. We both spent far more time there getting stoned than going to class. Now Sauly owns Zingerman's. He gives me a big bear hug. But frowns at the idea of helping us jump the queue.

"*Please*, Sauly," I whisper, with a quick jerk of my head at Janet, gazing at the cheeses.

Sauly looks Janet up and down. Pantomimes a silent whistle. Then breaks into a huge grin. "Okay. Just this one time."

Janet agrees to split a sandwich. But leaves me to design it.

Big mistake, I warn her. Cuz I like my sandwiches *complex*. Janet shrugs.

I choose free-range turkey breast and farm-fresh Wisconsin muenster cheese. On farm-baked, no-yeast bread. With orchard-fresh California avocado spread. Imported Greek kalamata olives. And hot Spanish piquillo peppers. Just your average Ann Arbor lunch.

I find us a picnic table outside. Make a small production of removing my jacket. Even though the October sun isn't all *that* hot. Because I'm hoping Janet will follow suit. Remove *her* loose business jacket. So I can check out her chest. But she keeps her jacket on. And buttoned.

Normally I try to be a little *indirect*. But I'm nervous. So I make no bones about interviewing Janet. Though I start with questions *only* about Janet. Better than diving right into my Davis & Nyman questions.

Janet tells me she was born on a farm outside Fort Wayne, Indiana. Worked in law firms in Fort Wayne for several years. Is married. To John Fickel. A car mechanic. (With regret I notice Janet wears a wedding ring.) John's boss asked him to transfer to Michigan last year to run the service department at Olson's Chevrolet, outside Ann Arbor. Janet came with, and landed the job at Davis & Nyman. But she hates Ann Arbor. As does her younger daughter.

"How old's your younger daughter?" I'm fishing, obviously, for a clue to *Janet's* age.

"Eighteen."

"No way! You can't be more than thirty yourself."

"Forty," Janet corrects me, while picking the Spanish piquillo peppers out of her half of our sandwich. "And—I have a four-year-old *grandson*."

"You don't look like any granny I ever met."

Janet laughs. Like I said, she has a *great* laugh.

"I got pregnant when I was seventeen. Dropped out. Married the guy. Had the kid. My older daughter, Carrie. She's twenty-three now. When Carrie was in high school, she made the same mistake. Pregnant at seventeen. Dropped out. Married the guy. Had the kid. My four-year-old grandson, Colin." Janet Fickel delivers this laconic explanation of how she became a grandmother at thirty-six without a trace of self-pity. In a voice as rich and throaty as her laugh. Remember Stevie Nicks? Fleetwood Mac? Janet's voice is like that. Plangent. Almost raspy. Like a torch singer. Sexy as hell.

"Did you ever go back to school?"

"No. Just got a job. Been workin' ever since."

"So you've been married twenty-three years?"

"No. I divorced my first husband right after Carrie was born. I've been married eleven years to John."

I do some quick math. She said her *younger* daughter's eighteen. Too young to be from the *first* marriage. Which ended in a year. But too *old* for John to be the father. Unless Janet was living out of wedlock with John for seven years before they got married. Which seems unlikely.

Janet reads my mind. "John's my *third* husband. Stacy is from my *second* husband."

Three husbands by age thirty! I censor myself from comparing Janet to Liz Taylor. Instead, I fall back on my kids' favorite teeny-bopper band, *Fountains of Wayne*. "*Stacy*? Like that song?" Off-key, I sing: "*Stacy's mom has got it goin' on/She's all I want and I've waited so long/I know it might be wrong/But I'm in love with Stacy's mom.*"

Janet laughs. "Yes. Like that song. Stacy's friends sing that around me all the time."

"Well you *do* have it goin' on—Granny."

"Stacy's boyfriends tell her 'your mom is so *hot*.' Probably *not* what Stacy really wants to hear."

"But Stacy's . . . staying out of trouble?"

Janet rolls her eyes. "I ground her twice a week. And still she defies me. John won't do anything. His own kids were more trouble than mine. So he says he's done worrying about it."

Janet reaches in her purse for something. Changes her mind. Brings her hand out empty. Instead sets about removing the imported Greek kalamata olives from her half of our sandwich. Since she's taken only one bite, I ask if Janet wants me to get her something else.

"No, I'm fine." She nibbles a little piece of the crust off the farm-cooked, no-yeast bread.

A yard sign across the street says: *Davis For Mayor: We Need Regime Change <u>Here</u>, Too.*

I gesture at the campaign sign. "Exciting times at Davis & Nyman?"

Janet snorts. "I can't wait 'til it's over."

"Really! Why?"

"So much bullshit! Fundraisers every day. Twenty million phone calls. And all the media morons. Constantly—" Janet stops. Probably remembering *I'm* one of those 'media morons.'

I smile ruefully. "It's okay. I've been called worse."

"Like what?" Janet teases.

"*Junkyard dog.* That's worse than a 'media moron,' right?"

Janet laughs. God, I could listen to that laugh all day. "Maybe. But you don't *seem* like a junkyard dog." Janet cocks her head. Raises a dramatic eyebrow. Gives me that sexy up-and-down look she gave me in the office. I can't tell if she's flirting. But I sure as hell hope so.

"That's cuz I'm on my best behavior here. Trying to be a good boy. To impress you."

"Good boys don't impress me," Janet teases.

At this I gaze into her eyes. Ready to flirt.

But Janet sees the danger in my eyes. Looks away at once. Starts picking at her olives again. "Anyway," she says, "you're not the kind of reporter who drives me crazy. It's the ones who call up *every day*. All they want is their daily quote. They wait 'til five minutes before deadline. *Then* they call. Gotta talk to Lane. Right away! To get Lane's views on whatever's hot news today. I explain he's already on the phone, with another reporter. Giving *that guy* his daily quote. Maybe they should think about calling a little earlier. They never do. They're so rude."

"Occupational hazard," I mumble. "You think Lane'll win?"

"God, I hope not."

"Why not?"

"Lane's a shit." Janet arches her heavy eyebrows. "This *is* off the record, right?"

"Of course," I assure her. "I'm not doing any story on Lane."

"Lane's way too left-wing for me. Plus, what happens to *my* job if he wins?"

"You could go with him to City Hall. Have your finger on the pulse of Ann Arbor."

"I'll pass, thanks. I don't know anything about politics. I like being a legal assistant."

"Well if you don't want Davis to win, you're in the perfect position to stop him."

"How?"

"Dish a little dirt. Tell those reporters who call every day about Lane *and Norma Lee*. No quote attributed to you, of course. You'd be a confidential source. Speaking 'on background.'"

Janet opens her eyes wide. As if *shocked* by my impropriety.

But the mischief in her eyes says she's really not shocked at all.

"Lane *and Norma Lee*?" Janet laughs. "I don't think so."

"I hear they used to be an item."

"Really?" Janet cocks her head. "Maybe. But these days Lane's . . . otherwise engaged."

"Oh, no," I groan. "Not the *Happily Married Politician*. That's such a boring story."

"Who said *his wife* is where he's engaged?" Mischief is now written all over Janet's face.

"Oh? Then who's Lane shagging? If not Norma Lee? *Tell! Tell!*"

Janet laughs. But shakes her head no. "Not to a reporter."

"I'm not a reporter. I'm a *journalist*. At least, that's what I tell my mom."

Janet laughs. "Does your mom buy that BS?"

"Not really. But Janet—I promise I won't do anything with the information. Lane's *my lawyer*. I'd never burn *my own lawyer*. I just . . . I'm curious, that's all. Who's Lane stepping out with?"

Janet shakes her head again. "I don't know you well enough, David Fisher."

Rather than admit this, I shift ground. "Does *Camille* know Lane's having an affair?"

"I think so. Lane's not very discreet, really. I kinda figured *everyone* knew."

"Except for me," I pout. "Does Camille *confront* him? Any *big scenes* in the office?"

"No. Camille looks the other way. I don't think she really *minds* not having Lane around all the time. He's kind of, you know—dull."

"Does Camille step out *on him*?"

"I doubt it. She's too sweet for that. I think she just stays wrapped up in her causes."

"The homeless, you mean?"

"And the Sierra Club. And the Interfaith Peace Network. And about fifty others."

"Well, we Ann Arborites do *love* lost causes."

Janet laughs. "Then you'll love Camille. She's the patron saint of lost causes."

"Ever hear Lane talk about Rachel Clark?"

"Not 'til today. When he started talkin' 'bout that new motorcycle helmet. Who's Rachel Clark anyway?"

"A lost cause from the sixties. I'd like to interview her. For my new magazine."

Janet opens her expressive eyes wide at this. "I got the impression she's a *fugitive*."

"That's why it would be a great interview. If only *you* would tell me how to find her."

"*Me?*" At first Janet is taken aback. "Why would I—?" But then she sees that I'm just kidding. So she smiles. And plays along. "Well, if you really wanna find someone, you should . . . take out a *personal ad*."

I play along, too. "OK. Let's see. How 'bout: *FLJ, 48, seeks RHF. For secret interview.*"

"FLJ?"

"Fun-loving journalist."

"RHF?"

"Red-haired fugitive."

Janet laughs. "I don't think *that's* going to inspire Rachel Clark to call you."

"How 'bout you? Would that intriguing personal inspire *you* to call me?"

This time Janet doesn't look away. My heart skips a beat. She's *very* pretty. Remember Donna Reed? Janet's face is shaped like that. A classic Midwestern beauty. And to me, Donna Reed was most appealing when cast against type. As the call girl in *From Here To Eternity*. Janet has the same appeal. The sweet innocent face. Cast against those teasing, sexy eyes.

"I'm not a fugitive." Janet doesn't take her eyes off me.

"But you're red-haired."

"This week I am."

I laugh. "What color is your hair naturally?"

"Who knows? Naturally is so long ago. When I was in high school my hair was brown."

This gives me an excuse to gaze a moment at Janet's hair. Which is also very pretty.

"Back to my personal," I say. "How can I make it better? So Rachel Clark *will* call."

"Well, I seriously doubt a fugitive would be looking for a *journalist*. Fun-loving or not."

"Good point. So I should pretend to be someone else. How 'bout I pretend to be Lane Davis? Here. Try this: *FECR, 58, seeks RHF. For enthralling evening of political palaver.*"

"FECR?"

"Frog-eyed closet radical."

Janet laughs. "Do you ever actually *read* the personals?"

"No."

"I could tell."

"Hey now!" I feign indignation. But laugh, too. "Since you're so smart, *you* write a personal."

"For who?"

"How 'bout Camille Davis?"

Janet chews on this a minute. Which is more than she's doing to her neglected half of our complex sandwich. "Camille Davis: *Lonely MWF, 54, seeks peaceful man for gentle companionship. Non-smokers, Democrats preferred.*"

I laugh. "Okay. I admit it. Yours is more realistic. But can't we spice it up some? How 'bout: *Lonely MWF, 54, seeks well-built non-smoker with liberal views, a mature man with a slow hand, who speaks softly but carries a big stick?*"

Janet laughs. "That's not a *personal* ad. That's more like a *porn* ad."

"Hmm. Maybe you're right. How 'bout Sheila Nyman? What would *her* ad say?"

"You want a realistic one? Or one like you would do, with the goofy initials?"

"One like I would do, of course. I *like* goofy initials."

Janet reaches in her purse again. Changes her mind, again. Comes out empty-handed. "Sheila: *FDFL, 54, seeks EDML. For long, quiet walks. Moody talks. And many library visits.*"

"FDFL?"

"Fairly dull female lawyer."

"EDML?"

"Equally dull male lawyer."

I laugh. "That's Sheila?"

"Maybe. Sheila's divorced. From a man. But these days she may want an EDFL."

"You're telling me my new business lawyer is a *lesbian?*"

"*I* didn't say that. Who knows? We're not as *frank* around the office as you are."

"Speaking of lesbians, do you know Raven LaGrow?"

Janet rolls her eyes. "Yes."

"Well then," I say, "here's Raven: *Pretentious feminazi law prof, 54, seeks docile male of any age. For kinky dominatrix games. Marital status: unimportant. Penetration: forget it. Handcuffs: mandatory. Dog collar: optional. But no tattoos, please. I'm not that young.*"

Janet's laughing hard now. A very good sign. "You *are* a bad boy, aren't you!"

"I suppose so," I say. Wishing I really were.

"The only thing you got wrong was the tattoos. Raven actually *has* a tattoo of her own."

"Really!" At the tabloids, we *crave* this kind of titillating detail. "Where is Raven's tattoo?"

"On her lower back."

"What kind of tattoo?"

"Some complex design. It's pretty spectacular."

"How do you know this?"

Janet raises an eyebrow. And looks away.

"No! Don't tell me! *Raven's* the one Lane Davis steps out with?"

Janet turns out to be no poker player. The look on her face says I guessed right.

"No shit!" I say. "But I always thought Raven was a lesbian."

"She goes both ways." Janet wags her finger at me. "But you didn't hear this from me."

"Janet who? I've already forgotten this entire conversation." I smile. "But *man*! Raven LaGrow! In bed with Lane Davis! That is *seriously* difficult to picture. Whoa!"

Janet catches me staring at her uneaten half sandwich. She offers it to me. I accept.

"Hey, Janet, have you actually *seen* Raven's complex and spectacular tattoo?"

"No."

"Then how do you know about it?"

"I told you, Lane's not real discreet. When his door's closed, he thinks he's in the Cone of Silence. But that's a very old house we work in. I hear lots of things I'm not supposed to hear."

"So what did Lane say? About Raven's tattoo?"

"It's spectacular. And big. Some complicated design. That's all I heard."

Janet starts to reach in her purse again. But this time changes her mind before her hand even goes in. "I should get back," she says. "I have a lot of work."

Reluctantly I nod. Offer to wrap up for Janet the few scraps of our sandwich I haven't devoured. She declines. We begin to walk back. Janet steals a glance at my left hand.

"What about you? You never told me anything about yourself."

"That's why I'm a good reporter."

"*Journalist*," Janet corrects. Smiling.

"Oh yeah, *journalist*. Whaddya wanna know about me?"

"You have kids?"

The moment of truth. We tabloid hacks know what to do in these situations. Lie. Early and often. Yet against all logic, I tell Janet Fickel the truth. "Two girls. Seventeen and sixteen. Great kids." I look down at my left hand. Which has no ring. I can still pretend to be divorced. But strangely I *persist* in telling the truth. "Married eighteen years. I just don't like jewelry."

"So how old are *you*?" Janet asks. "In one of your personals you said forty-eight. But in another one it was fifty-eight."

"Guess."

"Forty."

"Flatterer."

"Huh?"

"You're just being nice."

"No, I'm not," Janet says. "I'm not nice at all." No smile or laugh with this dark remark.

But I turn Janet's dark mood around in a heartbeat. "That's good. I *hate* nice girls."

*That* draws a throaty laugh. So I pull two steps ahead. Turn around. Face her. While walking *backwards*. This compels Janet to look in my eyes. And she doesn't look away. Several yards we walk this way. I'm thinking I could *lose* myself in Janet's big brown eyes. Until I nearly lose my head on the low branch of a tree.

Janet laughs. God I would love to listen to that woman laugh all day.

I'm not at all sure where we're headed. But I feel bees and butterflies in my stomach. Like I haven't felt since high school. Strange. I asked her to lunch for information. And because of those stockings. That great little body. And Her Strut. But at lunch, it's been Janet's lively patter that's made the strongest impact. She's a discerning little minx. Witty. Vivacious. And fun.

We stop and pick up the mums I got her. Janet thanks me.

"You said you hate Ann Arbor. I feel like I should defend my hometown. What don't you like? Besides the left-over hippies like Lane and Camille."

Janet shrugs. "The shopping's terrible."

"That's it? That's your entire indictment of Ann Arbor? Old hippies and bad shopping?"

Janet laughs. "I don't get to see much of Ann Arbor, really. We live out in Clinton. Cheaper. And closer to Olson's Chevrolet. I just come to Ann Arbor for work."

"What about the weekends?"

"John's president of his gun club. Most weekends he goes away to skeet tournaments. If I go with him, I sit all day at the bar. So mostly I stay home. And stare at the walls."

"No friends?"

"All my friends are back in Fort Wayne."

"Well, surely you go out to the bars here once in awhile. Evenings, or something?"

"Never. I used to go drinking all the time with the lawyers in Fort Wayne. But here, the Davis & Nyman people never go drinking. And even if they did, they wouldn't ask me."

"Well, this is just not right," I declare. "We have some really great bars in Ann Arbor. I'd like to appoint myself to be your official Ann Arbor drinking buddy."

Janet looks down at the sidewalk. Have I upped the ante too fast?

But then Janet stops. Looks me square in the eye. Her eyes are bottomless. With no more hesitation, she agrees. We make a date to meet tomorrow night at Dominick's. A campus bar across the street from the Michigan Law School. I write directions for her on the back of an extra Davis & Nyman brochure I've got in my pocket.

We finish our walk in silence. Walking beside Janet is exhilarating. Every male we pass checks her out. Great for my ego. Yet it's much more than that, too. I feel so alive. When was the last time anyone looked at me like that? Laughed at my jokes? Seemed so fascinated by me?

When was the last time I seemed even remotely interesting to myself?

We reach Davis & Nyman. Shake hands. I remind Janet of our date tomorrow night. Watch her walk inside. And rue the fact that her damn jacket never came off.

As I leave, I see a Latino guy in his twenties. Sitting in a parked Chrysler in the alley behind Davis & Nyman. Baseball cap. U of M sweatshirt. Studiously not looking at me. Or Janet Fickel. Maybe he's not interested in me. But *Janet?* No way. This guy is the only male on the north side of Ann Arbor who hasn't ogled Janet in the last hour. Clearly he's on a stakeout.

His Chrysler has local plates. Probably a plainclothes cop. One of Greg Hunter's minions.

But there's no way to be sure he isn't a rival tabloid hack. Or rival paparazzo.

\* \* \*

Rule #1 for the mainstream media: *If it bleeds, it leads.*

The dailies love violence. But they're embarrassed by sex. Monica Lewinsky was a huge problem for *The New York Times*. They knew they had to cover it. But they hated themselves in the morning. Wrote op-ed pieces apologizing for the salacious content of their own stories. Like they were going to confession.

At the tabloids, we know no such guilt. Have no such shame. The only comparable Rule at the tabloids is: *If you catch her with her lover, put her on the cover.* We love sex stories.

But that's my problem. Rachel Clark is not a sex story. Forget that line I gave you about how this could be the best tabloid story since Gary Hart and Donna Rice. Maybe you fell for that. But my boss, Graham Hancock, won't. Graham's in the trade. Gary Hart and Donna Rice were about sex, sex, and sex. Remember the pix of Donna sitting on Gary's lap? While the glazed eyes of the Man Who Would Be King were lost somewhere deep in Donna's décolletage? On a boat called *Monkey Business*, no less?

We've got nothing like that here. Just a foiled firebombing. And a dead cop. Thirty-five years ago. Sure, Rachel Clark's yearbook photo is hot. But so what? A hot little hippie chick had sex with her bomb-throwing boyfriend. Back in the sixties. That's not a tabloid story.

I'm not calling in. For just this reason. Because even with Hunter "ordering" me to stay in Ann Arbor, I know Graham will just tell me to come home. He'll praise me for the great cleavage pix of Norma Lee. Then tell me to give Hunter what he wants. And get my butt back home.

But I'm *interested* in Rachel Clark. (Not to mention Janet Fickel.) And I'd really like to stay at least through Saturday. For my high school reunion. So I go to the library. Again. To look for something—anything—to try to turn this into a tabloid story.

I start with the 1967 photos I stole. Good start. Especially the one from Rachel Clark's high school yearbook in Centreville. Like I said, she was built. Lots of chest. Long, shapely, slender legs, too. That devastating miniskirt. Pretty face. Striking long red hair.

Graham would love this photo.

But it gets me thinking about my four middle-aged suspects. No red-heads. Raven's the only one whose chest I even noticed. And hers are not on the, um, scale of Rachel Clark's. Women dye their hair. Get boob jobs, too. But breast-reduction? Uncommon. Though it happens.

How tall was Rachel Clark? You can't change your height.

I read the caption under the mug shot I stole: Rachel Clark—I.R. 246-021. F/W, 19, 5'5", 110 lbs. Thin build. Red hair, brown eyes. Fed Wt 60-3369. Wanted for mob action.

5'5" tall. Same as all four of my suspects.

I read more archived articles. In the fall of '69, Rachel Clark was a sophomore. An all-A student. Took Psychology. Poetry. Art History. Spanish. Her U of M profs were shocked that she was part of the plot. Her parents, Ray and Ruth, feel she was led astray by Paul Zimmerman.

I dig deeper. There's a 1981 *Time Magazine* story about Kathy Boudin's arrest. For the botched Brinks truck robbery in New York, which resulted in two dead cops and one dead security guard. Sidebar mentions Rachel Clark. The Fugitive Radical. The last Weatherman fugitive still free.

The 1981 *Time* sidebar says Rachel Clark was arrested at a housing riot in Amsterdam in 1980. Using the name "Rebecca Snyder." Got fingerprinted. Photographed. But then released. Just minutes before Interpol matched "Rebecca Snyder's" fingerprints with those of the fugitive cop-killer Rachel Clark. The Amsterdam Police searched high and low. But she eluded them.

I dig deeper still. Find a 1980 *Newsweek* article. About the near capture of Rachel Clark. *Newsweek* has the Amsterdam mug shot of "Rebecca Snyder." Who looks nothing like the 1969 hottie Rachel Clark. Short black hair. Can't see much of the boobs in a mug shot. But what's there looks pretty skimpy. Indeed, in the 1980 mug shot, Rebecca/Rachel looks downright gaunt.

So she changed her appearance in the seventies. A lot. So what? I'm getting nowhere.

I decide to drive to Centreville. Visit her parents. See what I can dredge up. To make this a tabloid story. Even though I'll be leaving town without giving Hunter his four hours notice.

But walking back to the Campus Inn to get my car, I find I'm not alone. I'm leading a regular parade. There's my Latino pal. From Davis & Nyman. Baseball cap. U of M sweatshirt. Tailing me in his Chrysler with local plates. And tailing him is another car. A gray Taurus with rental plates. I saw this Taurus an hour ago. On my way into the library. The Taurus has two blonde guys.

This is bad. No way Greg Hunter sent *two* cars to tail me. One of 'em's gotta be a tabloid rival. Or paparazzi. Those blonde guys in the Taurus. With the rental plates. Germans. Gotta be. Many paparazzi these days are Germans.

Probably spotted me at the Norma Lee press conference. Now they figure if I'm still in town, there must be a story close by.

I don't mind a cop tailing me. But I can't have paparazzi jumping my exclusive. And since I can't be sure which one is paparazzi, I gotta shake both cars. Before I go to Centreville.

Luckily, Ann Arbor's my hometown. I use my cell to call a cab. Arrange to be picked up in five minutes. At Huron and Fourth. Then I run my tails silly. I walk in the back of the Federal Building. Out the front. In the front of Afternoon Delight. Out the back. Half a block west through a parking lot. Vault a four-foot concrete wall. Half a block north through an alley. Half a block west on Washington Street. Then through the parking garage entrance to the Seniors' Downtown Housing. Out the Seniors' front door at Huron and Fourth.

No sign of my tails now. So I hop in my waiting cab. But not back to my hotel. My tails will go there once they see I've lost them. Instead I take the cab to a rental car agency on the edge of town. Rent another car. A Dodge. Just for the day.

Then I drive to Centreville. Alone. Laughing all the way. (I'm easily amused.)

* * *

The 1960s never made it to Centreville, Michigan. All the buildings on Main Street here are at least fifty years old. There's a barbershop with a gyrating candy-cane pole. A drive-in A&W Root Beer. With the swivel stools in front of the service counter. And a bank that looks easier to rob than my mom's house. No bulletproof glass. No surveillance cameras.

Four old geezers are sitting on a bench outside the barbershop. Suspenders. Flannel shirts. Watching the traffic light change colors. I *love* these guys. They remind me of my grandfathers. Guys who never get excited about *anything*. Because it's bad for the heart. And because they figure nothing in life really matters that much anyway. The old geezers point me to Ray and Ruth's house on Oak Street. Right around the corner.

Ray and Ruth Clark live in a small 1950s house. White aluminum siding. Small front porch. I drive by twice, looking for signs of a stakeout. Nothing. No parked cars on the street. No good stakeout place I can see. If someone's here watching this house, he's *very* good.

As I walk up, I see Ray sumo wrestling a big moving box in the living room. Ray is very small and very old. So the big moving box is winning their wrestling match. I shout "hello." Barge right in. And help Ray schlep that big moving box into the kitchen. Where Ruth (who is even smaller than Ray) profusely thanks me. Ray thanks me, too. When he finally gets his breath.

I introduce myself. Figuring they won't talk to a reporter, I flash my old 1980s DOJ ID. (I kept the ID when I left the DOJ. By falsely claiming I'd lost it. A violation of federal law.) I tell the Clarks I'm a federal law enforcement officer. (Another violation of federal law. Oh well.) I apologize for bothering them. Especially since they're obviously busy moving things. But I need a few minutes of their time. To talk about their daughter, Rachel.

Ray and Ruth exchange sad 'here we go again' looks.

I'm seldom guilty of tender feelings. But these sad little old folks pull at my heartstrings.

Ruth pours three glasses of water. We all sit down at a gray Formica table. We had the same gray Formica table in my house in Ann Arbor when I was growing up. My parents threw their's out about 1965. But the 1960s never made it to the Clarks. Except in the form of bad news about their prodigal daughter.

"We think Rachel is back in Michigan," I say. "Has she tried to contact you?"

"No, sir," Ray says.

"We haven't heard anything since the business with our grandchild," Ruth adds.

*Grandchild?*

"You'll have to excuse me," I say, "but I'm new to this file. I don't remember reading anything about your grandchild. This is *Rachel's* child?"

Ray shrugs. "We *think* so. We don't really know."

"Boy or girl?"

"Girl," Ray says. "Sarah."

"What makes you think Sarah might be your granddaughter?"

"We got a call," Ruth says. "Not long after the shooting. They—"

"Well, now, Ruth," Ray interrupts. "If you're gonna tell a federal law man about it, you'd best get it right. It was *more than a year* after the shooting. Fall of 1970."

"That's right," Ruth says. "Fall of 1970. Because after that call, we figured it out. That Rachel must have *already* been pregnant. The day they tried to bomb the Law School. In 1969."

"Who called?"

"Hippies," Ray says. "From Ann Arbor."

"Girl wouldn't give her name," Ruth says. "Wanted us to sign some papers. To let her and her hippie friends raise Rachel's child. A little four-month-old girl, she said. Named Sarah—with an 'h.'"

"Did you meet with her—or any of the hippies?"

"No," Ray says. "I told them on the phone. We wasn't gonna sign no papers. And we wanted our granddaughter. Right away."

"And—"

"Girl told us to go to hell," Ray says.

"She was not very nice," Ruth adds.

"How'd you know she and her friends were 'hippies?'"

"Girl lived in some kind of commune," Ray says. "A cooperative—non-patrician—"

"A 'non-*patriarchal* experiment in cooperative living,'" Ruth corrects.

"Yeah," Ray says. "Girl said they'd been raising Sarah since she was born. In this 'non-patriarchal experiment in cooperative living.' I asked, was it a *stable* home? Did they have the *money* to raise a child? Girl said they had many 'caregivers' for Sarah. And 'lots of resources.'"

"Anything else you remember?"

"They said Sarah was healthy," Ruth says. "Except she was born with a cleft foot."

"Anything else you can remember?" I press. "*Anything* at all—it may be important."

Ray and Ruth exchange blank looks.

"We reported this call to the FBI," Ray says. "Back in 1970. Like they told us to."

"I'm sure you did. My boss says you've always been fully cooperative."

Ray nods. "We try to be. We're awful ashamed of Rachel."

Ruth's eyes tear up at this. I offer her my handkerchief. Which, for once, is clean.

"Rachel was . . . she had . . . so much . . . *life* in her," Ruth says between sobs. "She was a *very good girl* growing up. Until she went off to school in . . . Sin City."

"Well, now, Ruth," Ray interjects. "If you're gonna tell a federal law man about it, you'd best get it right. Rachel was a good girl until she got to *high school*. When she fell in with the wrong crowd. Right here in Centreville."

"She was a little wild here," Ruth concedes. "But nothing like the trouble in Ann Arbor."

Ray nods, acceding to Ruth's compromise position.

"When was the last time you saw Rachel?"

"Summer of '69. Rachel came home for a few days." Ray shakes his head, eyes down. "Bad visit."

"Why?"

"We was still livin' on the farm back then," Ray says. "When she came home, we expected Rachel to do her share of the chores. Just like everyone else. Rachel didn't like that."

"We argued about almost *everything*," Ruth adds. "Her long phone calls back to her boyfriend in Ann Arbor. Her hippie clothes. Her loud music on the radio. Her tattoo."

I almost choke on my water. "Her *what*?"

"She had went and got a *permanent* tattoo," Ray says. "Like Popeye the sailor man." Ray frowns. "We *told* the FBI all about that tattoo. It was on her 'Wanted' poster."

"Oh, right," I say. "I remember now."

But I really don't. Evidently I missed the tattoo during my library research.

Ray and Ruth look suspicious. Like *how can a federal law man not know this detail*? So I risk a wild guess. Based on my lunch with Janet Fickel. And Janet's vague description of Raven LaGrow's tattoo. "The tattoo was on Rachel's *lower back*, wasn't it?"

"That's right," Ray says, relaxing. Evidently reassured. Because I got this detail right.

"Rachel tried to hide it," Ruth says. "But I saw it on her last day here. She was coming out of the shower. We had a big fight. And then she left. The last I ever saw my baby girl." Ruth tears up again.

I sit a moment in respectful silence. Then risk one more question.

"Help me remember—what *exactly* did Rachel's tattoo look like?"

Ray looks disgusted with me. "It had the group's *mark* on it," Ray says. "Their symbol."

"A rainbow," Ruth adds. "With a lightning bolt. You know. The Weathermen sign."

# CHAPTER THREE
# SHOELESS JOE

## Thursday 14 October 2004

Pembroke Watkins loved to preach: "*Those who do not remember the past are doomed to repeat it.*" Well I *do* remember my law school days. All too well. Yet here I am repeating them. Stumbling around U of M's Legal Research Building. Trying to find Raven LaGrow's office.

I love high school reunions. But I'll *never* go to a law school reunion. Haven't set foot in this place since the dark day in 1986 when they kicked me out. No happy memories here. All I remember is guys like Watkins. Who never answered a question except with another question.

I have a perfect legal right to be here. Yet I *sneak* around the stacks. Who knows why? Habit. Or guilty conscience. Sneaking around recalls Rachel Clark's stealthy five-minute visit here in 1969. Just before her boyfriends started throwing bricks. What *was* she up to?

It's taking me forever to find Raven LaGrow's office. Even though I've got her office number. Even though I went to school here. And even though supposedly I was once a crack federal investigator. Not to mention ace reporter. Because U of M's Legal Research Building is laid out like medieval Seville. A random warren of tiny winding corridors. All circling back upon themselves. With a Byzantine numbering system that defies logic. And, thanks to the Weathermen, a locked fire door every five steps or so. Which keeps forcing me into the dark interior. The ancient stacks. Rows of floor-to-ceiling bookshelves, packed with dusty legal tomes. My worst nightmare.

I grope through the stacks, looking for another tiny five-step corridor. *Hoping* it will be the corridor with Raven's office on it.

Could *this* be what Rachel Clark was doing for five minutes? *Finding Watkins's office?* That could easily have taken five minutes. Since it's taking me ten minutes to find Raven's.

Finally, I stumble upon it. Raven's not in. Her office is locked. Her office "hours" are posted on the door. Office *minutes*, actually. Tuesdays, 4:00 to 4:30. Or "by appointment." That's it.

At the student services desk, I get Raven's teaching schedule. Even more grueling than her office minutes. A seminar ("Feminist Critiques of Law") Tuesdays one to four. And a Constitutional Law class Mondays and Fridays ten to twelve. That's it. Seven hours of teaching a week. Tough life.

Outside, I don't see the Germans. Or the Latino cop. But I spend a half hour cleaning my tail anyway. To be sure I'm alone. Then I go stake out Raven's house. She lives in the faculty ghetto, not far from my mom. In a sixties house with lots of glass. Good for taking pix. And lots of leafy trees. Good cover. For an intrepid trespassing reporter. Excuse me. *Journalist.*

Raven is home. On the second floor. Writing. At a desk overlooking her woodsy back yard. I pretend to be a passing jogger until I get deep enough into Raven's woods that I'm pretty sure her neighbors can't see me. I close within thirty yards of Raven at her desk. Then sit down on a well-shielded tree stump. And shoot a few pix.

Of course I can't see Raven's lower back. Where Janet Fickel says Raven has a spectacular tattoo. Which I'm hoping turns out to be a Weatherman tattoo. *Rachel Clark's* tattoo.

*Could Raven LaGrow really be Rachel Clark?* If so, this is a tabloid story after all! Because last year Raven made herself a tabloid target. At that Yankee stripper trial I covered.

Raven has long been Rush Limbaugh's favorite "Feminazi" target. And there's a huge overlap between Rush's twenty million listeners and the ten million tabloid readers. So we trash lefties like Raven whenever we can. It sells. But we can't write a tabloid story about someone just because they're liberal. We need an occasion. A *pretext.* Like the Yankee stripper trial.

What a splash Raven made there. Testifying as an expert witness. On behalf of a stripper who sued her former boyfriend, an ex-Yankee ballplayer, for date rape. Raven looked hot. And intense. Lashing out at arrogant male chauvinists everywhere. With her big Sandra Bernhard lips.

But on cross-exam, Raven laid an egg. When she admitted she espouses the hard-core feminist mantra that "*all* heterosexual intercourse is rape." Oh. My God. We had a field day. "***ALL SEX IS RAPE****, Feminazi Law Prof Testifies At Yankee Stripper Trial*." All in huge red letters. Above a lovely photo of Raven on the courthouse steps. Scowling like a grim Victorian reformer. Snarling at the paparazzi. And flipping us off. My all-time favorite front page.

My wife Elaine says Raven threatens insecure men like me. Probably true. And though I would never admit it to Elaine, Raven's done a lot of good for this country. As a Senator's aide back in the early seventies, Raven drafted most of Title IX. Legislation that forced high schools to organize equal sports teams for girls. So instead of just cheerleading and puffing up the egos of insecure boys, my teenage girls get to *play ball themselves*. Which I admit is a very good thing.

But at the tabloids, we don't extol Raven's virtues. Not when *trashing* her sells so much better. So if I can *expose* Raven? Tell the world she's really the Fugitive Radical? Living a double life for thirty-five years? *That* would put *The National Spy* on the map. Put *me* on the map, too.

Maybe I can also expose Raven in another way. If Janet Fickel is right. If Lane Davis is really boning Raven. Usually we don't cover small-town scandal. *Mayoral candidate fooling around with law prof*? *Not* a tabloid story. But Raven's made herself a target. By saying *all* intercourse is rape. So what is *Raven*, of all people, doing boogying with a married *man*?

Still, Raven's affair with Davis pales next to the Rachel Clark story. If I can land *that*.

Buoyed by these thoughts I call in. Graham's unavailable. So I leave him a voice mail. Saying I'm on a really hot story. Too hot to discuss by cell phone. Won't be back 'til Sunday.

I sit out in the woods behind Raven's house. For *four hours*. My mind goes into low-power mode. Like a copy machine on the weekend. Like a hunter sitting in a deer blind.

The air is warm. The rotting autumn leaves beneath my feet smell like wet wood chips.

My thoughts drift back to 1969. When I was thirteen. My wise-ass pals and I sat out in these very same woods. Even then I was up to no good. We'd stuff towels into pants and a jacket. To make a life-size headless dummy. Then throw the dummy out into the road. In front of passing cars. So they'd think they hit someone. Little *fiends*, we were. We thought it was funny as hell.

Tabloid work requires the same style of juvenile recklessness. The same lack of concern for others. Rule #2 in the tabloid biz: *Never start caring about your target*.

With Raven, this is easy. She's so arrogant. I zoom in close with my camera. Raven's lips are snarling while she writes. No wonder they call her a "slasher in print." What a nasty bitch. But she's got fabulous skin. For fifty-four years old. Almost *too* fabulous. If she's really Rachel Clark, Raven must have had a lot of work. On the boobs. The hair. And maybe the skin, too.

More time passes. My left butt cheek falls asleep. Twice. I pee. Twice.

But still Raven never leaves her desk. Iron bladder. She takes two phone calls. On a land line. In her bedroom. But otherwise stays glued to her desk. Even *eats lunch* at her desk.

I can't sit out here all day, just waiting for her to leave. Raven's calls give me an idea.

Like all tabloid hacks, my hero is Fletch. The Chevy Chase character with the stupid disguises. Which always seem to work. So I come up with a plan Fletch would love.

I abandon the stakeout. Drive to a hardware store. Buy work gloves. And a tool kit. Big enough to hold my camera. My phone taps. My bugs. And my ultra-tiny pinhole video camera. (We have an ex-CIA guy at *The National Spy*. Another refugee from the *Enquirer*. He's *very* good. Keeps us on the cutting edge of surveillance technology. All the latest gadgets.)

I drive to my hotel. Fire up my laptop. Create a telephone repair form. Print it. Grab a gray wig from my suitcase. Take my contact lenses out. And put on my black-framed eyeglasses.

I drive back to Raven's house. By a tortuous route. To be sure the Germans and the Latino cop have not picked up my scent again. No sign of them. They've given up, I guess.

Raven's still at her post. Using the leafy trees in her back yard as cover, I dodge my way up to the outside back wall of her house. Scratch a small hole down to the place where her phone line enters the house. And cut it.

Next I don the gray wig. The black glasses and gray wig should keep her from recognizing me—in case she remembers the face of any tabloid hack from the Yankee stripper trial.

I put on my new work gloves. Grab my new tool kit. And ring Raven's front doorbell.

Raven doesn't open the door. "Who is it?" she calls through the door's glass lights.

I hold up my new tool kit for her to see. "Telephone service."

"I didn't call for any telephone service," Raven replies.

I pull out my computer-generated form. "Is this"—I squint—"2755 Devonshire Road?"

"Yes."

"Says here your phone is down."

"No, it's not." Raven starts to walk away.

"Ma'am? Would you mind checking it? Can't turn in the paperwork 'til it's checked."

Raven disappears. Comes right back. Opens the door.

"It *is* dead." Raven motions for me to come in. "Who called it in?"

"Dunno," I mumble. We move into Raven's kitchen. "Trouble in this whole neighborhood. Main trunk line. Hit six or seven houses, I think. Shouldn't take too long to fix."

Raven nods. Seems hassled. But not suspicious. I fiddle with her phone. Then say I need to check the line from the inside out. We troop down to her basement. Luckily, I *look* trustworthy. Especially in my gray wig. So Raven leaves me alone. Goes back to work upstairs.

I switch to my thin latex gloves. (Since the DOJ has *my* fingerprints, I have to be careful.) I ferret around the basement a minute. Find a locked file cabinet. In the back of a closet. Bingo!

With my pick gun I open the file cabinet's lock. Guess what I find?

Rachel Clark's old ID papers? Her love letters from Paul Zimmerman? No such luck.

Porn! Straight, hard-core, hetero porn. An unbelievably raunchy collection. The worst kind. Totally *gynecological*. Nothing left to the imagination. *Reams* of the stuff.

For an instant I'm elated. Imagine the headline: ***Feminazi Crusader Hoards Secret Porn Stash***. Above an article exposing Raven LaGrow's secret porn addiction. But then it hits me. This stuff can't possibly appeal to *a woman*. It doesn't even appeal *to me*. This must be some of Raven's old research. Trying to link pornography to violent assaults against women.

So I put the porn back. Return to the kitchen. Tap Raven's kitchen phone. Then I go upstairs. Poke my head in the study. And get Raven's permission to check her bedroom phone.

In her bedroom, I pull out an ultra-tiny pinhole video camera. Flip it on. And place it on top of a tall *armoire*. High enough that Raven won't spot it. Unless she dusts up there. I aim it down at her dressing table. The thing runs for twenty-four hours. Should be able to get some film of her lower back. Tonight. Or tomorrow morning. To see if she's got Rachel Clark's tattoo.

Next I tap her bedroom phone. Then conduct a quick—and very quiet—search.

In the bathroom I find just one toothbrush. Raven lives alone.

In the bedside table—which I open *very* slowly—I find a huge battery-powered dildo. Lord! I wish I were *half* as well-endowed as this rubbery devil.

Women always claim size doesn't matter. So why, if left to their own devices, do they choose a monster every time? Even Raven!

From the ceiling hangs an industrial-strength hook. In Raven's half-open closet I see the reason for the hook: a *Love Swing*. Hmm. Apparently she's a lot *kinkier* than I thought.

I pass Raven's study. Mumble something about "making good progress." Then walk outside. Splice back together the two ends of the line I cut a few minutes ago. And push the dirt back in the small hole I dug.

I go back inside again. Find Raven in her kitchen now. Chopping carrots for dinner.

I pick up the phone. Hand it to her. She hears the dial tone. Nods. Then returns to cooking.

I put on my best imitation of a phone repairman's drawl. "So yer a writer, huh?"

Raven nods. Doesn't look up.

"What kinda writing do ya do?"

"Legal topics. I'm a law professor." As if a mere phone repairman could not understand.

"Oh, *The Law*," I say. "The Law Is A Ass."

Raven looks up. Surprised, perhaps, that her phone repairman is quoting Shakespeare. "*Sometimes* it is."

"So do ya ever write about the faults in some of the laws?"

"Yes. I'm writing a feminist critique of laws applying to various crimes involving gender."

Gender is pretty close to sex—my specialty. "*A Feminist* critique of sex laws?"

Raven jerks up to look at me, clutching her carrot knife. Ready for a fight.

"That's great!" I say. "The laws on sex are a mess. They *need* to be looked at fresh."

Raven gapes. Amazed, I presume, to find that her phone repairman *supports* feminism.

So I launch into a rambling rant about Puritan laws "still on the books." Laws that make it illegal for two consenting adults to have certain kinds of intercourse. Laws that make it illegal, in some states, for married people even to have *affairs*. "Is that what yer writing about?"

"Sort of," Raven says.

"Do ya think it should be illegal for married people to have *affairs*?"

Raven frowns. "I'm not sure having an affair actually *is* illegal anymore."

"Oh? That's what I was *told*. But yer the law perfessor. Where'd you take the Bar?"

"Nowhere. I don't *practice* law. I *teach* it." Raven looks peeved. "Is there any paperwork you need me to sign today?"

"Oh, yeah." I hand her my pre-printed form. While reading the small print, Raven puts her fingerprints all over it. Signs it. And hands it back. I take it by the edge. And put it away. Carefully.

"There's no *charge* for this, is there?" Raven asks.

"Oh, no." I pack up to go. "I gotta ask ya though. Back in the sixties some radicals tried to *bomb* the Law School. Does that kinda stuff still go on?"

"No. The Law School's very safe these days. Very quiet."

"Did ya ever hear what happened to those bombers?"

"Police shot and killed 'em, I believe."

"But didn't one of 'em get away?"

"I believe that's right," Raven says. "A young woman."

"Yeah. A girl. Kinda like a Patty Hearst deal. Do ya know whatever happened to her?"

"No idea."

"You'd think if she was so hell-bent on bombing the Law School back then, well, maybe she'd come back and try it again sometime."

"I believe she and her friends were trying to kill a particular law professor," Raven says. "A very conservative gentleman. Pembroke Watkins. He's retired now."

"Oh, really? I thought they was just after the Law School cuz it's a *symbol*. Of The Law."

Raven grunts. But her attention is back on her carrots, which she's now dumping into a pot of boiling water.

"They say that little girl had herself *tattooed*," I continue. "With a *Weatherman* tattoo. You don't see many gals with *tats*, do ya?"

*This* provokes Raven to look up again. Her face betrays no emotion. But she's inspecting me hard now. "You sure know a lot about old revolutionaries. For a telephone repairman."

"I read a lot," I say quickly. "About free radicals. Nothin' wrong with that, is there?"

Raven returns to her boiling water. I let myself out.

\* \* \*

"*So what* if my guy is tailing you? You don't seem to have any trouble losing him."

"It just *feels* wrong," I say. "We're supposed to be *teammates*."

"Like hell," Greg Hunter snarls. "So. Are you here to claim the reward money?"

"*Not yet*, teammate. But I'm very close. Just gimme one more day."

I feel cocky. Those tattoos can't be a coincidence. Raven's *gotta be* Rachel Clark.

But I can't give Hunter the repair form yet. Because it has Raven's *name*. So if her prints match Rachel Clark's, Hunter will know whom to arrest. *Before* I can interview her. Better to wait a day. Let my pinhole camera film Raven's tattoo. *Then* interview her. *Before* I tell Hunter.

In the meantime, I've stopped by the cop shop just to be sure Hunter is staying calm.

"There's not an *expiration date* for this reward money, is there?" I ask.

"It stays in trust 'til 2019. If no one's earned it by then, it goes to the Police Officers' Widows' Fund." Hunter scowls. "But I'm not that patient, Fisher. You better come up with somethin' quick."

"Okay. But it would help if I knew more *details* about Rachel Clark."

"Isn't that why you went to the library? To read up on Rachel Clark?"

"Yeah. But there's lots of stuff that's not in the library. Like her Weatherman tattoo."

"Her tattoo's not important," Hunter says. "Tattoos only last about ten years."

"You mean they fade?"

"First they turn into dark bruises. *Then* they fade. Unless they get renewed. And guess what, boy-o? *Fugitives* don't generally go out and *renew* their tattoos. So by this time, there can't be much left of Rachel Clark's tattoo."

"Well, the tattoo is just an *example*." I mask my dismay. At learning this fact about tattoos that I did not know. "Without that kind of detail, I can't be effective. Gathering evidence for you. Teammate."

Hunter stares at me. Like he can't figure out if I'm crazy. Or just stupid. Or both.

"I'm not looking for state secrets," I say. "Just *details*. From 1969. What went down."

Hunter sighs. "Alright. October 27, 1969. 5:51 p.m. My brother Dale is on campus patrol. Alone. Sees two hippies in helmets, throwing bricks at the Law School. Dale hits his siren and radioes for back-up, then drives as close as he can.

He jumps out and yells at them to freeze. The short guy—Al Brown—whips out a .38. Gets off one round before Dale can get his own piece out. One *very lucky* shot. Hits Dale full in the stomach. Dale goes down. Returns six rounds."

"And kills them both?"

"Instantly. Dale's first shot catches Brown in the face. Two other shots hit Zimmerman—the tall guy. One in the side, one in the chest. The exact sequence of shots was never established."

"There was a lawsuit, wasn't there? By Zimmerman's family?"

"Total bullshit. Zimmerman conspired to firebomb the Law School and murder a law professor. His partner, Brown, had already shot Dale with a .38. Yet Dale's supposed to lie there, half-dead in the street, and say, what? 'Well, let's see now. Since Brown shot me, it's okay to shoot *him*. But Zimmerman hasn't pulled his gun. Yet. And he ain't running. Yet. So I can't shoot him. Not until he whips out his gun and tries to finish me off.' Is that it? That's total fucking horseshit!"

"What happened in the lawsuit?"

"City's insurer paid the Zimmermans some money to get rid of it. Not much."

"Was there any federal criminal civil rights investigation?"

"Naw. The Zimmermans tried to start one. But it went nowhere."

"No one to prosecute—Dale was dead," I murmur. "So what about Rachel Clark?"

"She was their driver."

"But she went *inside* the Law School, too," I say. "Before they got out to throw bricks."

"True. But we could never figure why. She was on the third floor by Watkins's office."

"How do you know she was up there?"

"We found two stacks of pennies in a corner of the hall. 'Bout six feet from his office."

"Pennies?"

"Pennies. Two nice neat stacks. Sixteen pennies in each stack. With her fingerprints."

"Maybe she dropped them there some other time?"

"Naw. Janitor cleaned that hall mid-afternoon on October 27. Said he saw no pennies then, or he woulda picked 'em up. And these were not *dropped*. They were perfectly stacked."

"What for?"

"Beats the shit outta me. But it proves she was on the third floor. For *something*."

"Tell me the details *after* the shooting."

"Rachel Clark jumped outta the van. Grabbed Zimmerman's gun. Dale saw her. He reloaded. But he didn't shoot her cuz he didn't know for sure she was with 'em. She heard my siren and the other cars coming. She got up on the loading dock just as we arrived. I saw an officer down and her running with a gun. I yelled 'halt.' She didn't stop. So I fired at her. One round. Hit her in that helmet you brought in the other night. But she got inside. And got away."

"How long did Dale live?"

"Twelve minutes. DOA at the ER. Toxins in his stomach leaked out cuz of the bullet hole. Poisoned him. Thirty-five years ago this month. Rachel Clark got away with murder."

"Why *Rachel Clark*? You said *Brown* shot him. She only picked up the other gun after."

"She's still a cop-killer. You went to law school, right? She was part of a conspiracy to firebomb a public building and murder a law professor. While acting out their plot, a police officer died. That makes all the conspirators equally guilty. Of first-degree *felony* murder. Counselor."

"Okay—but you have to prove they were all in the conspiracy. What physical evidence did you find at the scene to connect the conspirators?"

"Brown's gun. Matched the bullet in Dale's stomach. We also found two bricks in Professor Watkins's office. And a row of Molotov cocktails on the sidewalk."

"Fingerprints on any of 'em?"

"No. The two men wore gloves outside the van. But we found Rachel Clark's prints on the steering wheel of the van and on the pennies. Plus we found Zimmerman's and Brown's prints inside the back of the van. Where the smell of gas was very strong. If Dale had known that, he woulda shot Rachel Clark."

"Why?"

"No way Rachel Clark sat in that van with that gas smell and didn't know what was goin' down. But Dale didn't know about the gas smell, so he didn't know *for sure* she was in on it. So he gave her the benefit of the doubt. Let her escape. Like a good officer should. And *still* he got sued. Even though he was dead!"

"And you were able to identify their fingerprints because they all had records?"

"They'd all been arrested two weeks earlier at the Days of Rage in Chicago."

"Kids playing at being revolutionaries," I murmur.

"Not *playing*. Days of Rage was the first real Weathermen *action*. Marching down the streets screaming and throwing rocks. Breaking everything in sight. Storefronts, car windows, you name it. Half Chicago was scared shitless."

"But the whole thing was dumber than Pickett's charge, right? They didn't come *close* to taking over the Army Induction Center. They just marched, unarmed, right into the police lines."

"Even *dumb* punks are dangerous. Five hundred kids rioting in the streets is bad news."

"But the Chicago Police drove 'em off with just a few shots over their heads, right?"

"That's right. And arrested only the hard-core Weathermen who refused to disperse."

"Including Zimmerman, Clark, and Brown," I say. "Who all got out on bond. Came back here. And cooked up a plot to bomb the Law School. Was anyone else part of their plot?"

"We never found any evidence to connect anyone else to the bombing conspiracy. Though it wouldn't surprise me. Because Rachel Clark musta had help *afterwards*."

"How do you know that?"

"Most fugitives can't last a year without getting caught. And Rachel Clark was only nineteen. No money of her own. Someone *had* to be helping her. Probably still is."

"What details do you know about Rachel Clark *afterwards*?"

"You mean after she escaped from the Law School?" Hunter asks.

"Right," I say. "Rachel Clark runs into the Law School. With that helmet on. Gets out through the steam tunnel. In the basement, I assume. Then what happens?"

Hunter leans forward. Grips my left wrist. "How'd you know about the *steam tunnel*?"

"I dunno. Why?"

"Just a guess?"

"Am I wrong?" I wince to show Hunter his grip hurts. "*Isn't* that how she escaped?"

"Are you guessing? Or did someone tell you that?"

"What's the problem here, Greg?" I pry his hand off my wrist while he glares at me.

"Problem is, we never found any witness who saw her go into that steam tunnel. We only figured it out two days later ourselves. From her fingerprints on the tunnel door and along the tunnel walls, and then over by where she got out near the power plant. So how'd *you* know?"

"I musta read about it at the library."

"No. That steam tunnel escape was never made public. University was paranoid about it. Didn't want people to know you can travel all across campus by underground steam tunnels."

"But every U of M student knows about the steam tunnels," I point out.

"I know. But the U didn't want it *publicized*. So we never told *anyone* outside law enforcement that Rachel Clark escaped through a steam tunnel. We always made absolutely sure not to tell anyone. You see how I left that detail out today? Habit." Hunter grabs my wrist again. "So. *Teammate*. Who the hell told you about the steam tunnel?"

I can see I've made a serious mistake. Stopping by to see Hunter. But I can't tell Hunter it was *Lane Davis* who told me about the steam tunnel. Cuz then Hunter might go out and arrest Davis. Which might spook Rachel Clark into running.

"I really don't know *where* I heard that," I lie. Once again I pry his hand off my wrist.

"Check your notes," Hunter says.

"I don't take notes."

"Whaddya mean *you don't take notes*? You're a *reporter*, for Chrissake."

"Do *you* take notes when you work undercover?"

"I remember what people tell me 'til I get a chance to write it down."

"But I didn't know the steam tunnel was important. That's why I came to talk to you today. Because I don't know enough details to recognize the important ones when they come up."

"Well, I'm tired of your games." Hunter shows me the door. "Tomorrow you better remember about the tunnel. *And* where you got that helmet. Or I swear I'll hit you with a subpoena."

\* \* \*

On the way to Dominick's, I start thinking about pennies and doors. So I stop by the Law School. Borrow a ruler from the librarian. Walk up to the third floor. To Pembroke Watkins's old office, number 320. I measure the height from the floor to the bottom of the office door.

Three-fourths of an inch.

I fish four pennies out of my pocket. Stack 'em. Measure 'em.

Three-*sixteenths* of an inch.

You do the math. If four pennies are 3/16" high, then sixteen pennies must be 3/4" high.

* * *

"You were a *lawyer?*" Janet Fickel says. "And now you're . . . a *reporter?*"

"Journalist," I say.

Janet smiles. "I've heard of lawyers becoming *writers*. But not repo—er, *journalists*."

"Happens all the time. Lawyers and journalists have lots in common. Lying, for example."

We're sitting on the front porch at Dominick's. Right across the street from the spot where Rachel Clark's Weathermen pals shot Dale Hunter. Thirty-five years ago this month. Curiously, Dominick's serves its drinks in mason jars. A custom they started long *before* the 1969 action.

Dominick's is a magical place to sit on a warm evening in the fall. The twenty-one electric lights in the ceiling of the front porch cast a soft, warm glow over the café's many quirky details. Eccentric statuary. Old-fashioned ornate lamps. Brightly painted tables. And a huge selection of photos and posters from the ultra-liberal sixties, like *John Sinclair Freedom Rally*—featuring a vintage photo of the wild-haired prophet of the marijuana movement.

Janet's torturing me with another loose-fitting business jacket. But she still looks *damn* good. You should have seen her prance up the sidewalk. *Ever* so slowly. In her heels and short skirt. Ever since I saw her, my heart's been pounding harder than it should. For a man my age.

Now Janet raises a sexy eyebrow at me. "Lying?"

"Sure. When I was a federal prosecutor, I lied for a living."

"The prosecutors I know *never* lie," Janet says.

"Most don't. But my unit at the DOJ only did police misconduct cases. And racial violence cases. Jailhouse beatings. Klan cross-burnings. Teenagers fire-bombing black families' houses."

"Why'd that mean you had to lie?"

"Cops, kids, and the Klan all obey a Code of Silence. They *never* rat out their pals."

"Isn't that true of *all* criminals?" Janet asks.

"Not at all. Most cases depend on informants. And guys who roll over. The prosecutor finds a guy low in the chain. Cuts a deal. Gives him immunity. He testifies against the others."

"But couldn't *you* find someone 'low in the chain' to take *your* deals?" Janet asks.

"Only by lying. Here's an example. San Juan. It's still the Wild West down there. Cops there get just four hours training. Then they hit the streets. The rest they learn from *Miami Vice* reruns. Those guys shoot first, ask questions later. *If* they bother with questions at all. So. Three cops bust a kid selling marijuana outside a school. Kid runs. Cops chase him. Hundred yards. Down to the river. But they can't catch him. They're too fat and slow. It's hot. They're pissed. So one *shoots the kid in the back*. Kid's sixteen. Dead. For selling a joint to a pal at school.

"There's no witnesses. Except the two cops who didn't shoot. But they're not gonna rat out their brother-with-the-badge. So they fix the crime scene. Get a throw-down gun. Fire it a few times. At their squad car. Hit the windshield. Then stick the gun in the dead kid's hand."

I pause. Look deep into Janet's luminous brown eyes. Am I yakking too long? Probably. But Janet *seems* interested. And her eyes are even more beautiful in the soft evening glow of Dominick's twenty-one electric lights than they were yesterday in the sunlight at Zingerman's.

"So we bring in all the cops: the shooter, his two partners who didn't shoot, their sergeant, the lieutenant who signed off on their phony reports, and even the two cops who took the car to the shop to get the windshield fixed. *All* of 'em. Sit 'em in a waiting room, all together. They're talkin' tough. Pumpin' each other up. Very macho guys. You know the type."

"I married one," Janet murmurs.

I pause, curious about her macho husband. But Janet offers nothing more.

"We bring the first one back. The sergeant, Luis. We tell Luis the angle of the bullet through the windshield is wrong. Bullet came in too *high*, we tell him, to be the dead kid who fired it. He was a *short* little kid. Plus there were no powder marks from the gun on the dead kid's hand. So we *know* the kid didn't fire that gun. We tell Luis that *today* everyone gets a chance to tell the truth. But *tomorrow* the grand jury will indict anyone who doesn't tell the truth today. We stare at Luis with dead eyes. But Luis is a tough guy. He tells us to go fuck ourselves."

I take a long swig of the imported Belgian beer I'm drinking. Janet's drinking Bud Lite.

"Was it true?" Janet asks. "About the angle of the bullet? And the powder burns?"

"The bullet angle was a total lie. And the powder marks—well, that was a lie, too. It was true there were no powder marks on the kid's hand. But it didn't *mean* anything. Because the kid fell in wet mud. So the lack of powder burns on his hand was inconclusive. But those were just the *little* lies. They really didn't work. It was the *big lie* that worked."

I pause. For dramatic effect. And to contemplate Janet's sexy, thick, auburn eyebrows.

"We tell our little lies. Luis tells us to fuck off. After fifteen minutes, we walk him back to the waiting room. Let him go. He gives the thumbs up to his buddies. Swaggers out. Very macho.

"We bring the *next* guy back. Tomas. One of the cops who was right there. An eyewitness. Same drill. We tell Tomas he's goin' down tomorrow. Unless he tells the truth. Tomas tells us to go fuck ourselves. Tomas is even harder than Luis. Totally hopeless. But we keep Tomas back there anyway. *Ninety* minutes. Finally we let Tomas go. Out the *side* door.

"Then before Tomas can get back to the waiting room, we go out and get the third guy. Jose. The *other* eyewitness. And you can see the fear in Jose's face. Jose's looking at his buddies like, *why was Tomas gone so long? And why hasn't Tomas come back out here? Like Luis did?*

"We take Jose back. Same drill. We know what happened. The bullet angle. The powder burns. But now we add the kicker. *Tomas admitted everything.* We don't need you, Jose. We don't care what you do. We're giving you this one chance to tell the truth because, well, *we're just fair guys.* Take it or leave it. Tomorrow you won't have this chance. You'll be indicted with Luis. And anyone else who sticks to the bullshit story in those reports you guys wrote.

"And I swear to God, Janet, *the guy fell for it.* Old Jose spills his guts. Admits the kid was murdered. Admits the cover-up. Everything. What a riot! That job was so much fun!"

"Then why'd you leave it? Why'd you become a repo—a journalist?"

I have a standard rap I use, to avoid telling people I was disbarred. "Being a prosecutor is a *heavy* thing. Like being a cop. You send people to jail. Sometimes for life. I didn't like that part. Only reason I lasted as long as I did was, my boss Barry was a lot of fun."

"It does help if your boss is fun. I had the *best* boss in Fort Wayne. Simon. So *crazy*."

I get Janet talking about the good old days in Fort Wayne. About all her friends back home. And the entertaining antics of her old boss Simon. Turns out Simon is Jewish.

"Did you ever go to any Jewish holidays at Simon's house?" I ask.

"One Passover *Seder*," Janet says. "John hated it. But I thought it was pretty fun."

"Jewish holidays are a hoot."

Janet cocks her head, curious how *I* know anything about Jewish holidays.

"My wife Elaine is Jewish," I explain. "*My kids* are Jewish."

I pause. The best advice I ever got in my whole life was, *never talk to a woman about another woman*. But what the hell. This fling with Janet isn't going anywhere. She's married. I'm married. I'm going home Sunday. If not sooner. And even in my youth, when my dates were *single* and lived in the same town as me, *even then* I never learned how to get a woman to bed *fast*. With me, it's always been the *long siege*. I really have no idea how to *seduce* a woman. All I know how to do is just *wear 'em down*. So I decide to tell Janet a story about Elaine.

"One time before we were married, Elaine was really pissed at me. I forget about what."

"No doubt with good reason," Janet teases.

"No doubt. So it's Passover. Elaine decides to punish me. Seats me between her *mother*, who was Attila the Hun's wife in a past life, and her *aunt*, who was Lizzie Borden in a past life. Now I'm the only *goyim* there. These two grim little old Jewish gnomes hate the fact that Princess Elaina is dating me at all. So they're looking at me like I'm something smelly on the side of their shoes."

Janet's laughing hard now. Exactly what I want.

"Elaine figures she's got me fixed. But she fails to account for the wonderful effect of *alcohol* on the human spirit. It's *Passover*. Every few minutes, after you read a little more about the Flight from Egypt, the *Haggadah*—the Passover script—calls for you to take a sip of wine."

"I remember," Janet says, sipping her Bud Lite.

"Well pretty soon, we're not taking *sips*. Mom and Auntie and I are taking large *sloshes* of wine. In fact, we're not even waiting for *authorization* from the *Haggadah*. We're *freelancing* with the wine. Then they find out I can recite poetry from memory. Which I tend to do when I've been drinking. They really like this. They're from Canada. Where education is still about memorization. They think American education sucks because Elaine can't recite Wordsworth.

But *I* can give you Wordsworth out the wazoo. Especially when I'm well-lubricated. So the three of us are down at one end of the table, three sheets to the wind, reciting Wordsworth. And Elaine is looking at me like 'you are such a *cockroach*—I can't kill you, no matter *what* I do.'"

"And you're probably smiling that smug little shit-eating grin of yours," Janet adds.

I blanch. 'Til I see she's still laughing. Evidently she *likes* my smug little shit-eating grin.

"How'd you know?" I ask.

"Beginner's luck," Janet says.

Honest Reader, I want to give it to you straight. The good, the bad, and the ugly. At the words "beginner's luck," I feel the stirrings of a very strong erection. Who knows why? Just something about the way Janet says it. Something about how fun and witty and vivacious she is. Something about how she makes me feel like I'm so *enthralling*. For here, in the magic glow of Dominick's lights—and the magic glow of Dominick's beer—all my dumb old stories, which normally just bore my family to tears, have been magically transformed into riveting tales.

The way Janet *sits* also contributes to my erection. *Contrapasto* style. Like she's posing for Michelangelo. Torso turned left. Legs twisted sharply right. With that short little skirt hiked awful damn high up her lovely cinnamon-stockinged thighs. With her knees an inch from mine.

At age forty-eight, erections are a cause for *celebration*, not embarrassment. So I don't sweat it. I just *register* its existence. As an unusual phenomenon. Like a geyser in the Antarctic.

"Here I thought I was being Prince Charming," I say. "And all this time, you were thinking my grin is 'smug' and 'little' and 'shit-eating,' eh?"

Janet laughs. Even without the Belgian beer, I'd be drunk. On just that woman's *laugh*.

"Are you always this hard on men?" I ask.

"Only the ones who can take it."

"So if I start acting vulnerable and sensitive, you'll take it easy on me?"

"If you start acting vulnerable and sensitive, I'll leave!"

"Oh—you only like the tough guys?"

"Strong, silent ones," Janet says. "That's all I've ever known."

"*Silent* I don't do very well."

"I noticed."

I push my lower lip down and out. Like a kid who's lost his homework.

Janet laughs. "But it's okay." She pats my hand. "You're not bad. For a change of pace."

Janet withdraws her hand. But the electricity of her touch remains.

We drink in silence a few minutes. Just looking at each other. Enjoying the warm autumn air, and the smell of the pizza mixing with the autumn leaves. The mood is *very* good.

In fact, the mood is *so* good, I almost miss an old friend walking by. Tim Randolph. Tim knows Elaine. And knows this ain't Elaine I'm drinking with. I avoid Tim's eyes as he passes.

"Yesterday, you never *did* tell me how old you are," Janet points out.

"Boy, I can't put *anything* by you, can I?"

Janet smiles.

"Forty-eight," I say. "That's not too old for you, is it?"

Janet laughs. "Better not be. John's fifty-two."

We talk about John. He's at his gun club. Where he goes every Tuesday and Thursday night. For meetings and competitions. When they go to the movies, which isn't often, John insists on action movies. So Janet never sees the romantic comedies she prefers. She's not *trashing* John. Just noting his shortcomings. I wonder if I should reciprocate. Talk about Elaine. But that old advice about not talking to a woman about *another* woman seems much more relevant. Now that I have Janet laughing so much. Now that I've felt the electricity of her touch. Besides, I can't say much negative about Elaine. We both hate guns. And we both like romantic comedies.

"So," I say, "that was fun yesterday. Doing personals with you. But I forgot to ask. What's *Janet Fickel's* personal ad sound like?"

Janet meets my eyes. "You tell me."

"Okay: *SLA with sparkling wit, 40, seeks escape from humdrum life in Ann Arbor. Prefers strong, silent knight-in-shining-armor, prepared to ride off into the sunset. But will settle for a romantic poet who can hold his liquor. Sensitive wimps need not apply.*"

Janet laughs. "SLA?"

"Sexy legal assistant."

We lock eyes awhile. Janet ain't lookin' away.

"And how 'bout yours, David Fisher? What's *your* personal ad say?"

"You do it."

Janet swigs her Bud Lite. Looks me up and down. With warm dancing eyes.

"*FLJ with many surprises, 48, seeks a really good story to tell. And an even better story to live.*"

Damn! This Janet Fickel *is* a discerning little minx.

"This fun-loving journalist wants to interpret 'many surprises' as a compliment."

"Oh, *it is.*" Janet meets my gaze again.

"But there's a great story right here in front of me," I say.

"To tell? Or to live?"

"Both. Two different stories."

"What's the great story *to tell*?"

I point to the Law School across the street.

"That's the place Rachel Clark tried to bomb?" Janet asks.

"Yes. It's a great story to tell, Rachel Clark. Like those lost causes I love so much."

Janet cocks her head at me. People cock their heads all the time. But with Janet, it isn't just a quizzical expression. I can't tell you how incredibly sexy it is. It spurs me on.

"You know," I continue, "like Shoeless Joe Jackson."

This earns me an even sexier cocking of the head. And a very sweet smile.

"You remember Shoeless Joe?" I ask. "One of the greatest baseball players ever. Accused of taking bribes to throw the 1919 World Series. So the little kid on the courthouse steps says, '*Say it ain't so, Joe, say it ain't so.*' But Joe just hangs his head and walks off."

"Oh, yes! I *have* heard of him." Janet downs some more of her beer. "Okay. I'll bite. How the hell is Shoeless Joe Jackson like Rachel Clark?"

"God, for a minute there I thought you'd *never* bite."

"I only bite when it's called for."

*That* remark provokes more activity south of my belt. But I rattle on. "Well, after he was banned from baseball for life, Shoeless Joe knocked around the South for years. No job skills. No money. All he knew how to do was play ball. And he was in his prime. Best ballplayer in America. Except for Ruth. So what Shoeless Joe did was, he'd go anywhere he wasn't known. Give a false name. And play *minor league* ball. For peanuts. Anywhere Joe could find a team so *obscure*, so *far away*, that he thought he could get away with it. Just to be able to do the only thing he truly loved doing. Playing ball.

"Problem was, Shoeless Joe Jackson was way too good to be playing in Chucklehead, Texas. Or Bumfuck, Georgia. And way too *distinctive*. So after a few games, the whispers would start. See, Shoeless Joe's *swing* was so sweet, his *stride* so graceful, it never took long 'til someone would guess who he was. A few more games, and the whispers would turn into a roar. Some loser would tag Joe hard in the face as he slid into second base. Call him a cheater and a crook and a whore. A fight would break out. And then Joe'd be gone. On the first bus outta town. The Flying Dutchman of baseball. Unable to land in any port. Condemned to sail the seas forever."

Obviously, I've been drinking. *A lot.* My chatter is growing mildly incoherent.

But Janet seems *enraptured* with this wild stream of verbiage. So what the hell. You don't stop rolling the dice just because you catch a glimpse of yourself in the casino mirror and realize you look like the drunken fool you are. Hell no. You just keep rolling those dice!

"And that's how I see Rachel Clark. Unable to land in any port. The Shoeless Joe Jackson of Ann Arbor. Living a lie every day of her life. One false identity after another. On the lam the rest of her life. What would that *feel* like? Never able just to *be yourself.* Never able to see your old friends. Never able to go home and see your parents for Christmas."

"I would *die* if I couldn't go home for Christmas!" Astonishing passion fills Janet's voice. "That's the one thing I love best in all the world. Christmas Eve at home with my parents."

"Exactly my point!" Is that *moisture* in her eye? Not bad. If I can get tears from a tough little cookie like Janet Fickel. "Think how awful life would be, if you couldn't ever go home. Couldn't ever *be yourself.* That's Rachel Clark's life. And here's the worst part. You know, Shoeless Joe, *he wasn't even guilty.*"

Janet cocks her head again. God, I *love* it when she does that!

"The year he supposedly took the bribe, Shoeless Joe set the record for hits in a World Series. Which *still stands.* Eighty-five years later. And yet they said he took gamblers' money, to throw the Series? Nonsense. There's at least four books out now saying Joe was innocent."

"Then how come he wasn't acquitted back then?" Janet asks.

"Because Shoeless Joe was a poor boy from a farm. Never finished second grade. The lawyers talked him into signing a confession he couldn't even read. Told him it was all for the best."

Dimly through the haze of my fourth Belgian beer I remember that *Janet* was raised on a farm, too. Never graduated from high school. Has spent half her life in jobs that plainly aren't commensurate with her sharp wit and intelligence. Taking orders from lawyers. I'm guessing my account of farm boy Shoeless Joe getting railroaded by lawyers resonates with Janet. On the lower frequencies. Where, as Ralph Ellison said, the real gut checks occur.

"And I think Rachel Clark was innocent, too," I say. "Even though she definitely knew her boyfriends wanted to blow up the Law School. And she definitely drove them there. But when it came right down to it, I think she *abandoned* their conspiracy. Before the cop got shot."

"But Lane said *after* the cop got shot, Rachel Clark ran away."

"True. When the shit hit the fan, Rachel Clark hit the road. But put yourself in her shoes. Just *nineteen*. Facing those circumstances. Would *you* have had the guts to stay and stand trial?"

"What makes you think she abandoned their conspiracy before the cop got shot?"

"The pennies."

"The pennies?"

"They found two stacks of pennies. With Rachel Clark's fingerprints. On the third floor of the Law School. In the hall. Near the office her friends were planning to firebomb. Pembroke Watkins's office. Why would Rachel Clark leave two stacks of pennies up *there*?"

"She dropped them while escaping?"

"No. She escaped *through the basement*. And she didn't *drop* the pennies, either. They found 'em in two nice little stacks. Sixteen pennies per stack. Exactly the height from the bottom of Watkins's door to the floor. I think she was supposed to *penny* Watkins in his office."

Janet cocks her head at my use of the word "penny" as a verb.

"It's an old college dorm prank. You wedge two piles of pennies under a door. The person inside *cannot* get out. They musta sent Rachel Clark up there to penny Pembroke Watkins in his office. *Before* they threw the bricks at his window. So he'd *die* up there in his office. When they threw the firebombs in. Only—*she didn't do it*. Instead, she piled those pennies in a corner of the hall. I know it sounds weird. But there's *no other reason* for two stacks of pennies to be found on the third floor of the Law School, with Rachel Clark's fingerprints on 'em. I'm convinced she was supposed to penny Watkins in. But in the end, she backed out and *didn't do it*."

Janet nods. Reaches in her purse. Looks me square in the eye. "Do you mind if I smoke?"

"No, go ahead." Actually, I *hate* smoking. But we're outdoors. And frankly, if Janet Fickel wanted to slaughter a small defenseless child in front of me, I'd probably say fine. Go ahead. I *really* want to stay on this woman's good side. "I should have guessed."

"What do you mean?" Janet asks, as she goes through the smoker's light-up ritual.

"Yesterday I couldn't figure out what the hell you kept looking for in your purse."

Janet cocks her head at me. Blows a long ring of smoke out the side of her mouth, away from me. The whole effect is so enticing, I debate asking her to have sex with me on the spot. Right now. On the table. In front of everyone at Dominick's.

"You don't miss much, do you?" Janet asks.

"I try not to." We lock eyes a long, long time on that one.

We talk awhile longer. Drink another round. At last Janet says she's gotta get home. But luckily John's shooting skeet all weekend. Out of town. So Janet agrees to dinner tomorrow night. No hesitation. And a sweet smile.

I walk Janet to her car. Hands behind my back. As we walk, I swear Janet's heels tap out, in Morse Code, I-M-S-O-S-E-X-Y. But it's probably just my imagination. Running wild again.

At her car, I stand beside Janet's door while she opens it. Like an awkward teenage boy. Hoping for a kiss. But it's not in the cards. Janet isn't closing the distance between us. So I stick out my hand. Janet smiles. Shakes my hand. Very formal. Very proper. After all, we are both married. And standing in the street. In front of sixty or seventy people at Dominick's.

I'll spare you the grubby details of what I do when I return to my hotel room.

# CHAPTER FOUR
# THE FUTURE EVASIVE

## Friday 15 October 2004

Delmore Schwartz said, "In dreams begin responsibilities." Easy for old Delmore to say. Since he never suffered through *my* dreams. Mine are so *ir*responsible. Weird. And chaotic. I'm back in law school. I don't know the answer. And I'm naked. Or I'm back in junior high. I still don't know the answer. And I'm still naked. Except now I'm naked *for a reason*. Because I want to have sex with that really hot student teacher in the miniskirt who drove us all crazy in junior high.

How can any "responsibility" begin in dreams like these? But today is an exception. I'm not sure what I was dreaming about. But I wake up humming "Who Am I?" from *Les Miserables*. How *apropos* is that? Today I'm going to try to prove that Raven LaGrow is really Rachel Clark. And I wake up humming a song about *identity*. Maybe old Delmore Schwarz was right, after all.

I pack my lock-picking tools and latex gloves into a fanny pack. Then go for a long run. To be sure no one can follow me. I run down to the Huron River. East along the river to Gallup Park. Then emerge on a path just a few hundred yards from Raven LaGrow's house.

I ring the bell. No answer. According to Raven's schedule, she's teaching Constitutional Law now. So I pick the backdoor lock. Gaze a moment at the pretentious ultra-modern art on Raven's walls. And the sterile modern furniture.

Then I go up to Raven's bedroom. Retrieve my pinhole camera from atop the armoire. And stuff it in my fanny pack. But I leave Raven's phone taps in place. Even though, so far, they've netted exactly nothing. Just like the taps and bugs at Davis & Nyman. *Nada*.

I debate going straight back to my hotel. To view the video. To see if Raven's got that Weatherman tattoo. On her lower back. *Like* Rachel Clark. But Hunter's remark is still bothering me. About how tattoos only last ten years. And how fugitives don't often renew their tattoos.

So I decide to poke around the place. Look for *other* evidence of Raven's true identity.

Raven's files have some pretty wild stuff. Lots more porn. Long transcripts of interviews with prostitutes. And reams of information on various notorious serial-rapists and serial-killers.

But in the more mundane section of Raven's files, I find Raven's official resumé:

### Raven LaGrow

**Work**

| | |
|---|---|
| 1999-present | Marjorie Weinzweig Professor of Law & Women's Studies, University of Michigan Law School<br>• Teaching Constitutional Law and Feminist Critiques of Law<br>• Chair, Student-Faculty Committee on Diversity |
| 1989-99 | Assistant Professor, University of Michigan Law School<br>• Teaching Constitutional Law, International Law, and Feminist Critiques<br>• Organizer, Annual Symposia on Diversity |
| 1980-89 | Freelance political writer and grassroots political organizer |
| 1970-76 | Senator's Aide, U. S. Senator Birch Bayh, Indiana<br>• Drafted significant portions of Title IX<br>• Worked on other legislation outlawing discrimination against women in education |

**Education**

| | |
|---|---|
| 1976-79 | JD, Georgetown Law School, Order of the Coif |
| 1968-72 | BA, Georgetown University, Political Science, Magna Cum Laude |

**Personal**

Born February 13, 1950, New York City

The attached list of publications are mostly on Radical Feminism and the Law. And on Central American politics.

Raven's resumé gets me thinking. About my other suspects. They all have one thing in common with Raven. They're all a little vague about what they were doing in the 1980s.

Sheila Nyman's bio (in the Davis & Nyman brochure) says she got her BA from the University of Michigan in 1972. And her JD from U of M Law in 1989. Went to work for Lane Davis right after Law School. But *no comment* on what she did for seventeen years between '72 and '89.

Same drill for Naomi Williams. Her Davis & Nyman bio says she graduated from U of M in 1972. No more formal education. Went to work for Lane Davis the same year Sheila did. 1989. But *no comment* on what Naomi did between '72 and '89. What's up with that?

Camille Davis gives a little more information. Her internet bio says she graduated from U of M in 1972, back when her name was Camille Jensen. Volunteered for the Peace Corps and UNICEF for six years. Worked for Quaker Oats from '78 to '85. Then back with UNICEF, '85 to '89. From 1989 to now, she's been in Ann Arbor. Just like Raven and Sheila and Naomi. Except Camille's been married to Lane Davis and doing volunteer work here.

Raven's resumé—and my other suspects' bios—also get me thinking about *aliases*. How exactly—and *when* exactly—could Rachel Clark have become Raven LaGrow?

Generally speaking, changing your identity is much easier than you think. Even in today's computerized world. Because we still don't have a system that matches birth records with death records. So here's all you have to do. If you want to become a new person.

First pick a town you'd like to be from. *Any* town in the USA. Go to that town's library. Get the old newspapers for the year you were actually born. Then go to the obits. Find a child who died in infancy the year you were born and is the same gender as you. (Theoretically you could use a child from a year other than your exact birth year. But it would be a mistake. You'd be at constant risk of slipping up when asked for graduation years and other biographical data.) Take that dead infant's name. It's your new name. Get the name of the hospital from the obit, too. "You" were born there.

Next go to a store specializing in religious items. Buy a blank baptismal certificate. Fill in your new name. Then, using your new baptismal certificate, and the name of the hospital where "you" were born, apply for a birth certificate. It'll come in the mail. Two to three weeks.

Now, using your new birth certificate, apply for a Social Security number. If you're under thirty, no questions will be asked. The Social Security Administration is glad to have you sign up. It means they can start collecting taxes from you. If you're over thirty, they *may* give you a call. Just to ask if you've ever had a job. Because an above-the-counter paycheck would have required you already to have a Social Security number. But don't worry. They're not after *you*. They're after *your past employers*. To see if *they* owe back payroll taxes. So you assure the SSA person you've been a student. Or a drunk. Or a psychiatric patient. Whatever. They won't look any further into it. You'll get your new Social Security number in the mail. Two to three weeks.

Once you've got your Social Security number, it's Katie-bar-the-door. You can get a passport. Credit card. Driver's license. Library card. Fishing license. Go ahead. Knock yourself out. The sky's the limit. You're a new person. The only thing you don't have is a past.

And your past is something you can easily invent. The only hard part is remembering, each and every second of each and every day, to stay *consistent* with the lie you're living.

So I assume Rachel Clark followed this drill. With advice from experienced underground radicals. Back in 1969, it was even easier. No computers cross-checking the phony information Rachel Clark must have supplied. No tiresome calls from Social Security employees.

So Rachel Clark got a new name. Or more than one. "Rebecca Snyder," perhaps. That's the name she was using in 1980. When she was arrested at the Amsterdam housing riots.

But once she got her new name(s), you'd expect Rachel Clark—Rebecca Snyder—to *lay low*. Work odd jobs. Maid in a hotel. Night shift at a factory in a small town. Clean houses, maybe. Whatever. Something *inconspicuous*. So when and how did Rachel Clark become someone as flamboyant as Raven LaGrow? And why run such a crazy risk?

The resumé says Raven LaGrow was born in 1950. Same as Rachel Clark. But in New York City, not Centreville. I find her birth certificate. Raven LaGrow, February 13, 1950, Governor's Hospital, New York City. And her Social Security card. 176-33-2956. Both *look* real.

So there probably *was* a real Raven LaGrow. Born February 13, 1950. In New York. Who died sometime before Rachel Clark took over Raven LaGrow's identity. Which was *when*?

My first thought is—the 1980s. Sometime *after* the Amsterdam arrest of "Rebecca Snyder." Because there's that opaque entry on Raven's resumé:

"1980-89, Freelance political writer and grassroots political organizer." *Period.* No indication *where* she was. Or *what kind* of political organizer she was. An entire *decade*? In a single sentence on a resumé? C'mon. (Although it's better than Sheila and Naomi. Who offer no comment *at all* on the 1980s.)

Presumably "Raven" would say her political activity in the 1980s was too radical for a work resumé. But how *convenient.* With warrants out for both Rachel Clark and Rebecca Snyder, Rachel Clark would have seized any chance to get a new name. Like Raven LaGrow. And the 1980s was an easy time to make the switch. The ten years no one really knows where Raven LaGrow was. Or what she was doing. Or where Rachel Clark was. Or what *she* was doing.

But as I stare at Raven's resumé, I see a big problem with my theory. The *1970s.*

Raven LaGrow was not exactly *famous* in the seventies. But she wasn't *obscure*, either. As a Senator's Aide, and then a law student, Raven must have gotten to know a lot of people in DC in the 70s. How could Rachel Clark have stepped into Raven LaGrow's shoes in the 80s, and expected to pass herself off as "Raven" to people who'd known the real Raven in the 70s?

Of course, the law school on Raven's resumé could be bogus. Every few years you read about some big-firm lawyer who, it turns out, *never even went to law school.* Just faked it on his resumé and started practicing law. Because nobody verifies resumés. And law isn't like medicine, where you actually have to *know something.* In law, all you need is the lingo. And maybe half a lick of common sense. If that.

I've never heard of a law *professor* forging a resumé. But if practicing lawyers can do it, then a law professor can, too. Especially if you have lots of publications, like Raven LaGrow.

So I can explain away Georgetown Law School. But the *other* 1970s resumé entry is harder. Even a knuckle-scraping male chauvinist like me knows Raven LaGrow *really did* draft much of Title IX in the early 70s. While working for Senator Bayh. I'm not sure exactly how I "know" this, but it's so *widely* known, it can't be bogus. So how could Rachel Clark ever have dared to become Raven LaGrow *without Raven's old Title IX friends noticing the change?*

Then it hits me. There's an even bigger problem with my theory. The *1990s.*

Very seldom do fugitives, after taking a new name, go try to live the actual life of the person whose name they've usurped. *That's* risky business. Like I said, the real Raven must have had many friends from the 1970s. If Rachel Clark had really taken on Raven's identity in the 1980s, then you would have expected her to continue doing obscure "grassroots political organizing." *Not* apply for a high-profile job, like law professor at Michigan. *Not* begin testifying as an expert witness all around the country. *Not* start baiting Rush Limbaugh at every turn.

Maybe Rachel Clark felt confident, by the 1990s, that the FBI would never find her. Perhaps she yearned for something more challenging than an endless series of crappy jobs in an endless kaleidoscope of dinky towns. But even if so, why risk exposure by taking a job where she couldn't help but run into scores of Raven's old pals? Sooner or later, someone would be bound to bring up an old story that should have been familiar to Raven—except Rachel wasn't really Raven and so she couldn't go there.

The only way she could have pulled it off would have been for Rachel to become Raven *before* Title IX—i.e., in the early seventies. *Right after* the botched bombing. Yet it's hard to imagine Rachel Clark, with fresh warrants out for her arrest for the murder of a cop, blithely going to work as a Senator's Aide. A federal job *where they fingerprint you as a matter of course.*

Plus, if she became Raven in the early seventies, why was she "Rebecca Snyder" in 1980?

Face it: my theory makes no sense.

Still, if my videotape shows a Weatherman tattoo on Raven LaGrow's lower back, the woman—whoever the hell she is—is going to have a lot of explaining to do.

Raven's phone interrupts my ruminations. After three rings, Raven's message machine comes on. After the beep, the caller leaves a message: "*Hi, Raven. It's Sheila. You were right. About Sarah. She is back in Ann Arbor. And she says she's going to tell Hunter we know where her mom is. Sarah wants the reward money. So we've got to do something. Fast. Please call me as soon as you can. Thanks.*" Beep.

* * *

Ever wonder why, in every Faulkner novel, the lawyer is always an alcoholic?

It's because legal work is so deadly dull. It *breeds* depression and alcoholism. Even in the 19th century, when lawyers were revered as "doctors of jurisprudence," the actual daily grind of the lawyer was a grim business. Think Abraham Lincoln. The very paragon of a lawyer. Yet according to his law partner Herndon, Honest Abe was so depressed by the practice of law, he spent most afternoons flat on his back on the couch in his office. Literally paralyzed by depression.

I often ponder this image of Lincoln the lawyer, laid out on his couch. To console myself whenever the daily grind of life as a tabloid hack gets me down.

To remind myself it would be *even worse*, had I not been lucky enough to get disbarred. For example, few tasks in life are as dull as the tabloid hack's job of checking *hours* of surveillance tapes from bugs and phone taps. Particularly when the bugs and taps are at a quiet small-town law firm. Boring as hell.

Watching hours of surveillance videotape is not much better. My camera's fast forward is *very* slow. So it's like watching paint dry. Raven LaGrow does make a brief appearance. Around 5:00 last night, according to my camera's counter. Passes through her bedroom. But doesn't stop at the dressing table. Then hours pass. Even using fast-forward, I'm mightily bored.

So I resort to Faulkner's cure. Those little bottles of Scotch in my hotel refrigerator.

Now I'm half-crocked. When out of the blue two figures appear on the screen in my hotel room. Raven LaGrow and (drumroll, please) *Lane Davis*. Fully clothed. But Raven is lighting *mood candles* on the dressing table. A very good sign. I snap to attention.

They stand directly in my camera's sightline. The counter says 9:00 last night.

Raven pins Davis against the dressing table. With her back to the camera. Davis buries his mangy head between Raven's neck and her shoulder. Did he just *bite* her? Kinky. Whatever he's doing down there between her neck and her shoulder, she likes it. Gives a nice little moan.

But now Raven's pushing Davis away. Playfully.

"Bet you wish I was as big up top as Norma Lee!" Raven shakes her cleavage in Davis's face.

"Hey, c'mon!" Davis protests. "I didn't ask Norma to come out here. It was *her* idea. She insisted. And then *you* kept telling me I had to take advantage of her offer."

"But Norma would never have offered to come at all, if you weren't her old flame."

"Oh, let it go!" Davis tries to pull Raven close again. But Raven eludes his grasp.

"Not so fast!" Raven says. "First admit it: it was a *damn good idea* letting Norma come help."

"I'll admit anything you want. But you didn't think it was such a great idea when she brought out that helmet."

Instantly Raven's playful mood changes. "She was a damn fool to bring that helmet here!" Raven snarls. "God knows what you ever saw in her." Then just as quickly, Raven's mood lightens again. "Oh, I remember." Raven shakes her boobs in Davis's face again. "Isn't *that* what got you horny tonight? Thinking about Norma's big—"

Davis shuts Raven up with a long kiss on the lips. Raven unbuttons Davis's shirt. Davis paws at Raven's waist. Then hoists her pullover sweater over her head. Which gives my camera a clear shot of Raven's lower back.

The lighting from the mood candles is dim. And the image from my camera is grainy. Still, I can see that Raven's lower back does indeed feature a spectacular tattoo. But it's something astrological. Definitely *not* the Weatherman insignia. No rainbow. No lightning bolt.

Moral Reader, I'd like to tell you that, once I confirm Raven's tattoo is *not* a Weatherman tattoo, I promptly turn off the video. But that would be a lie. Instead I sit in the dark. Half-crocked. At noon. Watching two people on videotape. Two people in advanced middle age—fifty-eight and fifty-four—going through the familiar motions. The mating dance. The prelude to making love.

You gotta admire them. At their age most folks just mail it in. They forget about the passion. Forget the romance and the candles. Just get up each day with their assigned mate. Bump into each other's naked bodies in the bathroom. With no more reaction than when they bump into the sofa.

But Lane and Raven are *not* just mailing it in. They're *going for it*. I've tried to tell my kids the need for loving never dies. They don't believe me. My kids, of course, are completely *grossed out* by the thought of anyone over thirty even *thinking* a sexual thought about another human being. But here are Lane Davis and Raven LaGrow. Living proof. That the need for loving never dies.

Davis's shirt comes off. Raven's bra comes off. The kissing gets more passionate. Hands begin roaming freely. The focus on my surveillance camera is fairly soft. Just as well. They're both in pretty good shape. For their ages. And yet—soft focus is definitely best for this aging couple.

Still, it's pretty hot stuff I'm watching. Speaking professionally, of course. These video images could become great still photos. "*Feminazi Law Prof Caught In Candidate's Love Nest.*" Plastered above a titillating photo of the aroused couple. Half-undressed at her dressing table. With black-ink bars across any exposed breasts or sex organs. (After all, we are a *tasteful* publication. Suitable for display at your local supermarket.) And beneath the photo, the byline: "*If All Sex Is Rape, What The Heck Is The Feminazi Professor Doing?*"

I laugh out loud just *imagining* it. We might even run black-ink bars across the *eyes* of Raven and Davis, too. For no particular reason. Just to make the photos look a little *kinkier*.

Their pants come off. They move off camera. My last glimpse of them is from the back. Two naked people. Holding hands. And walking toward the bed. Their buttocks glowing a little whiter than the rest of their naked backs in the soft flickering light of the mood candles. So now I see only a dressing table. With a phalanx of flickering mood candles. But the *audio* is getting steamier. Heavy breathing. Lots of "oh Gods." And some *serious* squeaking.

At first I figure it's a squeaking *bed frame*. But that's not it. It's more like the squeaking from a universal joint. Then I remember. The *Love Swing*. That's gotta be it. Unbelievable. Raven LaGrow. The hard-ass feminazi. In a Love Swing. With a man. And squealing "oh God."

*Is it really a story?* Or am I just trying to *make* it into a story, out of habit?

Unlike the Rachel Clark story, this extra-marital affair is about sex. Not violence.

And unlike the Rachel Clark story, this extra-marital affair is simple. The Rachel Clark story is way too complex. The pennies that I'm convinced prove her innocence are awful hard to explain. At the tabloids, we don't do *complex*. We know what you, our readers, want. This shit right here. A Feminazi law professor caught *in flagrante delicto* with a married pol. *That's* what you want. And by God we give it to you. Week after week. By the shovel full.

The off-screen squeaking sounds from the Love Swing become steadier. Rhythmic.

I try to conjure an image of what they're doing. But I have no Love Swing experience. Though I do own a "manual" for one. Years ago Elaine and I bought a small hammock for the kids. The sleazy-looking Key West salesman slipped me a "manual." Which showed two hundred positions an acrobatic couple can try. So Elaine and I gave it a try. A short experiment. We couldn't even get ourselves into position #1. We were pitiful failures at Love Swing acrobatics.

My thoughts are interrupted by a disturbing image. Me. I've just glimpsed myself in the mirror. Sitting alone in my hotel room. In the dark. At noon. Half-crocked. Watching home-made porn. With middle-aged actors on a Love Swing. Like a pervert. How pathetic is that?

I switch off the film. Before their climax. Just to prove to myself I'm not *that* far gone. But now I'm *really* depressed. Up in smoke is my theory that Raven LaGrow is Rachel Clark.

*Or is it?* Hunter said tattoos bruise and fade after ten years. So Rachel Clark, in the late seventies, must have had a bruised and fading Weatherman tattoo. She wouldn't want to *renew* it. Because her FBI 'Wanted' poster described it. She'd want to *hide* it.

How better to hide an old tattoo than to put *another* tattoo over it? Like an Aquarius tattoo. So my theory might *not* be up in smoke, after all!

And even if the fingerprints show that Raven is *not* herself Rachel Clark, that phone message from Sheila sure made it sound like Raven knows where to find the Fugitive Radical. The reward money Sheila mentioned had to be a reference to the reward for Rachel Clark. And Rachel Clark's parents said she had a child named Sarah. Unfortunately, if Sarah's really back in Ann Arbor and about to tell Hunter that Raven and Sheila know where her mom is, well—I guess I'd better go see Hunter. See if I can build some trust with my "teammate." And maybe find out if Sarah's contacted him yet.

\* \* \*

"Look, asshole, I don't have time to crap around with you today."

"It's nice to see you too."

"What the hell do you want?" Greg Hunter growls.

"To help you. Teammate."

Hunter's eyes narrow.

"I remembered where I heard about the steam tunnel escape. Lane Davis told me."

"When did he tell you that?"

"Wednesday morning. Right after you and Cliff accosted me at the Campus Inn."

"You're *sure* it was Davis?"

"Positive. Davis said 'no one I know has seen Rachel Clark since 1969, she disappeared thirty-five years ago, through that steam tunnel at the Law School.' Then he said, 'After that, everything you hear about Rachel Clark is just urban legends, underground myths.'"

"You remember all this word for word, even though you have no notes?"

"I have a very good memory. But Davis knowing about the steam tunnel proves nothing. As you know, he was a prosecutor here, in the seventies. So he'll just say he heard about the steam tunnel back then." Using my handkerchief, I hand Hunter the telephone repair 'receipt' from Raven LaGrow's house. "On the other hand, *this* might really help you. Teammate."

Hunter inspects it. "How come the date on this is yesterday?" Hunter asks.

"She musta got the date wrong," I lie.

Hunter glares. He ain't fooled. But he hands the receipt off to his girlfriend for fingerprinting.

"Raven LaGrow?" Hunter looks skeptical. "You think *she's* Rachel Clark?"

"Maybe."

"You don't want me to arrest Lane Davis. But everything you bring me points to him. First, the helmet. With Davis's prints next to Rachel Clark's prints. Then it's Davis who told you about the steam tunnel. And now you tell me you suspect Davis's *girlfriend* is Rachel Clark?"

"Raven LaGrow is *Davis's girlfriend?*" I pretend this is news to me.

"Don't quote me on that," Hunter smirks. "*Teammate.* I forgot who you work for."

"We'll just call you a 'reliable source.'"

"I'm *not* your source!" Hunter barks. "You're *my* source."

"Have it your way. It ain't news. It's all over town."

"Davis is not real discreet," Hunter concedes.

"Doesn't Raven worry the affair will hurt her—politically? Ms. 'All Sex Is Rape' . . ."

"I don't know anything about Professor LaGrow's politics."

Somewhere down the hall a metal door slams. Angry voices shout obscenities.

"Hey, teammate," I say, "while we're waiting for those fingerprints. Would you mind telling me what you know about Rachel Clark *after* she escaped through that steam tunnel?"

"Ain't much," Hunter mutters.

"I heard she had a kid—Zimmerman's kid—named Sarah."

"FBI thinks that's true."

"So maybe Sarah could help us find her mom?"

"Not likely. If there even was a kid, she never lived with Rachel Clark. Probably never even met her."

"That's hard to believe—a mother who never saw her child after birth?"

"Happens all the time, boy-o, with adoptions. What choice did Rachel Clark have? You can't raise a kid when you're a fugitive."

I nod. Then stare at Hunter awhile, looking for signs that he might know more than he's telling me about Sarah. But the bulldog wears a poker face. If Sarah's tried to contact Hunter lately, you'd never know it from his face.

So I change gears. "Well if the kid's no help, what do you know about Rachel Clark after 1969?"

"I told you—not much."

"I read she was arrested in Amsterdam in 1980. Using the name 'Rebecca Snyder.' Got away just before Interpol's computers matched Rebecca Snyder's prints with Rachel Clark's."

"That's correct."

"Where was she from 1969 to 1980?"

"No clue. Amsterdam was the first peep we'd heard from her in eleven years."

"How 'bout *after* Amsterdam?"

"Amsterdam was the *last* peep, too. Trail went cold again after that."

"No leads at all?"

"Lots of *leads*. I've personally interviewed dozens of old hippies. Nothing."

"You mean they *know* nothing? Or they just won't cooperate?"

"Mostly they know nothing," Hunter says.

"And sometimes . . . ?"

"Sometimes they're like Alan Singer."

"Who's Alan Singer?"

"Small player in Berkeley in the seventies. Was hiding out in Amsterdam in 1980."

"Why?"

"Berkeley police wanted to question Singer about a campus fire. Suspicious origin."

"Is there still a warrant for Singer?" I ask.

"Never was a warrant. Not enough evidence. They just wanted to question Singer."

"But Singer didn't want to be questioned?"

"Evidently not. Skipped the country. Went to Amsterdam. Worked for Amnesty International. Helped a lot of the Amsterdam protestors get out of Europe after the housing riots."

"What's Singer do now?"

"*Stockbroker*. No more Revolution for Alan. Not now that he makes the big bucks."

"What'd Singer tell you?"

"Nothing. But he knows something. He was there in Amsterdam. Ran with the same hippie ex-pat crowd. And when I said 'Rachel Clark,' Alan turned white as a ghost."

"Can't really blame him, can you? Why would a rich stockbroker want to sit and shoot the breeze about his radical past? With a cop?"

"No one's looking for Alan Singer now. There never was a warrant. But man, when I said 'Rachel Clark,' Alan couldn't show me the door fast enough. I know a guilty look when I see it." Hunter socks his right fist into the palm of his left hand, hard. "If the goddamn US Attorney would get off his ass, he could *make* Alan Singer talk. But Singer'll never talk to me."

"How 'bout you let *me* take a crack at him?"

"What? You gonna pretend to be a phone repairman again?"

"Don't laugh," I say. "I can do some things you're not allowed to do."

"I don't wanna know about this."

"Exactly. I know how to get Alan Singer talking. And you definitely *don't* wanna know how."

Hunter gives me Singer's addresses, phone numbers, and e-mail. And Singer's resumé.

Lotta gaps. Like Raven's resumé. Like Sheila's and Naomi's, too. Singer got his BA in Political Science at Berkeley in 1974. MBA, Wharton, 1988. Partner, Kuhn & Huntley, 1995.

Seven years to make partner makes sense. But *fourteen years* to get through biz school?

Heck, it only took *me* eight years to get through law school.

Hunter fills in some of the gaps. Singer was arrested at a no-nukes rally, Livermore, 1977. Was named a suspect in the destruction of a campus laboratory where animal testing was conducted, 1978. Worked for Amnesty International in Amsterdam, 1979-1985.

Hunter's girlfriend pokes her head in. Says the fingerprints came back as belonging to a former federal employee named "Raven LaGrow." And no one else.

"So you're still just whistling in the dark, ain't ya?" Hunter sneers. "Teammate."

I prefer to think I'm *eliminating suspects*. One down. Three to go.

\* \* \*

Back at the Campus Inn, I check all my phone taps and bugs again. Nothing new.

I go online. Dig hard for a few hours. Find everything in cyberspace on my three remaining suspects. And on Lane Davis. Nothing new.

If only I were a character in a *real* novel. All I'd have to do is go provoke one of my suspects. Then get ambushed. Almost killed. In a hair-raising car chase. But then I'd know who was hiding the truth from me. I'd confront her. She'd confess. And the mystery would be solved.

But here, in this much more boring novel called *My Life*, I'm not even enough of a threat for anyone to *bother* ambushing me. Much less try to kill me. Heck, no one's even *tailing* me anymore. The Germans must've decided I don't have any story worth jumping, cuz they seem to have gone back to LA or whatever hole they crawled out of. And even Hunter seems to have lost interest in monitoring my movements.

*What* movements? With my Raven LaGrow theory up in smoke, my only remaining lead right now is my appointment with Sheila Nyman. Where I should be able to collect fingerprints from both Sheila and Naomi. On the legal documents I'll have them prepare for me. In my role as their new business client. Launching my new progressive magazine.

It's a pretty good plan, actually. Should be easy to take away their prints without them realizing that's what I'm doing. Then once Hunter runs the prints through the police computer, I'll know if one of them is Rachel Clark. Or if not, I'll know Camille Davis is the Fugitive Radical.

Problem is, my appointment with Sheila isn't 'til *Tuesday*. Still four days off. I may not be able to stay here that long. Plus that's a whole lot of time for something to go wrong in the interim. Like any of the following possible storm clouds I see gathering on the horizon:

(1) Hunter may get restless. Hit me with a subpoena. Arrest Davis. Or both.

(2) "Sarah" from Raven's phone message may contact Hunter. Seeking the reward. (Unless I can find her first *and* dissuade her. Which seems unlikely. Since I have no last name for her. No lead on where she is. And no money to offer her in lieu of claiming the reward.)

(3) Rachel Clark may get spooked. Disappear without a trace. Like she did in '69.

(4) My boss, Graham Hancock, may lose patience with me larking around in my old hometown. Order me to return to Florida. *Post haste*.

Actually, this last item is not just a possibility. It's a *certainty*. Graham's been quiet so far. Giving me a long leash. But it won't last the weekend. Sundays are never quiet in the tabloid biz. Since we go to press Monday morning. So as sure as iron man Brett Favre will suit up for the Packers this Sunday, so, too, you can bet Graham Hancock will call. And want my ass on the next plane home. To clean up whatever crap has landed in his lap in my absence.

And meanwhile, while all the above-listed storm clouds are building up pressure and any second might burst and rain holy shit down on me, what am *I* doing?

Basically standing out in the open. Waiting to get drenched. Diverting myself by flirting with Janet Fickel. And looking forward to my high school reunion tomorrow night. That's *it*.

What happened to the one-time crack DOJ investigator? The erstwhile ace reporter for the *Enquirer*? He must have grown old and fat. Because he can't seem to think of anything to *do* to track down Rachel Clark. He's a pathetic shadow of his former self.

In this dark mood I wander over to Davis & Nyman. Hoping a plan will hit me as I walk.

It's a beautiful autumn afternoon. Unseasonably *hot*.

A high school boys cross country team jogs by. It's so warm, the boys wear no shirts. On Main Street, the attorneys all walk in shirt sleeves, their suit jackets slung over their shoulders. Even the Goth kids, dressed head-to-toe in black, have removed their leather jackets. To let the sun strike their lily-white arms.

Everyone's enjoying the beautiful day. Except me. I gotta adjust my attitude.

As I approach Davis & Nyman, I see Sheila Nyman. Walking out. Since Sheila doesn't know me, I follow her. On foot. I'm elated. A suspect *on the move*! Something for me to *do*.

Sheila walks south on Main Street. Passes a drug store. Which, sad to say, I remember well. From my misspent youth. When my teenage fiend buddies and I used to shoplift candy there, every day after school.

Sheila goes into a coffee shop. Sits down at a table near the front. With Raven LaGrow.

Raven just talked to me yesterday. But I was wearing a gray wig and glasses then. Raven hasn't seen me blonde and unadorned with spectacles in over a year—and even then I was just one among many tabloid hacks. So I take a chance. Walk inside. But the place is deserted. No way can I sit near them. They'll clam up. And later remember my face.

So I stand at the counter. With my back to them. Order the most complex coffee on the menu. Even though I don't drink coffee. And when my triple-cap with double latte and a shot of hazelnut finally comes, I order a *second* one. Just to buy a little more listening time.

Sheila and Raven are having an animated conversation. But it's *whispers*. So I only hear a few words. Twice I hear them say "Déjà Vu." Like it's a *place*. Not a state of mind. Otherwise all I gather is that Raven will be the one to talk to "Sarah." About the "reward."

Still, at least now I have *something* to show for my afternoon. A place called Déjà Vu. A *lead*. I feel better. All I have to do is find out where Déjà Vu is. And figure out how to get "Sarah" to tell me—and *not* Hunter—where her mom is hiding.

Still seems like a long shot though. Probably best if I spend most of my time just developing a better plan to get fingerprints from my three remaining suspects.

I dump my coffees outside. Walk back to my hotel. And clean up. For my hot date tonight.

\* \* \*

The all-time best-selling *National Enquirer* issue was devoted entirely to celebrity breasts. I kid you not. *Eighty* pages on boobs. Fake vs. real. Big vs. small. Bras vs. no bras. All the burning questions. We reviewed dozens of *types* of breasts. Tastefully, of course. But in full color.

Sophisticated journalists decried our "puerile obsession" with "*décolletage.*" But almost five million Americans bought the breasts issue. And it wasn't just that one issue. It's *every* issue, really. Boobs are our stock and trade. Big ones, small ones, fake ones, real ones. Doesn't matter. Boobs are what tabloid readers expect to see. And we deliver. Week after week.

So I consider myself a minor expert in the field. And not just because of my tabloid experiences. Mine is a lifelong interest. ("Obsession," Elaine would say. But why be mean-spirited?) I've been an advanced student of female mammary glands since I was a wee lad.

So I'm sitting at Dominick's. Drinking Sangria. When, two blocks down the sidewalk, I spot the familiar sashay. *Her Strut.* Only it's much hotter out than last night. As Janet Fickel nears, I see she has her coat off. At last. And she's wearing a tight-fitting zebra-striped sleeveless sweater. Oh. My. God. She's only 5'2", 115 pounds tops. But she's sporting a chest like Sophia Loren in her prime. Janet's breasts are full. Round. Firm. And *very* large. *Schwing*!

"Is that my beer?" Janet points at the Bud Lite I already got for her.

"If you want it," I say. "Or I can get you something else."

"No, it's *exactly* what I need. After the day I had. I came within an inch of quitting."

"Why? Lane was misbehaving?"

"Lane was out all afternoon. It was *Sheila.* Jumping down my throat."

"For what?"

"Back in Indiana, I was taught to *cooperate* with law enforcement. Apparently different rules apply in Ann Arbor."

"Well, they do say Ann Arbor is 'fifteen square miles surrounded by reality.'"

Janet laughs. But it's a *grim* laugh. Clearly she's still upset.

"So what happened?" I ask.

"An Ann Arbor Police Detective came to the office. Wanting the guest list from the last fundraiser we had for Lane."

"Why?"

"Someone's car got hit in the alley behind our parking lot. Tuesday afternoon. He figures it was probably one of the guests at our fundraiser. So he asked for the guest list."

"And you gave it to him?"

"Of course. Why wouldn't I? But when Sheila found out, she hit the roof. She told me *never* to give out law firm information again, without first clearing it with her or Lane. She said I was 'jeopardizing the privacy of the firm's clients.'"

"Were the guests at the fundraiser all firm clients?"

"No. Hardly anyone there was a client. I made that point. Sheila didn't want to hear it. She shouted me down. It was *very* unpleasant." Janet takes a long swig of beer. "In fact, if it had been anyone *but* Sheila, I woulda quit on the spot."

"Why is Sheila different?"

"Most of the time, she's like me. Finds ways to *avoid* conflict. Instead of creating it."

I look at Janet's eyes. Although her *chest* is calling out to me. Like a homing beacon. "Here's a wild guess," I say. "This police detective. His name was . . . *Greg Hunter*?"

Janet's amazed. And impressed. "God, you really *don't* miss anything. How'd you know?"

"Friday's awful late to be investigating a Tuesday hit-and-run. Hunter thinks Davis knows where Rachel Clark is. Probably thinks one of the guests on Tuesday was really Rachel Clark."

"You mean . . . Hunter was *lying* to me?"

"'Fraid so."

"But I almost got *fired* trying to help him out."

"Hunter wouldn't care. He'll stop at *nothing* when it comes to finding Rachel Clark."

"*Rachel Clark*! *Rachel Clark!* That's all I hear about these days!"

"Oh? Who's talking about Rachel Clark 'these days?' Besides me?"

"Everyone! Wednesday it was Lane and that helmet. Yesterday, you. Today, Naomi."

"The paralegal? What did *Naomi* have to say about Rachel Clark?"

"I don't remember. Something about letting sleeping dogs lie."

"Tell me about Naomi," I say.

Janet cocks her head sideways. Looks me up and down. "Interested? I really doubt Naomi's your type."

I laugh. "Who do you think *is* my 'type'?"

"*Not* Naomi. She's very withdrawn. Not at all *verbal*."

"Does Naomi have a family?"

"No. Just a roommate. Female. And it's—just platonic. Naomi's *not* a lesbian."

"Has Naomi ever been married?"

"No. But she's definitely not a lesbian."

"Does Naomi have any love life at all?"

"No. Except I think maybe she carries a secret torch for Lane."

"*Lane*! Why do all the women go for fucking *Lane*?"

"Jealous?" Janet teases.

"Yeah I am! Next thing I know, you'll tell me *you've* got something going on with him."

"No chance in hell. I make it a rule. Never mess around with the boss."

"Why?"

"Because I'm already *living* that story. That's how I met John. He was my boss when I worked at the dealership. Before I became a legal assistant."

"And are you tired of living that story?"

"A little." Janet meets my eyes. "But that reminds me. Last night you said there were *two* great stories. Right in front of you. One to tell. And one to live. Then you told me Rachel Clark's the story you want to *tell*. But you never said, what's the story you want to *live*?"

"You really want to know?"

Janet nods.

"You."

Janet looks puzzled.

"This is kinda hard to say. Since we don't really know each other very well. But since you asked, I gotta tell you, Janet. I have really strong feelings for you. *Really* strong."

Janet looks stunned. And ready to bolt.

I kick myself. For being such an idiot. For upping the ante too fast.

I start debating if I should run after Janet when she bolts. Or just let her go.

But Janet doesn't get up. Doesn't look away either.

So I prattle on. Trying to *will* Janet to stay in her chair. By sheer force of verbiage.

"Please don't worry. I'm *very* well behaved. I'll never lay a finger on you. Unless you touch me first. But I feel I should just tell you straight out. You're an exceptional woman. I'm really having a great time with you. And . . . I really hope to get to know you a lot better."

Janet still doesn't say anything. But doesn't look away either. I'm scared to death. So I keep talking, hoping like mad she won't get up in the middle of one of my sentences.

"I'm sorry if I'm being too intense, too soon. It's just . . . this hasn't happened to me in a long, long time. So if I've offended you—please forgive me. I'm not very good at this, I guess."

Still Janet says nothing. But still she stays. I'm beginning to think she looks maybe more *thoughtful* than unhappy. So I decide to *go for it*. What the fuck.

"I can see maybe I've caught you by surprise, Janet. But please understand. I'm not fooling around. I mean what I say. If you want to be just friends, that's fine. I'll respect that. But if you ever decide you want to be *more* than friends, well, all you have to do is—say so."

You have no idea how close I came to stealing the famous Lauren Bacall line from *To Have And Have Not*: "*All you have to do is whistle. You do know how to whistle, don't you? You just put your lips together. And <u>blow</u>.*" Luckily I caught myself. But thinking of the near-miss has me smiling. And luckily, my smiling causes *Janet* to smile, too. Big smiles all around.

"In the meantime, though, I'll behave my butt. I promise. No more wild talk. Let's talk about something else. You know, I'm meeting Sheila Nyman next Tuesday. At your office. Tell me more about Sheila. Thinking about Sheila should cool me right down."

Janet laughs. God, she has *such* a great laugh.

"I don't think this is a good day for me to talk about Sheila." Janet pulls out a cigarette. Lights it. Takes a long drag. Cocks her head sideways. Blows out the smoke. *Very* sexy. Janet is a living, breathing tobacco ad. Then she gives me a level gaze. "Let's talk about *you* instead."

"Hard to do."

"Why?" Janet asks. "Because you're so evasive?"

"Bull's-eye." I laugh. "*Evasive* is exactly the word my in-laws use for me."

"I avoid my in-laws, too. Like the plague."

"Me, too," I confess. "But that's *not* why they call me 'evasive.' It's the way I avoid *answering questions about my future*. Especially when I first met them. They were trying to find out when I was planning to graduate from law school. And grow up. Stuff like that. I was so adept at dodging their questions, they said I'd invented a new verb tense. The 'future evasive.'"

Janet laughs. "So you didn't grow up fast like me?"

"Not at all. Dawdled through school as long as I could. I knew a good thing when I had it. Being a student is the best life you can ever have."

Janet takes a long drag on her cigarette. "Maybe for someone real smart like you. For people like me, school was total drudgery."

"I'm not buying that. You're plenty smart, Janet. And to be honest, I hated high school, too. Never did even one *second* more of work than I had to. Just like everyone else. But college was completely different. *There* I got hooked on learning for its own sake. If you'd had the chance to go to college, who knows how different your life might have turned out?"

"Well, it's too late now."

"It's *never* too late, Janet. Life is what you make it."

We lock eyes a long time on *that*.

Then Janet says: "Well, I'm *not* going back to school now. No matter what you say."

I laugh. "I won't make you go back to school. But I tell you what I would like. I'd like to see some pictures of you. From your high school days. And from your twenties and thirties, too."

Janet doesn't look away. Makes no promises. But looks flattered that I asked. All in all, I feel I'm on much safer ground than a few minutes ago. So I keep the mood light the rest of the evening. We stay another few hours. Eat dinner. Drink like fish. Banter. Laugh.

Around 8:00, the owner of Dominick's stops by our table. Marcus DaVanzo. A *junior* high school classmate of mine. Another friend who knows Elaine. And knows this ain't Elaine I'm drinking with. Marcus pulls up a metal chair. While checking Janet out. I introduce them.

"Glad to meet you," Marcus says to Janet.

"Great crowd tonight, hey?" I say to Marcus. "You sure there's gonna be enough room for our high school reunion here tomorrow night?"

"No problem." Marcus is answering me. But still looking at Janet. "You'll have the whole upstairs to yourselves. My regulars can sit down here."

"You mean we gotta fight the students all night to get our drinks?"

"No—I'll send up pitchers of beer ahead of time. We'll stay ahead of you until a half hour before closing."

"Beer's great. But don't forget to send up lots of pitchers of your sangria, too." I lift my glass to Janet. "Dominick's makes the best sangria anywhere outside of Spain." I turn back to Marcus. Who still can't take his eyes off Janet. "Hey, Marcus. Can I get your sangria recipe? So I can make it for myself at home."

"No way!" Marcus leans over to Janet. Conspiratorially. "Everyone wants our secret recipe. But I never give it out to anyone. Especially not to *lawyers*. They're the worst gossips!"

Marcus is one of my many ex-classmates who thinks I'm still a lawyer. So I hold my breath. Hoping Janet doesn't out me. As a "journalist."

Janet laughs. Looks at me. Eyes twinkling. Then looks back at Marcus. Turns on all her formidable charm. "What if David stopped being a lawyer? Would you give him the recipe *then*?"

Marcus considers. Then shakes his head. "No. *Retired* lawyers gossip even worse than the ones with jobs." Marcus turns to me. "Are you thinking of retiring, Dave?"

"Yeah, I am. But it's like most of my fugitive dreams. More fiction than reality."

Our conversation with Marcus DaVanzo is interrupted by a small imbroglio at the front gate. The guy checking IDs won't let one kid in. Insists the kid's ID is fake. Won't give the ID back, either. The kid's friends are getting belligerent. Marcus wades into the middle of the ruckus. Explains firmly that the law requires Dominick's to hold the questionable ID until the police come check it out. Explains the police will shut Dominick's down if they don't follow this law.

The prospect of Dominick's closing, for any reason, is universally deemed a bad thing. So the kid's support instantly evaporates. The belligerent crowd at the gate relaxes. They filter into the bar inside. The kid has no choice but to leave. Then Marcus disappears inside, too.

Janet and I stay out on the front porch. Drinking and talking awhile longer. At last Janet slips a breath mint in her mouth. And says she needs to call it a night. We make plans to get together again Tuesday after work. I don't bother mentioning I should be back in Florida by then.

We walk out into the street. Where her car is parked. Right in front of Dominick's.

The place is packed. But it's mostly students. And other people I don't know. Except for Marcus DaVanzo. Who has not come back outside.

Janet opens the driver's door. Leaning a little against the side of her car, I reach out to shake her hand. Like last night. But tonight Janet pushes right past my hand.

She puts her hand on my chest. Pushes up as high as she can go on her toes. Tilts her head up toward mine. Closes her eyes. Cranes her neck up even higher. And kisses me. Full on the lips. A really long, great kiss.

I know I was asking for it earlier. But from Janet's non-response, I figured there was no chance. At least not tonight. So I'm stunned. And—delighted. Apparently Janet's decided that if I'm not going to lay a finger on her until she touches me, then she'd better step right up to the plate and touch me. Which, I realize, means she *does* want me to lay a finger on her.

So I do. But *carefully*. I circle my biceps around Janet's shoulders. And cradle her lower back with my hands. We stand out there in the street. With at least eighty people on Dominick's front porch watching us. Making out like teenagers. We can't stop smiling. Because it feels so right. Even though, of course, it is *not* right. Not right at all. Not fair to Elaine. Not even fair to John the gun nut. Not *smart*, either. It's crazy and indiscreet for two married people—who are not married to each other—to stand out in the street kissing each other in front of eighty people.

But that's what we do. For ten minutes. Long, passionate kisses. Janet is the best kisser I've ever known. Soft, thin, moist lips. I always thought kissing a smoker would be like licking an ash tray. But the fresh taste of that breath mint covers up all the cigarettes. For each kiss Janet closes her eyes. Like each kiss is something special. That fabulous chest of hers heaves a little with each kiss, too. And best of all is the way she keeps her hand on *my* chest. Gentle pressure.

It doesn't matter what you call it. You can wax poetical. Put it in the vernacular. Or take it all the way down to the gutter. It's still the same thing. Poetically Emil Bergson called it "the life force." James Baldwin, more prosaically, called it "man's atavistic weapon." My high school buddies, all the way down in the gutter with me, just called it "having a boner."

But for now, I'll take the high road. The *life force* is surging through me. Feels great. And Janet, pressed up against me, must feel my life force, too. Pressing up against her.

Somewhere in the midst of all the kissing, we move our next date up. From Tuesday to tomorrow. Right here at Dominick's. At high noon.

At last we say goodnight. And Janet drives away.

* * *

Back in my hotel room, I try to make sense of the riot of emotions engulfing me.

I feel wildly *destabilized*. Voluptuously flung into a brave new world. Where anything is possible. I feel like this might really be the start of something that will change my whole life.

So, of course, my stomach aches like it just took a bullet. Bursting with toxins.

And my conscience—which I'm shocked to discover I actually have—is in overdrive. Bursting with blame.

So I call home. To try to assuage that guilt I told you I don't feel.

"Hey, sweetie, I've found some interesting, er, stuff up here." A mild under-statement.

"You mean besides Inga and Frieda?" Elaine teases.

"What? Who? Oh, yeah."

"Don't tell me you've forgotten their *names* already, David!"

"No, no. It's just—they're *resting* tonight."

"*You* should be resting, too. Tomorrow you'll be out half the night. You reunion junkie."

"Don't worry. I'll sleep late tomorrow morning. But I've stumbled onto a really great story. It's— "

"That's great. But my mother is driving me to despair. You know what she did today?"

Elaine launches into a long account of her mother's latest crimes against human-ity. Her mother insulted an old friend. At a fundraising meeting for the synagogue. With a snide comment about "changes" in the accounting reports. Elaine is beside herself. Her mother denies she was implying any *embezzlement*. She just doesn't like *changes*. So since she wasn't implying anything, she sees no need to apologize.

The whole thing seems pointless to me. Elaine's mother *never* apologizes. For anything. And she insults people left and right. All the time. Life goes on. But Elaine gets very upset about her mother's transgressions. Each one causes Elaine to relive, over and over, the worst parts of her childhood. To recycle all the destructive emotions she's never been able to let go of. I could write a whole novel about Elaine and her mother. Locked in a lifelong *danse macabre*. The mutual dance of self-annihilation. But luckily, I'll spare you that novel. For now.

Fifteen minutes later, when Elaine finally starts winding down, I debate try-ing to tell her the Rachel Clark story. But it's late. I'm tired. And I doubt Elaine would find my "Shoeless Joe" version of the Rachel Clark story anywhere near as fascinating as Janet Fickel found it.

So I just put a toe in the water. Tell Elaine I might have to stay on in Ann Arbor for a few more days. *After* the reunion. Because the story I'm on is awfully good.

I hold my breath. Figuring if I have to, I'll tell Elaine that Detective Hunter *ordered* me to stay in town. But it turns out I don't have to play that card yet. To my great surprise, Elaine does not object at all to me staying in Ann Arbor a while longer. Evidently Elaine's not minding a little free time, away from the old ball-and-chain.

It reminds me of when I worked for the *Enquirer*. Or even for the DOJ. In those days I was on the road a lot. Which was great for the marriage. Whenever Elaine was getting sick of me, I was off on another trip. By the time I came back home, Elaine missed me again. But ever since I landed the editor's job at *The National Spy* last year, I haven't been traveling anywhere near as much. Tensions have been running high at home. So it's probably all for the best if I stay away a little longer.

I wish Elaine goodnight. Without telling her about Rachel Clark. Or Janet Fickel.

And then I sleep the deep, sound sleep that only the truly wicked—and tabloid hacks—ever enjoy.

# CHAPTER FIVE
# ROLLER COASTERS LIKE THE PLAGUE

## Saturday 16 October 2004

My dad, a corporate executive, embodied the Protestant work ethic. Up at dawn. Work all day. Home for dinner. Then after dinner—work some more. Dad had zero leisure activities. Didn't know the meaning of "free time." The doctors say Dad died of heart disease. I don't buy that. I believe he died because he was forced to retire at seventy. Whereupon he lost all reason for living.

I was not exactly Dad's dream-come-true of a son. My wastrel tendencies were hard for him to accept. And my abrupt switch from lawyering to tabloid hacking was *very* tough on Dad.

Try to see it from his perspective. He believed with all his soul in the free market system. For my dad, it was an unassailable truth—an article of *faith*—that anything that stands the test of the free market must, *ipso facto*, have inherent value.

But tabloid journalism is a real challenge for free market zealots. Who can seriously argue there is any inherent *value* in the crap we tabloids crank out week after week? Yet our profit margins far outstrip those of Boeing or General Motors. Truly, only internet pornographers are more profitable than tabloids. So according to Dr. Keynes—and my dad—the tabloids *must* have value. Indeed, in my dad's value system, the fact that I make more money as a tabloid hack than I did as a lawyer means, *ipso facto*, that I was lucky I got disbarred.

But it was still hard for Dad to swallow my new career choice. For years after I joined the *Enquirer*, we hardly spoke at all. Then, at the end, when Dad was real sick, we had the only really great talks we ever had. Go figure. The guy's in terrible discomfort. Deeply depressed about dying. So suddenly, for the first time in my life, he's *chatty*. And instead of talking about sports, like we did for my first forty-five years, we actually talked about life. Imagine my surprise.

And Dad had some truly radical things to say. Told me I should be writing novels instead of screwing around making money as a tabloid hack. Though somehow I doubt this book you're reading now is quite what Dad had in mind. But it was nice to hear him acknowledge that maybe some activities have value independent of market rewards.

So then we talked about death. The only subject that really matters. As always, Dad was practical. Saw cemeteries as a huge waste of space. But I talked him out of cremation. Best closing argument I ever gave. (As it were.) Turned my dad around 180 degrees.

I persuaded Dad that cemeteries are the only tangible link we have to our past. The only places we can commune with the dead. See through a glass darkly. And grasp, however dimly, that the muddled and miscellaneous indignities of our personal lot—those endless miseries and injustices in our little lives that we all take so seriously—are really nothing new under the sun. Cemeteries are the only places where, as you read those archaic tombstone phrases from another time, you almost get it. Almost understand that Life is like one of those low-brow Broadway plays that runs forever. Every few years they change the cast. So the audience, which also changes every few years, *thinks* it's seeing something new. But it's really just the same old same old. They might change the clothes. Might even change the music. But it's the same old story, played out over and over again. Night after night after night. (To lukewarm reviews.)

So now I'm standing in front of my father's grave. In Forest Hills Cemetery. About five blocks from the house where I grew up. Where my mom still lives. I really should go see my mom. I know that. I like my mom. She's an easy soul to visit, too. Very undemanding. But I'm always too busy to go see her. Just like I was always too busy to go see my dad. Until the end.

But today I came to see my dad. I know why I'm here. To talk to Dad. Because *he* had an affair. In his late forties. With a married secretary. And now here I stand, on the brink of walking the same path. The path of exhilaration and freedom. The path of deceit and betrayal.

So I want to ask him: *Was it worth it?* Looking back, when all was said and done, if you could do it all again, would you still dip your wick into that admittedly scrumptious pie? (His secretary was pretty hot stuff. If I remember correctly.) I know it caused my mom some very serious pain. Cost both my parents some very hard days. Which of course, as buttoned-down Protestants, they never talked to *me* about. And which I never asked them about, either.

So how do I even know my dad had the affair? Same way I knew the lady fooling with the helmet in Lane Davis's conference room had to be Rachel Clark. I was born with a nose for news. But unfortunately, like most newsmen,

I wasn't born with any actual *insight* into the news I'm so good at uncovering. I find it. I report it. But I don't *understand* it at all.

Which is why I'm now poised to start acting like the people in my own tabloid stories. A depressing thought. Since the people in my tabloid stories are, by and large, fatuous fools.

Behind me a parade of cars winds slowly through the cemetery. Come to bury their dead. It's in their faces. The fear. Each one we bury takes us one step closer to our own burial.

But today I do not feel at all close to death. In fact, in all my life I've never felt so alive. I know I *should* be wracked with guilt. About kissing Janet Fickel. But I'm a tabloid hack. So I know no guilt. Have no shame. Instead, I'm wracked with—exuberance. Overflowing with anticipation. I slept great. Because I wanted to wake up and go straight to Dominick's. To see Janet again. I'm hoping like hell she still feels the same way today that she felt last night.

Unfortunately, I woke up too early for that. So I stopped by to see my dad. But like most guys six feet under, Dad's got little to say. So now I've got two hours to kill. Before my hot date at noon.

I walk the long way out of Forest Hills Cemetery. Meandering slowly through the grounds and graves. It's another spectacularly warm October day. The air is full of the smell of rich, black dirt and loamy leaves. The trees are packed with changing leaves, reds and yellows and oranges.

I pass through a section of the cemetery in the back corner where the graves are for people who died in the 1960s. I start reading headstones. Looking for something quirky.

All-time best tombstone? Gotta be the composer Alfred Schnittke's. I haven't seen it. But they say it has *no words*. Just a scrap of a musical score. And a single musical note. Above the note is the fermata, signaling this note should be held as long as possible. Beneath the note is "fff", signaling this note should be played as *loud* as possible. And the note itself? The *rest* sign— silence. How wry is that? *I've gotta rest forever now. But by God my silence will be as long and as loud as possible.*

Nothing I find in Forest Hills approaches the dry irony of Schnittke's tombstone. But I do find something even more interesting. Given my current investigation into the Fugitive Radical.

The tombstone of Dale Hunter. The cop who died at the Law School. Greg's brother.

Dale Charles Hunter
Born 13 June 1945
Died 27 October 1969

An Ann Arbor Policeman
Killed In the Line of Duty
Who Proved Eternally True
To The Policeman's Solemn Code:
*To Serve And Protect.*

Into my head come random images of policemen I prosecuted in my DOJ days. Macho San Juan cops. Fat southern deputies. Tough New York City detectives. Hip LA cops. All of whom lived up to a *different* "policeman's code" than the code on Dale Hunter's tombstone. Theirs was the code of *silence*. The code that says you never rat out your brother-with-the-badge.

Thinking of the policeman's code of silence gets me thinking about Rachel Clark's radical friends. Would one of them rat her out? And save me the trouble of collecting three more people's fingerprint exemplars? Somehow I doubt it. Old radicals have their own code of silence.

I decide to jog over to Martin Place. To look in on the Davises. Maybe I can dream up some way of getting Camille's fingerprints. Without Camille knowing that's what I'm doing.

Or maybe I can catch Camille alone. Convince her Lane's wading in deep shit. Cuz Hunter's so eager to bust him. Then see if Camille will rat out Rachel Clark. To save Lane's butt.

But as I jog down Martin Place, I see a problem. A stout middle-aged lady. Mashed-potato face. Looks like Janet Reno. In a blue SUV. I saw her on my way into the cemetery. And on my way out. No big deal. She might have had her reasons for being in the same place for thirty minutes while I visited my dad and Dale Hunter. But now she's over on Martin Place? Just when I happen to pay the Davises a visit? This is *not* a coincidence. This is a new tail.

One look at Janet Reno and I know she ain't paparazzi. She's too dowdy for that. She's a cop. Guess my "teammate" still doesn't trust me to bring him Rachel Clark when I find her.

I don't mind Janet Reno watching me as I watch Casa Davis. Hunter already knows Lane Davis is in this case. But I don't want Janet Reno following me when I go see Janet Fickel. *That* needs to remain a private matter. Between consenting adults.

So I pretend to stake out Casa Davis for half an hour. Jog around the house. Peep in the windows. Ring the bell. Determine the Davises are not home. Now what?

I could break in, I suppose. I've got my pick gun with me. But committing a B&E right in front of a cop seems, uh, ill-advised. Even for me. So instead, I leap the back fence. Jog half a mile over to my mom's house. Drop in for a surprise brunch. Catch Mom up on the latest news with her grandkids. And in the process, lose my tail. Poor Janet Reno. Hunter will *not* be happy with her. But in all fairness, I'm a slippery devil to try to follow. Especially in my hometown.

* * *

The *Guinness Book of World Records* does not list a world record for "Longest Continuous Mid-Life Crisis." But if they did, I gotta believe I'd top the list. My mid-life crisis started earlier than most. Age thirty. The day the bastards forced me to graduate from law school. And it's been raging unabated for eighteen years. Shows no sign of letting up anytime soon, either.

For this reason, I can sit at a college bar and rue the fact that I don't really belong here anymore. Most adults come to grips with this fact. They may not like it. But they accept it. Get over it. And move on. Me? I still haven't even accepted the reality of my premature graduation.

So here I sit at Dominick's, trying to pretend I belong. Waiting for my hot young date. (Well, forty is *sort of* young.) But thinking about Janet Fickel hurts even worse than thinking about how I don't fit in anymore with the college crowd around me. True, Janet is *somewhat* closer to my age. And we had a great time last night. But still. Who am I kidding? Janet's not going to come. She's way more woman than I deserve. What can Janet possibly see in me?

If I were a bookie, I'd give you three to one Janet won't show up today at all. Probably she'll go to the mall instead. She knows I don't have her address. Or her phone number. Probably she shook herself awake this morning. Conjured an image of making out with me in the street last night. Took a hard look at herself in the mirror. And said, "What the hell was I *thinking*?"

Or even if Janet *does* show up, it's two to one she'll immediately start back-peddling. No heels and stockings. I'm betting on shapeless slacks. Flats. And a baggy sweater. Her first words will be, "David, about last night . . . " I'll throw up my hands. To spare myself the painful brush-off. We'll agree it was all a "big mistake." We're better off as "just friends." Then we'll suffer through an awkward lunch. Agree to get together next week. But of course it will never be arranged.

This avalanche of doubts about Janet Fickel threatens to bury me. So I force myself to think instead about the supposed reason I'm still in Ann Arbor. My search for Rachel Clark.

Well, *search* is too kind by half, isn't it? *Search* implies focused, concentrated effort. Whereas my vague inquiry is so much more desultory. Amateurish. And inept.

But *so what*? Now that I've kissed Janet Fickel, why would I *want* to find Rachel Clark anytime soon? Once I find her, I'll have to go home. And face reality. With only distant memories of kissing Janet. Growing weaker, year by year.

*Fuck work*! What do I care about finding Rachel Clark? What I want to find is the Fountain of Youth. Or at least the Fountain of Love. I close my eyes. Re-live kissing Janet. Feel her soft lips. Her hand on my chest. Her own heaving chest. I re-live each word we shared the past three days.

Unfortunately my memory *is* very good. So I recall, among many good things, Janet's disturbing account of Greg Hunter obtaining the guest list. For Tuesday's Lane Davis fundraiser.

The bad news is, that guest list shows Hunter isn't going away. He's out there digging, too. He's not just waiting around for me to find Rachel Clark. He's hunting her himself. Hard.

But the good news is, that guest list shows Hunter's nowhere close. From my rooftop perch Tuesday afternoon I counted *fifty people* leave that fundraiser. Before Norma Lee and her pals had even come. Roughly half of those fifty folks were female. So until Hunter figures out that the fundraiser ended before the helmet arrived, Hunter's got about twenty-five red herrings to sift through. Whereas I'm down to three real targets.

On the other hand, Hunter's a cop. He knows what he's doing. Unlike me. I'm just a tabloid hack. I know I fed you some line about my DOJ days. So you'd *think* I'm a crack investigator. But the truth is, *the FBI* did all the investigations. At the DOJ, we just second-guessed the shit out of the FBI. After *they* did the investigations. *Why didn't you send an agent out to Nowheresville to interview the subject's third-grade teacher*? Crap like that. There's a huge gap between knowing how to second-guess someone else's investigation, and knowing how to actually conduct an investigation yourself. I'm on one side of that gap. Hunter's on the other.

Prying that guest list out of Janet was probably only one of a *hundred* things Hunter did this week that I don't even know about. To close in on Rachel Clark. So who am I kidding? I can't stall finding the Fugitive Radical, just so I can pursue my little romance with Janet Fickel. Hunter will track down Rachel Clark. Long before I track down Janet Fickel.

And if Hunter doesn't find Rachel Clark real soon, he'll just hit me with a subpoena.

Still, Hunter's options are limited. He can't bust into Davis & Nyman with a search warrant and start fingerprinting everyone. As long as I withhold what I saw Tuesday night and where exactly I got the helmet, he has no probable cause. Plus, with the election so close, the incumbent mayor would have to be dumber than Richard Nixon to risk the political fallout from letting the police search a rival candidate's law office.

Yet *without* a search warrant, all Hunter can do is what I'm doing. Interview suspects. Tail them. And hope for a break. I wonder if he's *bugging* these folks? Remember: Hunter said everyone thought Rachel Clark was in "Timbuktu." Just twelve hours after one of my radical targets used the same expression. Coincidence? Maybe. But if Hunter *is* bugging them, he sure isn't getting shit. The only hint of anything worthwhile from any of my bugs was that message from Sheila Nyman to Raven LaGrow. About how Sarah is ready to rat out her mom. For the reward money.

Which is the one place Hunter has a big edge on me. Because he's got control of the reward money. So I've got to hope Raven succeeds in persuading "Sarah" to shut up. Or else I've got to find Sarah myself. At "Déjà Vu." Real soon. And try to buy a few weeks of her silence.

Because I know Sarah hasn't talked to Hunter yet. If Hunter had Sarah, he wouldn't have sent Janet Reno out on a Saturday morning to tail me. Nervously I glance up and down Monroe Street. No sign of Janet Reno. I'm *sure* I lost her. So why am I so nervous?

The *other* Janet, of course. I'm going crazy with anticipation.

Sure, my rational mind gave you odds Janet won't come. Or that she'll come, but immediately quash my dreams. By dressing like a prim librarian. But in my foolish imagination, anything is possible. I'm back in school again. Excited about life and its endless possibilities.

Of course, when I was in school, I only dated women I could take home to Mom and Dad. No high school dropouts. No two-time divorcees. No married women. No Janet Fickels.

My mom would call Janet "cheap." *Elaine* would call Janet "cheap," too. If you think about it, "cheap" is a terrible thing to call anyone. But you know what they mean. Nice girls aren't supposed to dress to provoke. Or prance to provoke. Or meet a man's eyes with so much frankness as Janet does.

The problem, I'm beginning to realize, is I *like* cheap. A lot. Call it mid-life crisis if you like. I won't deny it. Hell, I'm gunning for the *Guinness* record. But isn't "mid-life crisis" just the label we apply to a guy who breaks the rules and starts living life the way he really wants to? And isn't "cheap" just the label we apply to a woman who decides to go for it, too?

Forty-eight years I've lived my life *for my parents*. Tried like a good boy to conform my conduct to *their* expectations. To meet the demands of *their* world. The world Rachel Clark and the Weathermen rejected. Go to law school. Marry a nice girl. Have kids. Get a house in the 'burbs. Sublimate all your rampant primal urges into the quieter joys of family life. Sure, I disappointed my parents some. By taking this wrong turn into the tabloids, for example. Still, at forty-eight, I've managed to live up to most of their values, most of the time. Key word. *Their* values.

Now as I wait for Janet Fickel, I wonder: why not live the rest of my life (what's left of it) for myself? Why not embrace the bad boy within? Get in touch with my inner rascal?

"Did you start without me?" Janet Fickel points at the empty mason jar in front of me. With that sexy cocking of her head.

"Just root beer." I try not to show I was so lost in thought I didn't even see Janet arrive. "Keeping up with you is hard enough. No point in getting buzzed before you even get here."

Janet laughs her sexy laugh. "Well I'm here now."

And Lord is she! No shapeless slacks. No baggy sweater. I lost *both* my bets with you, Gambling Reader. Not only is Janet here—she's also wearing a mini-dress so tight most *teenagers* couldn't fit into it. So short she has to hold the hem with both hands as she wriggles into her chair. Jesus H. Christ!

I stare shamelessly at Janet's lovely thighs. Tell her she has the most beautiful legs I've ever seen. Janet knows how to take a compliment. No blushing. No stammering. No words at all. Just a long, seductive gaze. Raising my RPM from zero to a hundred in a single heartbeat.

Janet didn't put this mini-dress on to *discourage* me. That's for sure. And I think I see a hungry look in her eyes that has nothing to do with food. Those eyes seem to be saying we'd better eat fast. Because our bodies are screaming for each other.

Janet fishes in her purse. Pulls out a square envelope. Hands it to me.

I open it. It's a Hallmark card. For something called "Sweetest Day."

Now I've never actually heard of "Sweetest Day." But I love Liar's Dice. So I bluff. Thank Janet for her thoughtfulness. And claim embarrassment that I forgot to get *her* a Sweetest Day card.

Janet laughs. "Don't bullshit me. You don't seem the type to remember Sweetest Day."

"Busted. But if you knew I wouldn't get you a card, why'd you get *me* one?"

"Because you're the sweetest man I know," Janet says. With no trace of irony.

I'm speechless. So I read the card:

**Dearest David – I feel like even though we just met, I can tell you anything and everything, which is good because I pretty much do anyway. And your kisses . . . well, let's just say they're pretty spectacular. It's really strange because they give me the same feeling in my stomach that riding on a roller coaster does, and I avoid roller coasters like the plague. So why can't I avoid you? Don't answer that. Happy Sweetest Day! Janet**

The mini-dress was so much more than I'd dared hope for. Now this?

"What's so bad about roller coasters?" I look up from the card. Straight into Janet's great big brown eyes. "I . . . I hope I wasn't out of line last night. I know I should be more discreet. It's just—wow. Kissing you felt so right. I couldn't stop."

"Don't apologize," Janet says. "*I* started it. And I couldn't stop either."

"I noticed. It was really fabulous."

I move my hand down to Janet's thigh. My fingertips tingle as they run back and forth along the smooth-grained texture of her cinnamon stockings. Janet watches me. No objection.

Remember when *you* were a teenager? "*Workin' on mysteries without any clues*," as Ann Arbor's own Bob Seger put it so well. First you held her hand. Then you stroked her hair. Then you hugged her. Then you kissed her. Next you caressed her thigh. Touched her waist. Her butt. Then—God help you—her boobs. And all the while she was making the same slow progress with your body. Each advance was at least a night unto itself. If not a week. (Or in my case, a *month*. I was extra slow.) And then the *real* fun began. Touching the erogenous zones. *Without* removing the clothes. Another month, at least. Before you finally got the clothes off.

Adults seldom get to enjoy the slow build-up. For all I know, maybe teens don't anymore, either. Everything's so much faster these days. Puberty at eight. Oral sex at thirteen. Retirement, with stock options, at twenty-five. But I suspect the romance gets lost in all the rush.

With my hand having established a new romantic beachhead on Janet's love-ly slender thigh, we order food. And I attempt to learn a few more things about the radicals Janet works for. Before things between *us* get too radical for words.

"If your boss wins the election, have he and Sheila decided who will take over his cases?"

"I don't think Lane seriously expects to win the election."

"Why would he bother to run then?"

"Ego trip."

"But that's true of all candidates, isn't it?"

Janet laughs. "Probably. But with Lane, the ego's *way* outta control. You shoulda heard him on the phone yesterday with Raven."

"Lane thought he was in the 'Cone of Silence' again?"

"Yeah. But in that old house, the walls have ears. Named Janet."

"And what exactly did the walls named Janet hear?"

"Lane compared himself to Ralph Nader. A true crusader. Doing the right thing."

"Regardless of the consequences to the compromising Democrats?" I ask.

"You got it."

"Was Raven trying to get Lane to pull out of the race?"

"No. But *Camille* thinks he should pull out. So Lane was justifying staying in the race. Oh—and you'll love this. He compared himself to Rachel Clark, too. Your favorite fugitive."

"What was the comparison?"

"Two idealists. Willing to sacrifice their personal comfort for their ideals. BS like that."

"Did you hear Lane say anything about Rachel Clark's daughter, Sarah?"

"No."

"Any mention of the reward money for finding Rachel Clark?"

Janet gives me a funny look. "No. But you should go on the Psychic Network."

"Why?"

"Detective Hunter called me at home this morning. Told me all about the reward money."

"Hunter wants to know if you have information about Rachel Clark?"

"Yes." Janet looks at my hand on her thigh. "That's what *you* want to know too, isn't it?"

"Hey now, this isn't—" Embarrassed, I withdraw my hand.

Janet laughs. "It's okay. I know you're not really interested in *me*," she teases.

"Like hell I'm not."

"Then prove it. No more questions today about Rachel Clark. Or Davis & Nyman."

"Deal. But hey—how come *Greg Hunter* has your home phone number? And I don't."

"He asked for it yesterday. When he almost got me fired over that guest list."

"And you were raised to cooperate with law enforcement."

Janet smiles.

"Well *I* used to work for the Justice Department. So I want cooperation, too!"

We write down our cell phone numbers. And exchange them.

"But David—please don't call unless it's important."

"I'm hoping you'll think *all* my calls are important."

"No, seriously. The phone bills go to John. If I'm over my minutes, he sees who I've been calling and who's been calling me. And even if I'm under my minutes, he checks the phone's call log."

"Possessive?"

"Very. When I go to work in a dress like this, he spies on me. At lunch. Or after work."

"What do you mean, 'spies on you?'"

"He gets a car from the dealership. One I won't recognize. Then he parks across the street. To see who I'm having lunch with. And to make sure I go straight home after work."

"How do you know he does this?"

"Naomi saw him once, Sue saw him another time. He wasn't in his own car either time."

"Does John have any *reason* to spy on you?"

"Not 'til I met you."

"So when you go home, what happens?"

"He gives me hell anyway. Just because he didn't catch me doesn't mean he trusts me."

"What kind of 'hell?' He's not *hitting* you, is he?"

"No. I wouldn't stand for that. But it's still—not nice. He pitches a fit. Yells. Throws things. I tell him, 'you *like it* when I dress like this.' He says, 'not when *I'm* not around.' The last time I wore this dress. Oh. My God. What a scene. Absolutely miserable."

"When *was* the last time you wore this dress?"

"Few months ago. I wore it to work. I forgot how—short it is."

"I'm not complaining."

"Lane wasn't either. Right away he was on the phone with his friend Bill Haffey. Telling Bill 'you'll like what Janet has on today.' Sure enough, Bill comes over within the hour. Asks me to lunch. So John sees me going out to lunch with a nice-looking lawyer in an expensive suit. Oh. My God. When I got home that night, John broke half our dishes."

"Why do you stay with him?"

"I don't know."

"You deserve better."

"Do I?"

We lock eyes a long time. I put my hand back on Janet's thigh. She ain't complaining. "Janet, I really don't give a damn about Rachel Clark. Or Davis & Nyman. It's *you* I want to know about."

"What do you want to know?" Janet teases.

"Everything. The stuff that's in your old photo albums. What did you look like twenty years ago? Who were you with? Why the hell weren't you somewhere *I* could find you?"

"Were you looking for me then?"

"*All my life* I've been looking for you."

I pay the bill. And challenge Janet to a game of pool. At the Michigan Student Union.

We cross the small lawn at the southeast corner of the Law Quad. Where red ivy climbs the gothic stones around Pembroke Watkins's old office. Cut through to the main Quad. Where dozens of students lie sprawled. Frolicking in the warm sun. Where one time, in our distant youth, Elaine and I lay. Making out so passionately, I seriously thought we were going to start copulating right here. On the Law Quad lawn. I kid you not. Elaine was so fucking hot that day!

Right now, another young couple is making out in a doorway. With great enthusiasm.

Janet's eyes meet mine. Detour time. I steer us to the next empty doorway.

Janet's arms go up. Around my neck. She presses her lithe little body close. Our lips meet. And linger. Long. We kiss like a sailor and his lover. Like it's our first time in a year.

I have to do *something* with my hands. I start slow. Under her armpits. An awkward place. I feel the sides of Janet's substantial bra through her dress. I'm dying to grab hold of those oversized breasts of hers. But I'm a chicken. And I don't want Janet thinking I'm a *complete* wolf. At least, not yet. So I move my hands down her sides. Slowly. End up with both hands on her hips. Which are small enough that my fingertips are basically on her butt, too.

We kiss long and slow. With each kiss I feel the heft of Janet's chest pushing against my ribs. Even in her three-inch heels, Janet is still eight inches shorter than me. Each time I tilt my head down to kiss her again, she closes her eyes. Each time we come up for air, Janet opens her eyes and gazes at me as if I am the best kisser she has ever known. So enraptured am I, it does not even occur to me to wonder if Janet gives this look to every man she kisses. Janet has me completely convinced I am her romantic dream come true. And she is certainly mine.

Eventually we stagger out of the doorway. Smiling. Holding hands. We walk toward the Union. But stop in another Law School doorway. For another twenty-minute bout of making out. Somehow we finally make it out to State Street. Cross the street. Dodge the political pamphleteers gathered outside the Michigan Union. And go inside.

They do have rooms for rent at the Union. But it's too soon for that. And I don't want to break the spell. The romance feels so sweet. So tender. So real. Don't get me wrong. I'm not the kind of guy who prefers the chase to the climax. Quite the opposite. But I remember those two quick flings I had at office parties past. The sex was fun. But afterwards: nothing. I don't ever want to feel nothing with Janet. So I hold off asking. I trust Janet to tell me when it's time for us to cross that line. If we ever get that far. Before I have to go home. To my real life.

So we just rent a pool table in the corner of the pool room. And shoot pool.

I'm a terrible pool player. Janet's worse. But we have a blast. Laughing over each atrocious shot. Marveling at Janet's unique pool-shooting style. Which attracts a lot of attention from the college boys too. Instead of bending at the waist, Janet bends from the knees to shoot pool. Like a cocktail waitress, balancing a tray of drinks. In that short little dress, it's sexy as hell.

Under cross-examination, Janet admits she did indeed once work as a cocktail waitress. Between marriage #1 and marriage #2. Her kid, Carrie, was living with Janet's parents. Janet was stubbornly trying to make it on her own. But she made so little money as a cocktail waitress in Fort Wayne that she had to live in her car. Slept in the backseat. Even in the winter. Waking up every two hours on cold nights. To turn on the engine and get some heat in the car.

Janet isn't looking for sympathy. Just sharing old stories. I share a few of mine, too. Like how I lived above a brothel in Amsterdam. Once a month I'd go downstairs to pay the rent. The hookers in their tight little teddies would hear the footsteps. Assume it was a customer. Perch up on their barstools. Splay themselves seductively across the bar. And then groan in disappointment when they saw it was only me. Very hard on my twenty-four-year-old male ego.

I run through more of my old stories while we shoot pool. I won't bore you with them. Elaine would tell you they're all the same anyway. But, as usual, Janet laughs at all the right times.

After shooting pool, we go back to the Law Quad and wander the halls. The halls Rachel Clark escaped thirty-five years ago. The halls I escaped eighteen years ago. We find a classroom where Pembroke Watkins used to torture me. Socratically. The door's unlocked. Our eyes meet. We enter. Close the door. And then make far better use of that classroom than I ever did in my law school daze.

We lie down. On one of the long tables. And shamelessly make out. For two hours. Things get pretty intense. I'm on top. Pressing against Janet's lovely little body. That oversized chest is an inch away. And her slender thighs are poking out from under that short little dress. Her thighs have to go somewhere. Pretty soon they're wrapped around me. In the missionary position. We aren't copulating. But we're as close as you can get with the clothes still on.

Eventually we come up for air. Stagger around half-dazed. We end up down in the front of the room. Standing on the raised platform from which Watkins used to deliver his lectures.

"It's been forever since I've been kissed like that," Janet says.

"Me, too," I confess. "I don't know if anyone's *ever* kissed me like that, Janet."

She gazes up at me. Utterly rapt. So I fold her in my arms. And start kissing her neck. Turns out Janet likes this. A lot. She starts moaning. Which is slightly unnerving. Because it reminds me of Raven LaGrow. Moaning on my videotape. When Lane Davis was biting her neck.

"John has diabetes," Janet whispers. "So he can't—we haven't had sex in two years."

Was that an invitation? Or a warning? I'm not sure what to say. So I stick with non-verbal communication. Continue kissing Janet's neck. But now she fends me off. By wriggling round so I can only kiss her lips. Of course, I don't give up easy. I waltz her over to the nearest long table. Ease her down on her back. Lie on top of her again. And resume chasing her neck.

"No, David," Janet says. Breathlessly. "I can't—I— "

I arch my neck up. "I'm only kissing your neck," I protest. "The clothes are still on."

"They won't be if I let you keep doing that."

"Would that be a bad thing?"

Janet takes my chin in her hand. So she can look me square in the eye. "For now, it would be. I only met you four days ago."

Well, three actually. But who's counting?

"Am I still allowed to kiss you on the lips?" I ask.

"Allowed?" Janet pulls my face back down to hers. "It's required."

"Let me see if I understand," I say between kisses. Sounding like the ghost of Pembroke Watkins. Socratically cross-examining a recalcitrant law student. "You like being kissed on the neck, yes?"

Janet nods.

"A lot, yes?"

Janet nods.

"So why, exactly, would you want me to stop?"

"I like champagne, too," Janet says. "A lot. But if I drink champagne around you, who knows what would happen?"

"Let's find out."

"Some day soon we will."

Two things seem certain. We're not going to be taking our clothes off today. And I'm not going home tomorrow. No matter what Graham says. So we make plans to meet tomorrow afternoon. At Island Park. Where I used to make out with my high school girlfriend.

Thirty years ago. But who's counting?

It's a long, sweet afternoon. A wonderful time. And it confirms I am heading for a worse kind of trouble than I've ever known before. Deep trouble. Trouble I have no idea how to resolve. Trouble that will definitely end in heartache. For someone I care about. And for me.

\* \* \*

Sigmund Freud said that all males, everywhere, at all times, unconsciously long to sleep with their mothers. He may have been right. Yet no one really knows for sure. Because no one can stay awake long enough, while unconscious, to test the truth of Freud's hypothesis.

But one thing we do know is true. At Ann Arbor Huron High School in 1974, all males—students, teachers, coaches, administrators, janitors—longed to sleep with Denise Maxwell. Denise was built. Like everyone's mother should be. If Rachel Clark was the Shoeless Joe Jackson of Ann Arbor, well, Denise

Maxwell was the Earl Campbell of Huron High School girls. Just as each of Earl Campbell's massive 38" thighs was the size of a normal man's waist, so too were each of Denise's massive 38-DDD boobs the size of a normal girl's head. And Denise oozed sex appeal. Huge pouty lips. Heavy makeup. And heavy eyelashes. Which Denise was always batting at all the males in the room. Denise was the whole package. Fulsome. Luscious. And ripe.

For our tenth high school reunion, Denise wore a low-cut prom-style gown. And radiated raw sex appeal. Denise was on her second marriage by then. Her new husband, a major stud, paraded Denise around like a prized show car. Even at twenty-eight, I was reduced in Denise's presence, to the stammering adolescent I'd always been whenever I tried to talk to her back in high school.

But by our twentieth reunion, I finally found the gumption to talk to Denise. By then we were all thirty-eight. Her stud husband was home with her four kids. Denise still looked damn good. But she wasn't a complete sex bomb anymore. She'd put on a few pounds. Which she packed under a sweater-and-slacks combo. Somehow the extra weight made Denise seem more human. More approachable. So I actually talked to her. Quickly discovered she's an airhead. And also learned Denise has some surprising self-esteem issues. Who knows why? Still. Just talking to Denise Maxwell was a fantasy come true. Except it happened to be twenty years too late.

So upon arriving at Dominick's for our thirtieth high school reunion, I immediately search for Denise. (I have much in common with Pavlov's dog.) And receive a huge shock. Denise has gone to seed. She looks awful. Gravity has finally taken its toll. All that heavy sexuality has become just plain old heavy. Denise must weigh two hundred pounds. Which precludes her from even bothering with the old Raquel Welch act. Denise just sits there. Like Jabba the Hutt.

But I sit and talk with Denise anyway. (I'm very loyal to my old wet dreams.) She's divorced the stud. Remarried. This time to an Ann Arbor lawyer. Todd Cook. Turns out Cook was a U of M Law classmate of Lane Davis. Denise knows Davis. Knows Sheila Nyman, too.

"Isn't Sheila Nyman a little too radical for you, Denise?"

Denise laughs. "That's all in the past. Sheila's a soccer mom now. Just like me."

"What do you know about Sheila's 'past?'"

Denise titters. "She was with the Weathermen. The real radicals."

"How do you know that?"

"Parent complaint. Didn't want Sheila driving on a school trip. Cuz of her criminal record."

"And?"

"The guy was wrong. There was no criminal record for Sheila Nyman."

I'm struggling to follow the logic. Denise was never the sharpest knife in the drawer.

"So then what makes you think Sheila was with the Weathermen?" I ask.

Denise bats her big eyes at me mischievously. Which thirty years ago would have induced cardiac arrest. But Jabba the Hutt batting eyes is not quite like Raquel Welch batting eyes.

"I told the guy—Bill Miller—that we checked, and Sheila Nyman had no record. But then Bill said Sheila Nyman is not her real name."

"Did Bill Miller tell you Sheila's real name?"

"Melanie McGeetchy. A fugitive from the seventies. He said he was a postal clerk back then. Stared at her 'Wanted' poster for weeks on end. Said he fell in love with her picture."

"How ridiculous!" I say. "To fall in love with someone just based on how they look."

Since Denise has zero sense of irony, my ironic interjection does not slow her down.

"I know," Denise says. "But it made me believe him. Bill said he had nothing *against* Melanie. Or Sheila. But he was dead sure she was a fugitive. Because he stared so many hours at her eyes in that picture, he knows her eyes like the back of his own hand."

"That's all? Bill was positive Sheila was a '70s fugitive named Melanie McGeetchy, for no reason except he thought her *eyes* looked like Melanie McGeetchy's eyes in a 'Wanted' poster?"

"That's all. But Bill was determined to confront Sheila about it. Since I was the president of the PTA, I decided I had to be there, too. We had a little meeting. At the school."

"And Sheila admitted she was Melanie McGeetchy, the fugitive?" I ask.

"Not exactly. Sheila—well, she's a lawyer." Denise pauses. Looking for the right words.

"You mean Sheila didn't say yes and she didn't say no?"

"Exactly!" Denise beams at me. A smile I would have *died for* thirty years ago. "Sheila was very smooth. Bill said he recognized her from the old 'Wanted' poster. Accused her of changing her identity. There was a long silence. *Very* long. *Very* awkward. Their lips weren't moving. But a lot was getting said anyway. With their *eyes*. You know?"

I nod. While gazing at *Denise's* eyes. Which are still sexy. If you ignore the rest of her.

"At last Sheila asked Bill what did he want. Bill said he wanted his kids to be safe. She said he had nothing to worry about. Because 'the Revolution ended in 1975.' And then Bill was happy. Thanked me. Shook hands with Sheila. And even walked out to the parking lot with her."

"Did you ever ask her about it later?"

"No. I don't know Sheila *that* well. But my husband, Todd, says that's what the Weathermen always said. 'The Revolution ended in 1975.' When the Vietnam War ended."

Hmm. Many *other* people have said that, too. Not exactly *conclusive proof* Sheila was in the Weather Underground. I'm about to get up. Then I realize Denise is still talking.

"Todd also said Lane Davis got in big trouble when he was at the prosecutor's office. In the late seventies. For crushing warrants. No, that's not the word."

"Quashing?"

Denise blushes. And laughs. "Yes. Lane Davis was *quashing* warrants. For old radicals. Like Melanie McGeetchy. Todd said Davis got fired for it."

"I heard Davis got fired for lending his car to Ralph Nader."

Denise opens her eyes wide. "I never heard that. Could be. I don't really know."

Over Denise's shoulder, across the room, I see two of my old cronies. Flailing their arms. They're giving me the international sign for a hand job. Which I choose to interpret as their way of saying they're impressed I'm hanging out with Denise Maxwell. Even in her present inflated condition.

I excuse myself from Denise and start crossing the room. To calm the boys down.

But en route two of my old basketball teammates intercept me. Phil and Joe. We catch up on life. Talk about their wives. Their kids. Their investments. Their European vacations.

In the background, the boom box is playing The Four Tops' "Same Old Song." I'll say.

Phil and Joe ask what "Wrong Way Fisher" is doing nowadays. I debate telling them. Let's see. Just the past five days. Committed five separate B&Es. A few petty thefts. And multiple violations of wiretap and privacy-invasion laws. Impersonated a law enforcement officer. An entrepreneur. And a telephone repairman. Destroyed public utility lines. Stalked a celebrity. And withheld evidence from a cop. Filmed illicit sex between a law professor and a politician.

Then screened it in the privacy of my hotel room. Not to mention dry-humped the hottest little skirt in Ann Arbor. In my old Civil Procedure classroom.

Just an average week for a tabloid hack.

Truly I would *enjoy* telling Phil and Joe all about it. But they couldn't handle it. They *need* me to be the same old Wrong Way Fisher they knew in high school. The timid scaredy-cat. Number Zero. The outsider who never quite fit in with any one group. Back then, the jocks didn't trust me cuz I was too smart and I was friends with lots of freaks. The freaks didn't trust me cuz I didn't do hard drugs and I played sports. And the braniacs didn't trust me cuz I never talked about academics outside of class and I had too many friends who were not college prep.

That's the only David Fisher that Phil and Joe know. And the only one they *want* to know. If I told them what a self-confident scofflaw I've become, they'd freak. And bolt. The Reunion Committee has enough trouble getting people to come to these reunions. They don't need me chasing folks off. By forcing them to confront this unwelcome truth: *people change.*

So I spend a few hours faking it with Phil and Joe. And all my other classmates. Telling them *variations* on the truth. Which sound consistent with the old Number Zero they knew. I still live in Florida. In the 'burbs. Still with the wife and two kids. Still a lawyer. Ex-prosecutor. Now I do "media work." In short, I follow Rule #1 at reunions: *Don't spook people with the truth.*

But there's one woman at our reunion who's breaking this rule. Big time. Lisa Williams. This is the first reunion Lisa's made. Oh. My God. In high school, Lisa was shy. Demure. Prim. Now, she's a forty-eight-year-old Walking Misdemeanor. Are *women* allowed to have a mid-life crisis? If so, Lisa's having one. She's wearing skin-tight, leopard-spotted leather pants. With a matching top cut just the way I like it: tight and low. Lisa's parading her husband around the reunion. Her *fourth* husband. A real live *biker*. In the flesh. Greasy, long black hair down to the middle of his back. Sleeves rolled up to reveal massive biceps. Sporting more tattoos per square inch than an NBA star. And wearing tight leather pants with medieval-looking *spikes* coming out the sides.

"What are you doing these days, Lisa?" someone asks.

In lieu of a verbal response, Lisa starts handing out business cards. I get one. The card says "Slumber Parties." And below the address: "Lisa Williams, Romance Specialist."

No one else has the gumption to ask. Except your favorite intrepid tabloid hack.

"What exactly is a 'Romance Specialist?'" I ask.

Lisa smirks. Raises her well-plucked eyebrows suggestively.

Her biker husband growls, "She helps you *get off*."

Lisa laughs. Nuzzles her biker husband. "Bruno, that's a little too—*rough*." Lisa turns to me. A twinkle in her eye. "We like to say 'I help you find the *romance* that may be missing in your life.' That's why I'm a '*Romance* Specialist.' If all you need is help getting off, I send you to Déjà Vu. But if you want *romance*, you come to me."

"Thanks," I mutter. "But right now I've got *too much* romance in my life."

The assembled crowd of my former classmates laughs. They think I'm joking.

"But just in case I develop any problems getting off, what's 'Déjà Vu?'" I ask.

My classmates erupt in laughter. At the sheer naiveté of old Number Zero.

Lisa smirks. Starts shimmying her tight little butt up against Bruno's pelvis.

"Strip club in Ypsilanti," Bruno grunts. Like I'm too dumb for words.

"Ah," I mumble. "I should have guessed."

The conversation moves on to Lisa's dogs. Orgasm (whom they call "Orgie") and Butt Plug (whom they call "Butt Plug"). I kid you not. Gradually I drift into other conversations. With other old classmates. But Lisa Williams is the highlight of the night. Who would have guessed, back in 1974, that shy little Lisa Williams would end up as a middle-aged "romance specialist?"

But that's why most people fear reunions. And why I love 'em. They're so *destabilizing*. You're forced to admit that people change. First you learn that your old judgments were way off. The people we all thought were so cool in high school mostly turn out to be losers. The quarterback who seemed so insouciant turns out to be just dull-witted. And the prom queen with the huge smile turns out to be so empty-headed she can't hold a job. Much less a husband.

These small reversals in fortune don't necessarily surprise us. They just force us to admit we were idiots in high school. But then come the bigger reversals in fortune. The shockers. The self-appointed gay-basher who turns out himself to be gay. (Causing class wits to murmur, "so the Lady *did* protest too much.") Or the shallow thug who spent his high school daze stealing hubcaps and beating up freaks by the flagpole for fun, who seemed utterly incapable of having any deep thought—until he shocked us by committing suicide last year.

And there are other big surprises, too. The ones we all *scorned* in high school, who grew up to be winners. The nerds who now live in California. Own dot-coms. And know how to talk at cocktail parties. Even the druggies turned out better than expected. At least the ones who are still *alive* for our thirtieth reunion. They've gone straight. Invested all the profits they made from years of dealing dope. And started legit businesses. Which thrive because they learned so much more about the realities of business from their years of drug dealing than they ever could have learned in biz school.

But happily, there's one old druggie at our reunion who hasn't cleaned up his act a bit. Tom Lacy. The Hunter S. Thompson of our class. It's a miracle Tom's still alive. No combination of drugs exists that Tom hasn't poured into his ravaged body at some point. Including combos fatal to the average Joe. But Tom doesn't go down easy. In his late twenties Tom did real time in a prison in Honduras or Jamaica or some such place. And lived to tell about it. Now *that's* a survivor.

Tom has never come to a high school reunion before. Someone talked him into coming to this one. And Tom looks like he regrets it. He's crouched in the far corner of Dominick's porch. Nursing a beer. When I sit down at his table to talk, Tom tells me he's about to leave.

"Reunions are too weird," Tom says. "You spend much time here in Ann Arbor after high school?"

I point at the Law Quad across the street. "I went to school there. For eight years."

"No shit! Remember my brother Jim? He dated the girl that tried to burn that down."

"*Rachel Clark?*"

"Yeah. Rachel Clark. The Fugitive Radical."

"Jim *dated* her? At U of M?" I can't conceal the excitement in my voice.

"Yep. Freshman year." Tom laughs at my awe-struck face. "Hey, 't'ain't no big thang! Jim had no clue the next year she was gonna try and burn the fuckin' Law School down."

"Did *you* ever meet Rachel Clark?"

"Yeah. She was—wow. Dynamite. Way out there, man."

"Was she as wild as Jim, Lace?"

"*Wilder*, man. *Much* wilder. Remember when I got into mushrooms in seventh grade?"

I wince. "I remember you were doing things I was, uh, afraid to join in on."

"Oh, yeah," Lacy says. "No hard drugs for Fish. I remember now. Well, anyway, it was *Rachel Clark* who first turned Jim and me on to mushrooms. And later MDM."

"MDM?"

"Designer drug. Early version of Ecstasy. Great for sex, man. Fabulous aphrodiasic."

Since I'm a *parent*, I don't regard Ecstasy as a "fabulous aphrodisiac." To me, it's the evil date-rape drug I warn my daughters against. But there's no point arguing drugs with Tom Lacy. A guy who, unlike me, actually *will* go to jail for what he believes in.

"Jim said sex with Rachel Clark on MDM was the best he ever had."

"I thought she had a steady boyfriend. Paul Zimmerman. The one who got killed."

Lacy shrugs. "So? Maybe she did. You forget. That was the age of *Free Love*, man."

"Those were the days." As if *I* knew.

"I'd *love* to know where Rachel Clark is now," Tom Lacy says.

"You're not the only one. Federal government still wants to know, too."

"Kind of amazing they never found her, huh?"

"Especially with that wild tattoo she had."

Lacy almost chokes on his beer. "How do you know about *that*? *You* make it with her, too?"

"Relax, Lace. I was only thirteen in 1969. Just like you."

"Oh yeah." Lacy takes a long stiff drink. "So how *do* you know about her tattoo?"

"Research. I'm doing an article about Rachel Clark. Learned a lot about her lately."

"No shit? You should talk to Jim. He was *real* good friends with her."

"Where is Jim now?"

"New Zealand. He'll be back next spring, though. When it turns cold Down Under."

"Can I call him down there?"

"Naw. He's a wilderness guide. No phones. You can leave him a message. But won't do no good. Jim never calls back. Better to wait 'til spring."

"Thanks. But I don't have that much time. Jim ever tell *you* anything about her, Lace?"

Two old hockey players from our class fall across our table. Seriously drunk.

The hockey players are wrestling each other. For control of a huge plastic rat. The Ann Arbor Huron High School mascot. The River Rat. We push the hockey players and their plastic rat away.

Lacy takes a long drag on his cigarette. Tilts his head up. Like Janet Fickel. And blows a huge smoke ring. Which drifts above us. Like a lazy halo.

"Jim never talks much about her. Not with so many cops after her." Lacy leans forward. Motions for me to lean forward, too. "But Jim knows a lot about Rachel Clark. Remember that motorcycle helmet she was wearing? That saved her life when she got shot?"

"Yeah?"

"Jim *kept it* for her. For thirty-five years. The most famous bullet hole in the Movement."

"Does Jim still have it?"

"Naw. Sold it. Just a coupla weeks ago."

"Aw, that's too bad. Jim needed the money?"

"Naw. He was scared."

"Scared? *Jim Lacy*? Scared of *what*?"

"The guy buying it was way too intense. Claimed to be a U of M history professor. A sixties memorabilia collector. But Jim smelled law man all over the guy."

"You mean, an undercover cop?"

"Yeah. Jim can spot a cop at a hundred paces. He really didn't want to sell the helmet. But he was afraid if he kept it, the cop might put *Jimbo* under surveillance. Jim, ah, . . . wasn't in a real good space for *that*." Lacy takes another long drag on his cigarette. "You know who you should talk to? If you really want to know about Rachel Clark? Her college roommate."

"Who's that?"

"Melanie McGeetchy."

"Where can I find Melanie McGeetchy?"

"I dunno. Heard she's a lawyer here in Ann Arbor. Main Street. Very respectable now."

Go figure.

# SECOND WEEK

# CHAPTER SIX
# A SHADOW WHITE AS STONE

## Sunday 17 October 2004

"Gimme a fuckin' break, Fisher!" My boss, Graham Hancock, publisher of *The National Spy*, is on the phone. Right on schedule. "You want another week in Ann Arbor? So you can try to catch a fugitive? Who do you think you are? Dick Fucking Tracy?"

"I've got fingerprints," I point out. "Fingerprints don't lie."

"I've got deadlines," Hancock replies. "Deadlines don't lie either."

"Hear me out, Graham. They're *Rachel Clark's* fingerprints. I'm the only person in the world who knows those fingerprints had to come from one of three women. And best of all, Rachel Clark *doesn't even know* her fingerprints have been found. So she's not running."

"David, I run a newspaper. Not a detective agency."

I decline to dignify this remark with a reply. Instead I rub my aching forehead. And resolve to stop drinking so much. (A resolution that likely won't last 'til noon. If the Past is any predictor of the Future.)

"It's a *weekly* newspaper," Hancock continues. "Your job was to get us a story *this week*. That's why I let you go up to Ann Arbor in the first place."

"I've *got* a story."

"I know you do. And it's a damn good one! I saw the pix you e-mailed to Larry. Norma Lee's cleavage. Tremendous! What a rack that bitch has! Where were you? Up a tree?"

"Roof next door. I've grown a little old for trees."

"Still—great work. You're way better than any reporter we've got. I mean that, David."

"Thanks." I hate it when Graham makes nice. Cuz I know he's just trying to disarm me.

"But that's why you're going to sit down right now," Hancock says, "write that story up, and e-mail it to Larry. Before noon. Today."

"Just gimme another week, Graham. If we run the story tomorrow, it'll spook Rachel Clark. She'll see a tabloid hack is getting too close for comfort. And she'll flee."

"We can't wait, David. Norma Lee's Ann Arbor visit was in the dailies last week. So all the tabloids will be running the story tomorrow, too. We can't miss the party."

"Yeah, but all they've got is maybe some pix of Norma at the press conference. Big deal. We'll blow them away next week. Not just the cleavage shots. We've got Norma Lee giving Rachel Clark's motorcycle helmet to Lane Davis. The candidate. Giving Davis a big hug, too."

I decide not to mention the spicy *video* I've got of Davis philandering with Raven LaGrow. *That*, I figure, might make Graham even *more* determined to run the story right away.

"Great!" Hancock says. "Now write it up. Your choice. Norma Lee the unrepentant radical. Or Norma Lee the hypocritical extra-marital cheat. Or *both*. I don't care. Just write it up."

"Huge mistake. If we rush to write this little story about Norma Lee *now*, we'll lose the big story. The biggest tabloid story since Gary Hart and Donna Rice." (Clearly, I'm desperate.)

"*Gary Hart*? You think catching Rachel Clark hiding in Ann Arbor would be like catching a *presidential candidate* on a yacht in the Bahamas with a bimbo? You're losing it, my friend."

"No, I'm not. Think about it. Rachel Clark is the last of the sixties radicals still on the loose. She's a big name. If we're the ones who capture her—"

"*Patty Hearst* is a big name," Hancock interjects. "*Kathy Boudin* was a fairly big name. But *Rachel Clark*? Nowhere near the same league."

"She's not Patty Hearst," I concede. "But Rachel Clark *is* a big name."

"Outside Ann Arbor?"

"*You* knew who she was. I didn't have to explain Rachel Clark to *you*."

"But does the *average person* know the name Rachel Clark? I doubt it."

"So what? The average person didn't know Kathleen Soliah either. Or Katherine Ann Power. But when *they* were captured, after all those years on the run, they were *big stories*. Baby boomers *love* these stories. Takes us back to our youth. *Everyone* loves these stories. The sixties flower child. Preaching peace, but throwing bombs. Forced underground for decades. Gone so long we almost forgot 'em. And then suddenly they're back. Looking like sad old ghosts of their former passionate selves. The best years of their lives gone forever."

"Kathleen Soliah and Katherine Ann Power were big stories *for the mainstream press*," Hancock counters. "The *tabloids* didn't bother covering those stories at all."

"But this'll be different. Because *we'll be the ones bringing her in*. It's big, Graham. It'll show people all our snooping is really in the public interest. We don't just catch celebs in the act. We catch *criminals*, too. We're the eyes and ears of the public. The man in the street. Rachel Clark may have eluded the FBI for thirty-five years. But she can't hide from *The National Spy*!"

"Hmm," Hancock says. Apart from Elaine, Graham has the most patronizing "hmm" on the planet. "You used to work for the Justice Department, didn't you, David? In your *youth*."

I smell a trap. Graham knows full well I worked for the DOJ. So I sit quiet.

"*That's* what this is all about, isn't it?" Hancock presses. "You were at Justice. In your *youth*. Now you're having a mid-life crisis. Wish you were back at Justice. Doing meaningful work. Hunting bad guys. Instead of celebrities. *That's* what's going on here, isn't it?"

"I won't deny the mid-life crisis part."

Hancock snorts. "How could you? Your sports car. Your serial flirtations with receptionists half your age. The backwards baseball caps to cover your balding head. These things speak for themselves."

"But you're wrong about the DOJ fantasy part. Really. I left DOJ behind long ago. I want to stay up here hunting Rachel Clark just because—there's a really great *story* here, Graham."

"Of course there is." Hancock speaks with such sincerity, for a second I think I've won.

"But that great story's *already been written*, David. It's called *The Company You Keep*. Fine novel. By Neil Gordon. Came out last year. About the sad lives those underground radicals led. On the run. Very literary. You'd like it. Perfect for a high-brow like you."

"But there's a *tabloid* story here, too," I insist. "Just gimme another week. I'll show you."

"You're playing with fire, David. This cop, Hunter, will hit you with a subpoena any day."

"Then we'll have a story right there. ***National Spy Resists Government Subpoena***."

"We wouldn't have a leg to stand on," Hancock says. "You know that."

"Okay. *National Spy Briefs Grand Jury On Secret Evidence Of Fugitive Radical.*"

"Hmm."

"Look. There's only three suspects left. It won't take me long to find Rachel Clark."

Long silence. Then Hancock asks, "Who are the three suspects?"

"Three women. Camille Davis. Sheila Nyman. And Naomi Williams."

"What do we know about them?"

"They're all connected to the Ann Arbor lawyer, Lane Davis."

"The guy running for mayor? The one Norma Lee flew out there to service?"

"Yeah. Only our tip was bogus. Norma Lee didn't come here to smooch his bone. Just came to endorse him for mayor. At a press conference. And to give him Rachel Clark's helmet."

"You *sure* that's all she did? That informant has never missed the mark before."

"Well, she did this time. Davis kept everything zipped up around Norma Lee. He—" I barely catch myself. Shouldn't tell Graham about Davis and Raven. Not yet, anyway.

"Tell me more about the three ladies," Hancock says. "How are they connected to Davis?"

"Camille's his wife. Sheila's his law partner. Naomi's his paralegal."

"Are you fucking *crazy?*" Hancock explodes. "If you were Rachel Clark, hiding in Ann Arbor, would you allow your *husband* to run for mayor?"

"Maybe hubbie doesn't *know* she's Rachel Clark. Kathleen Soliah's husband had no clue *she* was a fugitive."

"Hmm. Well, I suppose that makes more sense than your *other* idea—that Rachel Clark might be working *as a lawyer.* "

"Stranger things have happened. Sheila Nyman is the same age as Rachel Clark. Same height. 5'5". And I'm pretty sure Sheila was a hard-core radical in the sixties, too."

"Well now, *that's* convincing," Graham says with heavy sarcasm. "Two women. Both fifty-four. Both 5'5". *And* both dabbled in radical politics in the sixties? They *must* be one and the same. It's *obvious.*"

"Lemme finish. Sheila's bio doesn't say where she was for fourteen years. She just shows up in Ann Arbor for law school in the mid-eighties. And then goes to work for Lane Davis."

"So what? She was probably a *housewife* in the seventies and eighties. Then, when her kids got older, she went to law school. Many women do that, David. Here in the real world."

"Kathleen Soliah was a housewife, too." I'm clutching at straws. "In Chucklehead, Minnesota. Or wherever the hell they found her."

"Yeah, but Kathleen Soliah didn't go *to law school*. That's not how real fugitives act. Fugitives *lay low*. But why am I telling *you* this, Mr. DOJ? You already *know* this, don't you?"

I admit that *usually* fugitives lay low.

"In fact, you once told me, *almost all fugitives are caught within a year*. Didn't you say that?"

"Yes." One of Graham's worst qualities is that his memory is even better than mine.

"In fact, *the few who manage to elude capture more than a year*," Graham says, continuing to parrot my own words back at me, "*are the ones who blend into the background. Keep their heads way down. Lay very fucking low.*' That's what *you* once said. Isn't it?"

"I *did* say that. But that clearly didn't happen here. The fingerprints prove Rachel Clark is right here in Ann Arbor. And she's been here at least fifteen years."

"How do you know that?"

"Because all three suspects have been in Ann Arbor at least fifteen years. Rachel Clark must have tired of the underground fugitive thing. So instead of laying low, she went to the one place no one would ever think to look for her. Ann Arbor. And instead of working odd jobs, she hooked up with a radical lawyer. In broad daylight. Right under everyone's fucking noses!"

"Why the hell would she do something that stupid?"

"That's what I want to ask her. Though I think I know." I pause. To build suspense.

"Don't hold out on me, David."

"Her daughter. Sarah. Is still around here."

"Hmm."

I feel a new onslaught coming.

"Okay," Hancock says. "Let's suppose Rachel Clark did decide to return to Ann Arbor. She's willing to run the risk of getting caught. Just to be near her daughter. But let's be real. She didn't wake up one day and say, 'gee, I'm so tired of laying low, I think I'll go be *a lawyer*.' Real fugitives don't go to law school. Real fugitives don't take the Bar Exam, either. In fact—hey—you're the lawyer. Don't they *fingerprint* everyone who takes the Bar Exam?"

I admit this is true.

"Then Sheila Nyman is out. Just two suspects. At this rate I'll have you home for dinner."

"Not so fast," I say. "What if Sheila Nyman *never went* to law school? Never took the Bar Exam, either. Just put it on her resumé."

Silence from Graham. That's usually a very bad sign. Even worse than "hmm."

"People do it all the time," I continue, to fill the silence. "Every few years you read about some big-time lawyer who never even *went* to law school. Faked his whole resumé. Never took the Bar. Just started practicing law. That's the great thing about the Law. It's like Oakland. There's no there there. Anyone can do it. Really. All you have to do is pick up the jargon."

"I'm worried about you, David. You're starting to sound like one of our readers. Conspiracies and fraud everywhere. You're not hearing *voices*, too, are you?"

"The only voice I hear is the call of duty, Graham. It's my duty to save you from yourself today. Don't kill the goose that's about to lay us a golden egg. Gimme one more week up here."

I'm holding off telling Graham that Hunter "ordered" me to stay up here. I'll use it if I have to. But it's risky. Cuz Graham might get his back up then. About someone else usurping Graham's authority. Graham likes to be the only person who can tell me where I can and can't go.

"No problem," Graham says. "You can *have* another week in Ann Arbor. All I want is for you to write a story today. On Norma Lee's visit."

"Big mistake," I say. "It'll spook Rachel Clark. She'll run."

"No, she won't. You said she's been in Ann Arbor fifteen years. So she's *dug in*. Plus, fifty-four-year-olds don't run. That was the real point of the Kathleen Soliah story. Soliah was *relieved* the FBI finally caught her. She was *tired* of running. *Tired* of being someone else."

"But we can't be *sure* Rachel Clark won't run," I argue. "And if she does, we'll never find her. One thing she's proven. When Rachel Clark goes underground, *no one* finds her."

"Okay. Let's compromise. Suppose we run only the story everyone else will run? '***Norma Lee In Ann Arbor***.' Leave out Rachel Clark's helmet. Just run your pix. Short and sweet. Meanwhile, you stay up there another week. Hunt the Fugitive Radical. How 'bout that?"

"If we run my pix of Norma Lee, we'll spook Rachel Clark. She'll see a *tabloid hack* was right there at Davis & Nyman when the helmet was unveiled. I guarantee: she'll freak."

"Why? She'll figure the tabloid hack's already left town. Swam away in Norma Lee's wake. Ann Arbor ain't exactly a tabloid hot spot."

"She may not know that much about tabloid hacks. And she may not stop to think about it, either. Put yourself in her shoes. You find out a tabloid hack was right outside the office. Shooting pix when your old helmet was unveiled. If you're Rachel Clark, that's *gotta* spook you."

"It *is* kind of a weird coincidence, isn't it? Norma Lee just *happens* to bring Rachel Clark's old motorcyle helmet to the very place where Rachel Clark's hiding out?"

"That's my point, Graham! It *might* be a coincidence. But it probably is *not*. Probably *all* those people at Davis & Nyman know Davis has been sheltering Rachel Clark for years. *Norma Lee* probably knows it, too. Think about *that* story, my friend."

Silence. I debate telling Graham what Tom Lacy told me. That the last person who had the helmet before Norma Lee was likely an undercover cop. But I'm not sure this helps my case for waiting. Sure, it does show it's probably no coincidence the helmet turned up in the office where Rachel Clark was. But it would also remind Graham that cops are all over this story.

"Hold off one more week," I say. "And I'll nail the whole Rachel Clark story."

More silence. I debate telling Graham about Melanie McGeetchy. Rachel Clark's college "roommate." The fugitive Davis got fired for helping. Now rumored to be a Main Street lawyer. Except I found out this morning, before Graham called, that there is no lawyer by that name in Ann Arbor. No one by that name, period. Which reinforces the suspicion voiced by Bill Miller, the nosy school parent: maybe Melanie McGeetchy now calls herself Sheila Nyman.

But does that mean Sheila is *not* Rachel Clark? Or could the "roommate" named "Melanie McGeetchy" be just an earlier alias of Rachel Clark?

Trouble is, these unanswered questions show how little I really know about this story. Confessing ignorance won't help me get an extension from Graham. So I let Melanie McGeetchy ride.

At last Graham asks, "How do you know someone won't *jump* our story?"

"Right now, there's no one but me anywhere near the Rachel Clark story."

"What about those German paparazzi you saw?"

"They've got no clue about Rachel Clark. And I haven't seen 'em for three days now."

"What about Hunter? You said he's emotional. What if Hunter calls the *Enquirer*?"

"Are you joking? How do you think I dodged his subpoena? I convinced him the publicity would spook Rachel Clark. Which it would. Hunter's the *last* guy who's gonna go to the press."

"What about other possible leaks? The politico—Lane Davis?"

"He's a *candidate*. Last thing he wants is a story with his name next to Rachel Clark's."

More silence. "Alright already," Graham sighs at last. "We'll sit on it a week. But we've still got a deadline tomorrow. Unlike you, our real reporters have been *working*. There's ten stories stacked up on your laptop. Like planes at Miami-Dade. Waiting for your editing. Get cracking."

"I'll have them all done before noon. Boss."

*   *   *

After winning the battle with Graham, I open three Scotches. Toast myself. Then dive into work. And for a couple of hours try to forget about Rachel Clark. *And* Janet Fickel.

Turns out it's been a pretty good week for real-life tabloid stories. Some standard celebrity sightings. One recycled political scandal, brimming with illicit sex. And the usual wonderfully tacky Scott Peterson trial reports. So we won't need too many goofy believe-it-or-not stories to fill out our forty-eight pages.

First, I work on the celeb sightings. These stories need little editing. Since the pix tell the whole story. This week we've got all the usual suspects. The Royals: Charlie and Camilla, plus a nice shot of Prince William scolding Prince Harry. (Which I title: "Will to Harry: You're a Disgrace to Diana.") The Hollywoods: the Two Cruisers (Tom and Penelope), the New Brat Pack (Brad and George and Matt), and the self-styled Intriguing Women (Angelina and Oprah and Uma). And best of all we've got Jacko—Michael Jackson—in his standard tabloid pose. One hand shielding his face from the harsh glare of the paparazzi flashes. The other hand holding some little kid's hand. Truly, the guy is sick. But his fans love him. So we run pix of Jacko whenever we can get 'em.

Next I turn to the recycled political scandal. Last year Jesse Jackson hired Mel Reynolds, a former Chicago congressman. Reynolds was one of 176 criminals Bill Clinton pardoned back in 2000. Reynolds was serving six years for wire fraud, lying to the Election Commission, and *having sex with an underage campaign volunteer*. I kid you not. From a tabloid perspective, it's a perfect storm: an ex-congressman who had sex with a subordinate, wins clemency from a president who had sex with a subordinate, and then gets hired by a clergyman who had sex with a subordinate. We've got a few new details on the frisky subordinates, including some reasonably racy pix. Great stuff.

Now I work on the Scott Peterson trial reports. Which really need no editing. Even more than the celebrity photos, this story writes itself. Each and every week. The philandering husband. Who claims his pregnant wife "disappeared." Only to have her body, *cum* unborn child, wash ashore. With twenty clues and a long trail of lies pointing back at him. The Peterson story is lurid. Scandalous. And gripping.

You know why spousal mayhem like this grips our readers? Because it reminds us of the open secret we all wish we could talk about: that marriage-for-life is a crazy idea few of us can live up to. It's not that we fear our own spouse will actually try to do us in, *a la* Scott Peterson. Very few people ever cross *that* line. But we all know that marital vows don't really stop people from falling in love with other people. (A fact of which, these days, I personally am all too painfully aware.) And scandalous stories of intimate violence at least give us a chance to examine that painful open secret. To talk about it *under cover* of talking about a topical news story. In everyone's favorite forum for discussing topical scandals: the tabloids.

After editing the Peterson trial reports, I turn my attention to the filler. Normally my favorite part of tabloid work. Making up strange believe-it-or-not stories. Like "Study Confirms That 50 Percent Of All US Prostitutes Are Aliens!" (replete with a picture of an alien standing on a New York street corner in a slinky dress). Or "X-Rays Can Kill" (a story about an x-ray machine supposedly falling from a ceiling and crushing the chest of a Florida man).

But today I'm not feeling very creative. I'm still too preoccupied with chasing Rachel Clark. Not to mention Janet Fickel. No way can I sit here now and crank out the seven or eight side-splitting believe-it-or-nots we're going to need to fill out this week's issue.

Luckily I was a Boy Scout. *Be Prepared*, they always taught us. And I am. On my laptop I keep a large backlog of pre-written filler stories, all ready to go. My main source for these is an on-line internet service called "The Darwin Awards." These mock awards bestow ironic congratulations on people who have "removed themselves from the gene pool"—by harming themselves in such incredibly stupid ways that, inadvertently, they've demonstrated the truth of Darwin's evolutionary theories.

No one knows if the Darwin Awards' stories are actually true. But it doesn't matter. The Darwin web site *claims* these are true-life stories—so recycling their stories poses no copyright problems for us. It's no different than rehashing yesterday's AP news stories.

So I pick three fantastically stupid deaths from the Darwin Awards. And recycle them. In San Francisco, a forty-nine-year-old stockbroker, out for a jog, supposedly ran off a hundred-foot-high cliff. Died from the fall. Friends and neighbors all agree that he 'totally zoned out' whenever he went running. And in Detroit, a forty-one-year-old man got stuck and drowned in two feet of water. After squeezing head first through an eighteen-inch sewer grate. Trying to retrieve his car keys. His wife says he was "terrified" of being late for work.

I pad both these true-life stories with a few made-up quotes from fictitious people. Just so each one will take a full page. Then I turn to the third Darwin death. It's a classic. Replete with pix.

In a zoo in Paderborn, Germany, Stefan the elephant was badly constipated. First zookeeper Friedrich Riesfeldt, forty-six, fed Stefan twenty doses of animal laxative. Nothing. Next Friedrich fed Stefan six bushels of berries, figs, and prunes. Still nothing. So Friedrich climbed right up under the ailing pachyderm's tail. To administer an olive oil enema. But Friedrich forgot Rule #1 of giving enemas to elephants: *Stand to the side!* Before the enema was done, the laxatives, berries, figs, and prunes had their intended effect. The relieved beast let fly.

Investigators reconstructing the scene surmise the sheer force of the elephant's unexpected defecation knocked Mr. Riesfeldt to the ground. Knocked him *out*, too. Unfortunately, Stefan, with no malice, continued to dump. All told, Stefan unloaded *two hundred pounds* of poop on top of the unconscious zookeeper! Riesfeldt lay under all that dung for at least an hour before a watchman saw him, by which time Riesfeldt had *suffocated*. Flabbergasted Paderborn detective Erik Dern said "it seems to be one of those freak examples of how 'shit happens.'"

Now I realize, of course, that this story may be just an urban legend. But who cares? It's fun to read. So I add a few *more* "quotes" and turn the tale into a full two-page spread. With a great photo of an elephant from the Miami zoo. Shot up close. Where he looks so huge, you could believe he really *might* dump two hundred pounds of dung. *If* constipated.

I've still got a five holes to fill. So now I turn to my other favorite source of filler stories—our rival tabloid, *Weekly World News*. Their stories are clearly fictitious. But since they also present them as "news", they've never had the guts to sue us for borrowing their best ones. Because in order to sue us, they'd have to admit their stories are fiction.

The best available is ***Al Qaeda Plans To Drop Gay Bombs.*** With the sub-head ***Men Within 30 Miles of the Blast Will Instantly Turn Queer!*** Accompanied by a photo of two gay men hysterically embracing. We explain that Al Qaeda plans to release "potent waves of the female hormone estrogen into the air" in all major US cities. Within hours, formerly heterosexual men will be "making out with their buddies." Divorcing their wives. And "redecorating their living rooms." However, we can't depress our readers too much. So we end by quoting Homeland Security Czar Tom Ridge. Who is already "developing an *antidote*" to the Al-Qaeda bomb.

For the four remaining holes, I use four other short classics from *World Weekly News*. ***Bermuda Shorts Triangle!*** About a fifty-one-year-old North Carolina tourist. Who claims that over the years eight sets of car keys, twelve wallets, thirty condoms, and approximately fifty-five dollars in loose change have vanished without a trace. In that eerie no-man's land between his navel and his knees that he calls "The Bermuda Shorts Triangle." ***Monkeys Type Shakespeare Play***. About a researcher who proved if you leave enough monkeys alone long enough, they really will indeed type *Hamlet*. And two true-science pieces. ***Scientist Reveals: Thunder Caused By Fat People Doing Jumping Jacks***. And ***How To Tell If You're About To Burst Into Flames***. Both articles quote an "expert." The former advises that "eating Mexican food causes lightning." The latter advises "keep a fire extinguisher handy."

Like I said. It's a tough job. But at last I'm done. Time to go frolic in the park.

* * *

The greatest feeling in the world is to be young and in love. But a close second is to be *middle-aged* and in love. Nothing else in life comes close.

The euphoria of kissing Janet Fickel for hours yesterday is still fresh. I know I'm not supposed to be falling in love. With someone else's wife. Like a tabloid scandal story. But I am.

Some French filmmaker said, *"Lies are just dreams that got caught red-handed."* Well, I personally am *not* going to get caught red-handed. In this dream I plan to live this afternoon. Whatever happens out at Island Park will *not* be found in police reports. So I make *damn* sure Janet Reno's not following me. Drive out of town and back. Twice. Drive into two cul-de-sacs. And double back. Twice.

Then, after picking up sandwiches and champagne, I park several blocks west of Island Park. And *hike* in. Through the woods.

I find a secluded spot. Way in the back. A thirty-foot square patch of green. Surrounded by woods. With a few decorative rocks. And a view, through the yellow-leafed trees and the weeping willows, of the Huron River. Its dark-green waters sparkling in the warm October sun.

I spread a Campus Inn blanket out on the ground. Put out the sandwiches and champagne. Then spend the next fifteen minutes beating myself up.

I told you I have no guilt. And know no shame. But who am I kidding? I wish I really *were* a heartless, conscienceless guy. Who could come cavort with Janet Fickel in the same park where I used to cavort with my high school girlfriend, Renee, thirty years ago. And never think twice about how I'm betraying Elaine. But I'm *not* that guy, really. No matter how hard I try.

Two canoes pass by. College kids. Drinking beer. And trying to swamp each other. Another canoe passes by. Young couple. Romantic afternoon. He paddles. She lounges in his lap. Next up is a *family* canoe. Mom and Dad paddling hard. Two kids climbing around the canoe, like it's a mobile jungle gym on water. The kids' laughter carries across the water.

Like the laughter of my own kids. Stabbing at my heart.

What the hell am I doing? Putting at risk my kids' stability and self-confidence. Which Elaine and I have spent seventeen years building. Putting *Elaine* at risk, too. Elaine's tough on the outside. But if I were to leave her, she'd be devastated. Hell, I'm at risk, too. Because let's face it. Divorce is messy. And I'd be wracked with all that guilt I told you I don't feel.

Okay, four dates with Janet Fickel doesn't mean divorce is imminent. Or even inevitable. But the mere possibility of divorce fills me with dread. And yet—feeling guilty kind of *reassures me*, too. I must not be such a bad person after all. Or how could I be feeling guilt?

Embracing the guilt this way liberates me. I ignore my deep dread of divorce. And just work myself into a fugue state of excitement. Conjuring Janet's face. Her walk. Her smile. Her laugh. Fantasizing about kissing her. And whatever else might happen. Here in the park.

Strangely, my excitement about Janet Fickel is all mixed up with Rachel Clark. Thinking about Rachel Clark's lifetime of changing identities is giving me strange ideas. About myself. Whenever trouble got close, Rachel Clark changed her identity. *Reinvented herself.* It's worked for Rachel Clark. Kept *her* out of trouble. Why shouldn't *I* be able to do the same?

I told you, a new identity only takes four weeks. So. Out with David Fisher. In with . . . any dead infant's name I can find in the 1956 Ann Arbor obits. *David Fisher could disappear.* Mysteriously. Or leave a suicide note. Saying I drowned myself in the ocean. So they wouldn't bother looking for me. People would grieve for me for a few weeks. But they'd get over it. Give 'em thirty days tops. After that, I'd probably be dismayed to discover how unimportant I really am in the lives of my family, my friends and my co-workers. And then I'd be *free*. To resurface. With my new name. Work as a reporter. In Ann Arbor. I wouldn't even need plastic surgery. No one would be looking for me. And only once in a blue moon does anyone from the tabloids even come to Ann Arbor. Like Graham said, Ann Arbor ain't exactly a tabloid hot spot.

Then I remember: my *mom* still lives in Ann Arbor. Okay. So a few *details* still need to be worked out. In this fantasy. The devil is always in the details. My mom isn't the only problem. I have friends from high school and college who live in Ann Arbor, too. Saul Schwartz. Marcus DaVanzo. Tim Peterson. Denise Maxwell. And all the other locals at our reunion. So maybe I'll need plastic surgery, after all. Maybe disappearing has more problems than I realize. But it's still an appealing idea. To start over. A fresh shot at life. To do things right this time. To live life for myself this time, not for my parents. I'll just have to find a way to make it work.

Here comes Janet Fickel. Pulling into the Island Park parking lot. The Chevy's door opens. First out are her feet. In *high heels*. On a Sunday. At the park. You gotta love that.

Janet is also wearing a short, tight, blue-jean skirt. And a top straight out of my wildest dreams. Very tight. Very low cut. *Fiendishly* designed to look like a corset. Lots of visible structure. Vertical ridges cinching in the waist. And plenty of boning to accent the bust. Not that Janet's bust *needs* any accenting. But this low-cut corset top gives her more than just great cleavage. It gives her great *spillage*, too. As in the top third of her boobs spill out. We've come a long way by our fifth date here. No more covering up that fabulous chest under loose business jackets.

Janet's slow prance across the parking lot in those high heels is, by itself, worth the heavy price in guilt I paid to be here at the park. All my dread is going up in smoke.

Janet's carrying her purse. And a photo album.

"You said you wanted to know more about my past. So I brought you some pictures."

"Fabulous! Unfortunately, all I brought was lunch. And champagne."

Janet wags her finger. "I told you, if I drink champagne, who knows what will happen?"

"That's why I brought it." I grin. "For the sake of—science. Humanity needs to know: what *exactly* happens when Janet Fickel drinks champagne?"

Janet laughs. Sits down on the blanket beside me. Shakes her head. But smiles. So I uncork the champagne. We toast each other. And go through her album. I question each photo. When was it taken? Where? Who's in it? What are *their* stories? I meet Janet's parents. Her sisters. Her brother. All three husbands. Both her kids, too. And all her friends from Fort Wayne.

Janet's mother is clearly the most important person in her life. Judging from the stories I pull out of Janet to go with the pix. One day years ago, after the kids were all grown and gone, Janet's mother decided she was sick of living on the farm. So she told Janet's dad that she was moving to town. Which she did. Some months later, Dad limply followed, tail between his legs.

Janet tells this story with special zest. She clearly loves the way her mom told her dad how things were gonna be. Janet loves her daughters, too. And her sisters. Even though one sister has a bad drug problem she can't kick. And the other sister has an abusive husband she can't seem to leave. But the *men* in Janet's life don't get such rave reviews. The parade of father, brother, boyfriends, and husbands all barely get a grunt of semi-hostile acknowledgment.

Since I'm a cross-examiner at heart, I probe. And soon discover the husbands don't *deserve* any better than Janet's semi-hostile grunt. The first guy was an aimless idiot who knocked Janet up at seventeen. Married her under family pressure, with no clue how to support his new family. The second guy was worse. A mean drunk. Who disagreed with Janet's view that they couldn't afford another child besides Carrie. *Violently* disagreed. So one night he hid Janet's diaphragm. Then raped her. Spawning little Stacy. And inspiring Janet to divorce him. Compared to these two gems, John the gun nut is a regular Prince Charming. But John's also a guy who rules by fiat and by force. Who thinks everything in the marriage should be his way or the highway.

My cross-examination fails to elicit any anecdotes to explain Janet's feelings about her father and brother. But there's definitely hostility smoldering there, too. Which is why she relishes the way her mom put her dad in his place. By unilaterally moving back to town. The one anecdote from Janet's life where the woman, rather than the man, ruled by fiat. If not by force.

The album is spread out on Janet's lap. She sits on my lap. So I have to lean over her shoulder to see the pix. Which has me looking down into Janet's considerable cleavage. And her splendid spillage. A great view. Her breasts are so big. Solid. And *packed*. Granted, the corset top is giving them an extra boost. As is the well-structured black bra I glimpse from my bird's-eye perch. Still, Janet's breasts ride amazingly high. For a woman of any age. Much less forty.

Her high school pictures are amazing, too. Janet was very pretty. But she weighed only *88 pounds* when she first got pregnant. Which explains why she has such a great figure now. Most women put on thirty pounds with pregnancy. Then spend their whole lives fighting those thirty pounds. Janet's no different. She put on thirty pounds then, too. Only in her case, instead of taking her from just right to overweight, those thirty pounds took her from anorexic to just right.

Eventually we come to Janet's third wedding. Age twenty-nine. The face is still gorgeous. But now she weighs 115 instead of 88. Looks much healthier. One wedding shot has the bride-to-be posed sideways. One leg up on a short stool. Wedding gown hitched up over her thigh. Like Marlene Dietrich. Fiddling with her garters. And vamping it up. But something's missing. The legs look great. The face and hair look great. But missing in action is that bounteous chest.

I peer at the picture. Trying to figure out if it's a trick of lighting. Or if the wedding gown is just designed in a way that presses Janet's boobs in real far.

"This was before I had my surgery," Janet says. Very matter-of-fact.

I nod. As if I'd known all along her breasts were fake. As if it's no big deal. Which it isn't, really. Except it's disconcerting as hell to think that I, a self-proclaimed expert, could be so easily fooled. I've spent a fair amount of time the past forty-eight hours ogling Janet's boobs. Feeling them pressed against my chest, too. And it never once occurred to me they might not be real.

"When did you have the surgery?"

Janet cranes her neck back and to the left. To meet my eyes. "Five years ago."

"When you were *thirty-five*?"

"I got tired of John spending more time with his *Penthouses* than me. Growing up I never had any boobs. Two mosquito bites. So one day I decided to do it. John did not object."

"I'll bet."

"The decision was all mine. I did it for me. But I let John pick out the size."

I cock my head. And engage in a fully professional inspection of her chest. "Nice choice."

Janet laughs.

"I had no idea. Even when you pressed against me."

"Really? I always assume everyone knows." Janet sips her champagne. "First time I was home after the surgery, my father and brother kept staring at me. They were too chicken to *ask*. So they kept finding excuses to *hug* me. So they could press up against my chest."

I find this image a tad disturbing: Indiana farmers groping their surgically-enhanced daughter/sister. I rush to change the subject. To the *healthier* aspects of boob jobs.

"Did it change how you felt about yourself?"

"Absolutely. Before the surgery, I felt so invisible. After, I was like a new person. I got all the attention I always wanted. And some I *didn't* want, too."

"Which is why you wear those loose-fitting business jackets at work?"

"No—that's just because John wants his wife to be the shy little mouse. Except around him, of course. Pisses me off. Like I said, *he* picked the size."

"John sends you mixed messages?"

"Exactly! Like last month. When I went to the dealership to trade in my old car for this one." She points at her Chevy. "John kept me waiting out in the show-room. All he had to do was give me the damn keys. But he was busy. So finally I walked back to the service department. I didn't have a 'loose-fitting business jacket' on. John got royally pissed. Called me names. Told me *never* to walk past 'his men' again. I grabbed the keys and walked out. Right past all of 'em."

I nod sympathetically. Though I can well imagine *Her Strut* driving those car mechanics crazy. Since it drives *me* crazy, too. I put my arm around her. "Well, I have only one message for you, Janet. I love you just the way you are. You don't have to hide anything from me."

We fall into each other's arms. And kiss. A long time.

When the kissing stops, we get out the food. I eat like a horse. Janet eats like a bird. I comment on this. She says she has "irritable bowel syndrome." Meaning if she eats more than a little, she needs to use a restroom right away. So in public places, she tends to eat very lightly. To avoid emergencies. Especially public parks. Where restrooms are far away and often locked.

I ask if she wants to go somewhere else. *Indoors.* Our eyes meet. But Janet says no. She's happy out here in the park. And she'll get her calories from the champagne.

After lunch we look at some more photos. When we come to one of Janet's daughter, Stacy, I launch into my favorite *Fountains of Wayne* song again. *"Stacy's mom has got it goin' on/She's all I want and I've waited so long/I know it might be wrong/But I'm in love with Stacy's mom."* Then I cup Janet's chin in my hand. Gaze into her eyes. "And I *do* love Stacy's mom."

Janet answers again with her lips. We start making out. Janet on her back. Me on top.

I decide the talk about surgery was an invitation. So I begin handling those fake breasts. First, from outside her clothes. Then I reach down under her corset top and under her bra.

Janet turns out to be an enabler. With the skill of Houdini. Somehow she reaches under the corset top and, without taking the top off, removes her bra. Tosses the bra in her purse.

So we can *really* go at it. Like two teenagers. Which we do. We ignore the passing canoes and race through all the steps that can be executed with clothing still on. The steps that used to take me a month per step. Here, at age forty-eight, they're taking about *ten minutes* per step. Except the boobs take a little longer. Because I've never had my hands on a pair of fake ones before. I always heard they were *harder* than real ones. Not Janet's. They feel great. I'd never know they weren't real.

While exploring each other's bodies, we sometimes rest. And talk. I compliment Janet's candor. Talking so frankly about her breasts and her bowels. I tell her I wish I could reciprocate. But the only intimate surgery I've had is my vasectomy. Which I *rush* to disclose to her.

Then I fall back on the large inventory of old stories that bore my friends and family to tears. The ones Janet always listens to so intently. As if she's absolutely *enchanted*.

My best stories are from my *Enquirer* days. Unfortunately, I can't tell Janet these. Since I haven't yet come clean about where I work or where I live. So I stick with DOJ stories.

Like one time I go to see my boss. Barry. To report on a break in a big case. But Barry's on the phone. He motions for me to sit down. While he continues screaming into the phone. Gradually I gather he's talking long-distance to some private school headmaster. About Barry's juvenile delinquent daughter, Kymberly. Who gets kicked out of various schools about as often as Holden Caulfield did. So Barry's trying to intimidate the latest headmaster who's threatening to give Kymberly the boot. But it's not working. Evidently. Because Barry's losing control. Finally he screams into the phone at the headmaster on the other end of the line: "And furthermore, Mr. Goodmaster—*if that really is your name*—don't you dare take any action against Kymberly without first affording her full due process of law . . . " And blah-blah-blah. Who knows what else Barry said that day? Because I was on the floor. Laughing so hard I couldn't get up. Over "Mr. Goodmaster, *if that really is your name*." A minor classic.

Janet laughs as hard as I did that day in 1989. So then I tell her about the flash flood. Barry was driving a young woman prosecutor—Laura—and me in San Juan. It's raining so hard we can't see. The windshield wipers can't keep up with the buckets of rain. Doesn't rain much in Puerto Rico. But when it does, man, it *really* rains. The storm sewers there aren't equipped for *volume*. So water just sits on the roads. We come to an underpass. Down below there's a gulch, where we're headed. The water there is *seriously* deep. So Laura questions the wisdom of driving down into the gulch. But Barry says: "Don't worry, I led troops into combat in Vietnam."

About this time, the water lifts our car up *off the road*. I kid you not. We *drift* into the water in the gulch. We can't go anywhere. Because our wheels are not in contact with the road anymore. And then we notice the water level around us is *rising*. Above our windows. We're basically *sinking* into this huge lake of water on the road. So we roll down our windows and *swim* up to air. Then Barry remembers we have official government files in the car. So he and I dive back down to retrieve these water-logged files. From our submerged car. Needless to say, Laura is apoplectic. She calls in to Barry's boss back in Washington. Gives a colorful account of Barry driving us into a flash flood. While Barry claimed we had nothing to worry about. Because he'd "led troops into combat in Vietnam." Barry's boss, a wry fellow, doesn't miss a beat. He tells Laura it's *her* fault, not Barry's. Why? Because Laura failed to ask Barry if any of those troops Barry led into combat actually *came back*.

Janet likes my stories. A lot. So I just keep telling them. And we both keep drinking champagne. Which has a predictable side effect: I begin reciting poetry.

See, one of the five times I dropped out of law school, I went to grad school in English Lit. I was a lousy grad student. But I had a knack for memorizing poems. For the orals, I memorized over two hundred poems. To distract the professors grilling me. By giving verbatim recitations of their favorite poems. So they wouldn't notice how little actual *insight* I had into literature.

I never got my PhD. But I know a lot of poems. Which comes in handy at Island Park. Because Janet Fickel has never met a man who reads poetry. Much less a man who would bother to recite a love poem to her. In the park. Over champagne.

I go with Theodore Roethke. A Michigan man. Sylvia Plath's mentor. Very underrated. Wrote this great poem called "I Knew A Woman." About a middle-aged guy making a last stab at romance. And marveling at the lessons he can still learn from love. Seems right on target for us.

I recite the poem with passion. And lots of leering at Janet. During the sexual double-entendres. Like the part about "the rake *coming behind her* for her pretty sake." I also indulge in lots of physical contact with Janet. At appropriate junctures in the poem. Like the part about her "proferred hand." Her "flowing knees." Her "quivering hip." And her "mobile nose."

You may think you don't like poetry. But trust me. If you're ever hoping to get laid, this is a really great poem to know:

> I knew a woman, lovely in her bones,
> When small birds sighed, she would sigh back at them;
> Ah, when she moved, she moved more ways than one:
> The shapes a bright container can contain!
> Of her choice virtues only Gods should speak,

Or English poets who grew up on Greek
(I'd have them sing in chorus, cheek to cheek).

How well her wishes went! She stroked my chin,
She taught me Turn, and Counter-Turn, and Stand;
She taught me Touch, that undulant white skin;
I nibbled meekly at her proffered hand;
She was the sickle; I, poor I, the rake,.
Coming behind her for her pretty sake
(But what prodigious mowing we did make).

Love likes a gander, and adores a goose:
Her full lips pursed, the errant note to seize;
She played it quick, she played it light and loose;
My eyes, they dazzled at her flowing knees;
Her several parts could keep a pure repose,
Or one hip quiver with a mobile nose
(She moved in circles, and those circles moved).

Let seed be grass, and grass turn into hay:
I'm martyr to a motion not my own;
What's freedom for? To know eternity.
I swear she cast a shadow white as stone.
But who would count eternity in days?
These old bones live to learn her wanton ways:
(I measure time by how a body sways).

Janet likes the poem. A lot. Laughs at the sickle and the rake. The prodigious mowing they did make. The old bones. And her wanton ways. Even asks me to recite it again. Which I do.

Then I start jabbering energetically. About the meaning of "a shadow white as stone." How normally shadows are dark. And empty. But Love frees you to step outside yourself. To "know eternity." In the sense of understanding how you and I, each of us, at the moment we make love, become part of the long continuum of Time. Many things change over the centuries, I say. But not Love. When we make love, we feel *exactly* what Achilles felt. Exactly what Helen of Troy felt. Exactly what Cassanova and Don Juan, and Mata Hari and Marilyn Monroe, all felt. Even—if you believe the *Da Vinci Code*—what Christ himself felt. If he was really married to Mary Magdalene. The one universal aspect of being human: making love. Sex. The life force.

And that's why, in the poem, she casts "a shadow white as stone." Because in making love, she goes *outside* herself. Gets as close as we can ever get to eternity. So instead of casting a dark empty shadow, she casts a *white* shadow. Because the lover's shadow is full of light. Reminding us not to count eternity in days. But rather to measure time by how a body sways. Reminding us not to waste our short time on earth worrying how short our time on earth is. But rather just to go for it. Make love when we can. And then measure time by how a body sways.

Obviously I've been drinking. And you can see why I never got a PhD in English Lit. But in Island Park on 17 October 2004, I make perfect sense. To the only audience that matters.

Janet pushes me on my back. Climbs on top. And kisses me with even more passion than before. After awhile, I roll her over. Still kissing her. Janet's legs part. She wraps her knees around my waist. We're back in the missionary position. Oblivious to the passing canoeists.

We carry on like this, kissing and reciting poetry, until the autumn light grows pale. I ask Janet to lunch tomorrow. But she has a doctor's appointment. So I propose dinner Tuesday night after work. Coyly Janet says she'll "think about it." But her smile looks a lot like yes.

Then we stagger to our separate cars. And return to our separate lives.

* * *

"So how are you, Rachel?"

"Fine."

"What's new in your frantic life?"

"Nothin'."

"Miss me?"

"Yeah."

"Doesn't really *sound* like you miss me," I say.

"I *do*, Dad," my older daughter, Rachel, says. "It's just—I'm real busy right now."

"With what?"

"The MTV VMA Awards show is on."

"Oh. I *knew* there had to be a reason I've been short of breath all day."

"Very funny, Dad."

"Is your Mom there?"

Elaine gets on the phone. "I'm so glad you called, David."

"Really? Whassup?"

"Rachel's college application essays. What a hassle! I need your help."

"What can I do?"

"When are you coming home?"

"I'm not sure. Remember I told you Friday—I'll probably be another week up here."

"A whole 'nother *week*? Why?"

"I'm close to breaking a really great story. Best tabloid exclusive since Gary Hart."

"What's the story?"

"The Fugitive Radical. From the sixties. Still wanted. For an attack on U of M Law School. Left a cop dead. I've got proof she's still here. In Ann Arbor. Hiding under a fake name."

"So what's taking so long?"

A fair question. But I don't think Elaine wants to hear about Janet Fickel. "It's tricky. The proof she's here is fingerprints. But I'm still tracking down whose fingerprints they are."

"So you don't know *where* she is? Or even *who* she is?"

"Not yet. But I will soon. I've narrowed it down to three women. One is the fugitive."

"How do you know she's one of three women?"

"It's complicated."

"So? I'm pretty bright." Elaine sounds a little miffed. "Explain it to me."

"Okay. But Elaine, seriously, this has gotta stay super-confidential."

"Don't worry. My mother's not even talking to me these days."

"Because of the embezzlement imbroglio at the temple?"

"Huh? Oh, no. That was ages ago. It's—other things. You don't wanna know."

True enough.

"But I promise—super-confidential. So how do you know it's one of three women?"

"There were only seven people in the room when the fingerprints got left. I was outside on a roof. Saw it all. This past week, I've eliminated four of the seven. Three to go."

"How'd you 'eliminate' them?"

"Got their fingerprints. Secretly. Took 'em to an old basketball buddy. A cop. He checked the prints against the fugitive's prints. No match so far. So there's only three to go."

"And all you've gotta do is collect fingerprint samples from three people? Why's that gonna take a week?"

"May not take a *full* week. But I've gotta be careful to collect the prints without the women *knowing* I've collected 'em. Don't wanna spook the fugitive radical into running again."

"What about the cops, David? They must want to find the fugitive radical, too."

"Real bad," I concede.

"So if you're taking fingerprints to them—they must know you're close—they're—"

"On me like a cheap suit."

"—not gonna let you interview the woman *before* they arrest her."

"Not if I refuse to identify her until they let me interview her."

"What makes you think, if you walk into the police station and hand them the fugitive's fingerprints, they won't *hold you* as a material witness 'til you say whose fingerprints they are?"

Damn good question. Elaine has always been one of the brighter bulbs in the chandelier.

"Well, hopefully it won't come to that. I'm trying to track her down in other ways."

"Like what? David—don't tell me you're breaking into all their homes?"

"Me? Oh no, honey. Those days are way behind me." (Though it's not a bad idea.)

"David, we need you back here. This story doesn't sound all *that* important."

"Oh, but it is! She's the last of the sixties radicals still on the run. Finding her would be like finding one of those ancient cavemen, frozen alive in Siberian ice. Everyone's fascinated by these kinds of stories. You get this perfectly preserved artifact from the past. And when she's thawed out, here she is, plopped down in our time. As out of place as a caveman would be."

"David, have you been drinking?"

"Only a little," I lie. "But don't you see, Elaine? It's a *great* story. Plus it's a chance for our little start-up to make a name for itself. *The National Spy* catches a real-live crook!"

Elaine sighs. A *deep* sigh. A sigh of resignation. And exasperation. A sigh that starts somewhere back of her knees. A sigh I've heard a thousand times before.

"So you're just going to leave me to fight through these application essays by myself?"

"Not at all. *E-mail* 'em to me. I'll find time to edit 'em. And I'll e-mail 'em back to you."

Long pause. Then *another* huge sigh. "Okay. Hey, David. Is it because it's *your old law school* the fugitive radical tried to bomb? Is *that* what makes this so interesting to you?"

"Yeah, that's part of it. Think if she'd *succeeded*. You and I might never have met."

"Well, *that's* a nice thought."

"I don't mean—it's just—my whole life might have been different. You know?"

"Is that what you want? A different life?"

"Doesn't everyone?"

"Not me." Elaine starts to sigh again, but then catches her breath. "David, I just want you to come home."

"I will. As soon as my work's done up here."

"Goodnight, David. I love you."

"I love you, too, Elaine. Goodnight."

You know what's the worst thing about saying "I love you" to two women in the same day? I really think I meant it. *Both* times. How schizo is that?

* * *

For the first time since Friday my phone taps at Raven's home yield some good stuff:

| | |
|---|---|
| RAVEN: | Hello. |
| SHEILA: | Hi, it's Sheila. Have you talked to Sarah yet? |
| RAVEN: | Can't find her. |
| SHEILA: | Did you try Déjà Vu? |
| RAVEN: | Yeah. They claim they don't have an address for her. |
| SHEILA: | That's ridiculous. They need an address for payroll. |
| RAVEN: | Not if they pay her under the table. Which from the looks of the place . . . |
| SHEILA: | Did you look around for her? |
| RAVEN: | Ah, Sheila, have you ever been to a strip club? |
| SHEILA: | No. |
| RAVEN: | It's one of the lowest forms of hell on earth. And a woman, um, *patron*, is unheard of. I would stick out like a sore thumb. Plus I'd get so mad at all the exploitation there, in two minutes I'd be ejected for fighting. |
| SHEILA: | So how're you gonna find Sarah? |

RAVEN: I doubt I will. It's too late anyway. If Sarah told you Friday morning she's going to see Hunter, well, by now she's already gone and done it. Nothing we do now's gonna matter.

SHEILA: Shit! We can't just sit back and let this happen to Rachel!

RAVEN: It's really not our problem. Rachel made her own bed. She's gotta lie in it. Hey—I gotta go. I got a call on the other line. Talk to you later.

RAVEN: Hello?

LANE: Hi, gorgeous.

RAVEN: Don't sweet-talk me, you smooth-talking stud. Where've you been?

LANE: Sorry. Camille was feeling very needy this weekend.

RAVEN: Oh, great. Like *I* don't have needs, too?

LANE: That's not what I meant. It's just ... Camille didn't give me *any* space this weekend. This is the first chance I had to call. Honestly.

RAVEN: And now I suppose you want to come right over and fuck me?

LANE: Well, I wouldn't have put it quite that way, but . . . yes!

RAVEN: Then get your skinny old butt over here. Before I change my mind.

LANE: Be right there, gorgeous.

I laugh out loud. At the incongruity of Raven LaGrow, notorious feminazi hardass, scheduling heterosexual sex. In such a feisty way.

Then I wonder: does *Lane Davis* ever torture himself about having an affair? The way I was torturing myself this afternoon at Island Park? Before Janet came. And calmed me down.

Sure didn't *sound* like Davis has any qualms about cheating on Camille. He was pretty straightforward. And pretty ruthless. Making the necessary arrangements. With a minimum of fuss. But who knows? Beneath the surface, Davis may be as guilt-wracked as me.

I always figured guys who have affairs are *not* the type to be plagued by self-doubt. Faithful guys always assume adulterers are having all the fun. While we foolishly follow the rules. But now that I stand on the verge of being initiated into the secret society of adulterers, I wonder. Maybe adulterers are just caught in a more complex vortex of despair than those of us who behave our butts. Maybe adulterers are *not only* dissatisfied with the limitations imposed by their marriages, but also dissatisfied with the "cure" they found for their dissatisfaction.

Look at the way Raven was ragging on Davis. For not calling sooner. As if *they* were married. If you think about it, adultery is a very odd "cure" for feeling stultified in marriage. Replacing love grown routinized with—more love. Which will, itself, soon enough grow—routinized.

But I'm way ahead of myself, aren't I? Janet Fickel hasn't yet said, "I suppose you want to come right over and fuck me?" If only she would! I'd love to try to get bored with *that*.

In the meantime, though, while I wait and hope for Janet to get as frisky as Raven, I've got the *other* call I just overheard to think about. My first thought is, that byplay between Sheila and Raven means Sheila is definitely *not* Rachel Clark. Because Sheila alludes to "Rachel" like Rachel's *another person*. But then again, maybe Sheila's just being sly with Raven. Maybe Raven is trying to help the fugitive radical elude Hunter for political reasons, without knowing that her friend Sheila is really the fugitive radical herself.

An unlikely scenario? Perhaps. But stranger things have happened. In any case, I can't cross Sheila off the list for sure until I get clearer proof than this one ambiguous phone call.

\* \* \*

Inspired by Elaine's break-in idea, I walk over to Davis & Nyman. Thinking I'll break in again. Grab a few things off the desks of Sheila Nyman and Naomi Williams. For fingerprints.

But lights are on. Sheila—*if that really is her name*—is working late.

So I decide to pursue another lead tonight.

\* \* \*

As you might guess, I have no *moral* objection to strip clubs. Unlike Raven LaGrow, the idea that impoverished women are being "exploited" for the sake of male sexual fantasies doesn't trouble me one whit. Sorry. The fact that these women may have few serious career alternatives doesn't bother me either. Nor does the prevalence of drugs and violence around strip clubs. Hey, life is tough all over. And frankly, prostitutes have it a lot tougher than strippers.

My objection to strip clubs is they're just a stupid *tease*. Unlike prostitutes, strippers work you up—but don't get you off. How annoying is that? It's like being back with Renee, my high school girlfriend. Getting all steamed up. But with no hope of sexual *release*. Who needs *that* again? Why men sit for hours in strip clubs, shelling out hundreds of bucks for this aggravation, is a complete mystery. Why not just go bang your dick against a wall? At least *that's* free.

But here I sit. In Déjà Vu. Fully clothed. While "Chandra" straddles my chair. Backwards. Wearing only a G-string. And touching her toes. Which causes Chandra's very well-toned butt cheeks to twitch. As I stare at them from a distance of approximately three-quarters of an inch.

I'm planning to interview Chandra. *If that really is her name.* But I figure the conversation will be more productive if I can talk to Chandra's *face*. So I wait. Patiently. While Chandra slides her ass down into my lap. And rubs her twitching butt cheeks furiously against my zipper. Dry-humping me backwards.

But I got enough of that this afternoon. With Janet. So I'm not getting aroused here.

Chandra turns to face me. She's got implants, too. But unlike Janet, Chandra used no *restraint* picking the size. Chandra got the biggest ones on the menu. The volleyballs. Chandra starts swinging them back and forth. And lowering them toward my head. Jesus. I'm choking on cheap perfume. And now she's hitting me in the face with the volleyballs. Rhythmically. Whap! Whap! Her skin, pulled super-taut by the sheer mass of the volleyballs, feels like leather.

When I was at the DOJ, I prosecuted some cops in Louisiana for beating a guy in jail. To avoid leaving telltale bruises, the cops beat the guy with a weighted leather strap. That beating comes to mind. As Chandra smacks me repeatedly in the head with her twin leathery weights.

But I know I'm supposed to enjoy this. So I give Chandra my nicest smile. In between whaps. Though the assault—excuse me, the *dance*—continues long enough that it recalls another criminal case. Morganna, the notorious "Kissing Bandit," was once charged with assaulting a guy in a Texas strip club with her 36-HHH breasts. Her lawyer, the legendary Racehorse Haynes, stood up in court to enter her plea. "How does your client plead?" the judge asked Haynes. Haynes replied, "*Not guilty, not guilty.*" To make it clear he was representing *both* of the accused.

So as both of Chandra's twins assault me, I find myself mumbling "not guilty, not guilty" into her humungous cleavage. A plea Chandra takes under advisement. Without making any ruling on my actual guilt or innocence.

Eventually the "dance" ends. I slip a twenty in Chandra's G-string. While making sure she can see I have five more Jacksons at the ready.

"You want another dance?" Chandra's husky voice is cigarette-scarred. Like Janet's.

"No, thank you. I just wanna talk." I slip another twenty into Chandra's G-string.

"Sure, fine." Chandra plops down on the cushion beside me. "Can you buy me a Coke?"

I buy Chandra a Coke.

"Whaddya wanna talk about?"

I shrug. "How they treat you here?"

"Not bad," Chandra says. "Not bad at all."

"What's good about how they treat you?"

"This ain't like some clubs. Here the percentage we get to keep is fair. And the muscle—the bouncers—they leave you alone. Manager makes sure of that. So it's good. It's OK."

"How long you danced here?"

"Two years. Maybe three. I forget."

"You got kids?"

"Two."

"How old?"

Chandra smiles. "Six and four."

I nod. "Kids are the greatest. Who cares for your kids when you're here?"

"My sister. She dances here too. We trade off nights."

"Nice sister," I say.

"She's the best."

"What's her name? I'll ask for her tomorrow night."

"Her name here is Mystique."

"Know any dancers here named Sarah?"

"Yeah." Chandra sounds suspicious. "Why?"

"Friend o' mine told me come here, I should ask for Sarah."

"There's *two* Sarahs here." Chandra sounds unhappy referring me to other girls.

I pull out another twenty. Slip it in her G-string. Can't *over*pay. Or she'll get scared.

"The Sarah I heard about," I say, "has a small problem with one of her feet."

Chandra contemplates the extra twenty. "What kind of a problem?"

"A cleft foot. You know. Like a birth defect."

Chandra shakes her head. "Don't know any Sarah like that."

"Are either of the Sarahs here tonight?"

Chandra shakes her head.

"You know when they're gonna be here next?"

"One works tomorrow night. The other only works weekends."

To avoid creating suspicion, I pay for another session of Chandra's volley-balls slapping me in the face.

Like I said. It's a tough job. But someone's gotta do it.

# CHAPTER SEVEN
# NAMING NAMES

## Monday 18 October 2004

First thing Monday morning, I call Alan Singer's Wall Street office. Receptionist tells me Singer's there. But in meetings. She wants my call back number. Instead, I get her to give me his e-mail address. Then I e-mail Singer a message captioned "Alan Singer, Berkeley Arsonist":

Alan—

I'm a free-lance journalist. Doing a "where are they now?" *exposé* on former radicals from the '60s and '70s.

You have a choice. You can be an unnamed confidential source. Or you can be a named subject in the story. In other words, you can agree to talk to me this afternoon (as I pass through New York), or you can read your name in our story next week.

Your choice.

I only need an hour of your time. If there's a particular time you prefer between 12 and 3, e-mail me a response. If I don't hear from you, I'll call your office about 11 this morning when I get in to LaGuardia.

David Fisher

A variation on the old game we used to play at the DOJ. With the cops in San Juan, the choice was "be a witness, or be a defendant." For Alan Singer, it's "be a source, or be a subject."

Without waiting for Singer's response, I go to the airport. Cuz I'm *sure* he's gonna cave. They always do. En route I use my cell to buy a round-trip ticket to New York. Then I leave Greg Hunter a voice mail. Saying I'm leaving town. Just for the day. Forgot to give him four hours notice. Sorry. But I suggest Hunter arrange for Janet Reno to wait at the Northwest baggage claim this afternoon. So she can pick up my tail the instant I get back from New York.

At the airport gate, I open my laptop. Find a terse return e-mail from Alan Singer. Agreeing to talk to me. At a Wall Street bar. Patrick O'Flannery's. At 2:00 p.m.

I confirm by return e-mail that I'll be there.

In New York, I kill an hour leafing through old movie stills in a Bleeker Street shop. Buying a couple of Audrey Hepburn photos for my daughters. And a Brad Pitt poster for Elaine. Next I kill another hour editing Rachel's college application essays and e-mailing them back to Elaine.

Then I stroll through Washington Square. Watching the old guys playing checkers in the park. On what has to be about the last day of the year warm enough for checkers in the park.

On a kiosk I see an ad for "Musicians for John Kerry." Which includes Bruce Springsteen. And—whoa! Tomorrow night the Boss and his mates will be in Detroit.

I wonder if Janet Fickel likes the Boss? I know *I* do. Odds are *she* does, too. Bruce is very popular in blue-collar/pink-collar circles. And I know a guy in Springsteen's entourage who can always get me tickets. So I call Davis & Nyman. Ask for Janet. But she's out. At her doctor's appointment. Won't be back 'til 2:00. So this inspired idea will have to wait.

Patrick O'Flannery's is an imitation Irish pub. Not especially authentic. But dark. Lots of private booths. And very few customers at 2:00 p.m. Which I assume is why Singer chose it.

I sit at a booth with a view of the door. Order a Guinness. Place my notepad and pocket-size tape recorder out on the table. So Singer can see I really am a "journalist."

Singer arrives on time. He's fifty-two. But looks more like seventy. Overweight. Silver-gray hair, mostly gone. Blotchy complexion. *Cavernous* forehead wrinkles. Loose skin around his neck. Deep bags under his eyes. Teeth that are yellowed and cracked and wide-spaced, like the keys of an old piano. And a weary, haunted look in his bleary eyes. Singer looks like hell. Can he really be this worried about my story? Or is he just another Wall Street burn-out?

We order lunch. Singer orders a double Scotch straight up. I stick with my Guinness.

"I tried to look you up on the internet," Singer says. Icily. "Found nothing. David Fisher has zero publications."

"I write under a pen name."

"What's your pen name?"

I shake my head no. "I use the pen name so guys like you can't look me up."

"Then how do I know you're legit?"

Good question. But I've heard it before. So I have a pat answer I use. "You don't. But there's only two kinds of people who would even bother finding out that Alan Singer, successful stockbroker, is really Alan Singer, fugitive arsonist. Cops. And reporters. Cops aren't allowed to lie about who they are. So I must be a reporter."

"Whaddya mean, 'cops aren't allowed to lie about who they are?' Some of the guys in the FBI's Squad 47 pretended to be in the Weather Underground for six years. *Every day* they lied about who they were. For six years."

"Undercover is different. They get special authorization for that. But if a federal agent wants to interview you in a normal context like this, he's required by protocol to be honest about who he is. That way they don't risk having evidence thrown out of court."

I'm lying. As usual. I worked with some guys from the Bureau of Alcohol, Tobacco and Firearms who loved to pose as insurance investigators. They'd sit down with the bad guy's mom. Tell her a distant cousin died. They've got a check for her prodigal son. But they've got to deliver it to him in person. Mom would answer all kinds of questions. Thinking she was squawking to Mutual Life. Not BATF. And with any luck, she'd set up a meeting with her fugitive son, too.

Even better was the lottery scam the DC cops pulled. They published an announcement in the *Washington Post*. Listing five hundred men with "unclaimed lottery winnings." Directing them to go to RFK Stadium at noon on Saturday. To collect. About two hundred guys showed up. They were all fugitives. Mostly deadbeat dads. The DC cops arrested them all. En masse. Even down in lock-up, most of 'em still didn't get it. "When do I get my money?" they kept asking.

Alan Singer's still glaring at me. Like he's still not convinced.

"Look, Alan, I don't have time for this. Either you answer my questions. Or you read your name in my syndicated story next week."

"What do you want to know?"

"Rachel Clark. You knew her in Amsterdam. Where is she now?"

"Aw, c'mon. I don't know that. *No one* knows that. Rachel Clark's probably dead."

"Why do you say that?"

"It's awful damn hard to stay out of sight for thirty-five years. No one else stayed out that long. Even Kathleen Soliah finally got tracked down."

"You don't know anything about Rachel Clark's current whereabouts?"

"No. Look. Is that what I have to do to stay out of your story? Know where old-time radicals are *today*? Cuz if that's the deal, I might as well go back to work. Can't do it."

"Can't? Or won't?"

"Can't. That was another life, man. Long gone."

"Well, you should wait for your shepherd's pie, Alan. I don't expect you to know where old-time radicals are today. I was just asking."

"Good. I'm a stockbroker now. My old revolutionary friends don't trust me anymore."

"Then you can help me with information *from the old days*. Back when they did trust you."

"What kind of 'information from the old days?'"

"Details. About Rachel Clark. In Amsterdam. What she looked like. Who her friends were. Where she lived. What she did. How you met her."

"And if I give you that, you'll leave me out of the story?"

"You give me *useful* information, I leave you out of our story. That's the deal."

"Who decides whether my information is 'useful?'"

"I do."

Singer throws up his hands. "Not good enough, Mr. Fisher."

"It's the only deal I'm offering."

Our shepherd's pies arrive. Singer chows down for a few minutes in silence.

"How do I know you'll keep your word?" Singer asks between bites.

"Have you ever heard of *any* journalist, *anywhere*, burning a source? Our ethics *require* me to protect your name. To go to jail, if necessary. But never to give up your name."

Singer chews on this awhile. While chewing on his shepherd's pie. Then to my surprise, he just starts talking. With no formal deal. No wrap-up to the trust issue.

"I got to Amsterdam in the summer of '79. Bunked down with some Greenpeace guys."

"Who?"

"Guys I met a few years earlier. In Livermore."

"At the 1977 No-Nukes Protest when you got arrested?" I stare hard at Singer. To make him think I know a lot *more* details like this.

"Yeah. These guys helped me get a job as a waiter. 'Til the Amnesty job came open."

"Who were these guys?"

"Dutch guys."

"Who?"

"If your story is about *American* radicals, then you don't need their names."

"I won't name 'em in my story," I promise. "Their names are just for me."

"I don't name names."

"I thought your revolutionary days were done."

Singer snorts. "They are. But I still don't name names."

"Look, Alan. I may decide I need to *interview* the Dutch guys, too. If so, I need their names. But I promise they won't know I talked to you. Because *I* don't name names, either."

Singer stares a long time into his empty Scotch glass. Clutching it with a death grip.

"Pieter van der Loon was the main guy," Singer says at last.

"Where can I find him?"

"Sorrow Fields Cemetery. In Amsterdam. Pieter died in a car wreck."

"Who else helped you in Amsterdam?"

"Few other guys."

Singer orders another double Scotch. Clutches the new glass with the same death grip. Stares deep into the Scotch. It's scary to think people actually use Alan Singer for stock advice.

"I don't remember a lot of last names. One guy was named Dirk. Look. I really don't see why the names of my old Dutch comrades are so important. They're not in the Movement anymore."

"Gimme *one* full name, of a guy who's still alive, and I'll let it go."

I really don't need this name. But I don't want Singer running this interview, either.

"Jaap Roodhuis."

"Thanks. Where can I find Jaap Roodhuis?"

"Far as I know, Jaap's still with Amnesty. But I haven't spoken to him in twenty years."

"And van der Loon and Roodhuis eventually got you the job at Amnesty?"

"Yeah. In the fall of 1979."

"When you were—twenty-seven?"

Singer looks up at the ceiling. Calculating. "Yeah."

"When did you meet Rachel Clark?"

"1980. At a party. After work. *Wild* party. Pieter introduced me to an American girl. Rebecca Snyder. I found out later her real name was Rachel Clark."

"When did you find that out?"

"Summer of 1980. After the housing riots. A lot of our friends were arrested. Including Rebecca Snyder. Got booked, then released. But less than an hour after Rebecca was released, the Amsterdam police were *everywhere*. Looking to arrest her again."

"They'd found out who she was?"

"Yeah, man. They put up fliers with her picture. And the name Rachel Clark."

"That was the first you knew?"

"That was the first I knew."

"Did *anyone else* know who she was? *Before* the housing riot."

"Doubt it. She kept totally to herself. Didn't trust anyone she didn't have to."

"Kept to herself? But you said you met her at a wild party."

"Yeah. But she was off by herself. Doin' her own thing."

"Alan. I'm only a couple years younger than you. I remember those times, too. Everyone says Rachel Clark was hot stuff. Living the Free Love lifestyle. So c'mon, now."

"Maybe in Michigan she was into sex. But in Amsterdam, all she was into was hash."

Singer drains his second double Scotch. Starts sucking the ice cubes from the first glass.

"You were with Amnesty at the time of the housing riot?" I ask.

"Yes."

"And Amnesty helped Rachel Clark get away?"

"No."

"*No?*" I jerk forward. Glare at him. And almost spill my Guinness. (I'm not very smooth at pretending to be a hard guy.) "I have a very reliable source who says Amnesty *did* help Rachel Clark escape Interpol and the Dutch police," I lie.

"Your source is wrong. Amnesty was a new organization back then. Dedicated people."

"Dedicated *political* people. Radicals like you."

"They weren't all radicals like me. But they were political people, yes. Who hated seeing the Movement collapse in the late seventies. People dedicated to carrying on the fight. *Lawfully*."

"What does *that* mean? Amnesty helps political fugitives gain asylum. All over the world. To do that, Amnesty often has to break unjust laws of oppressive regimes."

"But we only helped true political fugitives. *Not* common criminals."

"Which group was Rachel Clark in?" I ask.

"Exactly. Some of us saw her as a political fugitive. But most saw her as a common criminal. And back then, Amnesty was new. Couldn't afford to take chances. Couldn't risk the bad press we'd get if we helped a cop-killer. So there was no way Amnesty could help her officially."

"But unofficially?"

Singer stares a long time into the creamy foam on top of my half-consumed Guinness. "You ever worry about dying, Fisher?"

Subjects often try to distract me during an interview. By asking questions back at me. Seldom works. I'm a pro. But this question is so odd, I bite on it. "All the time, Alan. Why?"

"Me, too. Though I think I got more to worry about than you."

"I don't know about that. Death comes for us all. Sooner or later."

"Sooner for me than for you. And when I go, none of this'll matter. Alan Singer, the successful stockbroker. Alan Singer, the fugitive arsonist. Who cares what you write about me? I'm no more important than the tiniest grain of sand." Singer fixes me with a stubborn stare.

"This is nothing personal, Alan. I got a job to do. But people *do* still care about old radicals. Now more than ever. As you draw closer to the ends of your lives. You're not just a grain of sand. You're—hell, except for the Civil War, you're the only white Americans who ever took arms against their own government. And you didn't do it for any of the usual reasons people commit crimes. Not for money. Not for sexual gratification. Not to indulge aberrant psychotic anger. You did it for *principles*. Which means you'll *always* be a story, pal. Like it or not."

"Where were *you* in 1975? When the Movement was still a force in America?"

"Doing my homework. And obeying the law."

"In other words, *sitting on the sidelines*," Singer sneers. "Where guys like you always hide. Too scared to get in the game and risk getting dirty." Singer stares into my Guinness foam. Then mumbles an old slogan: "*There are no spectators to a revolution.*"

"Well, then I guess it wasn't really a revolution. Because *I* was certainly a spectator."

Singer snorts. "You still don't get it, do you, Fisher? Our revolution was *real*, man. But it got killed by spectators like you. *If you're not part of the solution, you're part of the problem.* If you don't join the revolution, then you're a counter-revolutionary. Even if you *think* you're just a neutral spectator. *That's* what it means to say '*there are no spectators to a revolution.*'"

"I thought you left the Revolution behind when you became a stockbroker."

"I did. But I didn't stop believing that our cause was righteous. I just quit fighting. Because spectators like you killed the Movement."

"The end of the Vietnam War killed the Movement."

"Only because guys like you didn't care enough to keep fighting injustice."

"It wasn't that we didn't *care*, Alan. It was the *violence* we couldn't stomach. Which guys like *you* said was the ultimate 'gut check.' If I wanted to be part of the solution, according to guys like you, I had to sign up for burning buildings. And shooting cops."

"Big difference there. Burning buildings hurts no one. Shooting people does."

"Both are crimes. Both involve violence. It was the turn to violence that killed the Movement. Because 'spectators' like me weren't ready to sign up for the violence."

"There's no way to be committed to non-violence while living among the most violent society in history." Singer spouts this sixties bromide like it was yesterday.

"Alan, you're a hard case. But I didn't call you up to debate politics. I need to confirm that Amnesty people, acting unofficially, helped Rachel Clark get out of Amsterdam in 1980."

Singer stares into my Guinness foam some more. I wait him out.

"This is absolutely confidential?" Singer asks at last.

"Yes. If this goes into my story, it goes in *without names*. And if the police ask me for names of the sources for my story, they won't get them. *Ever*."

Easy promise to make. Since there is no story.

"Unofficially, Rachel Clark got help. From people connected with Amnesty."

"Tell me who. I need to hear you say their *names*, Alan."

Singer looks up. Suddenly startled by a scary thought that has overtaken him. Paranoia is written all over his blotchy, Scotch-addled face. "You *already know*, don't you?"

"Yes!" I lie. And lean forward. "But I need to hear their names *from you*."

Singer blinks rapidly. Grips his Scotch glass. Purses his lips.

"Time's running out, Alan. You—"

"Amy Pierce," Singer says. "And me."

*Amy Pierce*. The name rings no bells. I debate calling Hunter on my cell. To ask if *he* knows Amy Pierce. But I don't want to lose momentum here. Better to milk Singer while he's naming names.

"Go back to when you first met Rachel Clark. That party in 1980. When you got introduced to her as Rebecca Snyder. What'd she look like?"

"Short dark hair. Washed-out looking. Anorexic. She was doin' *lotsa* drugs."

"Back in Ann Arbor, in 1969, Rachel Clark had striking long red hair. She was slender. But healthy looking. Lots of curves."

"Right after the Law School action, she cut her hair. Dyed it. Went on a long fast. And had breast reduction surgery. Then she got way too deep into drugs."

"How do you know all this?"

"Amy Pierce. Amy helped Rachel Clark change her looks after the housing riot. Which required discussion about Rachel's *first* change of appearance. After the Law School action."

"What was the new look Rachel Clark went to? *After* the housing riot."

"*Older*. Heavier. Beehive hairstyle. Frumpy clothes. Amy suggested surgery to boost her figure. That's when Rachel told her she'd *already had* surgery on her breasts. To go the other direction. They decided there was no point in going back to looking like she did in Ann Arbor. So they left her chest alone. Just had her eat her way back to a moderate weight."

"What new name did you all pick out for Rachel Clark?"

"Sanne ter Spiegel. It was much easier for me to get a Dutch passport than an American one. And everyone was watching for an American woman."

"How'd you get her out of Europe?"

"*I* didn't do that. All I did was bribe a guy to get her a Dutch passport."

"Who got her out of Europe?"

"Amy."

"How'd *Amy* get her out of Europe?"

"Banana boat. To Central America."

"What did Rachel Clark do in Central America?"

"Who knows? Once she left Amsterdam, I never heard another thing about her. Few years later, I enrolled in biz school. My old friends like Amy Pierce stopped talking to me then."

"How 'bout *before* Amsterdam? Where was Rachel Clark between 1969 and 1980?"

Singer wrinkles his forehead. "She told Amy she was in the DC area in the early '70s."

"*DC*? What—so she could be as close as possible to FBI Headquarters?"

Singer shrugs. "Rachel Clark didn't have many contacts in the Movement. Her boyfriend in Ann Arbor was the one who knew people. And he was dead. So she got the hell out of Michigan. On her own. Drifted south. Somehow ended up in Eastern Virginia."

"When did she go to Europe?"

"I don't know. She got to Amsterdam before me. Before 1979. And she was in Madrid before she was in Amsterdam. I remember her talking about poetry classes she audited there. Before she came to Amsterdam. That's all I know about Rachel Clark. Really."

"Tell me about her Ann Arbor boyfriend. Paul Zimmerman."

"Never met him. I was a senior in *high school* when Zimmerman died."

I pretend to write in my notepad. Buying time while I think of more questions. But luckily Singer interprets the pause as a demand for more information about Zimmerman.

"The only thing I know about Paul Zimmerman is, Rachel Clark was *really hung up* on him. She wore an ankle bracelet he gave her. Amy Pierce told her to get rid of it. In case the Amsterdam Police had seen it when she was in custody. But Rachel would *not* let that thing go."

"Did she have any *other* prized possessions you remember? Like a motorcycle helmet?"

"Never saw a helmet. But she did have a ratty old checkered scarf. Wore it all the time in Amsterdam. It was from the 1971 HEW protest. They all wore checkered scarves."

"*Who* all wore checkered scarves?"

"The Weather Underground women. Not all the time. Just to the HEW protest."

"Wasn't it risky for Rachel Clark to participate in the HEW protest? So soon after the Law School action? With the fresh warrant out for her arrest?"

"Yes, it was risky. But Rachel was a committed revolutionary. And she had her new look. Her new identity. All she had to do was avoid arrest. Which she did—until that day in Amsterdam."

"Did Rachel Clark ever tell you anything about the Law School bombing action?"

"Not about the action itself. But Amy wanted to know who betrayed them. Most people in the Movement figured they'd been betrayed by *someone*. Yet Rachel Clark said no."

"What made other people in the Movement think they were betrayed?"

"The cop had perfect timing. Zimmerman and Brown were outside their van less than a minute. Yet just as they're getting ready to heave their bombs, here comes a cop? On a little side street in Ann Arbor? That cop was in exactly the right place, at exactly the right time."

"Did people think it was *Rachel Clark* who betrayed Zimmerman and Brown?"

"Oh, no. Rachel'd paid too heavy a price. People thought it was the old SDS leaders."

"Why?"

"Zimmerman and Brown had just taken over the Michigan SDS a few weeks before. With their Jesse James gang. They wanted violent action. The old SDS leaders opposed violence. So people wondered if the old SDS leaders ratted Zimmerman and Brown out. On the Law School."

"But how would the old SDS leaders ever have *known* about the Law School plot?"

"That was Rachel Clark's point. She said the only people who knew about the plot were Zimmerman, Brown and her. She said it was sheer, blind, bad luck that brought that cop."

"But if Rachel Clark said no one betrayed them, why was there *ever* any suspicion of the old SDS leaders?"

"Because right after the bombing, Rachel was gone. Far as I know, Amy Pierce and I were the first to hear what Rachel had to say. *Eleven years* later. Meanwhile, back in '69, the night of the Law School action, the old SDS leaders *immediately* disavowed any ties to the bombing plan. So fast, it was like they'd had their statement *pre-prepared*. Made people wonder. What's that old line? 'The Lady doth protest too much.' These guys denied the crime before they were even accused."

"You know a lot about this," I say, "for a guy who was still in high school in 1969."

"The botched action in Ann Arbor echoed down through the Movement *for years*. It was a . . . watershed. Before Days of Rage and the Michigan Law School, the Movement was unified. After the fall of '69, everything changed, man. Everyone splintered. The old SDS was dead."

"I was just in junior high then," I mutter. "What I remember most is, after the botched Law School bombing, the Jesse James gang lost all credibility."

"Definitely," Singer says. "Like you said before, the violence turned many people off. And even the real revolutionaries had to admit, Zimmerman bungled the action."

"So the *old* SDS leaders got labeled traitors. While the new SDS leaders like Zimmerman got discredited as bunglers."

Singer nods. And for the first time in our interview, smiles. Revealing those gruesome, cracked, yellow teeth. No wonder Singer doesn't smile much.

"That's why the conspiracy buffs decided *campus administrators* must have been behind the whole thing. A successful conspiracy to discredit *both* the Jesse James gang *and* the old SDS leaders."

I raise an eyebrow. Briefly consider pursuing this unlikely conspiracy theory. After all, tabloid readers love *any* conspiracy theory. No matter how old. No matter how ridiculous. But this one lacks punch. So I let it go. "Did Rachel Clark talk much about her daughter?"

Singer looks surprised. "I didn't know she had a kid. Never said a word to me about it."

"Where is Amy Pierce today?"

Singer looks at me a long time. "If I give you that, I'm out of your story?"

"Yes. *If* you tell me where Amy Pierce is. *And* how I can get her to talk to me."

"Not a word about me in your story?"

"Not a word."

Singer makes me write the promise down on paper. Sign it. And give it to him to keep.

"Amy Pierce is in Chicago. Works at the Public Defender's office. Downtown."

"Lawyer?"

"Paralegal. Amy's plenty smart enough to be a lawyer. But with her long record, they'd never let her in law school."

"Bernardine Dohrn teaches law at Northwestern. Bernardine had a long record."

"Not as long as Amy's."

"How can I get Amy Pierce to talk to me?"

"Say you're a friend of Rachel Clark's. And say you just saw Rachel *down in Key West*."

"Key West?"

"Rachel Clark's favorite poem. 'The Idea of Order At Key West.' Rachel uses 'Key West' like a password. To tell friends from foes."

\* \* \*

Who but a man, female readers will ask, would risk his entire marriage for "five minutes of fun?" Well, in my meager defense, first of all these days for me it's more like *thirty* minutes of fun. Since the old gun doesn't fire so fast as it used to. But more to the point: it's not *just* "five minutes of fun." It's a man's whole self-esteem. Wrapped up in having a beautiful woman go down on you. Or get on her back for you.

So I call Janet Fickel. At work. From LaGuardia.

"Hey, Janet. How'd you like to go to a Bruce Springsteen concert tomorrow night?"

"Um, I dunno. Maybe."

"I can get us great seats. The Boss. Live. I know he's getting old. But so am I. And he's still the Boss. It's supposed to be a great show. To help knock Bush out of office."

"I'm voting *for* Bush. I'm a Republican."

Somehow I'm not surprised. Indiana's not exactly Kerry country. "I'll try not to hold that against you, Janet. It'll still be a great show."

"Where is it?"

"Detroit. Cobo."

"I don't think so. We wouldn't get home until—too late."

"We could go for the first half. And still beat John home. He'll be in Detroit, too, right?"

"I really don't like Bruce Springsteen."

What's not to like about Bruce Springsteen? I take a deep breath. Collect myself.

"Well, okay. Forget that idea. I'm still hoping to see you three times tomorrow."

"Three times?"

"In the morning, when I finally get to meet with Sheila Nyman. In the evening, when I hope you'll still at least do drinks with me. And—if you'll say yes—at noon for lunch, too."

"Okay," Janet says. "For lunch."

"You're still thinking about the evening?"

"Still thinking."

"Don't think too hard. You don't want to get worry lines on your forehead."

Janet laughs. "They're already there."

"I didn't see any this weekend. And I got pretty damn close."

"Yes, you did. Close enough you *should* have seen them. Maybe you need glasses."

"Nope. I've got contact lenses. Twenty-fifteen vision. If you had wrinkles, I'd know about it. But I tell you what. Why don't we settle this debate *objectively*?"

"How?"

"Photographic evidence."

"You want me to bring *more* pictures?"

"Nope. I want you to get a *new* picture. There's a photographer on Main Street. Let's stop by there at lunch. I'll pay him to take your picture. With or without me. Or both. Your choice. But that way, I'll have a picture of you to take with me on lonely trips like this."

"What lonely trip? Where are you?"

"New York. Just for the day. But I miss you, Janet. Big time. Please say you'll wear something nice tomorrow and we'll get our pictures taken. It would mean a lot to me. Really."

"Okay. I'll wear my red jacket."

"The loose, shapeless one you had on the first time we had lunch?"

Janet laughs. "That's the one. It's very dressy. The red looks great in pictures."

"Fine. Though I'd really prefer you wear that little brown dress you wore on Saturday."

"No, you wouldn't. I'd be under surveillance all day if I did."

"Oh yeah. I forgot about that. Okay. Then the red jacket will have to do. And—thank you. I know it's a little corny. But it—you mean a lot to me, Janet."

"You, too. To me."

"This is a hard conversation to have at work?" Showing my usual keen grasp of the obvious.

"Yes."

"Okay. I'll pick you up at 11:45. At your office."

Janet pauses. "How 'bout we meet at the corner gas station? At Main and Miller."

"Fine. I love you, Janet."

Pause. "How can you be sure?"

"Believe me. I'm sure."

* * *

On the plane I write a love letter. It's so corny I'm not sure I should waste your time with it. But what the hell. You've hung in with me this far, Patient Reader. Here's the first part:

> *Dearest Janet—You ask me if I'm sure I love you. A fair question. As you say, it's only been six days. Or whatever. And I admit, I'm not someone who normally believes in love at first sight. Not at all. Yet I am absolutely certain I love you. So how do I know?*

*One way I know I love you is this: if I could design the ideal dream woman for me, you would definitely not be her. Please don't take offense. But I wouldn't choose a married woman. Much less a Bush supporter. And I wouldn't choose someone with your checkered past, either. Plus I hate cigarette smoke. And I've never been attracted to red-heads. And yet, in spite of all these things, I'm drawn to you. Like a north magnet to a south magnet. And it's precisely because you're not my ideal dream woman that I know I must really be in love with you. How else could we have carried on like we did this weekend?*

*Another way I know I love you is the magnitude of the risk I run to be with you. I'm not complaining. And I know you run the same risk to be with me. But it's not something I've ever done before. It's not something I'll ever do again. Not for any other woman would I run these risks.*

*But the real answer to your question is too deep for words. It's somewhere way below the surface, too. I know I love you because of how my chest clenches up when I see you strut down the sidewalk. Because of the exhilaration I feel just walking beside you or sitting with you. The tingle in my skin when you hold my hand. The thrill that runs through all of me when I hold you. And did I mention your big brown eyes? I could lose myself in your eyes, Janet.*

*And I know you love me too, Janet. I can see you're not ready to say it. That's okay. There's no rush. But your shyness with the words can't hide the truth about what's happening between us. A truth you can't run from, Janet. You might as well spend Tuesday evening with me. Because even if you cancel our tentative plans for Tuesday evening—which I really hope you won't do—you'll still be thinking of me. Constantly. Just as I'm constantly thinking of you.*

Enough. You get the idea. It goes on like that for *pages*. I can't believe I wrote it, either. Still, I know it's compelling. I'll drop it on Janet's desk tomorrow. When I go see Sheila Nyman.

\* \* \*

After a late dinner at the Campus Inn, I drop in on my mom. Borrow a photo album she keeps. With pix of me from birth all the way to the present. The "Greatest Hits" of David Fisher. My mom doesn't ask why I need the album. So I don't tell her I think Janet Fickel might enjoy these old pix. I also get my mom to write a retainer check for me to Davis & Nyman. She doesn't ask me why I need this, either. So I offer no explanation. What a great mom I have!

Then I swing by Davis & Nyman. It's 9:00 p.m. Tonight all the lights are out. Which means I'm in. With my pick gun. And my latex gloves, of course.

I know my way around. After all, I broke in three times early last week. But now I'm seeing the place with a fresh eye. Because I know so much more about the daytime occupants.

What I *should* do is simple. Go to Sheila Nyman's office. Riffle quickly through her drawers. Take something she won't miss. Hope it has her fingerprints. Next do the same for Naomi Williams's desk. And then get the hell out of here. Fast.

But you know me. Easily distracted. And mildly obsessed. So where do I go?

Straight to *Janet's* desk. Right outside Lane Davis's second-floor office. No question it's Janet's. There's a photo of her. Leaning on the shoulder of a huge *behemoth*. The Missing Link. Oh, it's hubbie John. I recognize him now, from the pix Janet showed me in the park. Only those pix didn't show me that he was so ginormous (as my kids say). Good to know the guy whose wife I'm chasing is *not only* a crack shot. *Not only* president of his gun club. He's also about 6'5", 250. With a fierce black beard. And glinting gray eyes. Looks like he should be on an NRA poster. Championing Second Amendment rights. So you always have a gun handy—to *eradicate* any tabloid snake who might be trying to steal your wife.

I turn the disturbing photo face down. Sit in Janet's chair. To get a feel for her world. There's a couple of other pix. Her kids. Carrie and Stacy. Whom I recognize from Janet's photo album. Surprisingly homely kids. Not cut from the same cloth as their hot little minx of a mom.

Janet's desktop is tidy. But her drawers are utter chaos. Crap all over. Cigarettes. Nail files. Brushes. Compact mirror. Lipstick. Breath mints. Pens. Pencils. Myriad other office supplies. Floppy disks. And a couple of issues of *Cosmo*. But nothing remotely *personal*. No letters. No books. No art work. Not even a bank statement. Just those three family photos on the desk. If Janet had quit on Friday, like she said she almost did, she could have packed all her stuff in five seconds. Out the door in thirty seconds. The fully portable legal assistant.

Still, the *Cosmo* magazines get me thinking. *That's* Janet. In a nutshell. Everyman's dream *Cosmo* girl. A girl with a short memory and a strong need to express joy. Who *enjoys* reading racy tips about "his trigger points." And how to give her man a better blow job.

Scoff if you like. Maybe I'm *supposed* to want a woman with more rarefied tastes. But James Joyce wrote puns in seventeen languages. Forgot more about life than I'll ever learn. Yet Joyce chose for his lifelong lover an illiterate barmaid. An Irish *Cosmo* girl. Because the high priestesses with the keys to Love's bitter mystery are not necessarily the ladies who score highest on the SATs.

I fire up Janet's computer. She's still logged on. Nothing personal in her e-mail. Not even in the deleted files. Nothing personal in her "cookies" either. The internet sites she visits are plain vanilla. A music trading site. MapQuest. A hotel information site. And the Detroit Gun Club site. That's it. So I go into Janet's personal computer documents. And at last strike gold.

*Divorce papers.* Already filled in.

At first I'm elated. Thinking Janet must be swept away in our passion. Just like me. Then I see the date. July 14, 2004. Three months ago. Long *before* Janet met me. Were these papers ever filed in court? No way to tell. Still, either way, they're a good sign. Even if Janet was only *thinking* this way three months ago, her marriage probably isn't in good shape *now* either.

I've learned all I can learn about Janet here. So I go to Sheila Nyman's office. Which is decorated with prints of *Tour de France* cyclists, racing en masse down narrow winding mountain roads, amid breath-taking Alpine scenery. And a close-up of Lance Armstrong.

Sheila's desktop is spotless, too. I riffle through Sheila's file drawers. Leaf through *her* divorce papers. Where I find her maiden name—Sheila Nyman. She didn't change it when she got married. A fully liberated modern woman. Then I find a file marked "medical." Inside are doctor's records pertaining to Sheila's hysterectomy. Two biopsies. And—bingo! Plastic surgery. On her nose. I *knew* it!

The plastic surgery was in 1990. A year after Sheila went to work for Lane Davis. A little late in the game. If Rachel Clark used plastic surgery to help change her identity, she would have needed it in 1970, not 1990. And even if she was getting a second or third plastic surgery to facilitate a second or third identity change, she would have needed it *before* she went to work for Lane Davis in 1989. Not *after*.

I'm not much good at reading medical records. But it looks like what Sheila had in 1990 was a routine nose job. Not a thorough facial reconstruction.

So I dig deeper. For evidence of identity. Copy Sheila's Social Security number from a credit card application. Her birth date. Her mother's maiden name. From a car invoice, I get Sheila's driver's license number. Best of all, I photocopy her signature off a loan application.

Then I strike real pay dirt. Way in the back of Sheila's file drawer. A file labeled "McGeetchy Trust." Filled with trust papers for Melanie McGeetchy and her family.

A client? Or Sheila's alter-ego?

I'm leafing through the McGeetchy documents. Copying the Social and the birth date and the mother's maiden name for Melanie McGeetchy, too. Also photocopying Melanie McGeetchy's signature. And trying to figure it all out. How Melanie McGeetchy fits in with Sheila Nyman. And how they both fit in with Rachel Clark.

I'm concentrating so hard, I almost miss the key scraping in the back door downstairs.

Shit! What kind of nerd comes back to work at 9:30? I kill my flashlight. Remove my shoes. And try to control my pounding heart. While also trying to take quiet, shallow breaths.

Downstairs the lights go on. I hear someone walk to one of the first-floor offices. Sounds like a man's footsteps. I'm guessing George Robertson. The thirty-two-year-old associate. Looking out Sheila Nyman's window, I see light from George's office spilling out into the parking lot. And amid the deafening pounding of my own heartbeats, I hear George puttering in his office.

I put my shoes back on. Take shallow breaths. And wait. In the dark. A long time.

Thirty minutes later, I hear George go into the bathroom downstairs. I *know* that bathroom. It has a really loud fan. Attached to the only light switch. Time to make my break. I debate taking the McGeetchy file. But I can't risk Sheila missing it. It's not *that* important. I'll get Sheila's fingerprints at our appointment tomorrow morning. Then I'll know who she is.

Three stairs creak as I walk down. But not too loud. No one bursts out of the bathroom.

The stairs land me by Debbie the receptionist's desk. The front door is right there. My hand on the doorknob trembles. Like a very old man's. But I manage to exit. Undetected.

* * *

Since I've aged thirty months in the past thirty minutes, I need rejuvenation. I drink three Scotches at my hotel. And three Jim Beams, too. For good measure. But then, since Janet's at home with The Behemoth, where better to find the Fountain of Youth than Déjà Vu? My second night in a row. (Which makes it "Déjà Vu all over again." As Yogi Berra would say.)

Turns out tonight is "Manic Monday." A promotion to boost attendance. Which features the dancers spraying each other with whipped cream. But I'm a little late. So by now it looks more like "Messy Monday." Call me old-fashioned. But to me, melted whipped cream running down a naked woman, like someone else's cum, isn't very *appealing*. I'd prefer just a plain naked woman.

Chandra isn't working tonight. But her sister Mystique is easy to spot. Same facial structure. Same build. Same volleyballs for boobs. Dr. Silicone must have been offering a family discount when the dancing sisters came to see him. But only on the humungous implants.

Mystique's busy slapping *her* volleyballs against the heads of two guys whose names, Bill and Ed, are stitched onto their shirts. Good to know my comrades—*mon semblables, mon freres*—are high-rent guys. I peruse the other dancers. Smile at a dark-haired woman who appears to have undergone no surgery. Of course, I thought *Janet Fickel* was natural, too. But here I've got a fully unobstructed view. This woman is *definitely* shaking only what nature gave her.

Her name turns out to be *Sarah*. So of course I invest heavily in lap dances with her. Sarah says she's twenty-nine. Six years too young to be Rachel Clark's daughter. If my Scotch-addled math is right. But women often lie about their age. Sarah says her last name is Watts. Not Clark. But women often change their last names, too.

After two dances, at my request, Sarah Watts shows me her feet. Close up. They look fine. She says she's never had any problems with her feet or legs. No surgeries. Doesn't know any dancer at Déjà Vu who's ever had any problems with her feet or legs.

So I ask Sarah point-blank, "Have you ever heard of a woman named Rachel Clark?"

Sarah Watts stops gyrating in my lap. Puts one hand under my chin. Lifts my chin up so she can look me straight in the eye. The way Janet Fickel did Saturday at the Law School.

"You've got the wrong Sarah. That's Sarah *Pierce* you want."

"Sarah Pierce dances only on weekends?"

"Correct."

"Why is *she* the Sarah I want? Her *foot*? Or because I asked for *Rachel Clark*?"

"You after the reward? Or you a cop?"

"No, sweetheart. I'm a friend. And I really need to find her. *Before* the weekend."

Sarah Watts wasn't born yesterday. She ain't buying it. And she looks *real* nervous. So I reach for the side of Sarah Watts's thong. To try to slip another twenty on her hip.

But my aim is poor. Maybe she moved. Maybe I had one too many drinks before I got here. (Or *five* too many.) In any event, instead of Sarah Watts's hip, I'm stuffing my twenty right down the middle. Her vagina.

Sarah Watts squeals. Loud. In less than half a nano-second, two well-muscled bouncers appear at my sides. And lift me off my comfortable cushion.

For reasons that surpass understanding, I resist. About as smart as running from a traffic stop.

The bouncers grin. They *love* resistors.

Now in *real* novels, even the most bookish of heroes will turn out to be a reasonably scrappy guy. Who can trade a few punches with anyone. Even burly bouncers. The hero may go down. May even get knocked out. But not before he gets a few licks in, right?

For your sake, Courageous Reader, I'd like to tell you I fight like a tiger. Indeed, for the sake of *my own ego*, I'd like to say at least I give these bouncers a run for their money before they take me down.

But that's not what happens.

The entire "altercation" lasts less than five seconds. For starters, they slam my head into a nearby wall. That's also for *enders*, I'm chagrined to say. At least, that's all I remember from my ill-advised resistance. Evidently they knocked me out cold. With the first blow to my head.

Because the next thing I know, I'm slumped on a bench in the drunk tank. At the Washtenaw County Jail.

Which I regret to report suffers from chronic overcrowding. I barely have half a bench to myself. On which to lie down. And feel the hard pounding in my head. From the bouncers' beating. And from my excessive drinking before I got to Déjà Vu. A pounding I feel each second. Of each minute. Of each hour. Of the long, sleepless night.

# CHAPTER EIGHT
# PEACE BY PIECE

## Tuesday 19 October 2004

Thankfully, no media attend my arraignment. But I'm not out of the woods yet. *The Ann Arbor News* still might report on the charge. When their reporter reviews the court docket.

I debate giving the court my mom's address. So if Janet Fickel happens to see a story on this, at least she won't learn I lied to her about where I live. But the police already have my Florida address. From my driver's license.

Now the judge is taking the bench. Oh great. He's an old high school classmate of mine. Patrick Flynn. Just what I did *not* need.

I didn't see Judge Flynn at our reunion Saturday night. And we didn't really know each other all that well in high school. Which may be why he's peering at me now. *Scowling*, actually. Could be he's just scowling at me the way he would scowl at any stranger who blew into his Midwestern courtroom from the crime-ridden miasma of South Florida. But I'm pretty sure Judge Flynn is scowling because he's recognized me. Yep. He's nodding at me now. Well, at least he's discreet enough not to mention our high school daze together in open court.

I plead not guilty to simple assault. (No sex charges were filed against me for inadvertently groping Sarah Watts. Thank God for small favors.) Judge Flynn asks if I'm going to represent myself at trial. Evidently he remembers hearing that I went to law school. But he doesn't say anything about me being a lawyer in open court. I tell him I'll try to hire a lawyer right away.

Judge Flynn sets trial in four weeks. Then asks if bail needs to be set.

The young assistant prosecutor suggests $25,000 bail. Since I live out of state. Which would mean I'd have to raise $2,500 to get out of jail now.

I stand. Ready to launch into a speech about my substantial ties to Ann Arbor.

"Do your parents still live in Ann Arbor?" Judge Flynn asks.

"My mother does. My father passed away."

"I'm sorry to hear that," Judge Flynn says. "You will be released on your own recognizance. But you must make all court dates. Or I'll have no choice but to issue a bench warrant."

"Thank you, Your Honor. I'll be here for all the court dates."

That's it. We're done. No one learns I'm a tabloid hack. No one learns I'm a lawyer. Best of all, by releasing me on my own recognizance, Judge Flynn got me out of having to call my mom or Graham or Elaine to bail me out. Hopefully none of 'em will hear of this. Until I'm good and ready to add it to my repertoire of silly stories. With the usual embellishments.

I'm halfway out the courtroom when I hear the Judge's mellifluous Irish lilt. Asking to speak to me privately. Back up at the bench.

"I won't be your judge on this, David. I'm a *circuit* judge. Felonies only. I'm just covering today for a district judge who's got a sick kid. So tell me. What's this all about?"

"It wasn't my fault, judge. I was at Déjà Vu—"

"The *strip club*?"

"Yeah. But I was there for work. To interview one of the dancers. They thought I was groping her. But I wasn't, really. See, they—"

Judge Flynn is shaking his head at me. He doesn't want to hear the gory details.

"You should try to work out a plea, Dave. You don't need all this aired out in public."

True enough. I thank him for the advice. He asks how the reunion went. And wishes me luck. Leaving the courtroom, I remember that my sister got divorced over an incident like this. Her husband was arrested at a strip club in their hometown. When he was supposed to be out of town on business. My sister, a reporter on the police beat, read about it in the next morning's police blotter. She was pissed. More about the lying than about him being in a strip club.

Would *Elaine* divorce me over something like this?

Given what I've been up to lately, who could blame her if she did?

I step outside. Squint in the sunlight. Rub my bleary eyes. And shiver.

It's much cooler than yesterday. Autumn has returned. No more making out with Janet Fickel outdoors this year. We're going to have to move our hot little romance indoors.

The clock across the street says 9:15. Only forty-five minutes 'til my appointment with Sheila Nyman. Barely time to walk to my hotel, shower, change, and walk back to Main Street.

Along the way I try to ignore my horrible hangover. So I can review what I know about Sheila Nyman and Melanie McGeetchy and Rachel Clark. Tom Lacy said Melanie McGeetchy was Rachel Clark's college roommate. Where? Which year? Unfortunately I didn't think to get those details. Lacy said Melanie McGeetchy's a lawyer on Main Street now. Just like Sheila Nyman. Denise Maxwell's husband, Todd Cook, said Lane Davis got in trouble for helping Melanie McGeetchy when he was a prosecutor. So Melanie was presumably some kind of political criminal. Now known as Sheila Nyman—at least if Bill Miller, who fell in love with her eyes in a 'Wanted' poster, can be believed.

Which makes me wonder: could *I* do the same thing? *Not* fall in love with Rachel Clark. (I've got enough love in my life these days.) But get pix of my three suspects. Hold them next to the old FBI 'Wanted' poster for Rachel Clark. And pick out the guilty party? By her *eyes*?

Seems like a long shot. But if Bill Miller could do it, why can't I? I resolve to try it later today. But what's my theory here, anyway? Sheila is really Melanie McGeetchy? Still helping her old college roommate, Rachel Clark? Or Sheila is really Rachel Clark?

Or *both*? Suppose Melanie McGeetchy died or disappeared in 1969. Suppose Rachel took over her roommate's identity after the bombing. Became Melanie in 1969. Then became Rebecca Snyder in the seventies. Next, Sanne ter Spiegel in 1980. And last, Sheila Nyman in 1989?

Seems like it would be hard to become your roommate. Though that was basically Lawrence Kasdan's plot for the movie *Body Heat*. Stranger things have happened.

My ruminations depress me. They show how little I know about any of my suspects. Except for the fingerprints eliminating Raven, I've basically accomplished nothing in a week in Ann Arbor. Dick Fucking Tracy, my ass. More like Son of the Keystone Cops. Mr. Incompetent.

I reach my hotel. Take the elevator up. Open my door. And get a nasty surprise.

My room's been trashed. Totally. Thoroughly. And professionally.

The dresser drawers have all been yanked out. All my stuff has been dumped on the bed. The mattress has been cut open. The box spring, too. And the sofa cushions.

My laptop's missing. And my pinhole camera. And all the rest of my surveillance shit.

I sit on the bed. My head aches from the night in the drunk tank. I can't think straight.

Then I remember. My laptop's in the trunk of my rental car. Along with my pinhole camera. And the rest of my surveillance shit. Which means the bastards did *not* get my pix of Norma Lee and the Rachel Clark helmet. Or my video of Lane Davis and Raven LaGrow.

Ha! But where's my rental car? The keys are in my pocket. Oh, yeah. The rental car is still parked in the parking lot across the street from Déjà Vu. Unless it's been stolen. Or towed.

I look again at the mess in my room. Someone wanted *something* I have. Real bad.

I'm pissed. But *scared*, too. Since they didn't get what they wanted, they'll be back.

* * *

"You're *wrong*," Sheila Nyman says. "Weather deplored violence against *people*."

"Oh, c'mon!" I reply. "The Brinks robbery in New York—"

"A splinter group. And that was 1981. Six years *after* Weather disbanded."

"The Greenwich Village townhouse bombing was 1970. And *that* was clearly Weather."

"An accident," Sheila says. "And the only people who died there were Weather members."

"Yeah, but the 'accident' occurred while they were building an *anti-personnel bomb*. Ten thousand little nails. Packed in with the explosives. Which they intended to use to blow up an Army Officer's Dance at Fort Dix. To kill *hundreds* of people. The bomb was so patently anti-human, the kid fiddling with the bomb—Teddy Gold—could only be identified by a single fingerprint they found on a small piece of human finger in the wreckage. The rest of Teddy Gold was literally blown to smithereens. And you're telling me Weather abhorred violence against people?"

"Yes!" Sheila flushes. Then her face softens. "Look. No group of people can agree on every point. There were definitely some within the Weather Underground advocating violence against other people. Like those kids that blew themselves up in Greenwich Village. But they were always outvoted in Weather. What they were doing in that townhouse was definitely *not* authorized by Weather. And they knew it."

"The people in that townhouse were Weather's *leaders*. Diana Oughten. Kathy Boudin."

"They were *some* of Weather's leaders. But if they'd sought authorization for that anti-personnel bomb, it would have been denied. And they knew it. In fact, Weather had a big meeting in San Francisco. After Greenwich Village. All agreed: no violence against people. *Ever.*"

I've already spent an hour and a half loosening Sheila Nyman up. At $275 per hour. For her legal services. We've incorporated my fictitious new business. We even named my new magazine. *Liberal Voices.* We figured out how much cash I'll need to capitalize the business. What I need in the printer's contract. And what my standard employee contracts will say. Best of all, Sheila Nyman's fingerprints are all over the documents I'll be taking home with me.

Once the business part of the meeting was concluded, I gently kidded Sheila about being an "unrepentant leftie." Which led us into talking about the Weather Underground.

"Sheila, I don't want to argue with my lawyer. Especially since you've given me so much great business advice today."

Sheila smiles.

"But your position is just a tautology. Whenever Weather engaged in a creatively violent act where no people got hurt, like the Pentagon bombing or the Capitol bombing, you say '*that* was Weather.' But whenever people got killed, like the Brinks robbery, or the townhouse bombing, or the botched bombing of the Michigan Law School, you say '*that* was an unauthorized splinter group.' So if you're going to define Weather not as a *group of people* but rather as a *result*, then of course, you're right. Weather was not about violence against people. But if you define Weather as *its members*—Kathy Boudin, Diane Oughten, Rachel Clark, etc.—then *I'm* right. Because *those* Weather members committed acts of violence that left people dead."

"You would have made a good lawyer, Mr. Fisher," Sheila Nyman says.

"David. Please. And yes. My mother *still* wishes I were a lawyer."

"Nevertheless, you're wrong," Sheila says. "Weather committed more than *fifty actions* from 1969 to 1975. Not just the Capitol and the Pentagon. Weather bombed the National Guard. The State Department. The Presidio. The New York Department of Corrections. The California Attorney General's Office. HEW. Gulf Oil. ITT. *Banco Ponce.* All with *no dead. No wounded.*

"Whereas you can point to only three examples where any person got hurt." Sheila holds up one finger, to signal the first example. "The 1969 attempt to firebomb the Michigan Law School. A completely unauthorized action. Led by Paul Zimmerman. A man kicked out of SDS for his homicidal views. Who would have been kicked out of the Weather Underground, too. Except the Weather leaders barely knew Zimmerman had joined Weather a few weeks earlier."

Sheila holds up a second finger. "The 1970 Greenwich Village bombing. Where kids playing with bombs blew themselves up. But no one else got hurt. Even Dustin Hoffman next door got out without a scrape."

Sheila holds up a third finger. "And the 1981 Brinks robbery. Six years *after* Weather disbanded. A robbery orchestrated by drug addicts masquerading as revolutionaries. Who manipulated a few ex-Weather people like Kathy Boudin and David Gilbert. Sad misfits clinging to their revolutionary dreams. Who couldn't find a place back in regular society. Easy dupes.

"And that's it! That's *not* the record of an organization committed to violence against people. It's just that the media"—Sheila gives her new media client (me) a nod—"forever sensationalizes those three isolated events. While ignoring all the good that Weather did."

"People *died* in those three 'isolated events,'" I point out. "Five good cops. Leaving grieving families behind. And six misguided kids died, too. Leaving grieving parents and siblings."

"That's *exactly* why Weather opposed violence against people. Those were tragedies. No question. Real human loss. And the fallout from those tragedies did just what Weather always feared. Overshadowed the many creative political statements Weather made, while hurting no one. Weather was once a serious political force. Accelerating change through creative violence that discredited the authorities. Forcing people to rethink their views about Vietnam. But in the end, because the press could not let go of those three tragedies, Weather's legacy was tarnished. Even people on the Left blame Weather for propelling the country into the Reagan era."

"Were *you* a member of the Weather Underground?"

Sheila purses her lips. "The attorney-client privilege gives *you*, Mr. Fisher—David—as the client, the presumption that everything we say here is confidential. I can't tell anyone what you say to me today, unless you authorize me to. But the attorney-client privilege does not give *me*, the attorney, any protection. You can tell anyone you want anything I say to you. So I'm not sure it's real *smart* of me to answer that question. Especially since my client is a journalist."

"How 'bout *off the record*?"

"Off the record, yes, I was a member of the Weather Underground."

"You joined with your close friend, Rachel Clark?"

"Off the record, yes. We were both recruited in the fall of 1969. Different cells though."

"And you helped Rachel elude the authorities after the Law School bombing?"

Sheila hangs fire. "I can't answer that, Mr. Fisher. Er—David. Not even *off* the record."

"Fair enough. But you can tell me about her daughter, Sarah, can't you?"

Sheila looks surprised I know about Sarah. And wary. "What about Sarah?"

"You helped raise her?"

Sheila hangs fire again. But she can't really blow me off. Her newest client. "The commune where I lived, on Packard Street, did care for an abandoned child. Named Sarah."

"From her birth in May or June of 1970 until—when?"

"Until the commune dissolved in 1976."

"What happened to six-year-old Sarah in 1976?"

"She moved to Europe."

"By herself?"

"Of course not. One of the commune members took over primary care for Sarah."

"Who had legal custody of Sarah?"

"A member of our commune."

"What about her grandparents? Ray and Ruth Clark."

"Never claimed her."

"Were they ever given a *chance* to claim her?"

"Not really," Sheila admits. "Rachel didn't want her parents to have her child."

"Was Rachel living at your commune on Packard Street?"

"Of course not. Rachel was far from Ann Arbor. Squad 47 was watching us all like hawks. They would have known if we were harboring a fugitive, Mr.—er, David."

"I know. It's just—well, the mother-daughter bond is so strong. It must have been very hard for Rachel Clark to stay away from her infant daughter in Ann Arbor."

"I suppose it was," Sheila says. Evenly. *Too* evenly. Like she's suppressing emotion.

"Especially since Rachel Clark never threw a bomb at anyone," I say.

"Never fired a gun at anyone, either," Sheila says.

"Did Rachel Clark advocate violence against people?"

"Absolutely not. That was all Paul. Rachel opposed violence against any living thing."

"But she went along for the ride? With her boyfriend?"

"Literally. And she's been paying the price for that ride ever since."

"Did she know Zimmerman and Brown were bringing guns that day?"

"Probably. But did she know they'd be stupid enough to *use* them? Certainly not."

"She could have refused to go unless the guns stayed home."

"Yeah. But little boys like their guns. Makes their little dicks get hard."

I try not to grin. But I can't help it. Sheila's so fuddy-duddy looking. My fifty-four-year-old corporate lawyer. Talking like—well, *like me!*

Sheila smiles, too. "Pardon my language. But Rachel had no *power* in that relationship. That's why Weather would have kicked Paul out. We didn't allow men to *own* women. But Paul owned Rachel. Mind, body, and soul. You remember the slogan 'Peace Now?'"

"Yeah. Sure."

"Some radicals did a parody poster. To depict the idea that violence might be needed to win peace. A picture of a gun. With 'Piece Now' underneath. P-I-E-C-E, instead of P-E-A-C-E."

"Clever."

"Paul went that one better. He took a picture of Rachel's naked ass. Slapped it over the gun in the poster. 'Piece Now.' That was his view of Rachel. His *piece*. Of ass. And she put up with that. So when it came time for his plan to hit the Law School, yes, she went along. For the ride."

"Well, she did a little more than *that*," I say. "She drove two gun-toting punks over to the Law School. In a van that must have reeked of gasoline. So they could get out and throw firebombs. At a particular office. Where the lights were on. Meaning it was occupied. By a particular person. Whose views they hated."

"Yes," Sheila says. Again, *very* evenly.

"What is throwing a firebomb at an occupied office? If not violence against a person?"

"Legally, you're probably right," Sheila says. Spoken like a true lawyer. "But as a practical matter, people almost never die in fire bombings. Unless the bomb lands in someone's lap. Otherwise, when the bombs go in one side of the room, the people just go out the other side."

"Unless they're *trapped* inside."

"True," Sheila concedes. "But Rachel did the recon on that building. She knew Pembroke Watkins had an easy escape route. Out his office door."

How does Sheila know what recon Rachel Clark did on the Law School?

"Did you talk to Rachel Clark before the attempted bombing?"

"No—I meant—" Sheila flushes. "I don't want to talk about this. Even *off* the record."

"I'm no threat to you, Sheila. You're my lawyer." I give her my best smile. But Sheila does not look at all convinced.

"In fact," I continue, "I'm no threat to *anyone*. All I want is a story. A major story. To launch my new magazine. What'd we decide to call it?"

"*Liberal Voices*."

"Right. So let's do this. I'll tell you a story. You don't even have to talk, Sheila. Except to tell me if any of my facts are wrong. Okay?"

Sheila nods. But still doesn't look happy.

"Paul Zimmerman wanted to burn down the Law School. To make a symbolic statement. Against the System. But he also wanted to kill Pembroke Watkins. Rachel Clark didn't like that part. But she was just nineteen. And in love. So she didn't rock the boat. Paul told Rachel it was *her job* to make sure Watkins was trapped in his office. By wedging some pennies under the door."

"I never heard anything about pennies," Sheila says. "Or trapping Watkins in his office."

"Didn't happen. But it was clearly Zimmerman's *plan*. The cops found two stacks of pennies. Right outside Watkins's office. With Rachel Clark's fingerprints all over 'em. No *other* reason for those pennies to be in that particular spot, with those particular fingerprints."

"Maybe Rachel dropped them," Sheila says. "When she was fleeing."

"No. She fled out *the basement* of the Law School. Not the third floor. Where Watkins's office was. And the pennies were *neatly stacked* on the third floor. Not dropped accidentally."

"So she was supposed to trap Watkins in his office—*with pennies*? I don't get it."

I stare hard at Sheila. Trying to figure out if this is *really* new information for Sheila. She's *very* convincing. If Sheila's really Rachel Clark, she's a great actress. On the other hand, if she's really *not* Rachel Clark, Sheila might well have spent her freshman year at Michigan engaged in more mature pursuits than I. So I explain about "pennying" someone into a room.

"And what those pennies in the hall really mean," I continue, "is that you and I finally *agree* on something."

"What's that?"

"Rachel Clark was innocent."

"*Morally* she was innocent," Sheila says. "But legally—"

"*Legally* she was innocent, too."

"How?" Sheila asks. "Rachel was part of a conspiracy. To commit fire-bombing. Murder, too, if you're right about the purpose of the pennies. She drove the bombers there. In a van which, as you said, reeked of gasoline. So she knew what was going down. And in the course of executing the conspiracy, a cop was shot and killed. Legally, that means *all the conspirators* are guilty of felony murder. Not just the one who shot the gun. *Everyone* in the conspiracy."

"Except *not* anyone who *withdrew* from the conspiracy, before the cop got shot. Which Rachel did. When she *disobeyed* Zimmerman. And set those pennies down in the hall. Instead of wedging them under Watkins's door. She *withdrew* from the conspiracy. And never rejoined it."

"But Rachel was the getaway driver," Sheila protests.

"But Rachel never actually drove anyone away. She was *in* the conspiracy when she drove them *to* the Law School. But she *withdrew* from the conspiracy when she stacked the pennies in the hall. Disobeying an order is a clear, unambiguous act of withdrawal."

"Rachel was sitting behind the wheel of the van when Dale Hunter was shot."

"But after disobeying Zimmerman about the pennies, Rachel committed no act *in furtherance of* the conspiracy. She had to go somewhere. So she went back down and sat in the van. But that's *all* she did. If she'd actually driven them away, or even *turned the key in the ignition*, it would be a different case. But that didn't happen. Her former co-conspirators died out on the sidewalk. Before Rachel ever did *anything* to signify that she was rejoining their conspiracy."

Dimly I realize I'm enjoying this legal argument. As if I *miss* being a lawyer. Weird.

"Rachel ran away," Sheila points out. "That's evidence of guilt, isn't it?"

"Yes. But it's only *rebuttable* evidence. Easily rebutted here. There's tons of innocent reasons for a nineteen-year-old in those circumstances to run. Flight alone doesn't prove Rachel Clark was guilty of first-degree felony murder. And there's *nothing else* to prove it, either."

Sheila gazes out the window. She's out of arguments. She can see I'm right. And she looks almost—troubled. By the news that Rachel Clark might have been, in a strictly legal sense, innocent all these years. "Your mother is right, David," Sheila says at last. "You really *should* be a lawyer."

"But instead I'm a reporter. Who badly wants to tell a story. Which you can help me tell."

"How?"

"Arrange for me to interview Rachel Clark."

Sheila flushes. And begins spluttering protestations.

So I hold both my hands up. Like a traffic cop at a busy intersection.

"Hear me out," I say. "Don't talk. Except to tell me if any of my facts are wrong, okay?"

Sheila nods. Again.

"Rachel Clark's daughter, Sarah, is in Ann Arbor," I say. "Right now. Works at a strip club. Raven LaGrow is trying to find Sarah. *You* want to find her, too."

I raise an eyebrow as I make this accusation. But Sheila doesn't stop me.

"Because one of you took custody of Sarah back in 1976. And raised her."

"No," Sheila says. "Wasn't me. Wasn't Raven, either."

"Who then?"

"Amy."

"Amy *Pierce*?" I say, realizing that this confirms the truth of the information I got last night from Sarah Watts at Déjà Vu—'that's Sarah *Pierce* you want.'

"Yes."

"Okay, but you and Raven both want to find Sarah now. Because you think Sarah knows where her mom is. And you're worried Sarah may rat her mom out to Greg Hunter. For the reward."

No argument from Sheila here.

"Which means time is running short. I don't want to see Rachel Clark arrested. I just want to *interview* her. Give her a platform. Let her state her case. Explain her innocence."

"Rachel doesn't believe she's innocent," Sheila says. "For thirty-five years, everyone has told her—even her friends—that she's guilty. Of first-degree felony murder."

I stare at Sheila Nyman. Is she secretly Rachel Clark? Sadness and guilt are written all over her face. Could be the sad guilt of the perp. Or just the sad guilt of the perp's best friend.

Of course, I don't have to figure it out right now. Because Sheila's fingerprints are all over the legal documents spread out in front of us. The incorporation papers for my new rag. *Liberal Voices*. Papers I'll take straight to Hunter. For fingerprint analysis.

"Well then," I reply, "it's time the whole story gets told. Then Rachel can gauge the public reaction. From a safe distance. While I get what I want. I won't lie to you, Sheila. Like anyone, I have my selfish motives. I'll be getting the best possible launch for my new magazine."

"The FBI would hit you with a subpoena the day *Liberal Voices* hits the news stands."

"Let 'em. A subpoena will just boost sales."

"But then you'll have to tell them where Rachel is."

"By the time the rag hits the stands, I'll make sure I have no idea where Rachel is."

"Then they'll force you to identify the go-between. The person who arranged for you to meet Rachel—i.e., *me*."

"I'll claim reporter's privilege."

"You'll lose that claim."

"Maybe. If I do, then I'll claim attorney-client privilege."

"You lost me," Sheila says. "How would attorney-client privilege apply?"

"You guessed my dirty little secret a while back. I *am* an attorney. Inactive. But I still have my ticket," I lie. "So. You refer Rachel Clark to me *for legal advice*. On surrender issues. That way, I'm not obliged to turn her in. And I'm not obliged to disclose the referring attorney, either. I just have to pay an extra hundred dollars in Bar dues. To get back on active status."

"And while she's receiving your legal advice, you'll interview her?"

"No rule against that."

"But *publication* of the interview would clearly *waive* the attorney-client privilege."

"Not if the interview was in a *separate conversation* from the attorney-client chat."

Sheila chews on one of her fingers. Nervously. "You've got it all figured out, don't you?"

I shrug. Try to look modest. But actually I'm very pleased with this clever little plan I've just cooked up on the spot. Even though my disbarment means, in truth, I could never be Rachel Clark's lawyer. But who cares? The goal here is just to get the interview.

"I wonder, though, if you really know what the hell you're doing," Sheila says.

Not exactly the ringing vote of confidence I feel my clever little plan deserves.

"This one time, Sheila, I do. Think it over. You'll see I'm right. Once you're satisfied, arrange for me to meet with Rachel Clark. Anytime. Anyplace. Any arrangements she wants. Any *guarantees* she wants. So she can be sure I'm not bringing the cops with me. And then she can tell her story. And correct the record. About herself. And about the Weathermen, too."

Sheila Nyman agrees to think it over. Gives me her home phone number. So I can call tomorrow tonight. After she's had time to think it over.

I decide not to grill Sheila about Melanie McGeetchy today. Why rock the boat? This interview is going so much better than I'd expected.

I reach for the pile of legal papers we worked on earlier. The papers incorporating my new magazine. With Sheila Nyman's fingerprints all over them. Along with my own fingerprints.

But Sheila throws me a curve. Sweeps up all the papers. Insists on *keeping* them all. So Sue Webber can organize them in a binder. Which Sheila says is part of what I'm paying for. My protestations fall on deaf ears. Sheila says everything will be ready for me on *Friday*.

*Fuck!* Somehow, I walk out of Sheila's office empty-handed. With nothing that Sheila touched. Except my hand. When she shook my hand good-bye.

On the way out, I introduce myself to Naomi Williams. The paralegal who will be working on my incorporation matters. I'm glad to see sad-eyed Naomi is still in town, of course. Don't want any of my suspects fleeing. But Naomi gets summoned to the telephone before I can even begin to interview her. Much less think up a way to get *Naomi's* fingerprints on something.

So I swing by Janet Fickel's desk. But her chair is vacant. The picture of her with big John is standing up. *Did I forget to turn that picture up again, before scampering out last night?*

Sue Webber notices me staring at Janet's picture. Tells me Janet just left. For lunch.

\* \* \*

To my relief, Janet's standing outside the gas station at the corner of Main and Miller. Smoking. And waiting for me.

"Sorry I'm late," I say.

"You're not late. I came early. To smoke. And get away from all the craziness."

"In the office? What craziness?"

Janet drops her cigarette on the ground. Steps on it. Viciously twists the toe of her high-heeled shoe back and forth across it. To rub out the flame.

"Oh. My God. You don't want to know."

"Sure I do. But we have an appointment to keep. Let's walk and talk." Which we do.

"Lane was completely out of control today. Absolutely paranoid."

"Over what?"

Janet laughs. "I started it. Though I didn't mean to. When I got to work, one of the pictures on my desk was face down. I *know* I didn't leave it that way. And we had no cleaners last night. So I mentioned it to Sue. No big deal. But Sue mentioned it to Lane. And Lane went *nuts*."

"Whaddya mean, 'nuts?'" Hopefully Janet thinks it's our *walk* causing my face to flush.

"Interrogating me about the picture. Like I was a witness in a deposition. What time did I leave last night? Who was there when I left? Was I absolutely *certain* the picture was upright when I left? Then George tells Lane he was working late last night. And thought he heard some funny noises. So Lane and George start looking all around. To see if anything's missing."

"*Was* anything missing?"

"No. But they found some things that didn't belong. *Bugs*. In the conference room."

Oh shit! Since we're walking, Janet's not looking at my face. Luckily.

"Insects?" I ask disingenuously.

Janet laughs. "No, *surveillance* bugs. Which *really* sent Lane off the deep end. For him, it's *Watergate* all over again. He thinks his *political opponents* bugged us. So he had Sue hire Burns Security. To sweep the office. While you were in with Sheila. Turns out our *phones* were tapped, too! So now Lane's hired Burns Security to guard the office. 24/7!"

"So even though Lane's paranoid, it turns out his opponents really *are* out to get him?"

"Maybe. But I'm not convinced this has anything to do with politics. I mean, do you think anyone really cares that much who's the mayor of Ann Arbor? To go around bugging an office? Plus—if you were gonna bug one of the candidates, why *Lane*? He has no real chance of winning."

"What *else* could it be? If not politics?"

"I think it's one of our *cases*."

"Hmm," I say. Sounding distinctly like Graham Hancock. Who's on my mind right now. Because I'm going to have to report the loss of our surveillance equipment. Which Graham won't like one bit.

Janet and I reach the studio. Get our pictures taken. It's fun. We strike some corny poses. For a few minutes I almost forget about my bugs being discovered at Davis & Nyman.

The proofs will take three weeks. But the photographer gives me some test shots he took with a Polaroid. And Janet seems truly touched. That I cared enough to bother with all this.

After the pix, we only have time for a quick bite. Not the easiest thing to find on Main Street anymore. Since Main Street's now so much more upscale than it was when I lived here.

But Janet suggests the Parthenon—the closest thing Main Street has to an old-fashioned lunch-counter place. Where she's apparently a regular. The staff fawns all over Janet. And we get great service. In and out in twenty minutes.

But the lunch counter affords no privacy. So I can't ask Janet any of the questions I've been dying to ask her. Since I saw those divorce papers on her computer last night.

However, Janet does agree to meet me for dinner tonight. At the West End Grill.

As we leave, I contrive to hand her the corny love letter I wrote on the plane yesterday.

* * *

After lunch, I take a cab to Ypsilanti. And enjoy a tearful reunion with my rental car. Which is still there. In the parking lot across the street from Déjà Vu. With all my equipment still in the trunk.

To keep anyone from breaking into my room again, I change hotels. To the Bell Tower. I clean my tail carefully. Coming and going. And for extra security, I put my laptop and camera in the Bell Tower's hotel safe. At the front desk. But I take my surveillance equipment with me. Just in case.

With three hours still to kill before I see Janet again, I decide to put Elaine's idea into action. Break into my suspects' houses. Get their fingerprints.

I start by driving over to Sheila's. On Devonshire. Not far from Raven's.

Unfortunately, a teen-aged boy is sitting in Sheila's family room. Slouched into the couch. Watching TV. At 2:15. Damn the public schools! They let kids out way too early these days.

So I drive over to the Davis's house on Martin Place. For once, my timing is perfect. A Burns Security truck is parked outside. Yet two minutes after I arrive, two Burns guys emerge from the house. Talking on the front porch with Camille. It's clear they've just swept the house. For bugs and taps and cameras. And found nothing. Because I haven't been here. *Yet.*

The Burns guys drive off. I figure now's a great time to interview Camille. Away from Hubbie Dearest. But before I get both feet out of my car, I see Camille's Volvo driving off, too.

I could follow Camille. But what would I learn from that? Camille's probably off to a political meeting. Or one of her do-gooder causes. Or the grocery store.

In the meantime, no one's home at Casa Davis. So I put on my gray wig and glasses. In case any nosy neighbors are watching. Grab my surveillance kit. Stroll up the front walk. Ring the bell. Then mosey around to the back. Where I'm chagrined to find my hands trembling. And my stomach doing one-and-a-half gainers.

Apparently the near-miss with George Robertson almost catching me at Davis & Nyman last night is still impacting my nerves. So I take a few deep breaths. Block out the negative image of me skulking down the Davis & Nyman stairs while George was sitting in the crapper. Pull my latex gloves on over my trembling hands. Pick the backdoor lock with my pick gun. And enter Casa Davis.

Unlike Raven's sterile, neat-as-a-pin, pretentiously-decorated house, Casa Davis is a real *home*. The furniture is soft and well-worn. Every available surface is cluttered with kids' junk. And the decorations are family photos and inexpensive arts-and-crafts stuff. Casa Davis looks like an Ann Arbor version of my own house in Florida.

I tap their phones. Bug the master bedroom. Bug the kitchen, too. The dining room. And the study. But I see no need to deploy any video cameras. No illicit sex *here*, I presume.

My heart is pounding hard. Down the street a car door slams. I jump halfway out of my skin. Man, I'm a nervous wreck! I wasn't kidding when I said I've grown too old for tabloid work.

Better limit myself to a *quick* search of the house. That's all my aging heart can handle.

The tiny basement is claustrophobic. Only one way out. The stairs back up to the kitchen. And the basement's packed with junk. Would take *days* to search it all. Empty luggage. Old furniture. Strollers. Cribs. Stacks of kids' games. Piles of old books. Heaps of boxes.

I sample the boxes. Kids' clothing. Adults' summer clothing. More books. And old files. Some are "Davis & Nyman" files. From the nineties. Others are "Davis & Associates" files. From the eighties. It would take *weeks* to go through them all. Not worth the trouble.

Plus I'm way too nervous down here. With only one way out.

So I go back upstairs to the ground floor study. Where I breathe a little easier. And feel much calmer. Cuz there's an easy exit to the backyard—if Camille returns unexpectedly.

The study is decorated like the conference room at Davis & Nyman. Except instead of Malcolm and Martin, here we've got the *real* radicals. Che and Castro. Mao. And old Vlad Lenin.

You don't see *those* guys much anymore. Not even in Beijing or Moscow.

I start with the files in Camille's desk. My God. Janet wasn't kidding. Camille must belong to *fifty* do-gooder organizations. All with a left-wing bent. She's got reams of crap. Brochures. Agendas. Leaflets. Position papers. Speeches.

But then I find her personal files. Including a medical file. Turns out Camille's had *major* work. She was in a car accident. 1985. The end of her Quaker Oats job. Broke her hip. Her foot. Her arm. And a dozen bones in her face. Major reconstructive facial surgery. I *knew* it!

I start digging deeper. Hoping for a photo of what Camille looked like before the 1985 surgery. But then I hear the damn garage door going up. Shit! Camille's back.

I replace the files. Grab a glass paperweight off her desk. And beat it out the back door.

Outside, I crouch down behind the garage. Watch Camille go into the kitchen. With two teenagers. She must have just picked them up from school.

Don't kids have after-school activities anymore?

After a few minutes, they all leave the kitchen. I see a light go on in the upstairs bathroom. So I walk quickly down the driveway. Staying close to the house. So they can't see me.

Once I get past the house, I walk down the driveway to my car. As casually as possible. Given that my heart is now pounding over two hundred beats a minute.

I get away. Unstopped. And as near as I can tell, undetected.

But *not* unscathed. My second near-miss escape in less than twenty-four hours leaves me trembling far worse than the first.

I take the paperweight over to Cliff Bryant. Cliff has it dusted for prints. No luck. No usable prints. The whole process takes twenty minutes. Yet when Cliff hands the paperweight back to me, I see my hands are *still* shaking. Cliff sees it, too. Raises an eyebrow. I shrug.

I gotta find another way to get information on these people. No more break-ins. That's it. I'm just plain too old for the excitement.

So I drive back to my new hotel room. At the Bell Tower.

Where I reach in my travel bag. And proceed to put on a skirt.

You heard me. A skirt.

Don't worry. This is *not* me getting in touch with my feminine side. (If I even have one.)

I've got a new plan. I'm going to pose as Melanie McGeetchy.

One of the few good things about being middle-aged is that now I can pass myself off as a woman. I've done this a few times before. Sure, I'm a little too tall.

And way too broad-shouldered. But you know how middle-aged men and middle-aged women all sort of start looking the same? The men are growing boobs and pear-shaped bodies. The women are growing facial hair and big calves. So I take advantage. I wear flats. Put on a loose-shouldered woman's business jacket, so my actual shoulders look like they're the padding. And cake a ton of makeup on. To soften my facial hair. Sure, I'm no Janet Fickel. But in the hotel mirror, I almost convince myself I'm not a bad-looking woman. *If* you like your women 6'1", 180.

At the University of Michigan Registrar's Office, I slump so as not to look too tall. Keep my mannish hands behind my back as much as possible. And put on a falsetto voice. I claim to be Melanie McGeetchy. And ask for a copy of "my" transcript. They hand me a form. And direct me to a nearby desk to fill it out. No problem. From Sheila Nyman's trust file, I've got Melanie's Social Security number. Birth date. Mother's maiden name. And most important, a copy of her signature. So I am able to trace a passable impression of Melanie's signature onto the Registrar's form. Even though my hands are *still* shaking.

So I get Melanie's transcript.

Turns out Melanie wasn't much of a student. She started in 1968. Same as Rachel Clark. Finished one year. But dropped out in the fall semester of 1969. Same as Rachel Clark.

The only other information on the transcript is Melanie's high school: Ann Arbor Pioneer. And Melanie's last known address. From her sophomore year. 432 Packard Street in Ann Arbor.

I go to the public library. Get an old U of M student directory for 1969. Turns out they *all* lived at 432 Packard. Rachel Clark. Melanie McGeetchy. Camille Jensen—now known as Camille Davis. And *Amy Pierce*.

The only name I *don't* see in the 1969 student directory is Sheila Nyman.

I want to go back to the U of M Registrar to ask for *Sheila's* transcript. Find out if there ever was such a person at U of M.

I've got Sheila's Social, birthdate, mother's maiden name, and a signature exemplar.

But can I convince the *same clerk* on the *same afternoon* that I'm a *different* 6'1," 180-pound woman? Doubtful. I'm a very good bullshitter. But I'm no David Garrick.

David Garrick was the greatest actor of the eighteenth century. Probably the best ever. Here's how good Garrick was. He's stuck in Brighton with a buddy. Needs to get back to London ASAP. He finds the Brighton–London stage coach. Four-seater. He and his buddy buy two seats. And ask the coachman how soon they can leave. "Not 'til all four seats are filled," the coachman replies. Garrick produces cash to buy the other two fares. "Nope," the coachman says. "Can't leave 'til I have four *passengers*." Rational argument has no impact on this phlegmatic coachman. Won't take Garrick's cash. And he ain't leavin' 'til he's got two more passengers in the stage. So Garrick and his friend enter the stagecoach cab by the door directly beneath the coachman. Garrick then promptly sneaks out the other door on the far side of the cab. Circles round the back. Approaches the phlegmatic coachman again. *No change of clothes, no disguise*. But Garrick changes his voice and his mannerisms to such an extent the coachman doesn't recognize him. Sells Garrick the third fare. Garrick goes in the coachman's side of the cab again. Sneaks out the far side again. Circles round the back of the cab. Again, *no change of clothes, no disguise*. But again, Garrick changes his voice and mannerisms to such an extent, the coachman sells him the *fourth* fare. And off they go.

*That's* a damn fine actor!

Unfortunately, I lack David Garrick's thespian skills. So I can't see how I'm going to fool the U of M Registrar into thinking I'm Sheila Nyman, the same day I was Melanie McGeetchy.

Instead I change back into male clothing. And drive over to 432 Packard.

It's a classic run-down student house. Beer bottles in the front bushes. Semi-rotting sofa on the ramshackle front porch. And two very stoned dudes on the sofa, smoking weed.

"Hey," I say.

"Hey," one of the stoned dudes on the sofa responds.

"I'm looking for Rachel Clark."

"Don't know her."

"Kinda figured. She lived here thirty-five years ago. You know if this house used to be some kind of commune?"

"Yeah, I heard it was," one of the dudes says. "Back in the seventies."

"You know who owns it now?"

"Abdul bin Wasim. Our landlord."

"You got a number for him?"

To my surprise, the two stoned dudes break up laughing at this question. "Yeah," one finally manages, between hysterical sobs. "Inmate #54321. Serving five-to-ten at Jackson."

"For . . . ?"

"Selling crack here, man. Don't you read the papers? This was Ann Arbor's leading crack house, dude. Just last year."

Next stop: Ann Arbor Pioneer High. No disguise needed. I locate the yearbook advisor. Ms. Wilkins. Nice-looking young black lady. I ask Ms. Wilkins if they keep a collection of old yearbooks. They do. She gets out the 1968 yearbook. And there's Melanie McGeetchy.

Does Melanie look like Sheila Nyman? Maybe. Maybe not.

I pay particular attention to the eyes. But I really can't tell. Melanie's seventeen or eighteen in the photo. Sheila's fifty-four in the Davis & Nyman brochure. Ever look at pictures of *yourself* taken when you were seventeen and fifty-four? Do *you* look like the same person?

This exercise reminds me to compare the Rachel Clark high school yearbook photo with the pix I have of Sheila Nyman, Naomi Williams, and Camille Davis. Same result. Even paying particular attention to the eyes, I can't say that any of them at fifty-four looks like Rachel Clark at seventeen.

\* \* \*

I meet Janet Fickel at the West End Grill. A high-end restaurant downtown.

Janet looks fabulous. Still wearing the red jacket she wore to our photo shoot. So I can't ogle those delicious big breasts under the loose jacket. But her long slender legs are to die for.

Several men in the restaurant are checking Janet out. Most are covert about it. But one gets busted by his wife. Who bops him on the head with her purse. Janet pretends not to notice.

That's when it hits me. Janet Fickel is my trophy date. While I truly hope and believe she's also *more* than that, there's no denying she's quite a sight in her tight little skirt. No denying that, by taking her out to a crowded restaurant, I'm flaunting my stacked little dreamboat.

Dimly I recall various times I've envied other guys flaunting hot dates. Airhead celebs with bimbo starlets. Denise Maxwell's husband at our twentieth high school reunion. And one time when I was a teenager at a ski lodge with my parents, and this college dude at the next table was groping his hot date in her miniskirt. My parents muttered disapproval. But I just wanted to know, *how do I become that guy*? He seemed so free. Doing exactly as he pleased.

So now at last, in advanced middle-age, I've become that guy. But is that all this little romance really is? A chance for me to live out some vague fantasy of being a libertine stud?

I admit I'm not the world's most profound person. But I truly hope my magnetic attraction to Janet is based on something deeper, something more romantic, than just the thrill of her great good looks. Because if it's not, I'm even more pathetic than I've ever realized before.

Janet looks nervously around the West End Grill. "This really isn't my kind of place."

"You wanna go somewhere else?"

"No, it's okay."

But for a while it doesn't seem to be. I order champagne. To calm her down. And food.

An exceptionally loud motorcycle roars by outside. Janet looks almost wistful. Staring out the window at the empty street left behind by the vanished racing machine.

"You ever ride a motorcycle?" I ask.

Janet rolls her eyes. "John and I used to ride every weekend."

"I'd love to see you perched up on a motorcycle."

"We were pretty wild. But those days are gone."

"Why?"

Janet shrugs. "We don't enjoy our time together anymore."

"Well, I'm nobody's idea of a psychologist, Janet. Or a marriage counselor. But if John can't have sex anymore, it's gotta be hard to maintain intimacy."

"It's not just the sex. It's—we've changed. Since our carefree motorcycle days."

"Have you ever thought about just filing for divorce?"

Janet's eyes open wide. Like she can't believe how uncannily *prescient* my guesses are.

"Yes, I have. I even wrote up the papers myself a few months ago."

"And?"

"John talked me out of it. He even agreed to go to the doctor."

"And?"

"And nothing. The doctor wanted John to produce a sperm sample. Oh. My God. John was such a baby about it. Just wouldn't do it."

"Well, in fairness to John, it's not all that easy. To jack off into a cup. I had to do it myself once. For a fertility test. I *missed* the damn cup."

Janet laughs.

"Laugh if you like. But I consider myself one of the world's foremost experts at jacking off. *Lots* of practice. Over the years. And yet even *I* couldn't do it into a cup."

"John said the same thing. More or less. So I offered to suck him off and then spit it into the cup for him. And *still* he wouldn't do it!"

Believe me, Gentle Reader, I *rarely* get to engage in candid conversation about oral sex like this. *Never before* in my whole life, to be honest. But what would you do in my place? Tell Janet to *behave herself?* Hell, no. You'd *keep the ball rolling*, right?

"How could any man in his right mind turn down an offer like that—from you?"

Janet shrugs. "Beats the shit outta me. John always said my blow jobs were the best. But I couldn't talk him into giving the sample. And the whole subject just kinda died away."

"Except by then he'd talked you outta the divorce?"

"Yeah. And instead it's just been one long argument the past three months."

"What do you argue about?"

"What *don't* we argue about? Take this afternoon. John calls me at work. Wants me to come watch him shoot this weekend. Like he always does. I say no thanks. Like I always do. He demands to know what I'll be doing instead. I refuse to say. And from there, it's all downhill."

"What *will* you be doing this weekend?"

"I have no plans," Janet says. "Like always."

"Would you like to spend some time with me?"

"Doing what?"

"Drinking champagne?"

Janet laughs. "Okay."

"And how 'bout lunch tomorrow?"

"Can't. After I was so vague about the weekend, John insisted *we* have lunch tomorrow."

"How 'bout lunch Thursday?"

"Can't do that either. I've got a dentist appointment."

I push my lower lip out. In my kid-who-lost-his-homework routine.

Janet laughs. "But Thursday *night* would be fine. If you're interested."

"Oh yes, I'm definitely 'interested.' Did you have a chance to read my letter?"

Janet smiles. "Yes. It was very nice."

"'*Nice?*' That's *all?* Janet, I put my *whole heart* into that letter."

Janet laughs. "I know. That's why it was so nice. I haven't gotten a love letter in ages. I *love* getting love letters."

"How 'bout love *stories?* Do you like hearing those, too?"

"I love to hear love stories."

"Be warned. Mine are not *conventional* love stories. No knights in shining armor. No lovers riding off into the sunset. No dripping syrup. But these are *true* stories. And if you think about it, they're *better* than typical love stories. The way *Dracula* is really the best love story."

"Try me," Janet suggests.

"Okay. First is Branwell Brontë. Promising young painter. In the 1840s. Made a name for himself in his twenties. But he liked the Scotch too much. And he had three younger sisters. Charlotte, Emily, and Anne. Each wrote a novel in *her* twenties. *Jane Eyre, Wuthering Heights*, and I forget the one Anne wrote. Famous novels that far eclipsed big brother Branwell's paintings."

"I read those books in high school. I liked *Wuthering Heights*. The hero— Heathman—"

"Heathcliff."

"Yes. He was what every woman wants. Dark and strong. Full of constant desire for her. And quite the bad boy. But I have to tell you. I hated *Jane Eyre*. Could *not* finish it."

"You're right, as usual. *Wuthering Heights* is great. But *Jane Eyre* is awful damn dull."

"I flunked high school English because of *Jane Eyre*. It was, like, the whole test. "

"Really? You know there's a poem that could have saved you. It's got the whole plot of *Jane Eyre*. Boiled down to just five stanzas. Funny as hell. Goes like this:

My love behaved a bit erratic
Our wedding day brought truth dramatic:
He *had* a wife, mad, in an attic.

I fled! I roamed o'er moor and ditch.
When life had reached its lowest pitch,
An uncle died and left me rich.

I sought my love again, to find
An awful fire his house had mined,
Kippered his wife, and left him blind.

Reader, guess what? I married him.
My cup is filled up to the brim!
Now we are one. We play. We swim.

The power we share defies all pain;
We soar above life's tangled plain,
He Mr. Rochester, me Jane!

Janet's laughing so hard she's almost crying. "You have a poem for *every* occasion!"

"*I* didn't write it. Guy named Maurice Sagoff wrote it."

"Still, it's amazing it stays in your head like that. What a *memory* you have!"

"Well, some people say my memory and I should spend more time in the *real* world."

"Are you kidding? You're *totally* in the real world. That's what's amazing. You talk about poetry as easily as you talk about producing sperm samples. I never met anyone who made poetry seem so real. If I'd had *you* for English, I'd have graduated from high school."

"But then you wouldn't be Janet."

Janet stops laughing. Cocks her head. Easily the sexiest thing any woman has ever done. At least since Anita Ekberg frolicked in that fountain in *La Dolce Vita*.

"See," I continue, "*you're* like Branwell Brontë, Janet. Bursting with life and talent. That never got a chance to express itself. He got suppressed by Scotch. You got suppressed by early pregnancy. So you know what old Branwell did? He had this one great painting he'd done. His best work. Portrait of himself and his three sisters. So when they became famous while he faded, he painted himself out of his own painting. Out of *love for his sisters*. So they wouldn't be dragged down by their association with their drunken brother, the failed artist. Can you imagine? He painted a pillar over himself. The picture hangs today in the National Portrait Gallery in London. It hung there for over a hundred years before X-rays discovered old Branwell hiding under that pillar. How unspeakably sad is that?"

"And you think *your girlfriend's* a sad case, too?"

"No! Not at all, Janet. But you're as hidden from sight as Branwell Brontë under his pillar. Only your pillar is John. Who keeps you hidden from sight because he doesn't want anyone—least of all, you—to know how beautiful and interesting and bursting with life you are."

Janet's eyes tear up again at this. But this time they're not tears of laughter.

We gaze at each other awhile in silence.

The waiter brings the check. I pay.

"I got another sad love story for you. Since I think you liked that one."

Janet smiles. Nods.

"There was another English painter. J.M.W. Turner. Way more successful than Branwell Brontë. But also way ahead of his time. Back in the 1830s Turner was already doing stuff the Impressionists made popular decades later. Paintings of light and fog and mist on the sea. Turner was appointed to give six lectures to the Royal Academy of Art. Very prestigious. But his jealous rivals organized a boycott. It was easy to do. Because lots of people in the 1830s felt Turner was just *too* damn radical. So. Turner shows up to give the first lecture. And *no one's there*. Except Turner's dad. *Imagine!* This huge lecture hall. Seating for thousands. And there's only *one guy* in there. An illiterate laborer. Who doesn't give a fart for art. Who's just there to support his son. So what does Turner do? He stands up at the lectern. And delivers *a two-hour* lecture. To his dad. And no one else. Never bats an eye. Just reads his lecture out into the air! In fact, he gave all six lectures. To an empty hall. Except for his dad. I *love* that!"

"Like your lost causes."

"Exactly! I love that guy—Turner—saying, 'Well, you paid me to give six lectures, so by God, I'll give you six lectures. Even though you've utterly humiliated me with your boycott. Cuz I still love talking about painting. *Even to the air*. And you can never take *that* away from me.'"

"Just like Shoeless Joe," Janet says. "Playing the game he loved, for peanuts. Because he couldn't do anything else."

"Yes!" God, she *is* a discerning little minx. "Just like *me*, too, Janet."

"How—like you?"

"Because I can't do anything else either. Except love you."

Janet stands up. Reaches for my hand. Pulls me up out of my chair.

Outside we walk back toward her car. Still parked at Davis & Nyman. I choose for our walk a long alley that runs parallel to Main Street. It's *not* a romantic alley. Overflowing garbage cans. Soggy cardboard boxes. A sleeping wino. And more garbage. But it *is* secluded.

I start gabbling some more about J.M.W. Turner. Janet steps in front of me. Kisses me full on the lips. In mid-sentence. Kisses me long and energetically.

"Was that a spontaneous burst of passion?" I ask. "Or did you just want to shut me up?"

"Both."

"So all I have to do is start jabbering about English painters if I want to get kissed?"

Janet smiles. Kisses me again. I steer her against a brick wall. She climbs up on me. She's about four inches off the ground. I'm supporting her against the wall with my hands under her thighs. While we kiss. Then she jumps up higher. Wraps her legs around my love handles. Good thing Janet only weighs 115. My weight training lately has not been all that it should be.

In this position—up against the wall—Janet's neck is very close to my lips. She does not try to stop me from kissing her neck. She starts moaning again. And kissing *my* neck.

"Thursday night," Janet says. Breathing unevenly.

"Ummn," I say. Chasing Janet's neck. Still without protest.

"John has to go to Indiana for a business dinner. Won't be home 'til real late."

I stop nibbling on Janet's neck. Look straight in her eyes. From a distance of two inches.

"We could go to a hotel then," Janet says.

"We could go to a hotel *now*," I point out. "They're open on Tuesdays, too."

Janet smiles. But shakes her head. "I need a little more time. To be sure."

"You mean there's a chance you'll change your mind?"

"A chance."

"Is there anything I can do to make it a very *slim* chance?"

"Just keep doing what you're doing."

So I do. Later, we make arrangements. To meet Thursday after work. At 5:15. At the Sheraton. (The Campus Inn is not an option. Nor is the Bell Tower. I am far too friendly with hotel staff to maintain the fiction, in front of Janet, that I live in Ann Arbor.)

"I'm okay with waiting until Thursday," I say. "On one condition."

"What's that?"

"The weatherman says it's going to turn even colder tomorrow."

"I saw that. Yesterday was probably the last warm day of the year."

"Exactly," I say. "So if I have to wait until Thursday, I don't want to get to the hotel and find you all bundled up. Like Nanook of the North. What will you wear when it turns cold?"

"You'll have no complaints." Janet's face turns mischievous. "Of course, if you *like* the Nanook-of-the-North look, you could always take *Naomi* instead of me to the hotel."

"Naomi *Williams*? Why Naomi?"

"As soon as it turns cold, Naomi gets all bundled up. She brings out the whole works—a giant parka, hat, mittens—and this truly awful scarf she has. Black-and-white checkers. At least thirty years old. Wait 'til you see it. It's the rattiest scarf you've ever seen. And she will *not* part with it. Last year Sue and

I bought her a really nice new scarf. For Christmas. But Naomi never wears it. Just stays with the checkered scarf. Every day. All winter long."

Whoa! Obviously the checkered scarf brings to mind Alan Singer. Telling me about the HEW protest. Could be a coincidence. Or it could just mean Naomi Williams was in the Weather Underground in the seventies. But then again, it could also mean Naomi Williams is Rachel Clark.

The reporter in me sees an opening. To ask Janet to help me collect Naomi's fingerprints. And Sheila's, too. My supposed purpose in staying here in Ann Arbor. But what if Janet takes offense? Accuses me again of only using her for information? Rescinds her hotel invitation?

I can't risk that. *Fuck work!* I'll just have to find another way to get those fingerprints.

"And what did Naomi get *you* for Christmas?" I ask, covering up my momentary silence.

"I don't remember."

"Well, I hope you remember *my* Christmas present when next fall rolls around!"

"What are you getting me?"

"Case of champagne, for starters."

Janet laughs. "You figure it was the champagne that got me thinking about a hotel?"

"Wasn't it?"

Janet shakes her head. "No, but you can believe that if you want. Because I never mind getting champagne."

"So what was it . . . that got you thinking?"

"*You*, David Fisher. Just you."

At Janet's car we kiss goodnight. Intensely. Rubbing against her, my balls begin to ache. I feel like Warren Beatty in *Splendor in the Grass*. I'm always kissing Janet goodnight. With blue balls. When what I really want to do—please pardon my French—is bang her silly. Right now.

Finally Janet drives away. I start walking back to the Bell Tower.

I pass a black guy. Whom I saw before. He passed through the alley when Janet and I were really going at it.

The black guy looks me in the eye. "Whoo-ee. That's a nice little woman you got there."

"Thanks," I mutter.

"So why you goin' home *alone*, man?" He shakes his head at me.

"Beats the shit out of me. Probably the same reason they used to call me Number Zero."

\* \* \*

I sleep badly. I dream about Rachel and Sara. They're caught out in a hurricane. Exposed to the wind and the rain. Crying for Daddy to save them. I want so badly to help them. But they're on an island. And I'm on the shore across the river. And the river is running really fast. And really deep. So each time I resolve to dive in and swim across to them, I chicken out. I point to the raging water. It would be pointless, I say.

But still my children's faces call to me. And their crying is getting worse.

So I close my eyes. And plunge into the roiling waters of the river.

Now I'm buffeted by strong winds. I can't see anything. Can't see my kids. Can't see the island they're on. Can't even see the river. It's all a blur.

I land on a street. No more wind and rain. But no sign of Rachel and Sara either. People are distracting me. With lots of little tasks they want me to do. Graham's there. And Elaine. With more jobs for me.

I keep trying to tell Graham and Elaine I don't have time. I have to go save Rachel and Sara. But they're not listening to me.

Now *Janet's* there. Janet's offering me chocolate. A big chocolate Easter bunny. I take a large bite out of the Easter bunny's head. But then, as I go to take another bite, I see it's not a bunny's head anymore. It's *Sara's* head. And I've taken a huge bite out of my daughter's head.

Sara's not complaining. But she doesn't look too good, either. With a gaping hole in her head. With *my* teeth marks on the edges of the hole.

I wake up in my hotel room. Sweating. And deeply disturbed.

Now I'm no Sigmund Freud. But even an uninsightful tabloid hack like me can figure out what *this* dream was about.

Guilt. The harm I threaten to do to Rachel and Sara. Each time I taste Janet's charms.

*Damn that Delmore Schwartz!* I don't *want* any responsibilities to begin in my dreams.

For once in my life, I want to be totally *ir*responsible. Totally selfish. Like a free radical.

# CHAPTER NINE
# FREE RADICALS

## Wednesday 20 October 2004

After barely making the early train to Chicago, I call the Chicago Public Defender's Office. And ask for Amy Pierce.

"Amy, my name is David Fisher. I urgently need to speak with you today."

"About what?"

"We have a mutual friend who needs your help. I would rather not say her name over this insecure cell phone. Could I meet you for lunch today?"

"I don't eat lunch with men I don't know."

"Okay. Can I just come by your office then? My train gets in at 11:45."

"Alright. I'll meet you here at the office. At noon. But I don't have time to waste."

"I promise I will not waste your time."

Amy Pierce meets me in a cheerless interior interview room. No windows. No decorations. Peeling paint on the walls. Stark translucent lights above. A rickety conference table between us. With the faux-wood Formica peeling off the corners of the table. In strips. Our chairs are sturdier. No wobbles. But not much cushion left, either. The springs beneath my chair's cushion press up hard against my aging haunches. Tough racket, the public defender biz.

Amy Pierce is pushing sixty. Deep wrinkles around her mouth and eyes. About 5'8". Slim, though a little broad in the beam. Crops her silver hair very short. Wears no-nonsense clothes. Flat shoes. Shapeless corduroys. An oversized chambray work shirt, worn over a loose white pullover. No makeup. No jewelry. Zero sex appeal. All work. No play. But her hazel eyes glisten with intelligence. And intensity. Amy Pierce's eyes are, if you'll forgive me, piercing.

"I'm sorry to be so mysterious," I say. "It's about Rachel Clark."

Amy Pierce's chair scrapes the linoleum floor. As she stands up.

"I have nothing to say about Rachel Clark."

I meet Amy's piercing gaze. But stay seated. "I've come from Key West."

Amy's chair scrapes the floor again. As she sits back down. "Who are you, Mr. Fisher?"

"David. Please. I'm a friend of Rachel's. From Ann Arbor, originally."

"I've never heard of you."

"Good. David Fisher is not my only name. But I've heard of you. And I need your help."

"With what?"

"Two things. First, Sarah. Sheila Nyman says Sarah's back in Ann Arbor. Says she needs help. Bad. But Sheila can't find her. I was hoping you might know where Sarah is."

"I don't."

"But you raised her."

"Yes."

I let the dead air hang between us. Hoping to force Amy Pierce to speak more than five words at once. But she hangs tough. Waits me out.

"Sarah doesn't stay in touch?" I ask at last.

"Not really."

"The last time you saw her was—when?"

"Spring of . . . 1999."

"Where was Sarah living then?"

"Toronto."

"Working?"

"Drifting."

"What was the occasion—that brought you together?"

"Sarah wanted money."

"You gave it to her?"

"No."

"Why not?"

"She wouldn't agree to go to detox."

"Detox for—what drug?"

"OC. Oxycontin. Hillbilly heroin."

"How long has Sarah been addicted to Oxycontin?"

"'Bout five years for OC. Before that, it was meth. And before that, coke. All told, Sarah's been on drugs for nineteen years. If she doesn't clean up her act soon, she won't see forty."

"So help me find Sarah," I say, leaning forward. "Before it's too late."

"Are you a drug counselor?"

"No," I admit.

"Then you can't help Sarah Pierce. Only a truly gifted drug counselor can help her."

"But *Rachel* hasn't given up hope for Sarah, has she?"

"Rachel's hope is fueled by guilt," Amy says. "But *I* did all I could for Sarah. More than anyone could ever expect. Even from a natural mother. So I see Sarah as she is. Hopeless."

"You were there all those years, giving Sarah the love Rachel couldn't give her," I say. "So love Sarah now. Help me find her."

"How?"

"Tell me where Sarah would go in Ann Arbor."

"Sarah Pierce is a drifter, Mr. Fish—David. She finds a man, rides him as long as she can. If she can't find a man, she latches on to a woman. Failing that, she lives like any homeless addict. When it's cold, shelters and soup kitchens. When it's warm, parks and trash bins. She steals, too. Any chance she gets. So lots of the time, Sarah's in lock-up. If I were you, I'd start there. The county jail in Ann Arbor. Or ask the cops if they've seen her."

"I didn't know she was this bad off," I say, somberly. "Have you ever known her to—*dance* for a living?"

"You mean a strip club? Used to she did. But Sarah's a little old for that now. And a little too—*strung out*. These days strippers have to look like fashion models. Or they can't get work."

"How'd she choose dancing? Wasn't she born with a cleft foot?"

Amy looks impressed. "You *are* a friend of Rachel's. To know *that*. But yes. The cleft foot was a problem at first. 'Til she got corrective surgery."

"Who paid for that? You? Or Rachel?"

"Neither. We had no money. No insurance. So Sarah got her grandparents to pay for it."

"The Zimmermans?"

"No. The Clarks."

"*Ray and Ruth*? The little people?"

Amy smiles. "Yes. The little people."

"I thought they disowned Rachel."

"They did. But Sarah's very good at—manipulation. She pushed all the right buttons. When it comes to getting cash, Sarah's a real charmer."

"Is there anyone in Ann Arbor Sarah would go see?"

"Not that I know of. We left Ann Arbor when Sarah was six. Never went back."

"You took Sarah to Amsterdam?"

"Yes."

"She lived there with you and Rachel—for a while?"

Amy Pierce nods.

"And then when Rachel fled to Central America, where did ten-year-old Sarah go?"

Bad question. Suspicion fills Amy's piercing hazel eyes. She's searching my eyes. Trying to figure how I know *some* details. But not others.

At last Amy answers. But guardedly again. "Sarah stayed with me. In Amsterdam."

"That must have been so hard. For all of you."

"You can't imagine the pain. The day Rachel left, Sarah locked herself in a closet. Refused to go down to the docks. Refused to say goodbye to her mom. It was—yes. Hard. On us all."

"But Rachel *had* to go," I say. "Because the Dutch Police were searching for her hard?"

"Rachel did a very foolish thing, getting arrested."

"And you—you couldn't go. Because you were doing important work. At Amnesty."

Amy nods. Still looks unsure how much she wants to tell me.

"So Sarah got caught in the middle?" I ask.

"Sarah wanted to be with both of us, yes. Which could not be."

"And Rachel couldn't take a ten-year-old along to run with her?"

"Of course not. But Sarah took it hard. Especially when we didn't hear from Rachel for years. Sarah spiraled down. A teen out of control. It was awful to watch. Do you have children?"

"Teens."

"Then perhaps you know what I'm saying. I felt responsible. I *was* responsible. For Sarah. But Sarah refused to take responsibility for herself. Like any parent who's lost a child to drugs, I kick myself every day. So pardon me if I'm a little cold with you today."

I nod. Let the dead air hang between us. Again. This time it works. Amy starts talking again. Spontaneously. For the first time.

But it turns out, Amy's got an agenda now. To test me. "There's a Catholic nun," Amy says. "Sister Marta Garcia Perez. Rachel's friend in Nicaragua. She never knew Rachel was a fugitive. Marta knew Rachel by her Dutch name."

Amy Pierce pauses. Her eyes challenge me to supply the name.

"Sanne ter Spiegel," I say.

"That's right." Amy lets down her guard again. "Sister Marta contacted me in 1985. On behalf of her friend Sanne ter Spiegel. Said Sanne longed for her daughter. Said Sanne had a suitable place for her daughter at last, in Nicaragua. Wanted me to send Sarah there."

"Did you?"

"Sarah was gone. Had run away from me three months before at age fifteen. Figuring she could get by on her looks. The last nineteen years, I've only talked to Sarah maybe ten times. Total. I've only seen her in person twice. But Marta may know more, because Sarah always wanted to find her mom, too."

"Sarah knew her mom's Dutch name?"

"Yes."

"When you last saw Sarah—in 1999—how'd she find you?"

"She heard from someone I was here. Came to Chicago. To visit. It was awful. To see how Sarah's destroyed herself. I loved that little girl so much." These last words stick in Amy's throat. She hides her face in her hands. Thirty seconds. When she emerges, there are no tears. But pain is etched deep in every wrinkle on her face.

"Did you take any pictures of Sarah when she was here in 1999?"

Amy roots around in her purse. Produces a photograph. Of herself, standing by the Lake. Beside a ragged ghost of a woman. The twenty-nine-year-old Sarah Pierce in the photo looks older than the fifty-something woman who raised her. Sarah Pierce looks like hell. She's forcing a smile for the picture. But there's no hiding the haunted look in her sunken eyes.

Sarah's pale, gaunt face recalls the Amsterdam mug shot of Rachel Clark at age thirty. Lines and blotches all over her face. Stringy, unkempt hair. An attitude of total disarray. Like mother, like daughter. Both were teenage knockouts; and by thirty, both were burnt-out cases.

"How do I find Sister Marta?" I ask.

"She's in Cleveland now." Amy gives me an address and a phone number.

"Do I need to tell her I'm from Key West?"

"No." Amy smiles. "Sister Marta never knew her friend Sanne ter Spiegel was a fugitive."

Down the hall loud voices argue about whether to accept a plea bargain. For "Murder Two."

"I have to get back to work," Amy says. "There's something *else* you need help with?"

"I've obtained Rachel's motorcycle helmet. Still has the bullet crease in it."

Amy Pierce stares at me. "Where'd you get it?"

"Friend out west. Jim Lacy."

"What do you need from me?"

"I'd like to give it back to Rachel."

"I doubt she'd want it. It would tend to—incriminate her."

"Are you kidding? After all these years? They'll never catch the Fugitive Radical. Not unless she decides to turn herself in." I lean forward. Put on my most earnest face. "That helmet's a piece of history. *Rachel's* history. I'd like to give it back to her. If she wants it."

"Okay," Amy says. We stare at each other.

"I was hoping you'd tell me how to find Rachel," I say. "Or if you're not comfortable telling me that, I was hoping I could send the helmet to you. And *you* could take it to Rachel."

"I don't know where Rachel is," Amy says. Flatly. "I'm sorry. Marta might know. She was very close to Rachel in Nicaragua. You should ask Marta."

On the train back to Ann Arbor, I nap fitfully. In the half-awake/half-asleep state, memories from the past mingle with images from the Amy Pierce interview. The result is disturbing. I see the long lines of addicts I used to avoid when I lived in Amsterdam in my twenties. Ragged men in ragged clothes. Washed-out women in washed-out clothes. The seamy underside of the drug capital of the world. Superimposed upon those old memories is an image, from Amy Pierce's photograph, of Sarah Pierce. Her haggard face. Those haunted, sunken eyes. Framed by the stringy hair. The eternal drifter. Always on the grift.

As I sink deeper into sleep, the images grow more chaotic. Sarah Pierce is a ghost. Piloting a ghost ship. Crewed by ragged Dutch addicts. Forever drifting. *The Flying Dutchman*. In search of Sarah's fugitive mother. The ghost ship tries to dock at Key West. With Sarah wailing "she's here, she's here, I know she's here." But the harbor pilots won't let her dock. So she's off again on the high seas. Now Sarah and her ghostly crew of addicts ride a flotilla of lifeboats in the rosy-fingered dawn. Seeking a mother ship they can never find. They arrive at Nicaragua. With Sarah wailing "she's here, she's here, I know she's here." But again the harbor pilots won't let her dock.

I wake to the conductor shaking me. "Sir? We're here. Sir? We're here."

Ann Arbor. Twilight. I stumble off the train. And stare down the dark meandering curves of the Huron River. The latest stop for Sarah Pierce. And for Rachel Clark.

\* \* \*

It's cold and raining. I'm tired. And I got almost nothing out of my nine-hour trip to Chicago. Except the name of a nun in Cleveland.

So I should feel like shit, right? But I don't. In fact, in spite of my grim dream, I feel *great*. If I were younger and more musical, I'd try the Gene Kelly thing. Singing in the rain. As I walk back to my hotel in the rain.

Mostly it's the exhilaration of my new romance. The thrill of how well things are going with Janet. But my search for Rachel Clark is going better now, too. Even though I struck out with Amy Pierce. Even though I failed to get Sheila Nyman's fingerprints yesterday. Because the meeting with Sheila went so much better than I'd hoped. The idea of asking Sheila to broker an interview with Rachel Clark just hit me there. But it turned out to be a great way to confront Sheila about Rachel Clark—without getting in her face. And Sheila's willingness even to *consider* it proved a lot. Sheila must know where Rachel Clark is. If she's not Rachel Clark herself.

So I'm feeling very pleased with myself indeed. Yet even at my most exuberant, I'm plagued by troubling thoughts, too. Falling in love with Janet is exhilarating—yet also anxiety-producing. How far will we go? How fast? When will I confess I live in Florida? And how will Janet react?

What am I looking for with Janet, anyway? A brief sexual encounter? You bet. But I want more, too. Much more. As I dodge the raindrops, I spin wild fantasies. What if I left Florida and moved back to Ann Arbor? To give the relationship with Janet a real chance.

I know I'd hate myself (more than I already do) if I just let drop this very special feeling that's growing between Janet and me. Life is short. And then you die. I don't want to die without finding out, first, if a much more intense love than I've ever known is possible.

But what a colossal fool I'd be, if I left Elaine and the kids, moved to Ann Arbor, and then things with Janet fell through. How do I know Janet is real? All we've had is six dates. Twenty hours of lively conversation. And several hours of passionate kissing. Hardly reason to leave a very good marriage. Not to mention two great kids. Elaine and I are nowhere near as passionate as in our youth. But we still love each other with middle-aged warmth. We have a very close friendship, too. And reliably great sex. Don't forget that. Plus shared history. What the hell's the matter with me? How can I even *think* of leaving all that—for a teenage-style crush? On a legal secretary. Whom I barely know. Who is, herself, married. Not to mention twice-divorced.

But perhaps I can have my cake and eat it, too. I could move to Ann Arbor *with Elaine and the kids*. Stay married. Just cheat—like everyone else does.

Carry on an affair with Janet. Until we know enough to decide. Whether to take the plunge. Into the deep dark abyss of Love.

Amorous fantasies crowd my thoughts. I try to picture what making love to Janet will be like. If she stays in the mood. And more important, what will it be like to be with Janet *after* making love? Will we still be able to make each other laugh? Will we really be able to get to know each other, in any meaningful way, while sneaking around behind our spouses' backs?

Dark fantasies crowd my thoughts, too. A disturbing image of hubby John from the desk photo. Somehow I can't see that gun-toting gorilla sitting pat if he learns I'm doing his wife. More likely, Big John will chase me through downtown Ann Arbor with his twelve-gauge shotgun. And we'll all land on the cover of *People*. Or, God help me, on the cover of *The National Spy*.

But what's the alternative to a dangerous liaison with Janet? A bittersweet goodbye once I find Rachel Clark? And then a lifetime of regret? For chickening out. Again. As always.

My dark musings are not limited to matters of the heart. *Work*, too, worries me. The success that seems so close—the exclusive Rachel Clark interview—is fraught with peril. What if my clever ploy with Sheila Nyman proves to be, like most of my clever ploys, not so clever after all? What if Rachel Clark up and runs before I get to talk to her?

Even worse, what if Rachel Clark *stays*—and actually gives me the damn interview? I'm a big believer in the wisdom of the old adage, *Be careful what you wish for, because you just might get it*. Were I to land that interview, the temptation to betray *The National Spy* would be strong. That exclusive could be my ticket out of the tabloids. It's really a mainstream media story anyway. Were I to stay with *The National Spy*, I'd never be paid anything close to what the Rachel Clark story is worth. Graham Hancock would promise me a raise, of course—*if* the paper ever starts making money. *Big* If. But *The New York Times*, or *The Washington Post*—they'd hire a guy good enough to get a story like this. No conditions. In a heartbeat.

I'm just a few blocks from my hotel. And here's *The Ann Arbor News* building. Right across the street. Just as I was thinking about where I could peddle the Rachel Clark story. This strikes me as a *sign*. Forget the *Times*. Forget the *Post*. I could parlay the Rachel Clark exclusive into a job at *The Ann Arbor News*. I'd have to take a massive pay cut, of course. But that would be a small price to pay. To have a respectable job. In the same town where Janet Fickel works.

Elaine's mother would do everything possible to keep us from moving. But Elaine might secretly support me. Might welcome an excuse to put 1,500 miles between her and her neurotic mother. The kids would grumble. But they'd adjust. Kids always do. And then I'd be in Ann Arbor permanently. Where I could find out if I'm just another middle-aged man grasping feebly and foolishly at one last chance for romance and youth. Or whether Janet Fickel is the real deal.

These fantasies are seizing control, as I stand here outside *The Ann Arbor News*. Why not drop in on the editor? Right here. Right now. No appointment. Just ask if he'll guarantee me a permanent job, if I deliver an exclusive interview with Rachel Clark. Of course, my rational mind recognizes that talking to a media competitor *before* nailing the story would be reckless. Beyond the pale. But the fantasies are running so strong, I swear I'm just about to do it.

Luckily Greg Hunter saves me from myself. As he pulls up beside me in a beat-up Olds. Tells me to hop in. Which I do. Anything to get out of the rain. And away from my dark thoughts.

"Where the hell you been?" Hunter asks. "Teammate."

"Nice to see you, too, Detective."

"Five days, not a peep from you. I figured you was in the wind. Duckin' my subpoena."

"Oh no!" I protest. "Don't serve me yet, Greg. I'm close, man. Real close."

"That's what you always say. Teammate. I need more than empty promises."

So I fill Hunter in on the Alan Singer interview. The lead Singer gave me to Amy Pierce. I hold back the Key West password. But I give Hunter the Dutch name Singer said was Rachel Clark's new identity in Amsterdam in 1980. Sanne ter Spiegel. And the information that Amy Pierce was the one who helped Rachel Clark/Sanne ter Spiegel go to Central America.

"You got all that out of Alan Singer?" Hunter says. "I'm impressed. But you been outta sight *five days*. What *else* you been doin'?"

"I went to see Amy Pierce. But she wouldn't talk to me."

"That didn't take five days. What *else* you got for me?"

"Rachel Clark had a daughter," I say. "Sarah Pierce."

"Raised by Amy Pierce?"

"Yes. First in a commune on Packard Street here in Ann Arbor. Then in Europe. Guess where Sarah Pierce is now?"

Hunter pulls into the Campus Inn's parking lot. Apparently he thinks I'm still staying here. I decide not to tell him I moved to the Bell Tower.

Hunter parks. Turns off the engine, which kills the wipers. Now the rain eddies and pools on his windshield. Blocking our view out into the night.

"Ann Arbor," I say, not waiting for Hunter to guess.

"*Where* in Ann Arbor?"

"I don't know. But I'm working on it. Gimme a coupla more days. Where the daughter is, the mother can't be far away."

Hunter does not challenge the flimsy logic of this proposition. Instead, he just keeps pressing me. "I'm runnin' out of time. Teammate. What *else* you got for me?"

I was hoping to leave Sheila Nyman out of this.

But I need to give Hunter more. To protect my exclusive.

"Davis's law partner, Sheila Nyman. Was one of Rachel Clark's best friends in college."

"So?" Hunter says. "I interviewed all those radicals back in 1969. At their free love commune on Packard Street. Right after Dale was murdered."

"You interviewed Sheila Nyman back in '69?"

"I don't remember that name. But if she was there, I interviewed her."

"She mighta had a different name back then."

"Oh? What name?"

"I don't know yet. I'm workin' on it."

"That's all you ever say. It's gettin' old, Fisher. What are you holdin' back on me? You think Sheila Nyman knows where Rachel Clark is now?"

"Maybe," I say. "But I'm not holdin' back on you. Teammate. Just gimme a coupla days. You've waited thirty-five years. You can gimme a couple more days."

"We'll see," Hunter growls. "No promises from me. That was our deal. Right?"

"Right. But hey—teammate. Since we're here, I wanna run something by you."

"Fire away, Fisher."

So I tell Hunter about the pennies. He's intrigued. And at first, genuinely appreciative. Says he's laid awake a lot of nights the past thirty-five years. Thinking about those pennies with Rachel Clark's fingerprints. A riddle with no solution. Hunter agrees my theory makes perfect sense. Compliments me. Imagine. Hunter—the bulldog—complimenting a tabloid hack.

"So let's take this one more step, Greg. If I'm right, then Rachel Clark's innocent."

Hunter jerks up in his car seat like he's just been electrocuted. "Like hell she is."

"Well, she's got one heckuva great defense. *Withdrawal from the conspiracy*. Before your brother was shot. And she never took any affirmative act to rejoin the conspiracy."

Hunter raises the same points Sheila Nyman raised. Only *much* more vociferously. Rachel Clark returned to sit behind the wheel of the van. Rachel Clark fled the scene. I refute these points, just as I did with Sheila. Rachel Clark never turned the key in the ignition after defying Zimmerman's orders. Never rejoined the conspiracy. And her flight wasn't *proof* of guilt—just a nineteen-year-old's normal reaction. Which any half-sober defense lawyer could explain away.

Hunter, of course, violently disputes each of my refutations. But the troubled look on his face speaks louder than his words. Hunter's smart enough to know I'm probably right.

"Look, Greg, I'm not tryin' to pick a fight. Cuz it doesn't matter what you or I think. It'll be up to the prosecutor to decide if he wants the case. And if he does, then some judge will have to decide if the case even has legs enough to go to a jury. I just thought you should know. That the issue is out there."

Hunter grunts. But still looks very disturbed. And he wants to keep arguing.

"If she was *really* withdrawing from the conspiracy," Hunter says, "then she would have run out the other side of the Law School. Left those two assholes behind. Called the police to come pick up her boyfriend and his trigger-happy playmate. Before they hurt anybody."

"You know the law doesn't require all that. She doesn't have to rat out her former conspirators to be innocent. All she has to do is commit a clear, unambiguous act of withdrawal. And then not rejoin the conspiracy. Setting those pennies down in the hall was clear and unambiguous withdrawal. And coming back to sit behind the wheel doesn't strike me as rejoining the conspiracy. But as Dennis Miller says, that's just my opinion. I could be wrong."

"*Damn right* you could be wrong! Our prosecutor wouldn't dare cut Rachel Clark that much slack. And no judge in this town would either. She came back out and sat behind the wheel. She was there when my brother got shot. In the middle of the conspiracy. That's enough to hang her."

"If I were you, I'd want to be completely sure the prosecutor agreed with me. Before I arrested a mayoral candidate for aiding and abetting a fugitive. Or arrested the fugitive herself."

"The authorization's already there for Rachel Clark. It's been there since 1969."

"Only cuz they didn't figure out the pennies back in '69. But if you explain the pennies, why would any rational prosecutor want to prosecute her? The case is thirty-five years old. She wasn't the shooter. She was only nineteen. The pennies create a reasonable doubt. And she's *already paid* for what happened. By living underground for thirty-five years. So why go after her *now*? And why go after a prominent politico, for aiding and abetting an ancient fugitive who probably wasn't even guilty in the first place? Everyone would scream that charging Davis is just politics. Not justice."

"I don't give a damn about Lane Davis's politics," Hunter snarls. "Or Rachel Clark's either. No matter what Davis tells you. For me, it's *only* about justice for Dale. Always has been. Always will be."

"So then why not tell the prosecutor about the pennies?" I press. "Let the chips fall—"

"Because I made a vow in 1969," Hunter interrupts. Then his voice gets very slow and measured. "If the prosecutor lets her walk, I'll have to take action myself. To keep my vow. And trust me—it'll be much better for Rachel Clark if it's the prosecutor who's after her. Instead of me."

I'm pretty sure I know what Hunter means by this dark remark.

* * *

After dinner I swing by Sheila Nyman's house on Devonshire.

"I thought you were going to *call* me." Sheila doesn't look happy to see me at her door. Doesn't invite me in, either.

"I was in the neighborhood." I give her a cheery smile. As if I haven't noticed the chilly reception. "Thought I'd save you the bother of a phone call."

I lean close toward Sheila. Intentionally crowding her personal space.

Which works. Sheila backs up and motions for me to come inside.

Sheila's house is not as warm as Casa Davis. It's decorated in a modern, minimalist style. The spartan furniture is hard and uninviting. And in spite of teenage residents, there's no clutter.

Sheila's kids are watching MTV in the family room. Including the teenage boy I saw yesterday. So Sheila takes me to her study. Which is decorated with photographs of the European countryside. Like the ones I saw in her office.

I sit down on a hard bench. Look up at Sheila. Expectantly. But Sheila does not sit down. Instead, she stands over me.

"I tried to tell you yesterday, Mr. Fisher."

"David. Please. 'Mr. Fisher' is my father."

"David. I tried to tell you. I don't know where Rachel Clark is. I really don't."

"But you *do* know how to contact her, don't you?"

"No. I . . . I have some ideas. That's all. Just people I could call."

"Okay."

"But I don't know if *they* know, either. Rachel is pretty careful. About the company she keeps. That's how she's managed to stay out of prison for thirty-five years."

"Okay." I let the dead air hang between us. Just sit there. Looking expectantly at her.

"So . . . I'll . . . make the calls," Sheila says at last.

"Who will you call?"

Sheila hangs fire. Lumbers over to another hard bench. Sits down. Heavily. Awkwardly. In stages. Like a camel dropping to its knees. Resignation is written all over her face.

"Old friends in the Movement," Sheila says.

"Who?"

"Mr. Fisher—David—I feel you're abusing the attorney-client relationship. I don't mind helping you with your new magazine. Up to a point. But *naming names*? To a journalist? I don't think so. That's not part of what you're paying for."

"If it's a matter of additional money—" I begin.

*Big* mistake.

"That's *not* what I meant!" Sheila's nostrils flare. Her dander is up. And so is she. Standing over me again. "I would *never* sell out my old friends. Do you hear me? *Never!*"

"I'm sorry," I splutter. "I hear you. I didn't mean it that way. I—"

"*Of course* you meant it that way! I don't know what you take me for, Mr. Fisher."

"David. Please."

"But I'm not part of your world. My friends are not for sale."

"I'm sorry, I—"

"You know why Hunter's reward money has sat there, unclaimed, for thirty-five years? Because people in the Movement *never* sell out their friends. *Never!*"

"Look. Sheila. I can see I offended you. I'm sorry. Truly I am. Can I tell you a story?"

"A *true* story?"

"All my stories are true." (What a lie that is! Although the story I'm about to tell Sheila is, in fact, true.) "I was living in England. Small village. One of the five times I dropped out of law school. I'm about twenty-four. I'm in this little grocery store. One shopkeeper. No other employees. There's a long line of English women, waiting to buy groceries. I'm in the back of the line. No one's talking. You could hear a pin drop. And all the English ladies in line are old and grim.

"Except the lady right in front of me is quite a bit younger. Cute, too. She's got her little three-year-old boy with her. The kid starts in on me. 'I like your hair,' the kid says to me. Everyone turns to look at my blonde hair. 'Thank you,' I say. 'I like your glasses,' the kid says. 'Thank you,' I say. 'I wish you were my daddy,' the kid says. '*Maybe I am,*' I say.

"It just came out of me, Sheila. That fast. Like a reflex. I swear I meant *nothing* by it. Wasn't even trying to be funny. Not in *that* place. No point. The words just slipped out. But once they were out, they hung there. Like a bad fart. I coulda died of embarrassment. All those English matrons glaring at me. And me trapped in that line, with a stupid smirk on my face. Sometimes I just can't help being a smartass. Or a dumbass. Depending on your point of view."

"Or both," Sheila says. Flatly.

"Or both," I agree. "And that's all that happened *here*, Sheila. I goofed. The words came out. Like a reflex. I swear I didn't mean to imply you'd sell your friends out. I *know* you're not like that. You and Lane are all about integrity. Passionate commitment to justice. I admire you. Really I do. What else can I do but apologize? Over and over. I'm sorry I said it. Really I am."

Sheila nods, sadly. "Apology accepted," she says at last. But does not sit down again.

"Good!" I say. "Thank you."

I gaze up at Sheila a moment without speaking, deciding I have to go after her. Now.

"Sheila. I have some other questions I gotta ask you. *Not* as your client."

"I don't think I want to hear these questions."

"You have to. Because you're in a precarious position. With your law partner running for mayor. And these questions hanging out there. Unanswered. Cuz if some *other* journalist gets hold of them—someone who's not as progressive as me—it will spell big trouble. For Lane."

"Maybe. But why would another journalist ask these questions? Unless you told him to?"

"Exactly, Sheila. I think we understand each other now. You don't name names. Not for money. Not for any other reason. And I don't name *sources*. Not for money. Or any other reason. But if you won't talk to me, you can't be my source. And then there's really no reason not to *sic my fellow yellow dogs of the press on you*, is there? So do we understand each other?"

Sheila sits down again. Heavily. "I understand. *Mr.* Fisher." She glares at me. Daring me to do the "David, please" thing again. "Either I answer your questions, or you rat me out?"

"Well, I wouldn't put it quite so baldly. But that does capture the basic spirit of the thing, yes." I lean forward conspiratorially. "So here's the first question: who was Melanie McGeetchy?"

"Rachel Clark's college roommate."

"Who became a fugitive—for what?"

"Throwing human blood on the walls of the Ann Arbor Draft Board build-ing in 1969."

"That's it?"

"That's it, Mr. Fisher. Melanie McGeetchy was no Rachel Clark. She didn't let any stupid little boys bring guns to the Weather Underground actions *she* was involved in."

"But there was an FBI 'Wanted' poster for Melanie McGeetchy."

"In those days, the FBI wanted *everyone* in the Weather Underground arrested. For political reasons. If we were off the streets, we were less of a threat to influence popular opinion."

"So there was a federal warrant for Melanie McGeetchy?"

"No—just a State of Michigan warrant."

"Which Lane Davis quashed? When he was a prosecutor?"

Sheila freezes. "That's old news, Mr. Fisher. Why would a self-proclaimed progressive like you want to dredge up that old dirt again?"

"Because now there's a new twist. See, I've looked through lots of old records at the University of Michigan. From the 1970s. Found records for Rachel Clark. Camille Jensen, now Camille Davis. Amy Pierce. Even Melanie McGeetchy. But there are *no records for Sheila Nyman.*"

Sheila stares at me. Blankly.

"I'm pretty sure if I checked enough obituaries, I'd find that Sheila Nyman died in infancy. And you've borrowed Sheila's name. Maybe even had some plastic surgery, too."

"What's your question, Mr. Fisher?"

"Are you Melanie McGeetchy? Or are you Rachel Clark? Or *both*?"

Sheila laughs. A high-pitched, half-hysterical squeak. "I'm *not* Rachel Clark."

"There's an Ann Arbor parent who thinks you're Melanie McGeetchy."

"Oh! So *that's* it! Well, if you've got Bill Miller as your source, why do you need me?"

"I like to confirm the information my sources give me. When I can."

"Why? Where is this going, Mr. Fisher? Are you going to write an article, just before the election, saying Lane Davis's law partner might be a very minor fugitive from the seventies who once threw blood on a building? *Who will care?* Sure, you'll make *my* life miserable. And Lane's. But it's not a real story. It's just the kind of mud that gets thrown before every election."

"I agree. I don't want to tell *your* story, Sheila. Or Melanie. Or *whatever* your name is. I want to tell *Rachel Clark's* story. So if you're not Rachel Clark, then find her for me. Fast. Before Greg Hunter bribes her daughter with that reward money."

"And what? If I find Rachel for you, then you'll keep me out of the news?"

"Absolutely."

"Don't you get it, Mr. Fisher? That's just another way of trying to buy me to name names. Which I *won't do*! So do your worst. I won't help you. In fact, I'm not going to be your lawyer anymore, either. Get someone else to incorporate your business. I wash my hands of you. There'll be no charge for the advice I gave you. But it's time for you to leave my house."

I feel my face flush. In thirteen years of reporting, I've never had *anyone* call my bluff like this. People *always* give in to the "be a source or be a subject" threat. Like Alan Singer did.

But not Sheila. She's on her feet a third time. And this time, she's motioning to the door. Frankly, I admire her. For standing up to the pressure. Even though it's thwarting my investigation.

Unlike Déjà Vu, Sheila has no bouncers to call. To show me out. So I show myself out.

* * *

Back in my room, I find the Bell Tower doesn't do mini-bars. So I have to do without my usual three Scotches. Good news for my liver. Bad news for my nerves.

I watch a little TV. As usual, the ads are more interesting than the shows. One ad fools me good. Guy is sitting on a nice sofa in a richly furnished room. He's talking. But his voice is a *woman's* voice. At first I can't figure it out. It's gender-bending. He/she is talking about how he/she bought all this great stuff. With a credit card. Turns out it's *someone else's* credit card. Of the opposite gender. Now I get it. It's a credit card security commercial. This is about *identity theft*. People pretending to be other people. Lord, what is the world coming to?

I change channels. Find the British movie *Love Actually*. Great flick. Except—there's a married man making a fool of himself. By starting an illicit affair with his voluptuous young secretary. Hmm.

I feel like Hamlet. *How all occasions do inform against me.*

I flip the TV off. With any luck, I can find better entertainment. On my surveillance tapes.

I have two tapes to check now. One from Raven's home. And one from Casa Davis.

Raven has another steamy call from Lane Davis. Apparently they use the phone for foreplay. They're far better than anything on TV. So I indulge myself in a little inappropriate vicarious living. As they arrange another "session" on Raven's Love Swing.

But the Casa Davis tape is more relevant. To my supposed purpose for staying up here in Ann Arbor:

CAMILLE:    Hello?

SHEILA:    Hi, Camille, it's Sheila.

CAMILLE:    Oh. Hi, Sheila. What's new?

SHEILA:    Oh—nothing much. Is Lane there?"

CAMILLE:    No. He just left to go back to the office. You can catch him there.

SHEILA:    Well, actually, it's *you* I want to talk to.

CAMILLE:    Oh, really? Why?

SHEILA:    There's a reporter. David Fisher. Asking a lot of hard questions. About Lane and—Rachel Clark.

CAMILLE:    Who's he work for?

SHEILA:    Freelance, I think. But David Fisher does his homework. He knows the real reason Lane got fired by the prosecutor. He knows Rachel Clark's daughter's here in Ann Arbor. He's . . . dangerous, Camille.

CAMILLE:    Well—is there anything we can do?

SHEILA:    I'm not sure. He wants to interview Rachel Clark. He's threatening to make trouble for Lane. Unless I—give him what he wants.

CAMILLE:    You don't have to make that sacrifice, Sheila.

SHEILA:    Thank you. I—I know I don't have to. But I don't want Lane to lose the election, either. Just because of me.

CAMILLE:    Are you kidding? We all know Lane's not going to win the election. And who cares who's mayor of Ann Arbor anyway? No one should stick their neck out over this election. Sheila, I mean it. Don't worry about Lane. Protect yourself.

SHEILA:    Thank you, Camille. Goodnight.

CAMILLE:    Goodnight.

I lie in the dark. Thinking "*sacrifice*" is an awful strong word to use. Unless Camille knows that Sheila is really Rachel Clark. Then "sacrifice" is exactly the right word.

I listen to this call. Over and over. Until *my* phone rings. It's Elaine.

"How's it going, sweetie?"

"Oh man, Elaine. I'm up to my eyeballs in alligators."

"That's the way you like it, right?"

"I guess. But I'm beginning to wonder if this time I'm in over my head."

"Why, honey?"

"Because these people aren't the usual tabloid suspects. They're real peo-ple. *Nice* people. Not pampered airhead celebrities. I feel kinda bad for 'em. Cuz the shit's gonna hit the fan up here, Elaine. Real soon. And some of these nice people are gonna get hurt. Real bad."

"It's that big a story?"

"I think so. And these people just happen to be living in the eye of the storm."

"You mean, like us, back in DC? When that Congressman got murdered next door?"

"Exactly, Elaine. One minute we were walkin' the fucking dog. Next minute we were on all three networks. In our PJs."

"You looked pretty good in your PJs, David."

"Back then I did. And *you* looked even better. You hot bitch. But we were lucky, Elaine. Not everyone is thirty-one and fit when the media comes calling. These people here in Ann Arbor are gonna get caught with their PJs down. And they're way past their prime."

"Can you help them?"

"Of course not. Not unless I tank the story. And even if I did, I have a feel-ing this thing's gonna blow much bigger than *The National Spy*."

"Oh. Well, at least—it sounds like you finally found a story worth your time."

"You got that right. I just have to decide *which* story it is that's worth my time."

# CHAPTER TEN
# FLOWERS FOR MISTER ROCKEFELLER

## Thursday 21 October 2004

All-time greatest tabloid scam? Easy. The *New York Post* reporter who wormed his way into the townhouse Nelson Rockefeller had bought for his "research assistant" Megan Marshak. Nellie had recently suffered a fatal heart attack at the townhouse. While supposedly working on a late night "art project" with Megan. So the Rockefeller people were guarding the place like Fort Knox.

The media knew what had really gone down. Nellie died while boning Megan on the townhouse floor. (What a way to go!) But no one could get any pix of Megan. Except the *Post* reporter. Who posed as a *flower delivery guy*. Got inside by insisting he had to deliver Megan's flowers *personally*. Five years later Eddie Murphy used the same scam in *Beverly Hills Cop*. "Flowers are my life," Eddie tells the doorman who tries to deny him entrance.

What the hell. It worked for Eddie Murphy. Better still, it worked for the *Post* in real life. So Thursday morning I dip deep into my suitcase of disguises. Go for a *younger* look. Kid Rock T-shirt. Jeans. Dark mustache and goatee. Dark brown wig. Sleek, hip, wrap-around sunglasses. And a backward baseball cap. The same cap Graham cited as evidence of my mid-life crisis.

I find a flower shop. Wait for it to open. Buy four different arrangements. All in cheap glass vases. I also get four nice cards. And a big box. Like a flower delivery guy might use.

Back in the car, I put on my latex gloves. Wipe the four glass vases clean. No fingerprints on 'em. Then I write out four nice cards. One for Sheila Nyman. One for Sheila *Newton*. One for Naomi Williams. And one for Naomi *Wilson*. I sign the card to Sheila Nyman as "David Fisher." And sign the cards for Naomi Williams and the fictitious people "Graham Hancock."

Next I call Davis & Nyman. Ask for Janet Fickel. Learn from Janet that Sheila Nyman is in her office. No clients this morning. I debate asking Janet if *Naomi* is in the office, too. But decide that might raise Janet's suspicions. So I just remind Janet of our date tonight. At the Sheraton. Whisper a few sweet nothings into the phone. Then let Janet put me through to Sheila.

Sheila's civil. But won't reconsider firing me as a client. I ask if she's willing to contact Rachel Clark for me. Absolutely not, Sheila says. I tell her if she changes her mind to call me.

Since Janet knows my car, I park a block away from Davis & Nyman. Walk in the front door. In my flower delivery guy disguise. Schlepping my box with the four arrangements in vases.

I'm expecting a confrontation. Since Janet said Burns Security now guards Davis & Nyman 24/7. After finding my bugs. In my febrile imagination, I expect Debbie Smith to be flanked by two burly rent-a-cops. So I'm ready. To launch into the "flowers are my life" routine.

But as usual, life falls far short of my imagination. Debbie Smith is away from her post. And there's no sign of any rent-a-cops. Little breakdown in security, here at Davis & Nyman. I walk straight upstairs. Unaccosted.

Janet looks at me as I pass her desk. Doesn't recognize me. Good sign.

Sue Webber looks at me, too. Also doesn't recognize me. But asks if she can help me.

"Flowers," I mumble without breaking stride. Relying on the weight and bulk of the box to excuse me from normal social niceties. As I barge right into Sheila's office.

"Sheila?" I pitch my voice much higher than normal. To disguise it.

"Yes."

I set my box down on her desk. And pull out the flower arrangement with the card for Sheila *Newton*. Carefully holding the vase by the very bottom and the very top, I hand it to Sheila Nyman. She has no choice but to put her fingerprints all over the middle of the vase.

Sheila looks pleasantly surprised. Finds the card. Then frowns. "These aren't for me," Sheila says. "I'm Sheila *Nyman*. These are for Sheila *Newton*."

I look shocked. Rummage around some more in my box. Pull out the arrangement with the card for Sheila *Nyman*. Hand Sheila the "right" arrangement. Take back the "wrong" one. Again carefully holding the "wrong" one only by the top and bottom, to preserve Sheila's fingerprints. And put the "wrong" arrangement back in my box.

Sheila inspects the second card. From "David Fisher." Agrees that this arrangement is, indeed, for her. Before she can reject the flowers from "David Fisher," I'm back out in the hall.

Unfortunately, I can't play the same game with Naomi Williams. Naomi is away from her post. Not expected until the afternoon, Sue Webber tells me. Bummer. So I leave the "right" flowers on Naomi's desk. Right in front of her computer. So she'll have to touch the vase to move it. I'm thinking maybe I can break in tonight and steal the vase. After Naomi has a chance to put her fingerprints on it. Since there's no evidence of the 24/7 security Janet told me about.

Now I duck into the file room. Since I don't have any use for the fourth vase, I remove the "Naomi Wilson" card. Grab a blank, unlined 3x5 card. And write out a trusty Yeats poem for Janet Fickel:

> Wine comes in at the mouth,
> And Love comes in at the eye.
> That is all we shall know for truth,
> Before we grow old and die.
> I lift the glass to my mouth,
> I look at you, and I sigh.

I sign the 3x5 card with the poem. Stick it in with the flowers. Turn to exit. And walk straight into the ample belly of a stern-looking employee of the Burns Security Service.

"What the hell are you doin' in here, sport?"

"I, er . . . there was a mix-up with the flowers. I was just trying to figure it out."

The Burns guy gives me a dirty look. Like he doesn't trust me as far as he can throw me. But he can *see* I haven't taken anything. So he doesn't try to stop me as I slither past him.

Janet's at the copy machine. So I just drop the flowers off on her desk. And beat it.

Outside, I notice a young dark-haired woman in a blue Toyota. Parked across the street from Davis & Nyman. Not looking at me. Even though I am a fairly silly sight. In my backward baseball cap. Carrying a big box with a single flower arrangement. The one with Sheila's fingerprints. I saw this same young dark-haired woman in the same blue Toyota on my way *into* Davis & Nyman, too. The plates are not rental plates. So I'm guessing this is Hunter's latest tail.

\* \* \*

"This time I got something for *you*, too," Greg Hunter says. "Teammate."

We're sitting at the Ann Arbor Police Department. While Hunter's girlfriend processes the fingerprints on the flower vase I brought in.

"Ann Arbor's favorite radical mayor-wanna-be," Hunter says. "The guy you don't want me to arrest. You know where he was in the summer of 1989?"

"Central America. In a moving van. Humanitarian mission."

"Correct. You inspired me yesterday. Telling me Rachel Clark was in Central America in the 1980s. So I got an INS agent in Galveston to look up some old immigration records. Guess what? Lane Davis went down alone. But when he *re-entered* the USA, he had company."

"Sanne ter Spiegel?"

"No. A Catholic nun. From Nicaragua. Named Teresa Rodriguez Lamas." Hunter raises an eyebrow. "Name ring a bell?"

"Sorry. No. Never heard of her."

"She was a very strange passenger for Davis to have in his truck on July 29, 1989."

"Why?"

"Because Teresa Rodriguez Lamas was murdered on April 20, 1989. In Nicaragua."

I swallow hard. Because I fear Hunter's closing in on Rachel Clark. Too fast.

"So you figure the woman was really Rachel Clark? Using the dead woman's passport?"

"Is there *another* explanation that makes sense?" Hunter asks.

"I'll bet *Davis'll* have another explanation. If you go confront him about this."

"So I suppose you want me to keep on waiting? For what? For you to bring in a new set of fingerprints every five or six days? From some unnamed suspect?"

From an interview room nearby comes a loud crash. I jump.

Hunter ignores the noise. Just keeps staring hard at me. "I need to know where you got that motorcycle helmet with Rachel Clark's fingerprints," Hunter continues. "Time for you to come clean. Teammate."

"Aw, c'mon, Greg," I plead. "We've already been down this road. Too many times."

"You're either gonna tell *me*, or you're gonna tell a *grand jury* next week. I'm outta patience. And in the meantime, don't try to leave town again."

"Why? Is that young lady in the blue Toyota having trouble following me?" Immediately I regret this smart-ass remark. Because now Hunter will just put a *different* tail on me.

"Yeah. You're too damn elusive. So if she sees you even *try* to leave town, she'll arrest you as a material witness. I'm not fuckin' around, Fisher. Don't leave town. I mean it."

"Whatever happened to freedom of the press?" I grumble. Strictly for appearances. In truth I'm *delighted* to be ordered, again, to stay in Ann Arbor. Even though I haven't had to play that card yet. This weekend I may need it. For the next round of calls with Graham and Elaine.

"Don't give me that First Amendment crap. Anyway, you should be happy to stay here in town. It'll give you a chance to spend a little more time with your new lady friend."

There are few things in the world as ugly as a bulldog trying to look *mischievous*.

I scowl. "Leave my private life alone."

Hunter laughs. "Oh, that's *good*! Coming from *you*. Mr. Gossip Reporter. Don't like it when the shoe's on the other foot, eh?"

"*Touché.*" I try to sound bored. So Hunter won't know just how nervous this makes me. To think my philandering behind Elaine's back is now a matter of police record. "Hey—you're not writing down any of that stuff about me, in your *reports*, are you?"

"Course I am. The law *requires* me to write down all facts material to our investigation."

"Since when are *my* whereabouts and actions material to your investigation?"

"Since you brought us Rachel Clark's fingerprints. Yet refused to disclose where you got them. And I can tell you—we're not the *only ones* who think your activities are material. We got a Freedom of Information Act request about you."

"From whom?"

"Coupla German guys. The Beckenbauer agency. Tabloid rivals of yours, I believe."

"*Fuck* those guys! Did you give 'em anything?"

"Not yet. We just got the FOIA request this week."

"You can't give 'em any information 'til Rachel Clark is located. Because 'til then, it's an ongoing criminal investigation. The FOIA has a specific exemption for that."

"That exemption *permits* us to withhold information for an ongoing criminal investigation. But it does not *require* us to withhold it. We can turn over public records anytime we want to."

We stare at each other awhile. In Hunter's eyes his meaning is clear: play ball with me, little tabloid prick, or I won't do anything to protect your private foibles from public disclosure.

"You understand they're just *using* the FOIA to try to make me do their work for them?"

"I don't care *why* those Germans want the information about you," Hunter says. "I just know that disclosing it isn't likely to compromise any aspect of our investigation."

"Oh really? You want the Beckenbauer boys promenading around town, snapping pix and spooking Rachel Clark? So she runs before either one of us finds her?"

"Telling them about your new girlfriend won't bring them back to town. Though it might bring *your wife* up here. If *she* files an FOIA request. You wouldn't want *that*, would you? Imagine! An FOIA request from *Elaine Fisher*. Seeking records regarding David Fisher's activities this past week."

"No, I do *not* want my wife to file an FOIA request. And if she does, I don't want you to have anything written down about my private life in your reports."

"How is any of this your 'private' life? Your lady friend is Lane Davis's secretary."

"So?"

"So it's all in the line of duty, right? I'm sure you're not out seducing Janet Fickel just because she's such a babe. You're doing it because *it's your job*. To get information out of her. For your story. You know what they say. It's a tough job, but someone's gotta do it."

Hunter is clearly enjoying himself. And I am *not*.

"Look. Greg. I don't mind if you tail me. Even though I tell you everything I'm doing. Everything I learn. Like the good teammate I am. But leave my private life alone, okay? Janet has a husband and kids. I have a wife and kids. There's no reason for those people to get hurt."

"Maybe you both shoulda thought of that before you started fucking around."

I shoot Hunter a dark look. "Nobody's fucking anybody."

"My report says it's only a question of time." Hunter leers at me. "Of course, I might be persuaded to remove certain *details* from my final report. *If* you were more forthcoming about that motorcycle helmet."

"Careful. You don't want me to accuse you of extortion."

"I'm not demanding money. I'm just exerting pressure. On a reluctant witness."

"Well, it ain't gonna work. All you're doing is pissing me off."

"Oh no!" Hunter says. "How will I ever sleep at night?"

We sit in silence. Just staring at each other. Listening to the police station's noises. Doors opening and closing. Footsteps clattering up and down the hall. Fax machines. Ringing telephones.

Finally Hunter's girlfriend returns. The fingerprints on the flower vase are *not* Rachel Clark's. They belong to *another* member of the Weather

Underground. Melanie McGeetchy.

* * *

After lunch I sit in my car. Kicking myself about the dumb move I made. Leaving the flowers for Naomi on her desk. Cuz with the Burns guy there—just like Janet said—I can't go back tonight and take them. Yet since I left the flowers for Naomi, now I can't plausibly bring *more* flowers to her later today or tomorrow. And try to pull the same stunt I did with Sheila.

Too bad. If I could get Naomi's fingerprints, I'd know if it's Naomi or Camille who's really Rachel Clark. Then I could make love to Janet tonight. Interview Rachel Clark tomorrow. And then—what? Who knows? Not me. I guess my next move would depend. On what happens with Janet tonight. And on what Rachel Clark says.

Normally if I see a criminal act, I report it. To the proper authorities. Never mind that I am, myself, a hardened scofflaw. Who often breaks laws relating to surveillance and trespass and theft. That doesn't stop me from getting up on my high horse. When I see *other* people breaking the law.

But Rachel Clark is different. I'm not sure I want to turn her in. To my "teammate" Hunter. For one thing, I really think she may be innocent. For another, turning Rachel Clark in would mean exposing her *friends* to possible prosecution, too. As aiders and abettors.

I realize I'm breaking Rule #2 in the tabloid biz. *Never Start Caring About Your Targets.* But I do respect Sheila Nyman's refusal to sell her friend out to me. And I'm even warming up to Raven and Lane and Camille. Their clumsy, late-in-life love triangle is oddly endearing to me these days.

Oh, well. I'm getting ahead of myself again. First I need to figure out which of my two remaining suspects is Rachel Clark. Naomi or Camille.

*Then* I can worry about the big moral questions. Like what to do with Rachel Clark. Not to mention what to do with *my own* life.

Since Naomi's at work this afternoon, I decide to visit my other suspect. Camille Davis. I don't bother cleaning my tail. Let the cops follow me. It's no secret the Davises are in this case.

There's a newspaper on the front stoop at Casa Davis. I pick it up by the ends. Slide the rubber band off. And put the advertising section on the outside. Thinking this could be how I get Camille's fingerprints. I'll hand it to her. Then contrive to have her hand it back to me.

I ring the bell. Camille opens the door. Behind her I see a cleaning woman in the living room. Vacuuming. I introduce myself as David Fisher. A client of her husband's. I tell Camille I'd like to interview her. About her work in Central America in the eighties. For *Liberal Voices*.

Camille clearly recognizes my name. Since Sheila warned her about me. Camille does *not* invite me inside. Even when I lean into her personal space. Camille says she doesn't mind being interviewed. But not now. She's on her way to a meeting. She's busy all day tomorrow, too. But she agrees to have lunch with me on Monday. At an Indian restaurant she likes. Raja Rani.

Then I act like I've suddenly remembered the paper in my hand. "This is your paper."

"Thanks." Camille takes the newspaper from me.

"Say. Do you mind if I keep the ads?" I gesture at the section I put on the outside.

Camille looks at the paper. Then gazes at me with sincere regret. "I'm sorry. But I promised an out-of-town friend I'd save the want ads. She needs a car for her teenager."

Thwarted. At every turn. So I remind Camille I'll see her at noon on Monday. At Raja Rani.

There's no point waiting for Camille to leave. Even if my nerves could stand another break-in, this ain't the right day. Not with the cleaning woman busy inside.

Next I spend forty-five minutes cleaning my tail. Before returning to the Bell Tower hotel. Where I fire up my laptop. And spend two hours trying to find a home address for Naomi Williams.

No luck. I Google Naomi. I use an online background investigation service. I even hire a more sophisticated witness-locater outfit. Which accesses utility bill databases. Nothing. No records for a Naomi Williams in Ann Arbor or environs.

Naomi's flying low. Below the radar. Must be a renter. Or her house is in her female roommate's name. I check local court records. Hoping Naomi was in a lawsuit. No such luck.

I'll have to follow Naomi home after work. To find out where she lives. Can't do it tonight though. I'm meeting Janet at 5:15. At the Sheraton. No way I'm gonna be late for that!

In the meantime, though, I gotta do *something*. So I drive by Casa Davis again. The cleaning woman is still there.

I swing by Zingerman's. Find Saul Schwartz. "Hey Sauly—I'm trying to find a homeless woman. Named Sarah Pierce. You know this new homeless shelter you worked on?"

"Yeah. Only we call it the DeLonis Center. Not the homeless shelter."

"Oh. Okay. How's the Center work? If I want to find out if a particular person's staying there?"

"You can leave a message for her at the Center. If she's there, she'll get it."

"Hmm. I'm not sure she's there. And even if she is, I'm not sure she'll respond. Sarah Pierce doesn't know me. At the Center, do they give out the *names* of people staying there?"

"Not the DeLonis Center. They're very protective of their guests' privacy."

"*You've* never met Sarah Pierce, have you?"

"Not that I know of, Dave. Sorry."

I swing by the shelter—the DeLonis Center—anyway. But Saul was right. They offer to take a message. But they're not letting on if Sarah Pierce is staying there or not.

So I've managed to waste the entire afternoon. Accomplishing zero.

Now it's time to get ready to see Janet.

\* \* \*

Waiting for Janet at the Sheraton, I feel enormous pressure. On several counts.

First and foremost, I have performance anxiety. I like to picture myself as James Bond. Always ready. For a quick throw in the hay. Whenever Pussy Galore calls. Walking around with a perpetual hard-on. But sadly, I know better. I'm forty-eight. Equipment failure is always a possibility.

My two quick office flings went fine. All systems go. No flaws in the hydraulic operations. Both times, when the zipper went down, I rose to the occasion. As it were. Both times, after a reasonably long but not excessive amount of time for foreplay and intercourse, the gun went off.

But those office flings were a few years ago. And they were low-pressure situations. I didn't even know sex was in the cards until a few minutes before the zipper went down. No time to get nervous. Plus, please forgive me, but I really didn't care about those women. They didn't care about me either. It was just fun. Nothing more. No pressure. One-offs know no shame.

Whereas I care for Janet a lot. I meant it when I said I loved her.

She may be a trophy. But she sure ain't no one-off.

And when I actually care for a woman, I have a history of equipment failure.

The last time I had sexual intercourse with a woman I cared about was twenty years ago. The first time with Elaine. A disaster. No fault of Elaine's. But I really cared about her. I loved Elaine. Tenderly. Romantically. Yet I also lusted after Elaine. Aggressively. Possessively.

For some reason I have always had a hard time (no pun intended) reconciling the huge inconsistency between these feelings. On the one hand, the tender romantic feelings. And on the other hand, the aggressive and violent nature of the sex act itself. So that first time, with Elaine, I came up utterly dysfunctional. Couldn't get it up. Completely struck out.

Luckily, Elaine is a patient and loving soul. We slept together that first Friday night without sex. And by the next morning I was a new man. That Saturday morning we went at it like Bob Marley in his prime. With holy zeal. A Jew and an Atheist. *Jammin' in the name of the Lord.*

But I remember that first-time failure. As my first time with Janet nears. Another woman for whom I have conflicting feelings. Tender romantic love. Mixed with raw aggressive lust.

Please don't get me wrong here. Love is life's greatest wonder. And sex is by far the best part of Love. In no other way can people communicate so deeply. Achieve such intimacy.

But Love is also a "wonder" in the sense that it is an unfathomable mystery. Violent assault and tender intimacy, co-existing in the same act. Love's bitter mystery, Yeats called it. Even Dr. Kinsey, the famed researcher who shed so much light on sex, admitted "when it comes to *Love*, we're all in the dark."

I remember the book Elaine used to teach our daughters about reproduction. The book had sketches. For kids under ten. Illustrating the mechanics of sexual intercourse. Non-graphic. Non-threatening. Depicting a benign-looking, roly-poly father. Picture Mr. Potato Head—with an undersized, drooping penis. Standing amiably before a serene-looking mother. Mrs. Potato Head. But don't worry. My elementary school-age girls were *not* fooled.

"You mean Daddy puts that THING into Mommy?" they cried.

Imagine what my girls would have thought if they'd seen sex as it *really* is. The raging stiff one-eye. Snapped to full attention. Then thrusting hard and deep. Like a frenzied piston. While Mommy moans. The victim of an animal attack. Fact is, sex is a close cousin to assault. (Grudgingly I admit this is *Raven LaGrow's* point.) That's why we lock our bedroom doors. That's why we try to keep our children from glimpsing the sex act. Because it's scary stuff.

Scary for adults, too. Even for the male aggressor. Because he knows he's in the throes of something too powerful to control. He has truly tender feelings for the female. All mixed in with his very strong libidinous desire to bang her silly. (And I cannot even begin to imagine what an adult *female* really thinks. When she sees that rampaging thing taking aim at her.)

At the same time, Love without sex would be just a poor shadow. Somehow the sex act takes all that power. All that violence. And channels it into something positive and life-affirming. Who knows how? Certainly not me.

So I await Janet Fickel's arrival at the Sheraton with dread. And not just because of performance anxiety. Not just because I recognize how little I understand about the mysteries of Love and sex. But also because there are all kinds of practical problems. Mundane worries.

How shall I pay for the room? Cash tells the clerk the room will be put to an illicit purpose. But credit cards leave paper trails. A bill someone will review. Graham Hancock. Or Elaine. Either of whom will likely ask why I needed *two* hotel rooms in Ann Arbor on the same October night. Not to mention Greg Hunter. Who enjoys collecting evidence of my infidelity. For his reports.

And how shall I explain the absence of luggage? To stave off questions, I've brought a small bag. (Don't worry. I didn't bring the Video Detective with me. My inner rascal isn't *that* kinky.) My bag's got a bottle of champagne. A backgammon game. And the photo album I borrowed from my mom the other day. But the bag isn't big enough to be a *traveler's* bag. It's more like a briefcase. So what shall I say when the clerk asks me if I need help with my luggage?

And what shall I say to all the *other* awkward questions clerks ask? What size bed? Smoking or non-smoking? Will you wait a minute 'til the bellhop can show you to your room?

I decide to face these awkward questions alone. Before Janet arrives. Clear the deck. So when Janet arrives, we can get right down to business. Without risking that any of these awkward questions might spook her. The way they're spooking me.

So I get the room. With a company credit card. (I'll deal with Graham later.) Endure the clerk's questions. Endure the walk up with the bellhop. Endure the bellhop's idiotic chatter.

Doesn't matter. Janet arrives on time. Under her jacket, she's dressed to thrill. Nice blouse. Short tight skirt. Stockings. Heels. But she looks distraught. *Very* nervous. No smiles.

"I'm not sure I'm cut out for this," Janet says. Her usual blunt, matter-of-fact voice. But I think I hear a little *quaver* in that voice, too.

I nod. Try to look sympathetic. Try to suppress any facial expression that might convey the enormous disappointment I feel.

Maybe I should be relieved. I'm off the hook, right? No need to confront performance anxiety tonight. No need to grapple with all that I do not know about Love's bitter mystery.

But I don't feel relief. No. I'm deeply disappointed. For just like at Island Park, even though I've been dreading it, I've *also* been in a fugue state of excitement. Over the prospect of sex with Janet. I've been anticipating it for forty-eight hours. Imagining what it would be like. Conjuring what Janet looks like naked. What Janet *feels* like naked. And the sequence of events.

Still, there's no point forcing the issue. Janet's clearly not up for it.

So I suggest we just have dinner. At the hotel. Janet agrees.

This time, we *both* eat lightly. I'm too keyed up to try more than a bowl of soup. And a glass of wine. Janet has a salad. And a glass of wine.

"Hey, did you get my flowers?"

"Yes." Janet's voice is flat. No enthusiasm. No thanks.

"Was there something wrong with them?"

"No. They were very nice. It's just—I had to give them to Sue."

"Why?"

"In case John stops by to see me at work. I can't have gorgeous flowers on my desk."

"Oh." I nod. "Did you give Sue *the card*, too?"

"No. I kept the card. It was very nice, David."

We eat in silence awhile. But I don't do silent well.

"Did Sheila say anything about the flowers I sent *her*?"

"No. But it was a big day for flowers at Davis & Nyman. *Naomi* got flowers, too."

"Naomi? I thought you said she has no love life."

"She doesn't. She was bowled over. Said she's never heard of the guy who sent them."

"A secret admirer?"

"Doubtful. She's taking the flowers over to the homeless shelter tonight."

"The *homeless shelter*? Why?"

"To give the flowers away. Naomi volunteers there a lot. 'Saint Naomi,' we call her."

I snort. "Well, if she gives away flowers from secret admirers, then I guess she really does have no love life. So sainthood is all that's left for her."

"I'm not complaining. Saint Naomi worked late tonight for me. Covering a late assignment from Lane. So I wouldn't be late . . . here." Janet looks chagrined. At remembering why she came here. Before she got the yips.

I smile. Put my hand on Janet's hand. "I'm sorry. I shouldn't have put so much pressure on you Tuesday night. I really didn't mean to force the issue."

"You didn't," Janet says. Matter-of-factly. "It was my idea to come here."

"And a damn good idea it was. But don't worry. There's no rush. Our time will come."

Janet relaxes. Smiles. For the first time this evening. "*Someday, Lady?*"

"Huh?" I'm not following her.

"You don't know that Bob Seger song? '*Someday, Lady, you'll accompany me?*'"

"Oh—yes! I *love* Bob Seger. You like him, too?"

"A lot."

"I don't get it. You don't much care for the Boss. But you like Bob Seger? Yet who's Bob Seger? The poor man's Bruce Springsteen, right?"

Janet shrugs.

"Well, okay, I'll go with it," I say. "And yes—I swear by this coaster here—someday, Lady, you *will* accompany me. All the way." I smile. "But even then, I'll be a nervous wreck."

"*You?*"

"Yes. I'm nervous as hell, Janet. I've never done anything like this before. Not that I'm a saint. But in eighteen years of marriage, I've only misbehaved twice. At office parties. With twenty-four-year-olds. Where it didn't matter. It was just for fun, you know? It was over almost before it started. But with you, it matters. I care very much for you, Janet. I meant it when I said I love you."

"I know you did. I think I . . . I think I love you too, David."

We sit holding hands. A long time. No more words. Just looking into each other's eyes.

At last I pay the dinner bill. We get up.

"I left a bag upstairs in the room," I say. "I'll just be a minute. To go get it."

"A bag? What's in it?"

"A photo album. I really liked your photos in the park. I thought I should reciprocate."

"It's upstairs?"

I nod.

"Let's go," Janet says.

I'm not going to argue with her. Walking up to the hotel room with Janet is almost an out-of-body experience. I have no idea what's going to happen. But I doubt I'm ready for it.

At the door, I put my arms together. For a fireman's carry. To carry Janet across the threshold. But she demurs. Darts out of my grasp. Scampers past me into the room.

"My second husband picked me up on our wedding night. To go through the door. Only he forgot to turn me sideways. Rammed my head right into the doorjamb. Knocked me out cold."

"True story?"

"Cross my heart. So it's a rule with me. No man *ever* carries me through a doorway."

On this gloomy note, we sit together in an oversized, cushioned chair. Flipping through my photo album. I supply a running commentary. Which gets Janet laughing pretty hard.

It's strange to see my whole life laid out in a few photos. Some pix from my high school daze. Old Number Zero. Wrong Way Fisher. My high school prom. With my girlfriend Renee. Some pix from college. Saul Schwartz and me. With our roommates. And our girlfriends. We look like loons. Hair past our shoulders. Those silly '70s bell bottoms. A shot of me and one of my many law school roommates. In our PJs at the U of M Law Library. Where we were protesting the early starting time of our Evidence exam by showing up in our PJs. Some grainy shots of me bartending in Boston. Backpacking in Italy. Holding hands with a buxom lass in Scotland.

"You always seem to be with women who are, um, well-endowed," Janet comments.

I feign innocence. "Coincidence, I'm sure."

"You were a handsome devil back then, weren't you?"

"I don't see why you have to say '*were*.'"

Janet smiles. Kisses me full on the lips. Then gets up. Goes into the bathroom.

When Janet comes back out, she stands directly in front of me. Between the chair where I sit and the bed. And gives me a look that is impossible to misinterpret.

The sexiest look any woman has ever given me in my life.

I stand and face Janet. We kiss.

"You're sure you want to do this today?" I ask.

"Are you trying to talk me out of it?"

"No, ma'am. I just—"

"Shhh." Janet kisses me again.

Best advice I ever got.

Now I realize, Delicate Reader, that we've reached the point where most writers chicken out. Fade to black. Leave you to imagine the lurid details. Lest they be accused of "indecency."

But I'm no coward. And I'm certainly not "decent." So those of you with faint hearts—skip ahead to page 251. Because I'm going to lay it all out here. As it were. All the lurid details.

I'm clumsy with buttons. So Janet has her blouse off before I get to my own third button. Janet intercedes. Unbuttons the damn thing for me. Runs her hand along my chest hair.

For a moment, my heart clenches. Just about stops beating. Then a jolt of pure adrenaline shoots through my entire body. My scalp flushes. My fingertips tingle. My stomach aches. And my cock snaps to full attention. All systems are fully operational. Thank God. (Or Janet.)

Janet removes her bra. Say what you will about fake boobs. But they definitely *look* better than real ones. At least Janet's do. They defy gravity. Defy Time. Truly I cannot believe how gorgeous Janet looks, standing there with nothing on her very ample chest. And it gets better. She slips off her heels and her skirt. She's wearing a very alluring stockings-and-garters combination. The stockings have a dramatic red satin band across the top. Which matches the wide red garter belt. Janet wears no panties. Must have slipped them off in the bathroom.

Down below, Janet sports an old-fashioned full bush. No Brazilian trims for this Cosmo girl. No landing strip. Just the natural curly pubic hair. Fine by me. I'm an old-fashioned guy.

Janet waits for me to take off my socks and shoes. And my pants. And my boxers.

I'm hoping she'll sit. Or kneel. And take me into her mouth. In light of that spunky talk we had at dinner the other night. About sperm samples and oral sex. But Janet comes from my generation. For us, oral sex is a bigger deal than intercourse. More intimate. Not the first thing you do. Not like kids today. Who think Bill Clinton was right. When he said oral sex is not sex.

Still, even without oral sex, Janet's foreplay is fantastic. Slowly she runs her fingertips—oh so *gently*—up and down my shaft. And back and forth across my balls. *Very* gently. All the while gazing into my eyes. Lord have mercy. It's unbelievably erotic.

I reach for Janet's bush. To reciprocate. But before I can even begin to warm her up, Janet lays back on the bed. And throws her legs way back high. So her heels are almost at her ears. I've never known any woman so flexible. But the message is clear. Forget foreplay.

So I enter her.

Janet turns out to be noisy. Lots of "oh Davids" and "oh Gods." I don't really like that. It reminds me of the sound track to a bad porn movie. Or this *Saturday Night Live* skit I once saw. Where two wild lovers are living next door to the Coneheads. Once you've heard Bill Murray do a series of "oh God, oh God, oh, GOD!" chants, it's hard ever to take "oh God" seriously again.

Still, with Janet it seems genuine. And I'm certainly not going to kick her out of bed for making too much noise.

The other strange thing about Janet is her eyes. Whenever we've kissed, she's always closed them. Demurely. But now Janet's eyes are wide open. Sometimes they seem to roll all the way back in her head. But even then, she doesn't ever *close* her eyelids. Not once. And much of the time, she seems to be trying to catch a glimpse of us in the hotel mirror.

There's really no good verb for the sex act. "Making love" is far too passive. But the active verbs—fucking, screwing, schtupping, boning, etc.—all overemphasize the *violence* of sex. And miss the *tender* side of Love's bitter mystery. So let's compromise. Half the time I'll call it "making love." The other half, I'll call it "fucking." To capture both sides of the mystery.

We get into a nice rhythm. Making love. After a few minutes, I reach one finger down to Janet's clit. Began rubbing little circles there. In response, she moans. Arches her back. And then the veins in her neck and forehead start bulging.

Now I recognize that *Cosmo* girls may sometimes fake orgasms. But no one can fake *bulging veins*. Janet's orgasms are the real deal. In fact, Janet's orgasms are *so* real, I start worrying she's having a stroke. Pulling a Nelson Rockefeller on me. But no, she's too young for that. Still very much alive.

Janet comes twice. And then, best of all, she realizes I'm suggesting *she* could use her hands on me. She goes back to running her fingertips fiendishly up and down my cock and balls. While I fuck her. She's teasing and pleasing at the same time. It's excruciatingly fabulous.

I try changing positions. So Janet won't think I'm a boring lover. (Even though, in truth, I am.) I sit back. Pull Janet on top of me. She's so much smaller than me, I figure she'll like that. But she doesn't look comfortable on top. Doesn't know what to do, either. Just sits there. Impaled on my cock. Not moving up and down. I guess big John the gun nut must not let her be on top. So I decide not to try any other creative positions. Better stick with the basics. Back to the missionary position. What's good enough for Albert Schweitzer is good enough for me.

We go at it quite awhile. Who knows how long? That's one of the best things about making love. The sheer *mindlessness* of it. You lose yourself. Lose all sense of time and place.

Some people even claim to lose all *consciousness* while fucking. Unfortunately, I'm not one of those people. Even in the throes of passion, I'm still painfully self-conscious.

With Janet I'm self-conscious about the disparity in our size. Even though her husband's much bigger than I am. I've never been with a woman this small. So I'm afraid to rest my full weight on top of her. Instead, I prop myself up on my forearms. While hovering a few inches above her. Then I rear up so the upper half of my body is almost vertical. Which affords me a spectacular view of the underside of Janet's thighs. Thrown back, as they are, toward her ears.

The undersides of a woman's thighs are the most beautiful parts of her body. Especially Janet's. Long and slender. With the hamstrings fully stretched. Janet's thighs are lovely to behold. But then again, lovely too are Janet's bounteous breasts. Which I cup in both hands. While I ride her like a jockey. On the last turn at Belmont.

But eventually I know I'm just not going to relax enough to come. And Janet's looking tired. So I ask her if she wants to stop. Janet nods.

"I'm sorry. I told you I was nervous. But you were wonderful, Janet. That was *so* nice. Next time I'll come. I promise. I just have to relax a little more."

Janet nods. Doesn't look particularly concerned about my failure.

"At least I didn't have any problem getting it up," I offer. In my meager defense.

"No, you did not. Very different from what I'm used to at home."

I'm not sure how to respond to this compliment. Because I'm not sure we really want to start comparing each other to our respective spouses.

Janet picks up the photo album. "You never finished showing me your pictures."

So we go through the rest of the album. My life story, in photos. This time I forego the running commentary. Just let Janet flip through the pix. My wedding. Elaine, looking damn good. Suntanned and voluptuous. My colleagues from the DOJ. My colleagues at a journalists' convention in New Orleans. And my daughters. At various ages. The gap-toothed smiles from the early years. Then a few shots of that middle time, when kids have a full set of adult teeth that seem so hugely oversized on such little people. And finally the teenage years, when they have a mouth full of metal braces. But for all their goofy dental looks, my girls are great-looking.

Janet comments on how attractive the girls are. And Elaine. We come to a shot of me horsing around with the girls. We're in a can-can line at a Miami football game. All decked out in team colors. Holding each other's shoulders. Kicking our legs up high. And laughing our asses off.

I flush at the sight of those Miami jerseys—fearing the photo might provoke Janet to ask why a Michigan resident (as I'm still supposed to be) was taking his kids to a Florida football game. So I quickly flip the album page to another shot of me and the girls. This time we're sitting on a couch in my study.

All three very somber. I've got a full-leg cast on my leg I got from sliding into third (I was out). And a real beard on my face. So my girls are wearing fake casts. And goofy fake cardboard beards they made to mock me.

"I wish I'd had a dad like you," Janet says. "I wish *my girls'd* had a dad like you."

I nod. Force a polite smile. But on the whole, in light of what we've just been doing, it seems like the less said about our families, the better. So when we finish with the album, I pull out the backgammon. And the champagne.

This turns out to be an inspired idea. Few things relax the mood as well as naked backgammon. Especially with champagne. Janet lies on her side. Leaning on her elbow. In just her stockings and garter belt. With those bounteous breasts scooped between her biceps. It's sexy as hell. Even though Janet's totally focused on the game. Sipping champagne.

We play an entire game. Start a second one.

At one point Janet shifts position, to pick up a stray die.

"You're an amazingly flexible person," I say. "Physically, I mean."

"I did a lot of gymnastics in school," Janet says.

"That was more than twenty years ago. You've kept yourself in fabulous shape. I couldn't believe how far over your head you can throw your legs. I *love* that."

"I always do that. It's more comfortable that way. Especially with you."

I cock my head. Inquisitively.

"I'm small," Janet says in a throaty tone. "You're—very large."

Now in reality, I may be *slightly* larger than the average male—but not very much larger. But who cares about *reality*? In my fugitive dreams I'm as big as Raven LaGrow's huge electric dildo. So if a woman wants to tell me I'm "very large," that's fine with me. While she's at it, she can call me a beast. Call me a monster. I won't stop her. Are you kidding? I *love* it.

Dimly I realize Janet may just be following advice she read in some back issue of *Cosmo*. "*Always compliment a man on his size—no matter how disappointingly puny he may really be.*"

Who cares? *Cosmo's* right. On me, it works like a charm. Immediately upon hearing Janet's comment on my size, I feel a strong erection stirring. Janet sees it, too. Stops rolling the dice. Pushes the game out of the way. And rolls over on her back.

I kneel above Janet. And bring her fingers where I want them.

Janet's got her oversized breasts cupped between her biceps again. Which only serves to make them look even bigger than they are. While her fingers flutter up and down my cock and balls.

This time I stay outside of her as long as I can. Enjoying the marvelous foreplay. Janet has such a delicate touch. I can't tell you.

When Janet finally throws her ankles back over her ears and pulls me inside of her again, I'm in high gear. I reach one hand behind her neck. Place the other on one of her oversized boobs. And enjoy the feel of her hands. Like two crazed marionettes, dancing lightly all over my shaft and my balls.

All the while Janet gazes at me. With that wide-eyed stare. And a steady stream of "oh Davids" and "oh Gods."

But this time I manage to ignore the verbal distractions. And the semi-catatonic stare.

And at last I come. Like a fucking fountain.

# CHAPTER ELEVEN

# THE RUNNING OF THE BULLS

## Friday 22 October 2004

No excuses. And no regrets. I'm glad I made love to Janet Fickel. It was fabulous.

But if I *wanted* an excuse, plenty abound. Half of all married people end up divorced. And of those who stay married, studies show at least fifty percent cheat on their spouses.

And statistics are not the only excuse. Anyone cheating on his or her spouse can find plenty of rationales. You start with every perceived injury or slight from your spouse. Every sexual rejection ("not tonight, honey—I have a headache"). Every harsh remark. By the time you tote them all up, you've convinced yourself you're a hero just for staying in the marriage *at all*. So *of course* you're justified to step out *this one time*. You're just *burning off some steam*.

You tell yourself this minor transgression is actually part of your larger fidelity to your spouse. You figure it's *a good thing* to blow off some steam once in a while. So you're able to be the faithful spouse the other 99.99% of the time. In the *big picture*, you're still faithful. (This is the time-worn excuse I've used to justify my two one-hour flings with receptionists past.)

But these excuses don't work for me here. Sure, I have my share of grievances against Elaine. Like any married person. But Elaine hasn't treated me badly enough to deserve this. And I wasn't just "blowing off steam" with Janet. No. I'm hoping to fuck Janet again. Real soon.

But I will offer one meager defense, Faithful Reader. You're probably too smart to buy it. But it's worth a try. Think of the great love affairs down the centuries. In history and in literature. Antony and Cleopatra. Romeo and Juliet. Abelard and Heloise. Dante and Beatrice. Emma Bovary and L'heureux. Anna Karenina and Count Vronsky. Tess Durbeyfield and Alec D'Urberville. Charles Dickens and Ellen Ternan. Prince Rudolf and Mary Vetsera (the "Mayerling" lovers).

What do they all have in common?

You got it. The great love affairs were all *affairs*. *Illicit* affairs.

You think this was just an accident of *history*? With no application to modern times?

Guess again.

What do these famous *twentieth century* love affairs have in common? Richard Blaine and Ilsa Lund from *Casablanca*. Laura and Alex from *Brief Encounter*. Yuri Zhivago and Lara from *Dr. Zhivago*. Katharine Clifton and Count Almasy from *The English Patient*.

You got it. Illicit affairs, one and all.

You can look long and hard for a model of romantic love that involves happily *married* people loving each other. Rhett Butler and Scarlett O'Hara? They were not exactly *happily* married. And Scarlett's ideal of romantic love was always the affair she longed to have with Ashley. King Edward and Wallis Simpson? They did finally get married. But their *romance* was all from the days when their illicit love scandalized the monarchy. Even the Eminent Victorians Robert Browning and Elizabeth Barrett Browning—the very epitome of the "marriage of true minds"—concealed the fact that Robert, that sly dog, got plenty of extra action on the side.

What's my point? We send ourselves terribly mixed messages. On the one hand, we celebrate the ideal of marital fidelity. We tell ourselves nothing is more admirable than the faithfully, happily married couple. Yet on the other hand, we also tell ourselves that the people who really get the most out of life are the great romantics. And then every picture we paint of what we mean by great romance involves illicit lovers breaking their marital vows.

Does this excuse my infidelity to Elaine? Of course not. It's just a *defense*. Not an excuse. But it may explain the deep ambivalence I feel this morning. Trying to function again in the clean world. While a constant stream of vivid images of Janet Fickel's wanton ways flashes fresh across my field of vision. Mixed in with vivid images of my own wanton ways with her. If it was so wrong, why did it *feel* so right? Why should I have to deny myself such unrestrained joy?

But *what about Elaine*? I know I did not set out to hurt Elaine. Not at all.

And despite what you may think, I still love Elaine. Just as much as I loved Elaine before I made love to Janet. Unfortunately, our culture says I *must* now love Elaine less, because now I love Janet. I think that's wrong. Though I know I could never convince Elaine of that.

Ironically, I'm torturing myself with these thoughts about Love and sex while driving to see a *nun*. In Cleveland. Sister Marta what's-her-name. The one Amy Pierce referred me to.

I could have *called* Sister Marta. Interviewed her by phone. Would have saved me this six-hour trip. But it's hard to press the tough questions by phone. Though honestly, that's not why I'm driving to Cleveland. The real reason is I'm awful close to finding Rachel Clark. She's either Camille or Naomi. So do I want to stay in Ann Arbor, and risk finding her today? Or do I want to run off to Cleveland, virtually ensuring that my little hunt will stretch out into next week?

If you'd been in that hotel room last night at the Sheraton, you'd know the answer.

On the way down to Cleveland, my cell rings. It's Graham. I can see his number. And I don't need tarot cards to know why Graham's calling. He wants me back in Florida.

I seriously consider not picking up. Then telling Graham later I was on a stakeout.

But what's the point? I'll have to face the music sooner or later. Let's get it over with.

"Scott Peterson Defense Fund. How much would you like to pledge today?"

"Very funny, Fisher," Graham says. "Are you on a plane yet?"

"We seem to have a bad connection, sir. You want to pledge an entire *airplane*?"

"Fisher, stop fucking around. This is *your boss* you're talking to. Show a little respect."

"Sorry, buddy. My bad. Whassup?"

"I need you back here. *Pronto*."

"Why? We got last week's issue out just fine. With me editing by remote control."

"Enough's enough, Dave. You've had your fun. No more Dick Tracy. Get back here."

"I don't suppose you want to hear how I'm progressing on the Story of the Century?"

"No, I don't. If you *had* anything, I'd already know it."

"How? Graham, did *you* send that goon to break into my hotel room?"

"David, have you been drinking again?"

"I'm stone-cold sober, buddy. And having the time of my life."

"Well it's time to get back to the daily grind."

"No."

"What?"

"You heard me, Graham. N. O. No. I'm not coming back 'til this story's done. If you want, I'll go on vacation. You can start docking my already meager bank of vacation hours."

"You're already in the hole on vacation, Dave."

"Good. This'll put me further in the hole. That way you'll know I'll never be able to afford to quit. Isn't that every publisher's dream? An editor who's an indentured servant?"

"I worry about you, David. I truly do. Have you considered going into therapy?"

"What self-respecting shrink would want to listen to me rant for an hour?"

"Fair point. Okay. Look. Anyone else says 'no' to me, I fire them. But I'm going to pretend I didn't hear you say 'no.' Still, I *am* going to put you on vacation. Starting Monday."

"It's only fair, Graham. Just do me one favor."

"What?"

"Don't tell Elaine. She worries I'm never going to have time to take her to Paris."

"One week, Fisher. That's it. And you still have to edit this week's stories."

"Wouldn't miss it for the world! Just e-mail 'em up to me. Say—they haven't convicted Scott Peterson yet, have they?"

"No verdict yet."

"Thank God. For a minute I thought I might have some real work to do."

"I'm glad you reminded me. If the Peterson verdict comes in today or anytime next week, your vacation is cancelled."

"Don't say that, Graham."

"Why not?"

"Because if you cancel my vacation, I'll have to quit. And truly, I like working for you."

"You feel *that* passionately about this story?"

"Yes, I do."

"Then let's hope the Peterson trial drags out another week."

"Amen to that, brother. Talk to you later."

I don't usually threaten to quit over a story. It's *Janet Fickel* that's got me acting so reckless. Go ahead. Fire me. Turn my life upside down. Might do me some good. *Fuck work*!

A strange virus has invaded me. I've contracted a life-threatening case of *desire*. The life the virus threatens is the life I've been leading. Which seemed fine until I met Janet. But which now lacks a vital ingredient. Lust. Libido.

And the virus has me feeling more than reckless. I feel *experimental*.

Anything's possible. I could quit my job. Or be fired. I could quit my family. (Or be fired from that, too.) I could move to Ann Arbor. I could romance Janet every day.

I'm sure this will never happen to *you*, Virtuous Reader. But imagine for a moment that it did. Imagine yourself in the highly contradictory position I'm in. Of having elected to live a life from which you now plot intricate escapes. Seeking to become a fugitive from yourself.

Am I going crazy? Perhaps. But I don't think so. We all crave connection. Love is the vital plasma we seek. So what if I've found Love in all the wrong places? It's still Love.

Isn't that a country-western song? *Looking for Love in All the Wrong Places*?

I gotta admit, I *love* country music lyrics. Not the music. But the *lyrics*. They're the best. Like, "I hear from my ex/On the back of my checks." Or, "My wife ran off with my best friend/And I miss him already." If only real poets could write that well.

But it's a little scary to think how much my life is beginning to resemble the plot of a country-western song. The only thing worse would be to have my life resemble a tabloid story.

So I do what we all do. In the absence of martinis. Or prozac. I focus on *work*. My job. After all, Graham didn't fire me. Yet. And I didn't quit. Yet. So I locate the convent.

Except it turns out to be more like an office. The modern church works in mysterious ways. This convent is in a low-rent office building. In a very rough neighborhood in Cleveland.

But the receptionist is one hot bitch. If you'll pardon my French. I mean, there's no other way to describe her. I drove down expecting nuns in wimples and robes. You know, the *Sound of Music* thing. And the first thing I see is a twenty-something African-American woman in the shortest, tightest skirt this side of Janet Fickel. Lord! I'm ready to convert. Where do I sign up?

Unfortunately, I'm not the first man to have noticed her. She shakes her head at me even as I approach. With a "don't-even-think-about-it" look. Too bad. I'm in fantasy overdrive today. Anything seems possible. But I settle for being escorted to Sister Marta's office.

Sister Marta Garcia Perez is forty-something. Dark-skinned. Pretty. Still wears the traditional nun's habit. The robe. The wimple. Even in her modern office setting. Here in the ghetto.

"The call to do God's work," Sister Marta says, "is strongest here amongst the poor."

"Did you ever read any poetry by Wallace Stevens?" I ask.

"Why no, I don't believe I have."

"Wallace Stevens has this great line: '*It is poverty's speech that seeks us out the most.*' I forget what poem that line comes from. But that's what you're saying. Isn't it?"

"Why yes. Wallace Stevens. I'll have to remember that."

"I came to see you about an old friend of mine. Sanne ter Spiegel. Sanne likes Wallace Stevens, too. At least she did in the old days."

"Oh, Sanne!" Marta clasps her hands together. Beatifically. "What a lovely soul!"

Sister Marta is laying it on pretty thick. For my cynical taste. Though she seems genuine.

"I need to get in touch with her. Amy Pierce thought you might know where Sanne is."

"Back home," Sister Marta says.

"Home?"

"Amsterdam. That's where Sanne's from."

"Do you have an address for Sanne there?"

"No."

"Then how do you know she's there?"

"That's where Sanne said she was going when she left Nicaragua. To look for her daughter Sarah."

"When was that?"

"Oh, goodness. After Sister Teresa was murdered. 1989. Yes. Summer of '89."

"By that time Sanne had been in Nicaragua how long—nine years?"

"That sounds about right."

"What made Sanne decide to leave?"

"Sanne had a large hole in her heart. From being separated so long from her daughter."

"How did Sanne leave?"

"An American lawyer came to our village. In a moving van with medical supplies. Humanitarian aid from the City of Ann Arbor. We were very grateful. You have no idea how desperately we needed those supplies. It was a very bad time for the people of Nicaragua."

"And the American lawyer was Lane Davis from Ann Arbor?"

"Yes," Marta says. "He brought the supplies down all by himself. A very brave man. Sanne was quite taken with him. A dashing figure, though a bit older than Sanne. Who knows? She may have been in love with him. Perhaps that is the true reason why Sanne left Nicaragua."

"But then she might not have gone back to Amsterdam after all?"

"I really don't know where Sanne went. She left with Mr. Davis in his moving van. She said she was going to ride up to Ann Arbor with him. Because she went to university there in her youth. And after that she said she was going home."

"You took that to mean Amsterdam?"

"Yes, of course. That's where Sanne was from. Amsterdam."

"Did you ever see Sanne's Dutch passport? Her identification papers?"

"Oh yes. The Military Police demanded them. Many times." Sister Marta raises a suspicious eyebrow. "Why? Is there a problem that makes you ask these questions, Mr. Fisher?"

"Yes. I can't find Sanne. I think perhaps Sanne is using another name."

"And why do you need to find Sanne?" Sister Marta is almost on the muscle now.

"Mr. Davis is looking for her," I lie. "He hired me to find Sanne. *And* her daughter."

Sister Marta relaxes at my explanation. But then a sad look crosses her face.

"Oh," she says. "Then I guess Sanne didn't marry Mr. Davis after all."

"I don't think she did." Although I'm thinking that's probably *exactly* what she did.

Because it all fits.

Lane Davis said he married Camille in 1989. After he drove the supplies down to Nicaragua. A dashing fellow. An heroic figure. In the eyes of the Fugitive Radical. So she falls in love. Rides back to Ann Arbor with Davis. Using the dead nun's passport. Then changes her name. Again. To "Camille." Marries Davis. He might not even know about her criminal past.

"Was there anything else I could help you with, Mr. Fisher?"

"Sanne's daughter, Sarah. Are you still in touch with her?"

"Goodness, no. I never met Sarah. Though a woman named Amy Pierce once called from Amsterdam. Friend of Sanne's. She'd received a letter from Sanne, asking her to send Sarah to Nicaragua. But Amy said Sarah was gone. A troubled child, was the impression I got."

"Yes. A troubled child. Sanne, too, was a troubled child."

I let the dead air hang between us. But Sister Marta sits demurely. Eyes downcast. No perceptible emotion. And no response.

"Amy Pierce said you were very close to Sanne," I say at last. "In Nicaragua."

"We were. Very close. We worked together on many projects."

"And?"

"Sanne said I'd given her life a purpose again. But of course the credit goes to God. *He* gave her life its purpose. I was merely His instrument."

"But if you were so close," I say, "how is it you lost all contact with her?"

Marta purses her lips. "Sanne's last few months in Nicaragua, we grew estranged."

"What was the problem?"

"Sanne was—disappointed. In me. She felt I should have done more to challenge the Nicaraguan authorities. About the murder of Sister Teresa."

"Who murdered Sister Teresa?"

"No one really knows. Sanne believed it was government agents. Which was certainly possible. The government there was not friendly to our work. And Teresa pushed the limits, always. As Sanne did. But the Nicaraguan government denied any involvement in Teresa's death. And the proof was not there. Our standing in Nicaragua was already—shaky. It would not have helped our cause to push for the government to investigate itself. What could come of such an investigation anyway? I grieved for Teresa. As much as anyone. But I felt, for the sake of the people who so desperately needed our help, that we had to leave the matter of Teresa's murder in the hands of the authorities."

"Whereas Sanne wanted—*justice*?"

"Precisely the word Sanne used! Justice. Since Sanne had never taken vows, she volunteered to be the one who pushed. For justice. But I told her to let it be. We quarreled. More than once, God forgive me."

"Was anyone ever charged with the murder?"

"No."

"What was Sister Teresa's last name?"

"Teresa Rodriguez Lamas, may she rest in peace."

"And a few months later, Sanne rode off into the sunset with Lane Davis. And you never heard from her again?"

"Never."

Well in my mind that about cinches it. Sure sounds like Camille is Rachel Clark.

On the drive home I consider the alternatives. I could lay it all out for Lane Davis. See if he wants to *join me* in confronting Camille. Or I could just confront Camille at home. While Lane's still at work. Give her one chance to give me the interview.

But do I really want the Rachel Clark interview *now*? On this Friday afternoon? Once I get it, I'll have to send it to Graham. ASAP. Then I'll be out of excuses. For staying in Ann Arbor.

Why not wait 'til my Monday lunch date with Camille? So I can have another weekend with Janet. *Fuck work*!

\* \* \*

"How you feeling today?"

"I'm fine," Janet purrs softly into the phone at work. "A little sore, but fine."

"*Sore*?"

"It's been almost two years since"—Janet dips her voice extra soft—"I've done that."

"Ah. Well it was really great. You were wonderful, Janet."

"You, too."

"I know you can't talk much at work. But I figured you'd rather have me call you here than on your cell. Would you like to have dinner tonight?"

"I can't."

"Oh." I wait. Hoping for some explanation. None comes. "How 'bout lunch tomorrow?"

Long pause. "Yeah, sure. But I have to be home by six p.m., David."

We make arrangements to meet at Island Park at noon.

"I love you, Janet."

"Same here."

\* \* \*

"Come home."

"I can't, Rachel."

"Why not?"

"I'm working on a big story. I need another week up here."

"But my Shakespeare paper's due next week. I *need* you."

"What's the assignment?"

Rachel makes a sound impossible to represent with letters. A cross between a sigh of exasperation and a groan of despair. After the sound, Rachel reads me the assignment. In a voice implying this is the most unreasonable assignment ever perpetrated by a teacher on a student. "'Take a scene from *Hamlet*. Explain why the scene is still relevant to modern readers. Include in your discussion examples of Shakespeare's use of *language* in the scene.' *That's it!*"

"What's so hard about that?"

"Dad!" Rachel makes that sound of exasperation and despair again.

"You know, at college you'll have to write your papers all by yourself. Without my help. Unless you're planning to call me every night. And become the laughing stock of your dorm."

"Dad. Save the advice. I'm not in college yet."

"Okay. Then do this. Did you read *Hamlet* yet?"

"Of course."

"Remember the scene when Ophelia's brother is going off to college? Or France? Or wherever the heck he's going?"

"No."

"Sure you do. It's in one of the first two acts. Before Polonius gets killed in the third act. In Hamlet's mother's bedroom. When Hamlet mistakes Polonius for his uncle. And runs him through with his—"

"Oh yeah, yeah. I remember Polonius getting killed."

"Good. Well *before* Polonius gets killed, there's this famous scene where Polonius gives some long-winded advice to his son. The son is Laertes, I think. And Laertes just wants to get the heck out of there. Kind of the way you feel. Whenever I'm giving *you* advice. But old Polonius keeps rambling on. And on. And on."

"Oh yeah, I remember now."

"It's a very famous scene. 'To thine own self be true.' And 'the apparel oft proclaims the man.' And 'neither a borrower nor a lender be.' These are very famous sayings."

"If you say so."

"I do. So here's an idea. Use that scene. It's not all that *long*. Really just one long boring speech by old Polonius. Focus on *each* of his sayings. The actual advice. But translate them into modern language. Like the language of advertisements. Instead of 'to thine own self be true,' use the Army's catch phrase,

THE RUNNING OF THE BULLS 

'Be all you can be.' Or something like that. Instead of 'the apparel oft proclaims the man,' use some slogan from Calvin Klein or Versace or some designer."

"Hey Dad, that's so tight!"

*Tight?* Is Rachel, too, accusing me of drinking? "Is 'tight' a good thing these days?"

"Yeah it is! That's tight! Meaning that's a *really good idea*, Dad."

Truly, I often wonder if my children and I speak the same language. "Why do you sound so surprised? Some of *Polonius's* ideas were good ones, too."

"Yeah sure, Dad. Thanks. Mom wants to talk to you now."

"That's what I'm here for."

Elaine gets on the phone. "When are you coming home, sweetie?"

"Sometime next week."

"That long? How many suspects have you got left?"

"Two. But that's not what's holding me up. The problem is the cops have *ordered* me to stay in town. Because I'm a material witness."

"Can they *do* that?"

"Maybe. Maybe not. Graham's working on it. But it won't get sorted out 'til next week."

"Oh. Well I need to talk to you about our December vacation."

"Go ahead."

"I mean when you're back home."

I hear a crashing noise in the background. At Elaine's end of the line.

"David, I gotta go. Sara just broke a vase. Can I call you tomorrow afternoon?"

"Ah—no. I'll be on a stakeout tomorrow. I'll call you Sunday."

\* \* \*

Friday night alone. No Janet. No Elaine.

I debate following Janet from work. To see why she can't go out with me. But I decide that's beneath even me. So instead I follow Naomi Williams. To see where *she* goes.

Naomi goes home. To a small, cedar-shake house on Ann Arbor's west side. Where she meets up with the female roommate Janet told me about.

Naomi and her roommate fix dinner. Eat. Clean up. Then sit down to read.

I try to think of a ploy to get Naomi's fingerprints. But I can't come up with anything. Other than waiting 'til they both leave. And then breaking in. So after a few hours, I abandon the dullest stakeout in history. Buy a bottle of Scotch. Return to my hotel. Break open the Scotch. And sit down to listen to tapes from the phone taps at Raven's house. And Casa Davis.

I'm half-crocked. And three-fourths asleep. When this one comes on. From earlier today:

RAVEN:      Hello?

SHEILA:     Hi, it's Sheila. Lane asked me to call. He can't make dinner tonight.

RAVEN:      Oh? And he couldn't call himself?

SHEILA:     No, he couldn't. Don't be mad, Raven. Lane's in a jam.

RAVEN:      What kind of jam?

SHEILA:     Greg Hunter's all over him. Lane and Camille are having a long meeting right now with Hunter. It's been going on for *hours*.

RAVEN:      About . . . the Fugitive Radical?

SHEILA:     I assume. But I don't really know. All I know for sure is, Hunter stopped by the office this afternoon. All business. First he leaned all over me. He told me he knows who I really am, and he told me I better tell him where Rachel Clark is. Or else.

RAVEN:      You mean the same kind of shit David Fisher tried to pull on you?

SHEILA:     Yes. So I told Hunter to go to hell. Then he insisted on speaking with Lane. ASAP. They talked in Lane's office for half an hour.

RAVEN:      About what? What does *Lane* know about any of this?

SHEILA:     I don't *know* what it was about. But it was serious as hell, because when they came out, Lane cancelled his interview with the *Free Press*. Then he had Janet call Camille, to tell Camille to meet him down at City Hall. And last he poked his head in my office, and asked me to call you and cancel dinner. He said he was going to be in a very long meeting at City Hall tonight.

RAVEN:      Shit! What can we do?

SHEILA:     I don't know. But if the press finds out Hunter's got Lane and Camille in for questioning, there's gonna be a huge shit storm.

RAVEN:      Sarah must have given Hunter what he wanted.

SHEILA:     Oh, God. I hope not.

RAVEN:      Look. We gotta do *something*.

SHEILA:     We need to find out exactly what's going on first. I'll call Lane at home tonight. As soon as I hear anything, I'll call you.

Even through the haze of my usual three Scotches, *this* call gets my attention. Damn that impatient Hunter! Rattling Davis's cage. Just when I'm poised to get my story.

I call the police station. Ask for Cliff. Even though it's late, Cliff's there. But the duty sergeant says he's busy. So I leave a message. What else can I do?

An hour later, Cliff calls back. "I'm busy now, Dave. What's up?"

"What's Hunter doing with the Davises?"

"You know I can't answer that question, Dave."

"Cliff, you gotta keep Hunter under control. I can find Rachel Clark for you. I'm so fuckin' close, you can't believe it."

"You're right, Dave. I can't believe it. Neither can Hunter. So we're through waiting for you."

* * *

As you know, my last visit to Déjà Vu ended unhappily. With their bouncers knocking me out of the box. Before I could finish interviewing Sarah Watts. Sent me to the drunk tank.

The sub-humans at Déjà Vu's door are *not* the sharpest tools in the shed. But even *they* will remember my face. It's only been four days. So I don the gray wig and black glasses.

Friday turns out to be the night they "run the bulls" at Déjà Vu. A big step up from the whipped cream fights of "Manic Monday." At Déjà Vu, the running of the bulls involves a scratchy recording of the "Toreador's Song" from *Carmen*. A few assorted capes and sombreros. And ten naked women running up and down the aisles. Holding their index fingers beside their temples. To simulate horns. The climax (as it were) involves the naked women gathering on stage. On their hands and knees. Taking turns charging a woman in a cape. This show is not ready for Broadway. Not even for the Catskills. But here in Ypsilanti? The crowd loves it.

The spotlight is harsh. Probably borrowed from the prison down the road. But it does the job. I can see the ladies' faces. Doesn't take long to spot Sarah Pierce. She's the woman in the cape. She's got ten pounds of make-up on. Looks better than she did in that Lake Michigan photo Amy Pierce showed me. But not a *lot* better. And she does have a very slight limp.

After the show, I duck into the bathroom. On the way out, I run into Sarah Pierce. Literally.

I hand her a phony business card I printed on my computer earlier today: "David Fisher, Claims Investigator, Mutual Savings Life Insurance Company." With my cell phone number on it.

Hey—it worked for my buddies at BATF. Let's see if it works on Sarah Pierce.

Sarah Pierce glances at my card. Tries to hand it back to me.

"No, please," I say. "You need the phone number."

"We can't date guys we meet here." Sarah slurs her words.

"I don't want a date. I believe my company owes you money. But I have to interview you first. To determine if you are, in fact, the sole living beneficiary of Rachel Clark."

Sarah Pierce narrows her eyes. She ain't sure she's buyin' it.

"I can't interview you here," I continue. "So if you want the money, you have to call me tomorrow morning. *Before noon*. If you get my voice mail, leave your call back number."

"Mister, I don't *have* a call back number. And even if I did, I sure as hell wouldn't give it to you."

"Fair enough, Sarah. So if you get my voice mail, be sure to call again later. Or I can't give you the money."

"Why you wanna give me money?" Sarah's slurring her words badly now.

"There's a life insurance policy on your mother. *If* Rachel Clark was your mother."

Before Sarah can answer, the manager accosts us. The gist of what he has to say is, he does not like to see his dancers involved in extended, non-remunerative conversations with patrons of the club.

"Can I buy a lap dance?" I suggest.

The manager flashes the phoniest smile anywhere outside a used car lot. Gestures to an open couch. Where I sit. And Sarah Pierce performs.

The cape turns out to be, for Sarah Pierce, what the scarf was for Isadora Duncan. A prop for all seasons. First Sarah hides behind it. Then she peeks over it. Then she rolls it up into a long snake. And pulls it across her shoulders. Pulls it between her large natural breasts. Through her legs. Across her twitching buttocks. And then across *my* face. And between *my* legs. Then she unrolls it again. Drapes the cape across her back. While she stands before me. Her long legs spread, Eiffel Tower style. Now she places her hands on my shoulders. And balances her knees on my thighs. With the cape like a screen. While she undulates in my lap.

Sarah Pierce is *very* close. As Bob Dylan said, "*I can feel the heat and the pulse of her.*" Which convinces me she's probably on hillbilly heroin. Right now. Because her breathing is *very* slow. Her pupils are dilated. And she's scratching herself a lot.

"I thought life insurance money only gets paid when someone dies," Sarah Pierce whispers in my ear. With very warm breath. And very slurred speech.

"Mostly that's true," I mutter. "But if a person's missing for thirty-five years, we're legally required to pay. *As if* she were dead. Unless we have evidence she's still alive."

Sarah Pierce nods. Rubs her big soft breasts in my face. Which is way sexier than having Chandra's volleyballs smacking me. Except Sarah's so high, it doesn't feel at all *personal*.

"I'll explain it all tomorrow. When I interview you. But basically, you get money either way. Whether your mom's alive, or not."

"How's that?"

"Because if there's no proof your mom's alive, we pay you the policy. On the other hand, if you have proof she *is* still alive, we'll pay you a percentage of the policy. Like a finder's fee. For being honest and saving us having to pay the whole policy until later. Plus—if you know where she is, we'll help you claim the reward money. Which is worth a lot more than the policy."

"What makes you think I'm even related to Rachel Clark?"

"Call me tomorrow morning, Sarah. Before noon. I'll buy you dinner. Answer all your questions. And if all goes well, I'll write you a check. For a lot of money. On the spot."

"How much?"

"I can't disclose that to you. Until I know for sure you're Rachel Clark's beneficiary. So please. Just call me tomorrow morning. *Before noon.*"

# CHAPTER TWELVE
# HOW A BODY SWAYS

## Saturday 23 October 2004

First thing Saturday morning, I write another love letter to Janet. I consider spilling the beans. About how I really work for a tabloid. And live in Florida. I'm going to have to tell her sometime. But as usual, I chicken out. Why run the risk that Janet'll get pissed *today*? Why do today what you can put off 'til tomorrow?

I'll spare you the love letter. But it includes a short poem. Which is *so bad*, I feel compelled to show it to you. In the interest of full disclosure. No false modesty here. It's inexecrable. Brace yourself. This is what love does to you. It drives you to write bad poetry.

> We gazed into the deep abyss
> Of what might be. I dared you. Dared—
> 'Til you called my bluff, and gave a kiss
> That sparked our dormant passion, flared
>
> Our mild flirtation into love
> So wild and reckless. Now your voice,
> Your eyes, your special grace, all prove:
> Even used hearts can still rejoice.
>
> But when I say, "I love you, Janet"—
> Still you demur. You try to douse
> My ardor. You tell me to can it,
> Behave my butt. Yet still your blouse
>
> Betrays you, for the telltale heave
> Each time we kiss just goes to prove
> This winter you'll get no reprieve
> From our reckless passion and our love.

Truly, when you start writing poetry like this, you need to *rush* yourself into therapy.

But I lack time for therapy. So I start trying to find out what's going on with Lane Davis. I call his home. His office. His campaign headquarters. No answer anywhere. I call Sheila's home and office. No answer. I leave another message for Cliff. Beseeching Cliff—my old *teammate*—to tell me if Lane Davis has been arrested. No call back.

I check the tapes from my taps and bugs at Raven's house and Casa Davis. Nothing.

I get in my car. Clean my tail. Then drive over to Casa Davis.

Eight boys are playing football in the front yard. They look like they're all eleven or twelve. And having the time of their lives. Using four "Davis for Mayor" yard signs as goal-line markers. The scattered piles of leaves on the lawn make nice soft landing places. Whenever they gang-tackle a guy. Or dive for a pass. The autumn air is perfect. Not too hot, not too cold. And the smell of the leaves, in this crisp clean air, makes *me* yearn to play football, too.

Is there anything as beautiful as a halfback's weave to set up a block? (Well, okay—*excluding* the undersides of Janet Fickel's thighs.) Or the warm sun on the leathery hide of a forward pass? Or the achingly beautiful hang time of a punt—even a fairly low-flying, twelve-year-old's punt? Or the fresh scent of grass on your sleeve when you dive to make a tackle?

I seriously consider asking these kids if I can join in their game. Even though next to them, I'd be like William "Refrigerator" Perry. Since they're all Janet Fickel's size.

But I talk myself out of this dumb idea. Walk past the football game. To the front door.

"My parents aren't home, Mister," a boy calls out. "They left about an hour ago."

"Oh. Thanks. D'ya know where they are?"

"Naw."

I drive to City Hall. Camille's Volvo is parked there. So I walk into the police station.

"Is Camille Davis here?" I demand of the heavy-jowled duty sergeant at the counter.

"I don't know, sir. Who are you?"

"David Fisher. I'm looking for Ms. Davis. Her car's been parked outside a long time."

"If she's here, you'll have to wait 'til she's done. *If* she's here."

"I understand. I'd just like to know if she's here."

"I can't tell you that."

"Is Cliff Bryant here?"

"Perhaps. Would you like to talk to Detective Bryant?"

"Yes, please."

"I'll see if he's available."

The heavy-jowled duty sergeant disappears. Returns five minutes later. In no particular hurry.

"Detective Bryant said he can't see you right now. He has your message. He'll contact you when he has some time."

I drive by Sheila Nyman's house. Sheila's not home. I drive by Raven LaGrow's house. Raven's not home. I drive by Naomi Williams's house. *Naomi's* not home, either. But Naomi's *roommate* is home. Painting. In the living room. Rendering any crazy break-in idea hopeless.

I'm out of ideas. Clearly my DOJ training is not all I cracked it up to be.

Sarah Pierce calls. Agrees to meet me for dinner. Anywhere. So I give her directions to Dominick's. We agree to meet at six. Though she says she'll have to leave for work at eight.

It bothers me a lot that Hunter knows about Janet Fickel. I was careless Tuesday night. Didn't clean my tail before going to the West End Grill.

I haven't spotted anyone tailing me today. But that means little. I'm sure the dark-haired young woman in the blue Toyota is off the case. Since I shot my mouth off with Hunter. And I might just be missing the new tail. So before going to lunch I clean my tail. *Thoroughly.*

* * *

"You said you liked this dress."

"I do!"

Janet's wearing that short brown dress she wore last Saturday. I'm *not* complaining.

I hand her my love letter. With the bad poem. She agrees to wait and read it later.

Janet reminds me she only has about five hours. Doesn't care what we do.

We go get lunch. In my car. Janet hands me a CD. It's a compilation of songs she put together for me. There's only time to hear two before we get to Café Zola. But they're both songs I've never heard before. I'm not even sure what type of music they are. They seem very modern. Techno-rock, maybe.

"These are songs Stacy listens to all the time," Janet says. "I picked out the best ones."

"Thank you. That was very thoughtful."

"Your daughters probably listen to these songs, too."

"I don't recognize these first two. But I don't pay as much attention as I should."

"I don't believe that! You never miss anything."

"I missed you. Yesterday."

I turn to give Janet an appropriately loving gaze. And nearly crash into a pickup truck.

"Hey! Watch where you're going, asshole!" The driver yells at me.

I flip him the peace sign. Janet laughs.

"Janet, I do hope you know I'm serious about our relationship."

"Yes. So am I."

"I don't want to rush things. But I'm thinking I should get an apartment. For that day."

Janet nods. Doesn't ask what "day" I mean. Good thing. I don't really know myself.

"Would you mind coming with me this afternoon while I look at an apartment or two?"

"Mind? Of course not. Sounds like fun."

So after lunch I call some numbers in the classifieds. Make some appointments.

First stop is a small house on North State Street. Your basic student dive.

The Landlady, "Charity"—*if that really is her name*—is a real trip. A total parody of the unrepentant flower child. Bell-bottoms. Tie-dyed shirt. Long gray hair with bangs. Looking at Charity, you'd never know the sixties ended. Except for the gray hair and a few worry lines near her mouth, Charity looks like she's still twenty. I almost ask if she ever knew Rachel Clark.

But when we start talking rent, Charity is all business. $850 per month, six-month minimum lease. Even though the entire "apartment" could fit inside my Florida bathroom.

Janet shudders at the galley-style kitchen. Which is too narrow for us to stand side-by-side. She turns up her nose at the peeling wallpaper, too. Janet's clearly not impressed.

Meanwhile, Charity's turning up *her* nose, too. At Janet. The short tight dress. The stockings. The heels. The big boobs.

"Will this be single or *dual* occupancy?" Charity asks. Staring hard at Janet's bust.

"Single," I say. "But I think this is not big enough for us. For *me*, I mean."

Janet and I hightail it out of there. Barely suppressing gales of giddy laughter.

Next stop: Barclay Condominiums. Northeast edge of Ann Arbor. Pretty far out of town. This place was woods when I was growing up. But I figure we'll get something *modern* here. Janet'll be happier.

On the way, we listen to several more songs on the CD Janet made for me. I recognize none of them. But that means nothing. I haven't listened to the radio since Bob Marley died.

Janet's songs are very sexy. Breathy female vocalists. Singing about guys who make them want to surrender. Guys who can get inside them if they play their cards right. I like the songs. Even more, I like the idea that Janet picked these sexy songs out for me. Good sign.

The realtor, Brian Fink, meets us outside. One look, no doubt: Brian's flamingly gay.

Brian turns out to be a lot of fun, too. He explains that normally the condos here are only for sale. No rentals. But there's one the developer wants to hold onto for a year. So he'll rent it for one year. No guarantee we can renew the lease. But we'll get a chance to buy, if we want.

"This is for two of you—right?"

"Just my name on the lease," I say.

Brian looks Janet up and down. Raises an exquisite eyebrow. Then takes us inside.

The place is brand new. Nice open floor plan. The kitchen is capacious.

We go upstairs. Janet leads. Then me. Then Brian. Which turns out to be a perfect arrangement. I watch Janet's tight little butt wiggle up the stairs. While Brian watches mine.

The master bedroom is large. The closets are all as big as bedrooms. And there's a jacuzzi tub in the master bath. The whole place is just $1,000 a month.

"Should be enough room here for my pool table," I say.

"In the *bedroom*?" Janet asks.

"Absolutely. So I can kick your butt at pool last thing every night before I go to bed."

"What if I'm not *here* last thing at night before you go to bed?"

"Should make it all the easier for me to win."

Janet laughs. Brian arches that exquisite eyebrow again. Like he's on *Queer Eye for The Straight Guy*. "I don't believe the bedroom is the optimal location for a pool table. I'd suggest the bonus room."

Brian shows us a second bedroom on the upper floor. Which he says only this unit has.

"I can't put the pool table in here," I say. "I need this room for the nights Janet kicks me out of bed."

Brian flings his hands into the air. In a perfect parody of a gay teapot. "Whatever!"

We carry on like this awhile longer. And then—impetuously, I must admit—I agree to rent the place. So I sign the rental agreement. Now Brian needs a check. Two and a half months' rent.

Janet's puttering around in the kitchen. So I whip out my Florida checkbook. Fast. Write the $2,500 check. Fast. Figuring by the time Elaine sees this check, next month, I'll either be living here—or, if things don't work out, I'll have had time to come up with some plausible story about the check.

"Usually we require certified funds," Brian says. "Especially with an out—"

"It's Saturday." I interrupt Brian. So he won't say "out-of-state" out loud. "We were really hoping to move in right away."

Brian looks around the starkly empty unit. "Without *furniture*?"

"We don't need a lot of furniture."

Brian looks at Janet in the kitchen. Raises *both* his exquisite eyebrows this time. Then sighs. "Well, you'll be saving me time. If I don't have to come back to do paperwork on Monday. Just *promise me* this check won't bounce."

"Brian, this check won't bounce. I promise."

Brian leaves the keys. Instructions for how to change over the utilities. And bids *adieu*.

"You *do* like it, don't you?" I ask Janet.

"Oh yes," Janet says. "It's very nice."

We fall into each other's arms. Start making out. Energetically.

"Did you ever see *Last Tango In Paris*?" I mumble into her neck.

Janet puts on mock disapproval. "What makes you think we watch movies like *that* in Indiana?"

"The guilty look on your face."

Janet laughs. "Okay. I admit it. I *did* see that one."

"*They* were in an empty apartment. Just like this."

Janet gives me a look of pure seduction. "Well, I hope you'll at least take your coat off. Unlike Marlon Brando."

I pick Janet up. Set her, fully-clothed, on the built-in kitchen desk. And slowly run my fingers up the insides of her thighs. By the time I reach her vagina, she's very wet.

We don't have a bed. Or a couch. The only choices are the hardwood floor. The carpet upstairs. Or this kitchen desk. Which is the perfect height.

I do remove my coat. Drop my pants. And then try something I've never tried before. Since Janet's so light and flexible. I slip her thong off. Balance her butt on the rounded edge of the desk. Throw her ankles over my shoulders. Put my hands on her thigh-high stockings. Lean her head against the cabinet above the desk. And make love to her. Me standing, Janet sitting.

Turns out to be a great position for fucking. For both of us. Her big boobs are right in my face. Her active hands can easily reach my balls. And my thumb has no problem finding her clit. Pretty soon she's moaning. Arching her back. And those veins in her neck and forehead are standing out again. A little later, I get dizzy. As the blood leaves my head. And I come.

"You do seem more relaxed today," Janet says. As we readjust our clothing.

"I guess I just like being in the kitchen."

"Not me! I should warn you now: I'm a *terrible* cook."

"We'll eat out then. Every night, if you like."

Janet laughs. "Well, how 'bout every *other* night? You wouldn't want to miss out on my nachos. My specialty. The one thing I can cook."

"Every *other* night is fine then. But I do hope you'll decide to move in here with me, Janet. No rush, of course. But eventually. When the time is right for you."

Janet kisses me. Long and sweet. Then excuses herself. To use the bathroom.

We sit on the hardwood floor in the living room. Leaning up against the wall. With my arm around Janet's shoulders.

"Have you ever been to New Orleans?" I ask.

"I've never been more than 150 miles from Fort Wayne. Chicago's my outer limit."

"New Orleans is a wild place. Very European. Great bars. Do you like music?"

"You mean jazz? Not really."

"Not just jazz. They have all kinds of music in New Orleans. Anything you like. They probably even have those techno-rock songs you put on that CD for me." I give Janet a squeeze. "How much vacation time do you have left this year?"

"Two weeks. I haven't used any yet."

"I'd like to take you to New Orleans."

"I can't get away, David."

"Sure you can. Tell John you've got to go to a firm training seminar. For three days."

"In *New Orleans*? Davis & Nyman isn't big enough to send its staff to New Orleans."

"Don't tell John you're in New Orleans. Tell him you're in Saginaw."

"He'll want to come stay with me."

"Okay. Tell him it's in Traverse City. Somewhere just far enough he won't try to come."

Janet smiles. Pats my hand. "It's a sweet thought. But I really don't think I could."

"It would be a great way for us to find out how we are together. You learn a lot about someone when you travel with them for a few days."

"Yes, you do."

"Promise me you'll think about it?"

"I'll think about it."

We sit in silence awhile. Even though Janet said no to New Orleans, the mood is still great. Mostly I'm thinking about the sex on the kitchen desk. By now you've gathered, I'm nobody's idea of a modern-day Casanova. Ask Elaine. I'm a *very* dull lover. With a very limited repertoire of "moves." If my fumbling can even be dignified by a word like "moves." Yet here I am. Acting like Marlon Brando in *Last Tango*. Sex *standing up*. Taking the hot little babe on a desk! As if I were a whole new man.

"John's feeling very touchy these days," Janet says.

"Touchy? I'm not sure I know what you mean."

"He took me to dinner last night. Which he almost *never* does. Spent a long time telling me all the things he loves about me."

"There's a lot to love. What specifically did he mention?"

Janet smiles. "The same things you always mention. In your letters. My wit. My liveliness. The way I dress. My, um, strut."

"What about your big brown eyes? He didn't mention those?"

"No."

"Guy must be blind. How 'bout your boobs? Did he mention those?"

"I think they came up, yes. But then he told me what he *doesn't* like about me."

"Uh-oh. What's that?"

"He said he doesn't like to *compete* for me."

"Meaning?"

"Meaning he thinks I'm seeing someone."

I arch an eyebrow. "What'd you say to that?"

"Nothing. I ignored it. But he made his point. That's one reason I don't think I could go away with you right now to New Orleans."

I nod. We sit in silence. While I contemplate jealous John the gun nut. Whom Janet says is prone to put her under surveillance. Could jealous John be the guy who ripped up my hotel room? But if so, why would he stop at ripping up my *room*? Surely he'd wanna rip *me* up too.

"How 'bout San Francisco?" I ask out of the blue. "That's a great town!"

Janet laughs. "I'd love to go to San Francisco with you, David. Or New Orleans. Or anywhere. I just don't see how we can do it. For now."

"Hmm. How 'bout Kalamazoo? I hear they have nice hotels there."

"*That* we might be able to arrange. But right now it's getting late. I should get back."

I help Janet up to a standing position. Which affords me a generous view of her thighs.

Janet sees me watching her. Gives me another one of those incredibly seductive looks.

There's a banister along the stairway. Somewhere in my misspent youth, I remember seeing a *Playboy* playmate splayed suggestively across a banister much like this one. A fantasy that has never come true for me. Until now.

Janet must be a mind reader. She stops a few feet from the base of the staircase. Spreads her legs. Eiffel Tower style. Bends over at the waist. Grabs the newel post in both hands. And offers herself to me. In an unmistakable invitation.

I cannot describe how beautiful Janet looks from this angle. The high heels cause her hamstrings to be fully tensed and elongated. Her thigh-high stockings are enticing. Her tight little butt is also fully tensed. And bending forward shows it off to its best advantage.

To get the right angle, I spread my own legs fairly far apart, and bend my knees down. I push the thong to one side. Since Janet always seems to be wet, entering her turns out to be easier than I would have expected in this position.

We go at it again. With reckless abandon. Two sex-crazed middle-aged romantics. Making love. Native-style. Ignoring our marital vows. Measuring time by how our bodies sway.

In this position, I begin to understand why native people around the globe *resisted* so ardently the importuning of the missionaries to have sex the European way. Truly, there's a lot to be said for the native way. Even though we civilized moderns call it "doggie-style," as if to put it down.

I turn out not to be the only fan of the native position in the Barclay condo. Janet's back arches. She comes. Twice. A few moments later, I come again.

I pull out of her. Look at my engorged cock a moment. Truly, I have never been prouder of the little guy in all my life. Who knew, at age forty-eight, I could still come twice in an hour?

Janet laughs at me admiring myself. "Men never get over having a hard dick, do they?"

"Not me." I laugh too. "It's just such a primitive *weapon*."

Janet stops laughing. "It's not a weapon," she says. Flatly.

"No," I agree. "I was just using a figure of speech. It's not really a weapon."

Janet still looks dubious. So I attempt further explanation.

"James Baldwin called it an 'atavistic weapon.' In a novel. *Another Country*, I think."

Janet seems uninterested in James Baldwin. So I let it drop. Since my foot's already way too far in my mouth to extricate.

Outside, Janet lights a cigarette. First she's had since we were at Charity's apartment.

"You know where I'd *really* like to go with you, Janet? Europe. Paris. Amsterdam."

Janet nods.

"I've always thought it would be great to live there. We could get away from everything. Get an apartment in Paris. You wouldn't have to work for Lane Davis anymore."

"Well, *that* would be a relief," Janet says.

"You'd like it there. They all dress like you."

"Then that means *you'd* like it there, doesn't it?"

I laugh. We banter some more. While Janet finishes her cigarette. When she's done, Janet drops the cigarette stub on the cement. Steps on it with the toe of her high heel.

And viciously rubs out the fire.

* * *

For dinner with Sarah Pierce, I clean my tail again. Even though Raven and Sheila think Hunter already found Sarah Pierce. I drive out to the mall. Circle the mall twice. Exit out the back. Drive downtown. Call a cab to meet me at the health food store on Fourth Avenue. Then I park in the Ann/Ashley parking structure. Walk out the side of the structure. Cross the alley. Enter the basement of the Heidelberg bar. Walk through the bar. Up the stairs. Out the front door. Cross Main Street. Cut behind the County building. Just in time to duck into my cab on Fourth Avenue. I'm telling you: *no one* can follow me in my hometown. Unless I'm careless.

In the cab, I don my gray wig and glasses. Since that's how Sarah Pierce knows me.

It's usually fun to see what strippers choose for everyday clothing. When they have a rare appointment away from the club. But Sarah surprises me. Nothing remotely flashy. Some nondescript jeans and a loose pullover. As sexless as anything *Amy* Pierce might choose to wear.

Sarah also seems much more alert than last night. No OC rails so far today, I gather.

"You got my check?"

"I have my check*book*. But I have to interview you first. Verify you're the beneficiary."

"Last night you said I get paid either way."

"You do. But only after I interview you. Please. Sit."

She sits. I get us some food. And a pitcher of sangria. With two mason jars for glasses.

Sarah inspects her sangria. Then quaffs it. Sarah likes Dominick's sangria. A lot.

"When was the last time you saw Rachel Clark?" I ask.

"Shit, I dunno. 1980."

"In Amsterdam?"

"Yeah. How you know that?"

"I'm smarter than I look."

"Well that ain't sayin' much."

I laugh. Tip my sangria jar against Sarah's. "Okay, wise-ass, tell me how you know you're Rachel Clark's daughter."

"She told me I am. When I was little and all. Who's gonna lie about that shit?"

"Rachel Clark lies about a lot of things, Sarah. Like her own name. She's had at least four different names. Do you remember what name she was using in Amsterdam?"

"Yeah."

"How 'bout you tell me that name. To help convince me you're really her daughter."

"Sanne ter Spiegel."

"You ever meet your grandparents?"

"The Zimmermans? Naw. They don't wanna know me."

"And the Clarks?"

"Yeah, I met them. They gave me money a couple times."

"They paid for your foot surgery, too, didn't they?"

Sarah looks at me sideways. "Yeah, they did. So? What's wrong with that?"

"Nothing. Do they know where your mom is now?"

Sarah gets a cagey look. "Beats me. Why don't you ask *them*?"

"Do *you* know where Rachel Clark is now?"

Sarah snorts. "Mister, if I knew that, I wouldn't be here shootin' the shit with you."

"Why not?"

"I'd be livin' large. Off that reward money. Fuck! Two hundred grand? If I had that, I wouldn't need to freeze my cold ass dancing in cold bars in this god-damn cold town."

"You know Raven LaGrow and Sheila Nyman?"

"Yeah."

"Why do *they* think you know where Rachel Clark is?"

Sarah snorts again. "Cuz they're scared of their own shadows. They think everyone's out to get 'em. And maybe they're right. You know that saying? *Just cuz you're paranoid don't mean they ain't out to get ya.*" Sarah breaks up laughing at her own joke.

I spend a couple more hours drinking sangria with Sarah Pierce. But get nowhere.

In the end, I have to give Sarah the bad news. No check today. No check *ever*.

Understandably, Sarah gets pissed. Emits a stream of obscenities that would make a sailor blush. I leave Dominick's with Sarah stalking right behind me, cursing my every step. But luckily she's gotta get to work. So she has to give up harassing me when her ride shows up.

*  *  *

Back in the clean world, I retrieve my car. And try again to find out what's happening with the Davises.

Their Volvo is still parked at City Hall. Still no return call from Cliff Bryant on my cell. And still no sign of Sheila Nyman or Raven LaGrow.

I debate breaking into Casa Davis again. But the Davis kids are home. Watching TV.

I debate breaking into Naomi Williams's house. But Naomi's there, too. With her roommate. Reading in the living room. I debate ringing Naomi's bell. Asking if Naomi knows what's up with the Davises. But that would be too dumb even for me.

Back at my hotel, I find a new phone call on my tape from Raven's phone:

| | |
|---|---|
| RAVEN: | Hello? |
| SHEILA: | Hi, it's Sheila. I went down to City Hall. |
| RAVEN: | And? |
| SHEILA: | They wouldn't let me in to talk to Lane. |
| RAVEN: | But I told you to say you're *his lawyer*! |
| SHEILA: | Didn't work. Lane *already has* a lawyer. Bruce Stuart. He's there. |

RAVEN:      Whoa! This *is* serious. Is this Stuart guy any good?

SHEILA:     He's the best lawyer in Michigan.

RAVEN:      Well, then there's nothing we can do, right?

SHEILA:     I guess.

RAVEN:      What about Camille?

SHEILA:     She's down there, too. Hasn't left. All day.

RAVEN:      Are they *holding her*? Or is she just there to support Lane?

SHEILA:     No way to tell.

RAVEN:      Any sign of the media?

SHEILA:     Not yet. It's Saturday. Everything's very quiet. I think we're the only ones in town who even realize Lane's missing.

RAVEN:      Wasn't there supposed to be a big campaign meeting?

SHEILA:     They went ahead without Lane. He begged off. Claimed he has the flu.

RAVEN:      Little *early* for flu, isn't it?

SHEILA:     Nobody questioned his excuse.

RAVEN:      And you're telling me, there's no way to tell if the police think Camille is the Fugitive Radical.

SHEILA:     That's what I'm telling you. Though they can fingerprint her and figure it out in fifteen minutes.

RAVEN:      *If* she's in custody. But if she's just down there to support her husband, they may not have fingerprinted her.

SHEILA:     Correct. In other words, we still don't know what's going down.

RAVEN:      Yeah, but we do know we're walking on the razor's edge.

# THIRD WEEK

# CHAPTER THIRTEEN
# STRANGE BEDFELLOWS

## Sunday 24 October 2004

Sunday morning I exchange e-mails with Graham. To get the gist of the day's work.

The Peterson trial is still dragging on. Thankfully. So I don't have to quit.

This week we've mostly got celebrity fluff. Such as, why is Lisa Marie Presley so heavy these days? We tease on the cover by hinting at the "secret reason" Lisa Marie's "packed on the pounds." Which turns out to be either of *two* "reasons": (a) she's sworn off dieting as unhealthy, or (b) she's got a new boyfriend so who knows, she might be pregnant?

We've also got two nice pix of Pamela Anderson. Masquerading as a "soccer mom." In one, Pam's grabbing her own shirt to cup one of her huge fake boobs, which looks almost as big as a soccer ball. In the other, Pam's balancing two real soccer balls in her palms—right in front of those ample fake soccer balls she's got strapped on her chest. I decide the best caption for these pix is, "Write Your Own Headlines For These Pictures."

I edit more celebrity fluff stories. Place the Scott Peterson trial reports. And find one AP story—a true story—that really grabs my attention. Yesterday in Douglasville, Georgia, Beverly Mitchell, fifty-four, came home from a three-week vacation. Only to find a complete stranger, Beverly Valentine, fifty-four, living in her house. Wearing her clothes. And repainting a room in which she'd already ripped out all the carpeting. Turns out the interloper, Beverly Valentine, had basically decided to *become* Beverly Mitchell. Except she had apparently not developed any plan for what to do when the real Beverly Mitchell came home.

No doubt you can see why this true life story of changed identities—involving fifty-four-year-old women, no less—grabs me. But that doesn't stop me from having fun with it. I place a quick call to Beverly Mitchell. The victim.

"Beverly, this is David Fisher from Mastercard. I'm sorry to trouble you at home on a Sunday. But I just read the news story about this crazy woman living in your house. I need to remind you that you should check right away to see if this woman has been using any of your credit cards."

"Oh, goodness! Thank you so much for calling. But I already checked that. Right away. She seems to have been using her own cash and checks to pay for her expenses."

"Even the new carpet and paint?"

"Yes, sir. There were no charges on my cards the past three weeks except the ones I put on the cards myself. While I was on vacation."

"Well, Beverly, that makes this one of the strangest cases of identity theft we've ever seen. Why do you think this complete stranger marked you?"

"I—I dunno. I have a real nice house. You know, it wasn't really 'identity theft.' She didn't change her name. She even switched my utilities into her name."

"Do you think she was planning to kill you when you got home?"

"I—I dunno. Might be. She had a gun in her car. And all my jewelry, too."

"In *her* car? How much is your jewelry worth?"

"$23,000."

"Wow! Sounds like you're lucky to be alive. How'd you get her out of your house?"

"The police evicted her. When I got home and saw the lights on, I didn't go inside."

"You're a smart woman, Beverly. And very brave, too. Are you having any difficulty sleeping at night, knowing that a deranged killer was stalking you?"

"Well, I—it's only been one night. But I—I guess a little, yes."

"And is it true she was wearing your underwear when the police arrested her?"

"Well—I didn't see what she had underneath—but she had on one of my dresses."

Next I call the Douglas County Jail. They won't put me through to Beverly Valentine. Just as well. I'd rather make up *her* quotes anyway.

In the mainstream press the headline was **Breaking, Entering, And Moving In**, with a sub-caption **Georgia woman returns from vacation to find stranger living in her house**. But in *The National Spy*, the headline is **Deranged Stalker Steals Woman's Home, Identity**, with the sub-caption **"She stole my name, my jewelry, and my lingerie," tearful victim moans. "And she was going to kill me with a gun—after repainting my kitchen!"**

This is why ten million Americans prefer to get their news from the tabloids.

Finally it's time for my favorite part of tabloid work. The filler stories. I need five. This week, again, I have no time to make them up myself. So I loot the Darwin Awards repository for two doozies.

*Man Killed By His Own Farts*. In rural Montana, 350-pound Thomas Carswell went to sleep in his unventilated bedroom with the windows closed. The next day he was found dead in his bed. No marks on his body. But a poisonous cloud of methane gas hanging over his bed. Three rescuers got sick from breathing the gas in the room. One was hospitalized. The autopsy disclosed that Carswell had a huge amount of methane gas in his system. Which the coroner ruled resulted from Carswell's large intake of beans and cabbage. So I stretch this allegedly true story into half a page. Replete with fictional quotes from the family. And a fictional summary from the coroner: "He was a big man with a huge capacity for creating deadly gas. Frankly, we're lucky he was sleeping alone. Anyone in that room would have died from those lethal farts."

The second Darwin story is even sillier. A series of catastrophes that seldom happen anywhere outside a law school exam question. My headline is: *Frogs Drown When Man Accidentally Shoots His Own Privates*. In Woodruff County, Arkansas, two men, Thurston and Wallis—*if those really are their names*—were driving home at night. From a "frog gigging trip." (That's Arkansas talk for catching frogs.) The headlights on their pickup truck failed. Malfunction in the fuse box. No replacement fuse available. But these good ole' boys discovered that a twenty-two-caliber bullet fit perfectly into the fuse box—and caused the headlights to operate. They drove twenty miles before the bullet overheated and discharged. Right into Thurston's testicles. Just as they were crossing a bridge. Thurston lost control of the pickup. They crashed through the bridge's railing. Into a river. Miraculously, both men survived the crash. But Thurston's future ability to procreate is in grave doubt. And the captive frogs drowned in their metal cages.

Last but not least, I recycle three classics from *Weekly World News*. *Medical Industry Holding Back Cures For Major Diseases—Because It's Good For Business!* We quote "Dr. Edward X." A whistle-blowing cancer specialist. Who says virtually all patients who died medical deaths last year could have been saved. By an inexpensive assortment of shots, pills, and therapies. Which doctors are well aware of. But don't want you to find out about! "Doctors let patients get sick for a damn good reason—they'd go bankrupt if they didn't," says Dr. X. Who lives in fear of "lethal reprisals" from the medical industry.

Then there's ***Supreme Court Judges Are Naked Under Robes!*** With "Insider's shocking allegation" blazoned across a group photo of the Justices in their black robes. The "insider," who speaks only "on condition of anonymity," says it's an ancient tradition. Going back to the first justice, John Jay. We "explain" this is where the expression "naked as a Jay-bird" comes from. Back in 1794, Jay spilled coffee on himself just before a court session. With no other clothes handy, he pulled his robe on over his "birthday suit." The other justices razzed him. But then it caught on. And they've all been doing it ever since.

And finally: ***Real-life Rocket Man Lands on Moon***. About a thirty-year-old Arizona ditch-digger. Who strapped a thousand bottle rockets to his body. And landed safely on the Moon. Except (his vindictive wife gleefully notes) he has *no way back.*

I chuckle a few times while editing these goofy stories. But I'm not enjoying them as much as usual. I wonder if chasing Rachel Clark is turning me into a serious person? Or is it chasing *Janet Fickel* that's turning me into a serious person? Whatever it is, it's clear I need help.

Instead of seeking professional help, I turn to the bottle of Scotch I presciently bought yesterday. What the hell. It's Sunday. And it's raining outside. So I get drunk. Stare at the walls a few hours. And idly fantasize about the new life I could live. With Janet Fickel. In Europe. My new identity could be Sandy Hill. I could get a job as an international stringer for the wire services. In Paris. Or London. We could get a nice apartment. I bet Janet would like not working.

How exactly would I make the switch? Maybe I wouldn't have to bother with faking my death. Maybe I'd just disappear. Just hop on a plane with Janet. And start using my new name. No one would look for me in Paris.

But that would be cruel. To leave Elaine and the girls wondering about my fate.

Oh, who am I kidding? Even if I could find the gumption to leave Elaine— which is highly doubtful—I know I'd *never* have the heart to leave my kids.

So I'm back to Plan A. I'll go to work for *The Ann Arbor News*. Move my family up here. And then meet Janet regularly. For secret romantic trysts. At my Barclay condo love pad. Wow! Imagine. Every night after work. On the kitchen desk. Over the banister. Or what the heck. I might splurge. Buy a bed. Might even buy a Love Swing. So we could really go at it. Like two animals in heat. So these old bones could live to learn Janet's wanton ways.

Hopefully Janet would decide in time to leave the Missing Link. So we'd get mutual divorces. I'd buy a gun. To protect myself. From Big John. Though hopefully he'd take it like a man. Let the little woman go. Move on. Meanwhile, my kids would already be ensconced here in the Ann Arbor schools. So we'd all be in the same town. Elaine would be angry. About being "traded in" for a "younger woman." The "trophy wife." But my kids wouldn't quit on me.

Or would they?

Even through the haze of my third or fourth Scotch (who's counting?), I feel a cold wave of sobriety pass through my brain. As I contemplate the awful possibility that my darling girls could learn to hate me. For "trading in" their mom for a "younger model." It wouldn't be the first time that the spurned woman fought back through the kids. By teaching them to hate their dad.

I really don't think Elaine would fight like that. Elaine truly values the strong bond her kids have with their dad. Elaine would never hurt them. Even to get back at me.

Or would she?

I slap myself. On the cheek. Gotta stop thinking this way. I'm getting way ahead of myself again. I was having a nice fantasy. Imagining Janet Fickel as my secret love-slave. In Paris. Or in the Barclay condo. Wherever. Let's forget about the divorces. And all those messy *details*. Let's just focus on the fun part of the fantasy. The sex. Every night after work, I stop off for a quick fling with Janet. On the desk. Over the banister. Or in the Love Swing.

Lord. What a thought. Janet Fickel spread out in a Love Swing. My motor might overheat. At the sheer *gorgeousness* of the sight. But if so, what a way to go. Like Nelson Rockefeller. *Someday, Lady.* Indeed.

My cell phone rings. Interrupting my debauched reveries.

"Tabloids-R-Us", I answer.

"Hey, Dad."

"Hey Sara. Whassup?"

"Nothing much. I hear you're working on a great new story up there."

"Tru dat."

"Ah, Dad? Want a little advice?"

"Sure."

"Don't try to talk like a teenager. You just don't have the right inflection to pull it off."

"Thanks, Sara. I appreciate being reminded I'm as old as the dinosaurs."

"It's for your own good, Dad. You really do need to grow up."

Drunken paranoia seizes me. What if Sara has filed an FOIA request? And learned from Hunter *exactly* how immaturely I've been acting up here. Between my hot new "girlfriend" (as Janet calls herself) and my B&Es and my Scotch abuse.

But then I get a grip. Sara is sixteen. Sixteen-year-olds don't file FOIA requests.

"Why?" I ask. "Peter Pan didn't grow up. It worked for him."

"Peter Pan was a character in a book, Dad. You're a real person. Here in the real world."

"Says who? And since when did you become so cold and heartless, Sara? Did Graham Hancock put you up to this call?"

Sara laughs. "Hey, Dad. The reason I called is, I thought you should know. Rachel just got in an accident. With the car."

"Oh, no! Is Rachel okay?"

"Rachel's fine. The car has a few dents. But mom is pissed. They're having a small war. Thought you'd want to know."

"Thanks for the heads-up. Hey, why don't you tell Elaine I called?"

"Dude, that would be a lie. *I* called *you*."

"Lying is underrated, Sara. This lie would make your mother happy. For once, she'd say, '*David was thinking of me. Instead of just himself.*' That would be good for the marriage. And what's good for the marriage is ultimately good for you. So it's in your own self-interest to tell this lie, Sara."

"That sounds as fishy as this dude we're studying in History. John Stuart Mill. He was always making up justifications like that for lying. As long as it's *useful*, you should lie."

"Hey, old John Stuart Mill was one *very smart* 'dude.' This may shock you, Sara. But I'm *seldom compared* to John Stuart Mill. If old John Stuart says I'm right about lying, then I'm right! Is your mom there?"

"Yeah. I'll get her. I love you, Dad."

"I love you, too, Sara."

Elaine comes on. "It's so nice of you to call, David."

"Yeah, well, every ten years or so, I think of my loved ones. Back home. But then it's off to hunt the whales again. Out on the treacherous open seas. Where death is a daily risk."

"David, have you been drinking?"

"Guilty as charged, my love. It's a slow Sunday here in my hometown. Would you rather have me drunk—or out chasing *poon tang*?"

"Why don't you go see your mother?"

Good question. What *is* the matter with me?

"She's busy today," I lie. "With her bridge club. Hey, Elaine—tell me about Rachel's accident. Where, when, why—and who was *at fault*?"

"*Rachel* was at fault. She pulled out of a parking space without looking. At the mall this morning. With three of her friends in the car—and the CD player cranked up."

"How do you know about the CD player?"

"Who do you think drove out to help Rachel talk to the police? *In your absence.*"

Ouch. I maintain a tactical silence in the face of this delicate point.

"David, do you think we should ground Rachel?"

I wince. I don't like grounding. Neither does Elaine.

"If you ground Rachel, the person who gets punished is you, Elaine. Because you'll just end up having to drive her everywhere. To school. To tennis practice. And to all her volunteer activities. Unless you want to punish the homeless, by not allowing Rachel to volunteer there? And punish those elementary school kids she gives the anti-discrimination workshops for?"

"No, I don't want Rachel to stop doing those things."

"So how 'bout this instead? Ask Rachel what *she* thinks would be the appropriate response from her parents."

"I already know what Rachel thinks. She thinks I should be nicer to her. Because she's been in an accident."

"But you *were* nice to Rachel, weren't you? Until you knew for sure she was okay?"

"Yes."

"So remind her how concerned you were. And then tell Rachel the reason we think there needs to be *another* response is precisely because we're concerned about her safety. We don't want her to think it's just another day at the office, la-de-da, when she gets into an accident. So we want *her* to think of an appropriate sanction. To help her remember that she needs to be more careful with the car. Then give her some ideas. Suggestions."

"Maybe no friends in the car for a month."

"Great idea! Come up with a back-up, too. In case Rachel's got some good reason up her sleeve to shoot down the no-friends-in-the-car idea. Maybe no *music* in the car for a month. Or whatever. Then see if you can get her to *agree* to the sanction."

"It would be a lot easier to get her to agree if *you* were here."

"Maybe. But you're damn good at this parenting stuff, Elaine. You can do it without me."

"What choice do I have? Since you seem to have taken up permanent residence in Ann Arbor?"

\* \* \*

After another Scotch, I check the tapes of my Raven LaGrow phone tap. And hear this:

| | |
|---|---|
| RAVEN: | Hello? |
| LANE: | Raven, it's Lane. I need your help. |
| RAVEN: | Of course, darling. What is it? |
| LANE: | I've been charged. With aiding and abetting a fugitive from justice. |
| RAVEN: | Rachel Clark? |
| LANE: | Yes. Though I have no idea where she is. But they won't believe me. |
| RAVEN: | Why not? |
| LANE: | Hard to know. Greg Hunter's playing his cards very close to his vest. |
| RAVEN: | Is this all politics? |
| LANE: | I think so. I assume the mayor's behind it. But then again— |
| RAVEN: | Then again, what? |
| LANE: | Hunter's a little out of control. This may be all Hunter. For all I know. |
| RAVEN: | What can I do to help? |
| LANE: | I'm going to be arraigned tomorrow morning. 9:00. There'll be a shit storm in the press. Can you write up a pro-active statement for me? Saying I'm innocent. I have no idea where Rachel Clark is. Never met her in my life. And I've certainly never knowingly aided and abetted her. |
| RAVEN: | Sure. Are you still in custody? |
| LANE: | Yes. They offered to arraign me this morning. Quietly. But I told my lawyer I want the media there. This is an outrage! I'm not going to let them get away with hiding this behind closed doors. |
| RAVEN: | What makes you think the media won't find out *today*? |
| LANE: | They *may*. But I doubt it. There's no one here. No one knows about it. But just in case, it would be good to have a statement ready. Today. |

RAVEN: Where are you?

LANE: Police station. City Hall. I'm not even in lock-up. I'm just hanging out in an interview room.

RAVEN: Is Camille under arrest, too?

LANE: No. They aren't charging her. She just came down to stay with me.

RAVEN: All weekend?

LANE: She went home late last night to sleep. But came back this morning. She's here with me now.

RAVEN: Oh. Lane—are they arresting Rachel Clark, too?

LANE: I don't think so. I don't think they even know where she is.

RAVEN: If they don't know where Rachel Clark is, how can they charge you with aiding and abetting her?

LANE: This seems to be all about that motorcycle helmet Norma Lee gave me. The one you said Norma was stupid to bring here. God, Raven, were you right about *that*!

RAVEN: That's *all* they've got? You got Rachel Clark's helmet as a gift?

LANE: Apparently it has fresh fingerprints on it. Mine. And *Rachel Clark's*.

RAVEN: Oh.

LANE: But there's more. They've got something they think proves I helped her escape back in '69. They won't say what. And something they say proves I helped her *again* years later. Plus, they keep talking about me quashing that warrant for Melanie McGeetchy.

RAVEN: What does your lawyer think? This Stuart. He's supposed to be good, right?

LANE: Bruce is the best. Bruce says he thinks they're just whistling Dixie. But he wants me to say as little as possible until we get to the preliminary exam. He's going to push for the earliest possible PX. Which we should get. Because of the election.

RAVEN: And then try to get the charges thrown out at the PX?

LANE: You got it.

| | |
|---|---|
| RAVEN: | Lane. After the arraignment tomorrow, I need to talk to you. ASAP. |
| LANE: | Okay. Why? |
| RAVEN: | I don't want to say now. Not on a police line. But be sure we talk tomorrow morning. I'll come to the hearing. If it's too much of a mob scene for us to talk, then I'll come straight back home. Call me here as soon as you can after you're free. On a safe line. They *will* let you out, won't they? |
| LANE: | Oh, yes. They really want me to go home today. But I'm not giving them the satisfaction of a quiet arraignment. And they can't bring themselves to just release me on my own recognizance. Even though they know that's what the judge will do tomorrow morning. Stupid bastards! |
| RAVEN: | Lane. About Camille. |
| LANE: | Yes? |
| RAVEN: | It's—oh, nothing. I just, well, you know—I want you to remember: *Rachel Clark is not your fight.* |
| LANE: | I'm not following you. |
| RAVEN: | Rachel Clark made her own bed. Now she has to lie in it. There's no reason for *you* to go down, just because *she's* unwilling to go public. |
| LANE: | I agree. I'm not protecting anyone, Raven. Believe me, I have no idea where Rachel Clark is. Truly. |
| RAVEN: | Good. I'm just saying, it's time Rachel Clark turned herself in. She's way too old for the fugitive life. |
| LANE: | Rachel Clark can do whatever she wants. It has nothing to do with me. But see, Hunter wants me to start naming names. From the Movement. Just because I'm up for election, he figures I'm scared of the publicity. But heck, my chances of getting elected are already slim. This might even help. Turn me into a martyr. |
| RAVEN: | Maybe. Look, I'll bring a draft statement down to City Hall. ASAP. |
| LANE: | Thanks, Raven. |

Next up, Raven calls Sheila. Fills her in. They agree Sheila will come over to Raven's. To help draft the statement for the press.

I debate calling Raven. Asking for a preview of the statement. Or for a comment.

But the problem is, if Raven learns one member of the media is on this, she'll probably go ahead and release the statement to the mainstream press. The dailies. Whereas, if I keep my trap shut and just write, *The National Spy* might be able to scoop *everyone*. Even *The Ann Arbor News*. Which might help me someday. If I apply for a job there. And I can show the editor I beat his own reporters on a local story.

So instead of calling Raven, I call Graham. But not from my room. I know this sounds paranoid. But I still don't know who broke into my *last* room. So how do I know he/she didn't break into this one, too? But instead of ripping it up, maybe planted taps and bugs?

Better safe than sorry. So I go out to the main campus sidewalk, the "Diag." Ogle a few bundled-up coeds. And call Graham on my cell. Fill him in. And agree to do what Graham wanted me to do last week. Write it up. Cuz *now* it's a story. For the front page of *The National Spy*.

## NORMA LEE ENSNARED IN SHOCKING COLLEGE TOWN SCANDAL!

### *ANN ARBOR AUTHORITIES SAY NORMA LEE'S PAL, LANE DAVIS, HAS BEEN HIDING FUGITIVE RADICAL COP-KILLER FROM 1960s*

*Television celebrity Norma Lee, 54, is living in terror—that her radical past has come back to haunt her! The bosomy star learned today that her ex-flame Lane Davis, 58, has been arrested in a shocking scandal in Ann Arbor, Michigan—just 12 days after Norma Lee came to Ann Arbor to throw her support behind Davis, a radical lawyer running for mayor of the mid-size college town. Worst of all, the evidence against Davis leads directly back to Norma Lee herself!*

[Beside this paragraph I insert the best of my pix of Norma Lee and her cleavage exiting the taxi. And slap a red banner across the photo with the words: CELEBRITY SUSPECT.]

The National Spy *penetrated behind the scenes of the police investigation. Got an exclusive interview with a knowledgeable source close to the investigation. And obtained exclusive photos of the perpetrators and the evidence.*

## THE 1969 SHOOT-OUT WITH POLICE

*The prime evidence against Davis is the infamous motorcycle helmet worn by fugitive radical Rachel Clark in a 1969 attack against the University of Michigan Law School. The 1969 attack was foiled by an Ann Arbor policeman, Dale Hunter, who died in a shoot-out with the radicals. Two of the radicals died in the shoot-out, too. Only Rachel Clark escaped the scene.*

*Rachel Clark was shot in the head while trying to escape—but her motorcycle helmet, emblazoned with the "Weatherman" rainbow insignia, saved her life. Clark, 54, who also sported an exotic "Weatherman" tattoo on her back, has eluded authorities for the past 35 years.*

[Below these paragraphs I place two pix. I slap a red banner marked "EVIDENCE" across the best photo of the helmet on Davis's conference room table. And I slap another red banner marked "FUGITIVE RADICAL" across the Centreville High picture of bosomy seventeen-year-old Rachel Clark—the picture I razor-bladed out of the Ann Arbor Public Library magazine section.]

*But Rachel Clark's famous helmet surfaced last week, when Norma Lee gave it to Lane Davis. Authorities have identified fresh fingerprints on the helmet as belonging to just two people: Lane Davis, and RACHEL CLARK!*

## FINGERPRINTS DON'T LIE

*Authorities are still unsure exactly what connection Norma Lee has to the long-missing fugitive radical, Rachel Clark. But our source close to the investigation confirms that Norma Lee will have a lot of explaining to do.*

*Where did Norma Lee get the helmet? Why does the helmet she gave Davis have "fresh" fingerprints from the fugitive cop-killer Rachel Clark? Where is Rachel Clark hiding today? These are just some of the questions authorities will put to Norma when they grill her this week.*

*Lane Davis proclaims he is innocent. Says he never met Rachel Clark. And has no idea where she is. But Davis is being arraigned today on charges of aiding and abetting Rachel Clark. And he cannot explain how his own "fresh" fingerprints came to be next to Clark's fresh fingerprints on Clark's helmet. As our source close to the investigation pointed out: "fingerprints don't lie."*

[Below this paragraph I insert one of the bosomy pix of Norma Lee hugging Lane Davis. With the red banner: NORMA LEE AND EX-FLAME LANE DAVIS.]

*Adding to the mystery is Norma Lee's radical past. During the 1970s Norma was arrested at several left-wing demonstrations around the country. Our sources say Norma Lee's ex-flame Lane Davis was also present at some of the demonstrations where she was arrested.*

*But the biggest mystery is this: why weren't Norma Lee's fingerprints found on the helmet, too? Did Norma Lee wipe the helmet clean before she gave it to Lane Davis? Or did Davis unsuccessfully try to wipe it clean, obliterating Norma Lee's prints, but not his own and Clark's?*

### THE SECRET RADICAL UNDERGROUND

*Authorities confirm that the same radicals who brought wide-spread terror to college campuses in the 1960s and 1970s are still in secret contact with each other. While many now hide behind respectable daytime jobs as lawyers and stockbrokers, they haven't changed their dangerous radical views. "Tigers don't change their stripes," our source said. Authorities believe that some of these old-time radicals continue to help Rachel Clark elude justice.*

*This week's continuing* National Spy *investigation will seek the answers to two burning questions: Is Norma Lee connected to the secret radical underground that is protecting Rachel Clark? And where exactly is Rachel Clark hiding now?*

*—SANDY HILL and staff reporters*

(It always makes the story sound bigger if lots of people were needed to crank it out.)

I read this draft story over. Debate going into the pennies. Raising the possibility that Rachel Clark is innocent. Since I truly believe she is. And since going into the pennies would piss Hunter off. Big time. Which would be great. But proclaiming Rachel Clark's innocence is *her* job. Not mine. The pennies are way too complex. Our supermarket readers don't have time to read about the law on withdrawal from conspiracies. They've got groceries to buy.

If I find Rachel Clark, *then* I can go into the pennies. *If* she gives me an interview.

So instead I work up a side bar story I know our readers will *love*. On Lane Davis and Raven LaGrow.

## NORMA LEE'S EX-FLAME ALSO CAUGHT IN LOVE NEST WITH FAMOUS FEMINAZI!

### *FEMINAZI LAW PROF RAVEN LAGROW, WHO SAYS ALL SEX IS RAPE, IS LANE DAVIS'S SECRET LOVER*

*Politics makes strange bedfellows. And few bedfellows are stranger or more shocking than the couple pictured here. Raven LaGrow, 54, long-time "feminazi" antagonist of Rush Limbaugh, espouses the radical feminist mantra that "all heterosexual intercourse is rape." Yet here Raven is, on her way to bed with a man— and a married man, at that!*

[Beside this paragraph I insert a reasonably discreet frame from the videotape from Raven's bedroom. A shot that *conceivably* could have been taken from outside the home. So Raven can't prove criminal trespass from the photo alone. I place black ink bars across their privates. And their eyes. Just to make it look kinkier. And a red banner with the words: ILLICIT LOVERS CAUGHT IN THE ACT.]

*And who's the mystery lover canoodling with the outspoken radical feminist? None other than Ann Arbor mayoral candidate and radical lawyer, Lane Davis, 58. The same Lane Davis who is being arraigned today on charges of aiding and abetting the fugitive radical Rachel Clark!*

*The athletic Davis—whom our sources describe as a "real Lion in Winter—58, but still feisty"—sure gets around! Writers are already lining up to buy the rights to Davis's life story.*

[Beside this paragraph I insert a blown-up version of the photo of Lane Davis from the Davis & Nyman firm brochure.]

*Lane Davis is an ex-Marine. But also a life-long radical. He's a former prosecutor—fired for dropping charges against political radicals, and also for lending his car to Ralph Nader, so Nader could lead a protest against General Motors. Davis is also a leading left-wing lawyer. And a popular city councilman in Ann Arbor. Who is now running for mayor of Ann Arbor on the radical "Human Rights Party" ticket.*

*Lane Davis is also an ex-lover of Norma Lee. Now married to a prominent Ann Arbor social reformer, Camille Davis, 54. And yet somehow lover Lane also finds time to canoodle on the side with the spirited Raven LaGrow. Our source describes Lane and Raven as "aging but very passionate lovers, who refuse to go gentle into that good night."*

*Lane Davis, who was still in custody when this story went to press, was unavailable for comment. Feminazi Queen Raven LaGrow was also unavailable for comment on her shocking and notorious affair with Davis. Which is too bad. Because we're dying to know: does Raven feel she herself is being "raped" every time she has consensual sex with Lane Davis?*

*—SANDY HILL and staff reporters*

Beyond the pale? Perhaps. But in the tabloid biz, this is what passes for a very good day's work.

Now you're probably wondering. Did I have any *qualms of conscience* writing this snide piece? Not really. Though I'll admit it did occur to me that my wisecracks about the "Lion in Winter" and the "aging but very passionate lovers" apply with equal force to me (and Janet).

But so what? So I'm a hypocrite. Just like Raven. Big deal. Unlike these minor celebrities, I don't have the misfortune to live my life under the glare of media scrutiny. It's the price they pay for their fame. I know I told you I find them kind of endearing. And I do. But they're still people who made themselves media targets. It's my job to expose 'em. If I didn't do it, someone else would. So fuck 'em if they can't take a joke.

Once I send these stories off, my thoughts return to the hunt for Rachel Clark. My prime suspect, Camille Davis, has spent the weekend in the cop shop. Yet did *not* get charged.

Did the cops fingerprint Camille?

Surely they must have. Hunter's no dummy. He knows Camille was in Central America in 1989. Knows she came back to the States in '89. And married Davis. Hunter *also* knows Davis returned from Central America. With a passenger. Using a fake name. Who Hunter presumes was Rachel Clark. Under these circumstances, with Camille right there at City Hall, how could Hunter *not* have fingerprinted her? It would have been a breach of professional standards *not* to fingerprint her. Investigatory malpractice, if there is such a thing.

Yet Hunter let Camille go.

Which means my *other* suspect, Naomi Williams, is now my prime suspect. What do I know about sad-eyed, hunched Naomi?

Janet told me Naomi has a ratty old checkered scarf. Like the women of the Weather Underground wore at the HEW protest. And Lane Davis told me Naomi's been with Davis & Nyman fifteen years. Meaning she joined them in 1989. Davis also told me Naomi did "humanitarian work" in Central America, before she joined Davis & Nyman. Meaning Naomi, instead of Camille, could have been Davis's mystery passenger. Riding back with him in 1989. Using a murdered nun's passport.

How much of this does *Hunter* know?

Quite possibly *none* of it. Gray-haired Naomi's very good at blending into the background. Her checkered scarf wouldn't catch Hunter's eye. The Davis & Nyman brochure does not recite *her* Central America connection. Hunter might not know any reason to suspect Naomi Williams of being Rachel Clark.

But what about Lane Davis? After a long weekend of listening to Hunter's questions, *Davis* must see there's a damn good chance his paralegal is really the Fugitive Radical. After all, *Davis* knows who his passenger was in 1989. Yet still he refused to "name names" to Hunter.

Why? Davis must be protecting his passenger. Sticking his neck out for her.

A man will do that for his wife. Or even for his lover. But would he really do that *for his paralegal*?

Hard question to answer. Without knowing more about Davis's relationship with sad-eyed Naomi. After all, Sister Marta thought she saw romantic sparks between Davis and "Sanne." Back in 1989. So if Naomi's really Rachel/Sanne, maybe she had a little fling with the boss. Before he married Camille. Or after. And then she settled down to be his paralegal.

But one thing's certain. There's little point in staking out Camille. She's not going anywhere. Because either she's been cleared, or the cops are watching her like a hawk. So my time is best spent staking out Naomi. Who's still flying below the cops' radar.

I drive over to Naomi's house. Naomi and her roommate are home. In their living room. Reading. As always. I can see them from down the street.

For the rest of the afternoon I watch Naomi. Reading.

At six Naomi and her roommate get up. Make dinner. Eat it. Clean up. Then back to their living room. For more reading.

At ten they get up. Go to bed.

If Naomi Williams is really Rachel Clark, she's the calmest damn fugitive in history.

As I drive back to my hotel, after seven fruitless hours on stakeout, I struggle to suppress a depressing thought.

What if my original premise was all wrong?

What if *none* of the women in Lane Davis's conference room twelve days ago is secretly Rachel Clark? What if Rachel Clark's fingerprints got on that helmet sometime *before* the helmet got to Ann Arbor? And I'm just up here tilting at windmills?

# CHAPTER FOURTEEN
# THE SHIT HITS THE FAN

## Monday 25 October 2004

I arrive thirty minutes early for Lane Davis's arraignment. Yet still barely get a seat in the back row. Because the mainstream press is now *all over* this story. Like the cheap suits they are.

Too bad. *The National Spy* goes to press in an hour. But we won't hit the supermarkets 'til tomorrow morning. *The Ann Arbor News* will be on the stands today. By noon. So much for scooping them. Although at least the Detroit dailies can't get a story out 'til tomorrow morning.

The Washtenaw County Circuit Court allows cameras in the courtroom. Which gives me an idea. I give up my back row seat. Run back to my hotel. Get my *camera* from the Bell Tower's hotel safe. And run back to court. Still ten minutes before show time.

But now a dense crowd throngs the small sidewalk plaza outside the courthouse. Lane Davis supporters. Holding signs. *Don't Let Them Steal Our Election. End Oppression.* And the one I saw two weeks ago: *Davis For Mayor: Time For Regime Change <u>Here</u>, Too.*

I slither through the crowd. Pass through security. Run upstairs. Flash my press credential at the courtroom deputy. And end up with a better view of the proceedings. Standing along the side wall. With the media photographers.

The tension in the courtroom is palpable. Electric. Very dramatic.

Two Ann Arbor police officers bring Lane Davis in from the back. Davis looks great. Fierce. Determined. Unbowed. Cameras are clicking like crazy. Including mine.

Davis sits down at the defense table next to Camille and his lawyer, Bruce Stuart. Who's fifty-something. Very tall and lean. I'm guessing 6'6", 190. Stuart has a single thick, bushy black eyebrow. Which runs all the way across the beetling ridge above his dark, brooding eyes.

I ask the *Ann Arbor News* photographer beside me about Stuart. She says most Ann Arborites call Stuart "One Brow." She also says One Brow Stuart doesn't usually do criminal cases. But Davis obviously isn't fooling around. Because One Brow Stuart is absolutely the best lawyer in the state.

Stuart and the Davises sit quiet. But at the other table, Prosecutor Ed Barnett is busy with paperwork. Which gives him a reason to avoid Davis's angry eyes. Next to Prosecutor Barnett sit Greg Hunter and Cliff Bryant. Hunter looks right through me. No sign of recognition. Even my old teammate, Cliff, barely acknowledges me. With an almost imperceptible nod.

You could cut the tension in the air in this courtroom with a knife. Unfortunately, however, not much actually *happens* at most arraignments. So for all the drama in the air, there isn't likely to be much drama to report. The best we can hope for is some inflammatory speeches on the courthouse steps. Afterwards.

The judge comes in. It's Judge Flynn again. My high school classmate. Who arraigned me last week. Apparently he's covering for the district judge again. Judge Flynn looks *very* serious. The clerk calls the case. Ed Barnett and Bruce Stuart state their appearances. Judge Flynn recites that both sides agreed to permit cameras in the courtroom. Barnett acknowledges he has no objection. Stuart steps to the podium and says: "That's true for us, too, Your Honor. My client has nothing to hide from the public he serves."

Stuart advises the judge his client waives a formal reading of the charges. Judge Flynn thanks him. Then the judge addresses the media. In a voice normally reserved for small children. Explains that copies of the indictment will be available immediately after the hearing. At the prosecutor's office. *Not* in his chambers. We nod. Like the small children we are.

Meanwhile, I get a nice shot of One Brow Stuart. That wild bushy eyebrow is the kind of thing that makes lawsuits more fun. For our readers.

Judge Flynn asks Lane Davis how he pleads to the charges.

Davis stands. "Not guilty, Your Honor. Not guilty at all."

Not guilty, not guilty. Just like Morganna the Kissing Bandit.

Stuart then steps to the podium again. "As Your Honor knows, my client is a candidate for mayor. The election is just eight days away. I don't wish to impugn the integrity of the prosecutor. But the timing of these charges is nothing short of astounding. The charges relate to acts allegedly committed fifteen—and even thirty-five—years ago. So why now, after so many years, did these charges suddenly have to be brought *today*? Just eight days before the election?"

"What's your point, Mr. Stuart?" Judge Flynn asks.

"The public has the strongest possible interest in a fair and impartial election process. Yet if these charges are still pending on election day, the election will be tainted. There is no legal mechanism for delaying a public election. Accordingly, we respectfully request that this court set the preliminary examination for this case at the earliest possible date. This afternoon, if possible. In addition, we request that trial be set so that it will be completed *before* the election."

Prosecutor Barnett rises. "The People don't object to an early preliminary examination. But this afternoon is absurd. We need time to serve subpoenas. One witness we may need to call is out of state."

"What is the earliest you could be ready to go?" Judge Flynn asks.

"A week from Wednesday," Prosecutor Barnett says. That is, the day *after* the election.

"*This* Thursday would be better." Judge Flynn's tone brooks no disagreement.

"That only gives us three days," the prosecutor grumbles.

"Correct. Preliminary examination is set for Thursday, October 28 at 9:00 a.m."

Stuart rises. "Thank you, Your Honor. We appreciate your willingness to make this accommodation. We intend to prove my client's innocence at the preliminary examination. However, as you know, the question at the preliminary examination is only whether probable cause exists to think my client *might* be guilty of the crimes charged. Only at a trial is the question of innocence or guilt determined by the constitutional standard of beyond a reasonable doubt."

"What's your point, Mr. Stuart?"

"If at the preliminary exam, you bind my client over for trial, we must respectfully request that the *trial* take place before the election, too. Otherwise, the election will effectively be decided by the police and the prosecutor, rather than by the voters."

"Mr. Stuart," the judge says, "I realize you don't regularly practice in the criminal arena. So please understand. I probably will not be your judge on Thursday. I'm only filling in for Judge Haggerty this morning. But regardless of who your judge is at the preliminary exam, if that judge finds probable cause exists, he or she is legally obligated to bind your client over *to the circuit court* for trial. It will be up to *the circuit court* to assign a judge. And it will be up to *that* judge to set the date for trial. So I can't do anything about setting a trial date now."

Call me a cynic. But somehow I think this guy Stuart already knew that. Somehow I think that whole speech he just gave was for the benefit of the media. Not the court.

"Would Your Honor consider conveying the very strong public need for a trial *before the election* to the chief judge of the circuit?" Stuart asks.

"I will definitely do so." The judge turns to the prosecutor. "Any position on bond?"

"We have no objection to releasing Mr. Davis on his own recognizance."

"So ordered."

Judge Flynn slams his gavel. And the proceeding is adjourned.

Everyone except the judge and his clerk troops back downstairs.

We all gather in the small plaza outside the courthouse. The reporters, photographers and other members of the audience. Plus the prosecutor, the cops, the Davises, and Stuart. There's barely room in the small plaza for everyone. So we crowd in tight. People lean against the historical monuments. One young guy even stands, perfectly balanced, on a fire hydrant—to get a better view.

Lane Davis holds a small wireless microphone. And reads a statement to the crowd. While Davis supporters hand out printed copies of Davis's statement. To anyone who wants one.

"These charges are completely baseless," Davis says. "Like many University of Michigan graduates, I have heard of Rachel Clark. But so far as I know, I have never *met* Rachel Clark. So far as I know, I have never *spoken* with Rachel Clark. So far as I know, I have never *communicated* with Rachel Clark in any way.

"On October 27, 1969, Rachel Clark and others tried to firebomb the Law School that I myself later attended. On that same day in 1969, I was a Captain in the United States Marine Corps. Serving my country in Vietnam. I had no connection to Rachel Clark or her deadly plot at all. By the time my tour of duty ended and I returned home, Rachel Clark was long gone.

"As you know, I served as an assistant prosecutor here in Washtenaw County. In the same office that issued the warrant for Rachel Clark's arrest. The office that has now seen fit to charge me. I have spent the past three days talking with detectives from the Ann Arbor Police Department. Men I used to work with when I was a prosecutor. Trying to understand how they developed the misconception that I have ever known or assisted Rachel Clark in any way.

"When the evidence is brought forward on Thursday, I predict you will be shocked. You will be shocked that charges could ever be brought against *anyone* on such ephemeral and utterly illusory 'evidence.' Because this case is a complete travesty of justice. A mockery of all American values. There is nothing close to probable cause to support the charges against me.

"These charges have been brought for one reason only. They are part of a blatant and shocking attempt to take next week's election out of the voters' hands. The incumbent Democrats are hoping that you, the voters, will be leery of voting for someone facing criminal charges. No matter how baseless those charges may turn out to be. Because the incumbent Democrats are betting I will not get a chance to clear my name before the election."

Davis looks up from his text. Ad libs. "Judge Flynn today took an important step in preserving the voting rights of the citizens of this county. By insuring that the prosecutor, this Thursday, will have to put up or shut up."

Davis looks back down to his pre-prepared text. "We believe it will be abundantly clear at the preliminary examination that the prosecutor cannot meet even the minimal standard of 'probable cause' to believe a crime has been committed. Much less the proof beyond a reasonable doubt that is required, in our great system of justice, to convict anyone of a crime.

"We will call upon Judge Flynn and the independent judiciary of Washtenaw County to throw out these baseless charges. So that you, the voters, may go to the polls next week and decide who you want to be your mayor—based on the merits of the candidates, rather than on the speculation and innuendo that the incumbent Democrats hope these charges will provoke.

"We also call upon the ladies and gentlemen of the media to report fairly on these charges. Do not pander to the sensationalism of the incumbent Democrats. Do not engage in the wild speculation and innuendo that they hope you will engage in. Ladies and gentlemen of the media, do not allow yourselves to be *manipulated* by the incumbent Democrats. The voters deserve better from you!

"I would also remind the voters: I am not the *only* person up for election next week. Our county *prosecutor*, Ed Barnett, is up for election next Tuesday, too. I urge all voters to come to the polls. And I urge all voters, when voting, to remember this travesty of justice. Surely there are better uses for public tax dollars than to spend them paying the salary of a prosecutor who would allow his office to be used as a political tool.

"In the final analysis, what is happening here today is a bald-faced attempt to end-run the political process. Instead of letting the voters decide who shall be mayor, based on the merits of the candidates and their positions on the issues, my opponent has orchestrated a behind-the-scenes campaign to smear my name unfairly. However, I vow that I will do everything in my power to prevent this travesty of justice.

"My attorney, Bruce Stuart, and I are prepared to go to trial today. We will press for the earliest possible hearings at every juncture in the court process, so that this matter can be fully resolved before the election. While we are mindful of the burdens on the courts, we call upon the courts to work with us, in the public interest, to ensure that this matter is resolved before the election. Thank you. I have no further comments."

The crowd surges forward toward Davis in a mass. Like rioting European soccer fans. If Davis is saying anything more, I can't hear it.

But now the prosecutor deftly weaves through the riotous crowd. He's watched the whole spectacle from the side of the little sidewalk plaza. Now it's his turn. He doesn't have a hand-held mike like Davis. But he holds up his arms. Like Richard Nixon used to do. Gets the attention of the crowd. And makes his own short statement. In a loud, clear voice. With no notes.

"My office has never made a practice of trying cases in the press. We will not do so now. However, we vigorously deny that politics played any part in our decision to bring these charges at this time. Our office is required to evaluate each case on its own merits, independent of outside concerns. Including the timing of elections. Late last week we received very strong evidence, some of which will be presented at the preliminary examination, that shows that Mr. Davis has knowingly aided and abetted a notorious fugitive, Rachel Clark.

"Rachel Clark has been wanted in this jurisdiction, for thirty-five years, to answer to very serious charges arising from the murder of a uniformed, on-duty Ann Arbor police officer. I would not have delayed bringing charges against anyone else in this community who aided and abetted Rachel Clark. And I was not about to delay bringing charges against Mr. Davis, simply because he is a prominent politician in this town. Thank you."

Again, the crowd surges forward. But if Prosecutor Barnett says anything more, no one can hear it. Because the Davis supporters now erupt in a loud chant. "*Drop the bullshit charges now! Drop the bullshit charges now! Drop the bullshit charges now!*"

The Prosecutor picks his way back to the courthouse doors. And disappears inside.

The crowd swarms. Reporters try to interview Raven LaGrow. Lane Davis. Camille Davis. Bruce Stuart. The only one they miss is Sheila Nyman. Because they don't know who she is.

So I try to wend my way through the crowd to get to Sheila.

But now Greg Hunter's at my elbow. So is Cliff Bryant. Hunter waives a subpoena in my face. Rolls it up. And stuffs it in my shirt pocket.

"Consider yourself served! Teammate." Hunter slaps my back. "We'll see you Thursday. For your testimony." Hunter puts a huge paw on the back of my neck. Pulls my right ear very close to his lips. And snarls, "You better cooperate with us, asshole. Or your wife may receive a very interesting package in the mail. With *details* you don't want her to know." Hunter releases my neck. Glares at me a moment. Then stalks off with Cliff Bryant.

Out the corner of my eye, I glimpse two blonde guys. Standing against the side of the courthouse. Watching me get served with the subpoena. It's the two guys who were tailing me the week before last. The Germans. They're back in town.

Once the shit hits the fan, you can count on all the flies to find the shit.

* * *

Back in my hotel room, I call Graham. Fill him in on the subpoena. Graham makes some calls. Gets the name of a local media lawyer. Jonathan Lowe. Gets me an appointment with Lowe. For 2:30 this afternoon. Graham also compliments me on yesterday's stories. Which are in the *National Spy* edition that's just come out today. And we agree to put an LA reporter on Norma Lee. To see if she's the prosecution's "out-of-state witness." And to get some quotes.

Then I listen to a fresh tape of a phone call Raven LaGrow just had with Lane Davis:

| LANE: | Hey. Thanks again for writing up that statement. It was perfect! |
| RAVEN: | Oh you're welcome, of course. But Lane— |
| LANE: | I really think this is going to blow up on the Democrats! They're going to look *so* bad! Cuz the evidence just isn't there. |
| RAVEN: | Yeah, well— |
| LANE: | The media is already having a field day! And I'll come out smelling like a rose. With way more visibility and name recognition than before! |
| RAVEN: | That depends on how the media plays all this. Not the most *reliable* people, the media. You never know what they'll do. Or say. |
| LANE: | Well they've gotta call this one the way it is. Candidate charged eight days before the election? C'mon! It's obviously bullshit. |
| RAVEN: | Not if Rachel Clark keeps quiet. As long as she's in the wind, people will figure *someone* must be help- |

ing her. And you're made for the part, Lane. Old-time radical. With a documented *history* of helping radicals. Even at the expense of your own career. Like when you helped Melanie.

LANE:     What's your point?

RAVEN:    You need to give her up.

LANE:     Who? Melanie? Or—you mean, Rachel Clark?

RAVEN:    Yes. You've done everything anyone could expect. But now you need to give her up.

LANE:     Raven. Listen to me. I know my phone's not bugged anymore. This is just between you and me. I have no idea where Rachel Clark is. Or who she is. I have no idea how her fingerprints got on that helmet next to mine.

RAVEN:    But you do know who rode back with you from Nicaragua. In the moving van.

LANE:     Yes. But I have no reason to believe she was Rachel Clark.

RAVEN:    So just tell them. Who rode with you. *That's* what they want to know.

LANE:     Why should I tell them that? I promised to protect her. She had her own reasons for coming into the country that way.

RAVEN:    Has it occurred to you she might have *lied* to you about those reasons? Has it occurred to you she might really be Rachel Clark?

LANE:     A lot of things have occurred to me. While cooling my heels at police headquarters the past three days. But idle speculation is not a good enough reason to break a promise.

RAVEN:    How 'bout saving your own neck? Is *that* a good enough reason?

LANE:     No! I'm not the kind of guy to name names. But you're working yourself up over nothing, Raven. My "neck" is in no jeopardy. They've got no case. All they're doing right now is helping my campaign.

RAVEN:      You are a hopeless romantic, Lane.

LANE:        I know. That's why you love me. Remember?

* * *

There are worse places to sit than the steps outside Raja Rani in Ann Arbor. But after thirty minutes, I face the cruel facts: Camille Davis has stood me up. On our lunch date.

Thinking of dates inspires me to call Janet Fickel.

"Hey, Janet," I say into my cell phone.

"Hello."

"Wild day at the office, I bet."

"You got that right."

"Lane looked good at the courthouse this morning. Especially after his arraignment."

"He's got me pretty busy right now. Getting things ready for Thursday."

"What kind of things?"

"I can't really say."

"I assume his supporters will be out in full force on Thursday."

"Sooner, too."

"What was Naomi's reaction to the news that Lane's being charged?"

"Same as everyone else," Janet says. "Why?"

"The cops may be watching Naomi. And Camille. Because Rachel Clark was in Central American in 1989. When Lane went down there. On his humanitarian mission. Just like Naomi and Camille were. And the cops think Davis brought Rachel Clark back from Central America. In that moving van. Using an alias. So they're bound to be watching Naomi. And Camille."

"But I thought this was all just politics."

"Bull. Like you said, mayor of Ann Arbor just isn't important enough for all this. I think they really believe Davis knows something. Or at the very least, they figure charging Davis will spook Rachel Clark into running. Which is why I think they'll be watching Naomi and Camille."

"Well, so far no one's going anywhere," Janet says. "At least, as far as I can tell. But I've got to get back to work."

"Would you like to have lunch with me today?"

"Can't. Too much work. I already ate a sandwich at my desk."

"How 'bout lunch tomorrow?"

"Can't do that either."

"How 'bout dinner tomorrow night?"

Pause. "Okay."

"Where you want to meet?" I'm hoping, of course, that Janet will say something frisky. Like 'the Sheraton.' No such luck.

"The gas station."

"Miller and Main? Okay. I'll meet you there at five tomorrow night. I love you, Janet."

"I know."

* * *

Across the street from Raja Rani, I see the Germans. Parked. In a new rental car. A big SUV. Moving up in the world. The Germans smirk at me.

I let them follow me awhile. I drive over to the homeless shelter. Park across the street. Let the Germans pull up nearby. Give them a friendly wave. Then I aim my camera at the door of the shelter. And take a photo of the first person who walks out the door. Who turns out to be a wild-haired woman. Let the Germans wonder what the heck I'm up to.

Now it's time to lose them. So I drive over to my mom's house. On Hill Street. She's home. As always. So I pop in the front door. Have a nice chat with my mom.

The houses on Hill Street are packed close together. The Germans are parked down the street. So they do not have a sight line to my mom's back door. After a few minutes of chit-chat with my mom, I slip out the back, Jack. Walk twelve blocks. Over to Casa Davis.

Turns out I'm not the only hack with the bright idea of trying to interview Camille. Four other members of the Fourth Estate are patrolling the sidewalk in front of Casa Davis.

I walk past the Davis front yard. Nod to my fellow hacks. Glance briefly at the Davis for Mayor yard signs. Lined up in front. No longer marking out two end zones for football.

Four doors down, I cut through a driveway. Then circle back to Casa Davis. From the back. Peer in the kitchen door. Camille's right there. Making a sandwich.

I rap on the glass in the kitchen door. And wave.

Camille jumps. Then puts her hands on her hips. And glares. Looks ready to explode.

"Did you forget our lunch date?" I yell through the door.

Camille peers through the glass. Recognizes me. Shakes her head. But softens a little, too. Even opens the door. "I'm sorry, Mr. Fisher. It's been a hectic day."

"I'm sorry, too, Ms. Davis. And I really hate to bother you at home. But in lieu of our lunch date, could I just ask you a couple of questions?"

Long pause. "How many is 'a couple?' Two?"

I smile. "No more than ten."

Camille steps outside. Looks at me expectantly. Like I'm suppose to ask my ten questions here. On the back steps. Even though it's fairly chilly.

"Can we do this inside? I'm very well-behaved. I'm sure Sheila Nyman told you. When she asked me to leave her home, I left. Right away. No fuss."

Camille raises an eyebrow. "No, Sheila did not tell me that. Why did Sheila have to ask you to leave her home?"

"She didn't want to help me find Rachel Clark. For an interview."

"I'm not going to help you find Rachel Clark either, Mr. Fisher."

"Is that because you're Rachel Clark?"

Camille laughs. "The police already asked that question, Mr. Fisher. You're a little late."

"Did they fingerprint you?"

"Yes. And they let me go. You don't think they'd let Rachel Clark go, do you?"

"No. So then I guess we both know who Rachel Clark is, don't we?"

Camille doesn't flinch. "I don't know who Rachel Clark is. I don't know if you know."

"Naomi," I say. "Naomi is Rachel Clark."

Camille says nothing. But looks distressed.

"I'm right, aren't I?"

"I promised Lane I would not speculate about things like that."

"Why is Lane sticking his neck out so far for Naomi?"

Camille shakes her head. "That question, Mr. Fisher, is like asking 'when did you stop beating your wife?' It presumes facts not in evidence. As you lawyers say."

"How'd you know I was a lawyer?"

Camille looks me up and down. Not quite as provocative as when Janet does it. But close.

"It's written all over you. Also, Sheila told me. But you're almost out of questions."

"I still have three left. But who's counting?"

"I am." Camille smiles. "Now you have just two."

I grin. "Shoot! I better make these last two count. Okay." I take a deep breath. "Has Lane ever had a romantic affair with Naomi, either before or after you married him, and regardless of what name Naomi was using at the time?"

Camille looks sad. "Now I see why Sheila had to ask you to leave her home, Mr. Fisher. That's not a proper question. That's just bad manners. And it's not even fair."

"I'm sorry. Truly I am. But I think it *is* fair. I'm not digging for dirt. Like a tabloid hack would. I just want to understand why Lane isn't telling the prosecutor he met Naomi in Central America. And brought her back here in his moving van."

"There you go again. Assuming facts not in evidence. And you managed to do it without even asking your last question."

I laugh. "You got me there, Ms. Davis. You would have made a good lawyer."

"I doubt it. I'm surrounded by lawyers. Lane and Sheila and Raven. And many other friends. But I want no part of their world, really. I'm someone who thinks, when you get asked an unfair question, you just don't answer it. Even if lawyers—and reporters—might later try to use your silence against you. And it *is* an unfair question, Mr. Fisher. How do you think your wife would feel if I asked her whether you ever had a romantic liaison with Janet Fickel?"

I blink so hard my contact lenses almost fall out.

I assume Hunter must be the one who told Camille. About Janet and me. During his weekend grilling of the Davises. But I can't afford to use my last question just to verify my suspicion on this collateral issue. Unless I can get Camille to allow me an extra question.

"Checkmate, Ms. Davis. You're right. And I'm wrong. So I withdraw the question."

"Too late. You only have one question left. Better make it count."

"Oh, I will. It's the $64,000 question. Or I should say, the $200,000 question."

Camille cocks her head at me. Again, not as sexy as when Janet does it. But not bad.

"What should I do?" I ask.

Camille cocks her head even further. Looks genuinely puzzled.

"Unlike Greg Hunter and Prosecutor Barnett, I know who Rachel Clark is. Should I nark on her and claim a big reward? It would help your husband. I think. Or should I sit on it? And respect her privacy."

"That was way more than one question. But there's only one answer. You have to do what we're all doing, Mr. Fisher. You have to do what your conscience tells you to do."

Camille spins on a dime. Walks back inside. Locks the door behind her.

'Follow your conscience.' Ha! Easy for her to say. She's not a tabloid hack. She *has* a conscience.

\* \* \*

"Actually, Mr. Fisher," Jonathan Lowe says, "there would be no point even arguing reporter's privilege. We'd get laughed out of court."

Lowe's the regular lawyer for *The Ann Arbor News*. The guy Graham Hancock hired to represent me. I'm trying to pay attention to Lowe. Since we're paying him five bucks a minute. But it's a little hard to concentrate. Because on the wall behind him in his office, right above his head, is a huge 30" x 40" framed portrait of . . . Abe Lincoln? No. Clarence Darrow? No. A giant rat. I kid you not. The biggest, ugliest rat I've ever seen. Lowe's role model? His muse? Who knows.

"Didn't Graham Hancock tell you we're hiring you to *fight* the subpoena?" I ask.

"Mr. Hancock retained me to review the matter and protect your rights in the best way possible," Lowe says. "But your rights won't be protected if I act like Custer and charge us up a hill we can't possibly take."

"Custer charged down hill," I say.

Lowe raises an eyebrow at me. "Mr. Hancock warned me you have some, ah, focus problems. We need to focus here, Mr. Fisher. We need to work a deal with the prosecutor."

"How can we work a deal if we have no leverage?"

"We'll threaten to invoke your Fifth Amendment rights, not your First Amendment rights."

"You lost me."

"I thought Mr. Hancock said you're a lawyer." Lowe smiles a smug little smile.

Why is everyone such a wise-ass about my failed legal career?

"You have a Fifth Amendment right not to incriminate yourself," Lowe continues. "So if the prosecutor asks you where you got that motorcycle helmet, you invoke the Fifth. Until he agrees to give you immunity. That way you won't have to worry about being prosecuted for breaking and entering into Lane Davis's law offices."

"That's not protecting my rights! I don't want to take the Fifth. And I don't want to admit in open court I broke into a lawyer's office. To plant bugs. This is my hometown. My mom lives here. All my old friends. If this becomes public, and I ever decide to move back here, I'll never get a job in this town. Heck, I won't even be able to get dinner at my mom's house."

"Maybe you should have thought of that before you broke into the man's office."

Very helpful guy. You'd think a rat-lover like Lowe would admire my sneaky B&E faculties. But apparently not.

We go on like this awhile. But Jonathan Lowe insists the reporter's privilege would be of no use in a criminal prosecution. Especially where I am the only person with the particular evidence the prosecutor seeks. And it's highly material evidence. The location where I obtained the helmet. With the fresh fingerprints of the Fugitive Radical and Lane Davis.

"Bottom line, Mr. Fisher. I'm not going to lose my credibility with the judges in this town by making a silly argument. I'll be happy to negotiate an immunity deal. And I'll be happy to represent you at the PX. To be sure the questions are strictly limited. Just the evidence they can't get from other sources. But if you want to argue that the reporter's privilege shields you from having to testify at all, you'll have to find another lawyer. I won't do it. Not on these facts."

So I give in. Agree to let Lowe call the prosecutor. And start negotiating.

\* \* \*

Back to the Bell Tower. Stop to get my surveillance equipment. From the hotel safe.

Then up to my room for a quick shower and change. Because I may have a long night. Staking out Naomi Williams.

I open my door. And get another rude surprise.

My room's been trashed. Again. Totally. Thoroughly. And professionally. Fuck! Same drill. Mattress slashed. Drawers yanked out. Clothes all over the bed.

Who is doing this to me? And why? And how'd he find my new hotel?

There are only two groups tailing me. Hunter's minions. And the Germans.

Hunter certainly hates me enough to do it. But he seems—I dunno. Smarter. The Germans, on the other hand, are idiots. Tabloid low-lifes. Like me. This seems like their work.

Especially since this week's *National Spy* just got released today. Supermarket readers won't see it 'til tomorrow. But the independent photo agencies all get their tabloids on Monday morning. Hot off the presses. So. The Germans saw how far ahead we are. On this Ann Arbor story. They'd love to steal my outtakes. So I'm guessing they found me at Raja Rani. Tailed me 'til I lost them at my mom's. Then instead of getting mad, they got even. While I was playing "ten questions" with Camille Davis, the Germans went and trashed my room. Looking for my outtakes.

But how'd they find out I was staying here at the Bell Tower?

I must have been careless one time coming back here.

Oh well, fuck it. I'll just switch rooms. I'm done running from these ass-holes. They obviously aren't going to hurt me—just my room.

While I'm here, I check the tapes from my phone taps. Hear this call. On Raven's phone.

SHEILA: Hi Raven. It's me.

RAVEN: Hi Sheila.

SHEILA: Look. I know we don't see eye-to-eye on this. But you gotta let Lane decide for himself. He should do what his conscience tells him to do. Not what you or I think is best.

RAVEN: Oh, that's *good.* Coming from you! And if *I* stop telling him to turn her in, are *you* going to stop trying to convince him to protect her?

SHEILA: I'm not doing anything of the kind. I'm only trying to be a good friend.

RAVEN: To whom?

SHEILA: To everyone.

RAVEN: Sure, Sheila, all you care about is *other people.* And you're not the least bit worried that, if Lane starts talking, *your own* dirty laundry will get washed in public? *That* couldn't possibly be the *real reason* you always advocate silence and non-cooperation with the authorities, could it?

SHEILA: Fuck you, Raven.

RAVEN: Fuck you, Sheila.

\* \* \*

Well. On that sobering note, I leave my room. In a shambles. Report the break-in to the front desk. Supervise the movement of my things to a new room. And then drive over to Davis & Nyman, shortly before 5:00. Pick out a nice stakeout spot in the alley. The same spot where I saw Hunter's Latino buddy sitting two weeks ago.

At 5:00 on the dot, Her Strut sashays out. God, Janet's a good-looking woman! It takes all my willpower to resist the urge to run out and talk to her at her car. Just for five minutes. But I'm on assignment. And my target is Naomi. Not Janet. So I watch Janet drive away.

At 5:15, Naomi comes out the back door. Bundled in an oversized winter coat. With her ratty checkered scarf wrapped round her neck and face. But even through the scarf I can see she's deeply agitated.

Naomi hops in a Hyundai. Zips out onto Main Street. I follow in my Sebring.

Naomi doesn't go far. Two and a half blocks. Right on Huron. Two and a half more blocks. Right into the parking lot of the Robert J. DeLonis Center. Ann Arbor's homeless shelter.

I circle the block once. Then pull in and park near the front entrance. Pull out my binoculars. I can see Naomi Williams in the lobby just inside the front door. She's talking to a woman with wild stringy hair. Oh. My God. It's Sarah Pierce. Rachel Clark's daughter.

Naomi Williams hands something small to Sarah Pierce. I can't tell what it is. A ring? A letter? A weapon? Who knows.

Naomi comes back outside. I duck behind my steering wheel.

Naomi's in her car. Oblivious to me. Oblivious to pretty much everything. She's wired.

I follow Naomi back to her house. Naomi parks her Hyundai in the one-lane driveway. Because her roommate's car is already parked in their single car garage.

Here's my chance. Gotta go for it.

"Naomi!" I double-time it across her small front lawn. Like Geraldo Rivera used to do. Invading the privacy of some poor Midwestern schmo. "Naomi! I just need to ask you a few questions."

"It's too late for that."

Naomi disappears into the house. The last glimpse I get is of her ankle. Crossing the threshold. No surprise what's on her ankle. An ankle bracelet. Paul Zimmerman's, I presume.

I ring the bell. Repeatedly.

Finally Naomi's roommate comes down. Yells through the closed door.

"Leave us the fuck alone!" The roommate goes back upstairs.

So I go back to my car. Push the seat back as far as it goes. And wait.

For what exactly, I don't know. But I wait.

I put a call in to my conscience. Like Camille recommended. But I get a busy signal. My conscience is overloaded with traffic these days. So all lines are down. Just my luck.

* * *

So I call Elaine. *Her* line is open.

"Hi, David! I'm so glad you called. Guess who just dropped in out of the blue?"

"Beyonce?"

"Who?"

"You know, the curvaceous rock star. I think Beyonce's always had a thing for me."

"You've met *Beyonce Knowles*?"

"No. But I'm absolutely convinced that if we *did* meet, we'd really hit it off."

Elaine laughs. "Truly, David, even I can't tell anymore when you're in the real world and when you're off on Fantasy Island. But no, it was not Beyonce. It was Matt Harmon."

"No kidding! In from the Hague?" Matt is an old DOJ crony. Who is now the lead prosecutor in the International Court of Justice. Matt prosecutes Bosnian war criminals. While I write about celebrity cleavage. Matt is one of my many over-achieving friends. And a very nice guy.

"You should see him! Matt looks almost as good for his age as you do."

"Well now, *that's* a very nice thing to hear you say, Elaine. Seriously. You have no idea how that lifts a man's spirits. When he's sitting on a dull stakeout. Feeling like warmed-over shit."

"You're welcome. God, I wish you were here, David. Matt was so anxious to see you. And he's only here for two days."

"What brings Matt to Miami?"

"Some witness he needs is here. Matt came to persuade him to come back and testify."

"Oh, man—my specialty! That was the one thing I did well at the DOJ. Bullshitting regular people into doing something they knew in their hearts they really didn't want to do."

"That's exactly what Matt said. He wanted to take you with him to the guy's house."

"Elaine, do you remember the time—"

"—you got that poor old guy in Puerto Rico to testify, by pretending there was a problem with the translation? Yes! Matt reminded me of that one. He said you kept smiling and shaking the guy's hand. Telling him you were proud to shake the hand of someone who would stand up to tyranny. Even though the old guy was actually just trying to tell you to get lost."

"It worked! Finally the old guy got so fed up with what he thought was a problem with the *translator*, he just agreed to testify. To get me off his fucking back."

I laugh. Recalling the good old days at the DOJ. When my life had a purpose. Maybe Graham's right. Maybe this whole Rachel Clark thing *is* about me yearning to be back at the DOJ.

"Did Matt bring pix of Deborah and the kids?"

"Yeah. The kids look great. Deborah—well, she's gotten older."

"Haven't we all? Not everyone can age as well as you, Elaine."

"Oh, you're just saying that because I complimented *you*."

"No. I'm not. I really don't like the idea of you running around with Matt Harmon. Without me there to chaperone. That guy is way too charismatic."

"David! You know I would never cheat on you!"

"I know."

Actually, I *do* know that. Elaine had a young tennis pro hit on her a few years back. Big time. Great for her ego. But she walked away from it. No second thoughts. As far as I know.

Why couldn't *I* walk away from Janet that way? Especially since I really do love Elaine.

The answer, I'm afraid, is either (1) I'm an asshole, or (2) Janet strikes a very special chord with me. Deep in the core of my soul. How could I ever explain either of these to Elaine?

Elaine goes on awhile longer about Matt Harmon. And the old days at the DOJ. We have a really nice chat. Which only serves to remind me how lucky I am to be married to Elaine.

What the hell am I doing with my life?

And what am I supposed to do, now that even my own thoughts are turning against me?

\* \* \*

It's hard to sleep deep while sitting upright in your car. But I'm pretty sure I'm dreaming.

I sure *hope* I'm dreaming. Because things are getting pretty wild.

I'm in a nightclub. Not a strip club. A stand-up comic club. I'm the emcee. Introducing some terrible acts. The audience is clearing out. Understandably. But I'm begging them to stay.

Elaine's in the audience. Supporting me. As always. Elaine looks great. Dark tan. White blouse. Very low cut. Lots of cleavage. The way Elaine knows I like it.

But I'm not paying attention to Elaine like I should. Because *Janet's* in the front row too. I'm trying to be sly. Sneaking peeks at Janet. But Elaine can see Janet's got me mesmerized.

Janet's getting ready to leave the show. Packing up her purse. With my eyes I implore Janet to stay. She gets my meaning. But mouths back at me "I'm bored." So now she's leaving.

Janet's wearing a really skin-tight motorcycle suit. And a motorcycle helmet. With a bullet crease. Janet hops on a motorcycle. I figure I can follow her. Find out where she lives. So I slip away from my responsibilities at the show. Which is awkward. Since I'm on stage.

But now Janet's wearing a super-short mini-skirt. Lord! It's *so* short, it's up around her shoulders. And otherwise she's naked. She's leaning forward, provocatively cupping her breasts.

But now Janet's breasts are just two empty sacs. Someone drained her saline implants.

I wake up in the dark in my car. Damn that Delmore Schwartz!

# CHAPTER FIFTEEN

# THE WRITING ON THE WALL

## Tuesday 26 October 2004

Daylight comes. And you want to go home.

Unfortunately, though, if you're me, you're still sitting in my rental Sebring. Across the street from Naomi Williams's house. Truly, I am too old for all-night stakeouts. My mouth tastes like the inside of my old basketball locker. Stale. Dry. And more than a little rancid. From all the Scotch I drank to keep myself warm through the cold part of the night.

In the mirror I see that my eyes look like two piss holes in the snow. But they're functioning well enough to see that Naomi's Hyundai is still there. Right in the driveway. Right where she left it last night. Blocking her roommate's car, which is still in the garage.

I flip on the car battery. To get the time. 7:45 a.m. The radio comes on, too. Bob Seger. "Against the Wind." Singing, *"Wish I didn't know now what I didn't know then."*

Amen to *that*, brother Bob. Here I thought I really wanted to know which one of the four ladies was Rachel Clark. 'Til yesterday. When I found out. And saw the deep distress in Naomi's sad, tired eyes. And the fear.

But all I want to do is interview her. *No way* am I going to nark on this sad little soul.

So I go over my plan. The one I cooked up in Sheila Nyman's office last week. How first I'll be her lawyer. So she thinks we have attorney-client privilege. I'll give her some advice on the pros and cons of surrendering. Then I'll switch to my journalist's hat. And interview the Fugitive Radical. Find out if I'm right about the pennies. Find out how she found the steam tunnel. How she got the dead nun's passport. All the gory details. And then watch her disappear into the mist.

Unless, like me, she finds she's got a conscience she didn't know she had. Cuz she's got to decide what to do about her boss. Whose ass, right now, is flappin' in the wind. Cuz of her.

I drink some water. Throw some water on my face, too. Eat two Power Bars. I glance at Naomi's car every minute or so. Still sitting there. Motionless. Silent. Around 8:50 I get antsy. Time to go to work, sweetheart.

By 9:00 I realize I'm a sap. But I don't want to admit it. So I wait another ten minutes.

I'm too proud to pray. So I keep telling myself she's coming out any minute.

At 9:10 I get out of my car. Stretch my old stiff legs. My old aching back. Amble slowly to the front door. Ring the bell. Repeatedly. No answer.

Could be they're inside. Unwilling to talk to me. But I don't think so. I think they're gone.

I walk round to the back. Put on my gloves. Pick the back door lock. And walk in.

"Hel-*lo*?" I'm talkin' to myself.

The inside of Naomi's house looks like your grandmother's. Small. Neat as a pin. Fussy old-fashioned furniture with flowery patterns. Antimacassars. Lace doilies. The kind of stuff Elaine hates. And judging from her photo albums, the kind of stuff Janet Fickel loves.

First I check all the rooms. To see if anyone's hiding inside. But the place is empty.

In the bedroom I pat my hands around the unmade bed. It's cold. But *my* bed's cold at 9:15 in the morning, too. Even when I slept in it the night before.

Since I'm inside at last, I poke around. Find Naomi's personal files. Riffle through them. I find bills. Tax returns. Receipts. Warranties. But nothing personal. Nothing personal about Naomi Williams. And nothing personal about Rachel Clark either.

The whole house is like that. Spartan. Uncluttered. In fact, Naomi Williams's house is like Janet Fickel's work desk. You could pack up everything that mattered in thirty seconds.

In the living room I find a photo album. But it tells me nothing. It starts when Naomi's already got gray hair. In the nineties. A few pix of Davis & Nyman folks. (None of Janet. To my regret.) Many pix of people at the old homeless shelter. And a few at the DeLonis Center. But that's it. No pix of anyone who looks like they might be Naomi's family. Or close friends.

In the basement I find two large suitcases. Empty. But what does that mean? Maybe Naomi and her roommate own *six* large suitcases. Took four. Left two. But still aren't planning to come back anytime soon.

One thing I know for sure. Naomi ain't here.

And since her car's still in the driveway, it's highly unlikely she went to work today.

But I gotta check. Even though I can plainly see the writing on the wall.

\* \* \*

No more clever scams. No more dressing up as a woman. No more pretending to be a phone repairman. Or a flower delivery guy. Or an insurance claims adjustive. Or anything else.

I walk right into Davis & Nyman. At 10:15 a.m. Just like any other client. Ask Debbie if I can please speak with Naomi Williams.

"Naomi's out sick today, Mr. Fisher."

I was afraid of that. Obviously I waited too long. Rachel Clark's in the wind again. And I missed my chance. To be a hero. To get the interview. To nail the Fugitive Radical's story.

"Mr. Fisher? Are you alright?"

"Huh? Oh, yeah. Fine. Can I just pop upstairs for a quick word with Janet?"

"She's out in back. Smoking."

I find Janet in the parking lot. With another woman. Her smoking buddy.

"Hey."

Janet takes a drag on her cigarette. Nods. But doesn't introduce her smoking buddy.

"I came looking for Naomi. But she's out sick."

"Yeah," Janet says. "Must be that cold going round."

I gaze into Janet's eyes. But get no *return* gaze. No warmth at all. Apparently Janet doesn't want to give away anything about us in front of her smoking buddy.

I stick out my hand to the smoking buddy. "David Fisher."

The smoking buddy is about Janet's age. Heavier. Nowhere near as sexy as Janet. But not bad looking. She looks at my hand with deep mistrust. Laughs. A harsh laugh.

"I don't shake hands during flu season," the smoking buddy says.

I withdraw my hand. Nod. At the sheer wisdom of this advanced public health policy.

"Do you give out *your name* during flu season?" I ask.

The smoking buddy laughs. Still a harsh laugh. "Not to men I don't know."

"How does a man get to know you?"

"Takes time. Plus he has to behave his butt."

I glance at Janet. She's smoking. Not even *looking* at me during this banter. No hint she's going to help me out here. Instead, just a slight, almost imperceptible smirk on her face.

Something is very strange here. I feel like I'm back in that dream I had last night.

Time to exit. Exiting *gracefully* would be nice. But I don't think I can afford to be greedy. Better just settle for exiting *soon*.

"Well, unfortunately I don't have a lot of time today. My loss, I'm sure." I give a mock old-fashioned bow to both women. "See you later, Janet."

I retreat back inside Davis & Nyman. Ears burning. Trying to figure out what I'm missing. But it's a total mystery to me.

I walk back to my hotel. Fuming. Why would Janet be so cold? So distant? But I can fume all I like. I still can't figure it out.

* * *

I'm at a crossroads. If I'm going to tell Hunter that Naomi Williams is Rachel Clark, I need to do it *now*. It may already be too late. Wait any longer, it will *clearly* be too late.

But do I want to tell Hunter? No. Because I truly *hate* to help the bulldog in any way. He's such an asshole. Yet I must admit, I lack the resources to chase a fugitive. Hunter is really the only hope for catching Naomi Williams. Which is my only chance to get the story I want.

I stop by the police department. Looking for Hunter. To check on Camille Davis's fingerprints. And *maybe* talk to him about Naomi Williams.

But Hunter isn't here. No one knows where he is. Cliff Bryant isn't here, either.

So I drive over to a supermarket. To pick up this week's *National Spy*.

On the way to the supermarket, I see the Germans. In their new SUV. They've picked up my tail. At City Hall, probably. I give them a friendly wave.

My stories are on the cover of *The National Spy*. The cleavage shot of Norma Lee is huge. Man, Graham is right. What a rack! Jane Russell would have died of envy. Most of my other pix look good, too. Though Rachel Clark's *Days of Rage* motorcycle helmet ended up looking like some kind of bizarre artifact from the *Sutton Hoo* excavation. But the grainy video of a half-naked Lane Davis canoodling with a half-naked Raven LaGrow is very titillating.

I briefly skim the articles I wrote. To be sure no one edited the editor's work.

I'm so absorbed in reading my own stories I don't realize the guy behind me in line is talking to me. When he finally gets my attention, he starts laughing. It's my pal Saul Schwartz.

"Boy you really get *into* those tabloids, don't you?"

I've never told Sauly I work for a tabloid. He thinks I'm still a lawyer in Florida.

"Well this is pretty hot stuff." I show him the articles by 'Sandy Hill.' And point to the picture of Lane Davis canoodling with Raven LaGrow. "That's your future mayor, buddy."

"Fat chance. *Channel 7 News* last night said Davis got charged with hiding Rachel Clark. The Fugitive Radical. That's pretty much gotta be the end of his political career. Don't you think?"

"Maybe. Then again, maybe Davis'll prove he's innocent. And discredit the Democrats. But in the meantime, *this*"—I point again to my picture of Davis with Raven—"can't help him."

"Aw, no one believes the tabloids. Who but you even *reads* 'em?"

"You're wrong," I say. A little defensively. "Ten million Americans read the tabloids."

"Yeah but how many of 'em are *voters*?" Saul slugs my shoulder. "I'll bet not many."

I concede this is probably true.

"Hey," Saul says. "Remember last week you were asking me about Sarah Pierce?"

"Yeah."

"A woman by that name almost got *killed* last night. At the DeLonis Center."

"You're kidding. What happened?"

"Guy went ballistic on her. Yelling she killed his father. Bad scene. Very bad for the Center. We don't need that kind of publicity."

"You catch the guy's name?"

"Boyce Hunter."

Somehow I'm not surprised.

\* \* \*

Boyce Hunter's arraignment is in front of Judge Haggerty. Not Judge Flynn. Boyce gets a different prosecutor than Lane Davis or I got, too. And a different defense lawyer. A public defender. No big crowd, like Davis's arraignment. No media. A trivial event. Like mine.

But otherwise it's the same basic drill. Boyce's lawyer waives the reading of the charges. Judge Haggerty sets a date for a preliminary examination. In a couple of weeks. Bail gets set at $25,000. No one objects. No one's going to post bail for Boyce Hunter.

Boyce stands in an orange jailhouse jumpsuit through the entire proceeding. Hands shackled in front of him. Ankle chains, too. Thick, matted, dirty brown hair hangs down in front of his face. He doesn't bother to push the hair away from his glazed eyes. He stands motionless. Almost comatose. His public defender has to nudge him. In order to get Boyce to utter the only two words he utters. "Not guilty."

The only spectators are Greg Hunter and me. Hunter glares at me the whole time.

I spend the arraignment trying to decide if I should tell Hunter about Naomi. When it's over, I still haven't made up my mind. I catch up with Hunter out in the courthouse hallway.

"Hey, Greg." I have to double-time it to keep up with Hunter's brisk walking pace.

"No dice." Hunter doesn't break stride.

"Boyce thought the woman he assaulted was Rachel Clark, eh?"

Hunter doesn't break stride.

"But she was really Rachel Clark's *daughter*, hey?"

Hunter *still* doesn't break stride.

"What made Boyce think Sarah Pierce was really Rachel Clark?"

At last Hunter stops. "Boyce got a letter. From Rachel Clark. Apologizing. About his daddy. It set him off. Who knows what makes Boyce think whatever it is he thinks?"

"You saw the letter?"

"Yeah."

"Authentic?"

"Who knows? Maybe."

"Did you fingerprint it?"

Hunter looks disgusted with me. "We do *function* without your advice and counsel, Mr. Fisher. Yeah. I had it dusted for prints. Nothing. Only prints on it were Boyce's."

"Let me talk to Boyce."

"We ain't teammates no more."

"Sure we are. I carry no grudge. Just cuz you hit me with that subpoena. I know you're just doing your job. And that's all I'm doing, too."

"Why the hell would I want a gossip reporter talking to my crazy nephew? So you can plaster his pathetic picture all over your front page? Like you did to Lane Davis and Raven LaGrow? You told me they ain't even news. But now *they're* on the front page, ain't they?"

"Greg, I promise you we will never print word one about Boyce Hunter. No pix either. Like you said before, Boyce's story is not one the tabloids care about."

"Then why you wanna talk to Boyce?"

"There's gotta be a *reason* he went off on Sarah Pierce like that. He can help us find Rachel Clark. Which is still what we *both* want. Teammate."

Hunter hangs fire. A long time. But finally agrees to let me talk to Boyce. Down in the courthouse lock-up. Before they take him back to the county jail.

The courthouse lock-up in Washtenaw County is primitive. No rats. And no leaking water. But also zero amenities. A single room. With a single bench. One harsh overhead light. The standard single-piece stainless steel toilet-sink combo. Grim.

Boyce sits on the bench. Face buried in his hands. Greg Hunter and I stand before him.

"Boyce," Greg Hunter says, "this man wants to ask you some questions. He might be able to help you. You should listen."

Boyce Hunter looks up. "He's a friend of yours?" Suspicion fills Boyce's voice.

"No," Greg Hunter says. Emphatically.

"But he's a cop?" Boyce guesses.

"No," Greg Hunter says.

"He wants to be my lawyer?" Boyce guesses next.

"No. He's just a guy who knows a lot about Rachel Clark. But you can trust him, Boyce. Maybe he can help. Maybe he can't. But you oughta talk to him. Just a coupla minutes."

I know my cue. "What made you think the woman at the shelter was Rachel Clark?"

"She gave a letter to Naomi," Boyce says.

"Naomi Williams?"

"Yeah."

I wait. But Boyce says nothing more.

"So?" I prompt him.

"A few minutes later, Naomi gave the letter to me. It was from Rachel Clark."

"What did the letter from Rachel Clark say?"

"Said she was sorry. For what they done to my daddy. Fuckin' bitch."

"And you figured it was the same letter you saw the other woman give to Naomi?"

"Yeah. It was. See, they didn't know I was watching. When she gave it to Naomi."

"But how do you know it was the *same* letter? People send lots of letters. Every day."

"Not with *no postmark*," Boyce says.

"The letter Naomi gave you from Rachel Clark had no postmark?"

Boyce nods.

"So you figured it must be the same letter you saw Sarah Pierce give to Naomi?"

"I don't know Sarah Pierce," Boyce says. "But it was the same letter. No one sends letters with no postmark. Unless you hand-deliver 'em. Like Naomi does to me."

"Naomi hand-delivers you *other* letters?"

"Sometimes."

"What's in those other letters?"

Boyce looks at Greg Hunter. Then back at me. "What do you care?"

"You're right. It doesn't matter." I don't press. Because I realize I really don't want Greg Hunter to hear the answer. In case it implicates Naomi.

"Alright, Boyce," I continue. "So you figured the letter Naomi gave you from Rachel Clark must be the same letter that you just saw the lady at the shelter give to Naomi, right?"

"Yeah."

"And that's why you figured the lady at the shelter was Rachel Clark?"

"Yeah," Boyce says.

Outside Hunter and I stand a few moments in the cold wind. Truly, in Ann Arbor it's a thin line. Between summer and winter.

"Get what you want?" Hunter asks.

"I guess. Thanks."

"Fuck you, Fisher. Don't try to be my friend. You need to understand. What's happened to you so far"—here Hunter's eyebrows dance suggestively—"is nothin' compared to what's gonna happen. If you don't cooperate on Thursday."

"I have no idea what you're talking about, Greg. Unless—are you telling me *you're* the person who's been trashing my hotel rooms?"

Hunter smirks. But says nothing.

"Man, that's *pathetic*. Junior high kids could do better than that. But what makes you think I won't 'cooperate' on Thursday? I got the damn subpoena. I gotta show."

"Your goddamn lawyer keeps talkin' about the fuckin' reporter's privilege."

"Really?" I'm glad to hear Jonathan Lowe is doing *something* to earn his outrageous fee. Even if he is just bluffing. "Well, I'll tell you what, Greg. Just for you. Old teammate. I'll tell Lowe to back off. And let me tell the judge exactly what I saw. If you give me what *I* want."

"Which is what?"

"I want you to promise me, that *if* Rachel Clark turns herself in, and *if* the prosecutor decides not to charge her, you won't go after her, vigilante-style."

"No deal. Fuck you, Fisher. But I got a deal for *you*."

"I don't want to hear it."

"You tell Jonathan Lowe to back off. You tell the judge exactly what you know. Or else your wife finds out exactly what *I* know."

"Fuck you, Hunter."

\* \* \*

My cell phone rings. The only people who have my number are Graham Hancock, Elaine, and my kids. So I answer. But it's Janet Fickel. I forgot I gave *her* my number.

"David, I can't make dinner tonight."

"Oh, no. What's up?"

"John's meeting was cancelled. He's going to be home. Looking for dinner."

"Oh. Can we have lunch tomorrow then?"

Long pause. "Sure."

"I'll meet you at the gas station at twelve?"

Longer pause. "Call me in the morning. We'll figure out where to meet then."

\* \* \*

I see no sign of the Germans. But I spend half an hour cleaning my tail anyway. Then I drive over to the University of Michigan Hospital. Where Hunter told me Sarah Pierce is laid up.

Sarah Pierce is flat on her back. Two IV tubes running into her left arm. A black eye. A large gauze dressing on her forehead. And her right arm in a sling. She doesn't look at all like the sexy stripper with the Spanish cape. She looks more like the woman in the Lake Michigan photograph Amy Pierce showed me. Washed out. Burned out. And old way beyond her years.

Sheila Nyman is sitting at Sarah's bedside. On the opposite side of the bed from me.

Sheila greets me with surprising cordiality. "Mr. Fi—I mean—David."

"How is she?"

"Sarah's okay. They're getting ready to discharge her."

I raise a skeptical eyebrow. Glance at the IV tubes that run from Sarah Pierce's left arm to a couple of cellophane bags. Which presumably contain dextrose and painkillers.

"As soon as they unhook her," Sheila adds, in response to my skeptical eyebrow.

Since I'm not wearing my gray wig and black glasses, Sarah doesn't recognize me as her not-so-helpful insurance claims adjustor.

"Sarah, I'm David. A friend of Sheila's. And a friend of your mom's."

I cock my head at Sheila. Daring her to contradict me.

Sarah glances at Sheila. To my surprise, Sheila nods confirmation.

Sarah looks back at me.

"I need to find your mother," I say.

"I don't know where she is," Sarah says. "No matter what that crazy man thinks."

"You gave a letter to Naomi Williams," I say.

"Yes."

"Who was it from?"

"My grandparents."

"The little people? Ray and Ruth Clark?"

Sarah smiles weakly. "Yeah. The little people."

"How'd you get a letter from them?"

"They gave it to me."

"Out in Centreville?"

"Yeah."

"When were you there?"

"Last week."

"What made you go out there?"

"Raven LaGrow said they might be able to help me out. With some money."

"Did they?"

"Yeah. I spent a few days out there."

"With Ray and Ruth?"

"Yep. Woulda stayed longer. But it gets kinda boring out there in Centreville."

"The letter your grandparents gave you," I say, "who was it for?"

"My mother."

"Why'd they give it to you?"

"Guess they figured I knew where she was."

"But you don't know where she is?"

"No, I don't."

"So why didn't you tell your grandparents you don't know where your mother is?"

"I did. They said I was more likely to see Rachel than they were."

"The letter they gave you. Was it sealed? In an envelope?"

"Yes."

"Why'd you give it to Naomi Williams?"

Sarah turns to look at Sheila. To my *great* surprise, Sheila nods her head up and down. I have no idea why Sheila is helping me. Maybe she thinks I let Naomi get away last night *on purpose*.

But I never argue if someone wants to help me.

"Naomi came up to me in the dining room. Pulled me aside from the others."

"At the shelter?"

"Yeah. Naomi said she knew I was Rachel Clark's daughter. Said she's in touch with people who know where my mother is."

"Did she tell you who those people are?"

"No. But Naomi gave me a letter *from* my mother. So I asked if she could get a letter *to* my mother. And she said yes. So I gave her the letter from my grandparents."

"Did Naomi tell you anything else?"

"No. But she also gave a letter to that man—" Sarah turns her head to Sheila.

"Boyce Hunter," Sheila interjects.

"Yeah. And I guess he also saw me give the letter from my grandparents to Naomi. So he jumped on the idea that I must be Rachel Clark. People say I look a lot like my mom."

* * *

I'll admit it. I'm feeling low. First Janet treats me like a stranger. When I pop in on her and her smoking buddy. Then she cancels dinner. At the last minute.

When your love life's in the crapper, there's only two real choices. Drink. Or work.

Normally I would drink. As you know. But I'm interested in all the surprising new things I've heard the last few days about the little people. Ray and Ruth Clark.

So I drive out to Centreville. Drop in on the Clarks. They're cleaning up after dinner.

"Yo. Special Agent Fisher again. With a few more questions."

Ruth gets me another glass of water. We all three sit down at the gray Formica table.

"Any word from Rachel?"

They shake their heads no. Solemnly.

"Any word from your granddaughter, Sarah?"

They shake their heads no. Solemnly.

I gaze at them a long while. In absolute silence.

"You're nice people. So I don't want to call you liars. But I know Sarah was here last week. I know you paid for her foot surgery. Contrary to what you told me two weeks ago. And I know you wrote a letter to Rachel last week. The daughter you claim you disowned."

Ray and Ruth exchange worried looks.

"All of that could get you in a heap of trouble. Except, luckily for you, I'm a liar, too. I'm no Special Agent with the DOJ. I'm just a reporter. I mean no harm to Rachel. I just want to tell her story. Where can I find her?"

Ray and Ruth exchange worried looks again.

Then Ray takes charge. "If you're not a federal law man, we don't gotta talk to you."

"No, you don't. But if you toss me out, you won't be helping Rachel."

"Why is that?"

"Because I'm the only person in the state of Michigan who believes Rachel's innocent. And I can prove it, too. If she helps me. All I want to do is give her a chance to clear her name."

Ray and Ruth exchange worried looks a third time.

"Mister," Ray says, "we don't know where Rachel is."

We all sit awhile at the gray Formica table. Staring at each other. A Mexican stand-off.

In the sink I see dirty dishes. Seems like a *lot* of dishes. For just two people's dinner.

"I don't suppose you care much about Rachel's *friends*," I murmur at last. "But one of them is about to get hurt real bad, if Rachel doesn't come forward and talk to someone."

This time Ruth speaks up. In a voice clear as a bell. "Rachel will never leave her friend hanging in the wind. I'm sure of that."

Now how does Ruth know *that* for certain? If she hasn't seen Rachel in thirty-five years?

\* \* \*

Back in my new hotel room. Just me and a new bottle of Scotch. Until my cell rings.

"Tiger Woods's Wedding Consultants."

"Hi, Dad."

"Hello, Rachel. What's new?"

"Halloween, dude. Are you gonna be home for Halloween?"

Playful Reader, I confess: I *love* Halloween. You can keep *all* the other holidays. Just give me my memories of walking my kids around on Halloween. Dressed as clowns. Or bunnies. Or pirates. Life is short, and then you die. But at least, before you go, you get the simple joy of seeing your kids dressed up in goofy costumes. And hoarding candy like it's about to be banned.

"Yes, Rachel." I choke back an alcohol-induced tear. "I'll be home for Halloween."

"You sure? It's *this Sunday*, you know. Dad."

"I'm sure I'll be back by then. But aren't you guys a little too *old* for Halloween?"

"No way, dude. I'm gonna be an eco-terrorist. Raise people's consciousness."

"While liberating their environmentally-unsound candy?"

"Exactly."

"And how 'bout Sara?"

"She says she's gonna be a half-baked idea."

"Huh?"

"Don't ask me. Sara says she's gonna go as a half-baked idea. That's Sara for you."

Yes, it is. That's Sara for me. One of the two kids I claim I'm going to leave. For Janet.

# CHAPTER SIXTEEN
# DEATH'S IRONIC SCRAPING

## Wednesday 27 October 2004

The memorial service for Dale Hunter begins at 10:30 a.m. Outside City Hall.

They've cleared the entire City Hall parking lot of cars. To make room for all the people. They have a podium set up near City Hall. Right by the door to Police Headquarters.

The temperature dropped thirty degrees overnight. Indian summer in Ann Arbor is now officially dead and buried. The chill in the air warns everyone that winter is coming. Very soon.

But they go ahead with the service outside. There's a color guard. Lots of flags. And a big crowd. Dozens of uniformed policemen. Dozens of non-police people, too. For a guy who died thirty-five years ago, it's pretty impressive. Turns out cops in Ann Arbor almost never get killed in the line of duty. One guy in 1935. And Dale in 1969. That's it. So this memorial service has become an annual event. Supported by the Police Union. The Fire Union. The City Hall Employees' Union. Many people here weren't even *born* when Dale Hunter died.

First the incumbent mayor thanks people for coming. Comments on how important this sad occasion is in the life of the community. Drones on for awhile. But makes no mention of the charges brought against Lane Davis. For allegedly harboring the only fugitive still at-large after the Dale Hunter shooting. The omission speaks louder than words. Plainly the mayor is determined not to give Davis any fodder for alleging the prosecution is politically motivated.

Next Greg Hunter gives a eulogy to his brother. Hunter's pretty emotional. And fairly disorganized. Bounces back and forth between recalling the grim events of October 27, 1969, and talking about the present. Hunter's main message is an exhortation to everyone to remember October 27, 1969, as long as they live. But he lacks the mayor's self-control. So he makes a murky reference to how "past events" are still caught up in "present events." But right away Hunter looks guilty. Like he was warned to steer way clear of mentioning Lane

Davis. And he knows he's damn close to the line. So Hunter quickly moves on to talking about how you have to remember the past. Or you're doomed to repeat it. Pembroke Watkins's favorite bromide.

Last a minister gets up. I don't catch his name. But this guy is pretty good. He plays off what Greg Hunter said. But he's much more coherent. And he takes it to another level.

The minister begins with the famous passage from *Ecclesiastes*. About how there's a season for everything. A season for loving. A season for hating. You know that passage. Then he moves into a discussion about how each person's life consists of different seasons. The season for living. The season for loving. And the season for remembering those whose sacrifices make all *our* seasons possible. How important it is for each of us to preserve the memory of people like Dale Hunter. A brave man who gave his life while keeping our community safe.

The minister goes on like this a long time. The crowd is very quiet. Just a few crying babies. And the occasional coughs. But even at the outer fringes of the crowd, people are paying very close attention to the minister's speech. Except for me.

My mind is wandering. As it always does during ceremonies. Funerals. Weddings. Award presentations. Doesn't matter. I'm sorry. I can't stay focused on the speaker for more than about five minutes. Then I'm off in the ozone. Daydreaming. Like Walter Mitty.

I begin imagining a new life with Janet Fickel. This time I try to be *realistic* about it. I don't want to succumb to wild and lurid fantasies about making love to Janet morning, noon, and night. I assume we would find our way, eventually, into a daily grind. The way all people do.

Except the great lovers of history and fiction, of course. Who *never* get into a daily grind. Because they never actually get together for the long haul at all. They have their quick burst of passion. The flames leap brightly. But then, almost as quick as it starts, it ends. The fire burns consumes itself. Cleopatra poisons herself. Romeo and Juliet poison themselves. Pierre Abelard is defrocked. While Heloise is sent to a convent. Emma Bovary poisons herself. Anna Karenina jumps under the train. Tess Durbeyfield murders her lover. And is led away from Stonehenge by the constables. The Mayerling lovers shoot each other. Mister Rick puts Ilsa Lund on the plane to Lisbon with her husband, while Rick stays put in Casablanca. Yuri Zhivago puts Lara in the sleigh to Kamchatka with Viktor, while Zhivago stays put in the Urals. The passionate lovers in *Brief Encounter* find they can't sustain their passion because of all the sneaking around they've had to do just to hook up. Katherine Clifton dies in the Cave of Swimmers. While Count Almasy suffers horrible burns trying to rescue her.

But in my *tempered* imagination, Janet Fickel and I are not destined to be among the great lovers of history or fiction. I just imagine us living quietly together. She as a legal assistant; I as a reporter for *The Ann Arbor News*. Nothing dramatic. We'll drink beers. Enjoy witty conversations. Shoot pool. And kiss passionately. We'll travel. To New Orleans. San Francisco. Europe. Our parents and our children will eventually see this was what we had to do. That it was the right thing to do. Even though we'll leave the wreckage of two marriages behind us.

Standing there at City Hall, listening to the minister droning on, reminds me how fifty percent of all marriages end in divorce. The minister stands there before the crowd. Eliciting vows from the happy couple. Promising they will love each other "'til death do us part."

And literally half the time, the vows prove to be a lie.

Elaine and I were married in her parents' backyard. Beautiful summer day. Friends and family. Certainly I did not intend my vows that day as a lie. But I also didn't intend to keep on *living* a lie, just to keep my vows. People say you have a duty to try to live up to the vows. To "work" at your marriage. But what a funny concept. If you think about it. We generally understand "work" to mean something that is alienating. Routinized. Deadening. Something we only do because we are *forced* to do it. So why would we ever want to "*work*" at love?

A tap on the shoulder pulls me out of my thoughts. It's some guy I've never seen before in my life.

"Sorry," the guy says. "Thought you were someone else."

Indeed. These past two weeks I've sure been *trying* to become someone else. I'm just not quite sure who it is I want to be.

The guy disappears into the crowd behind me. I re-focus on the minister.

He's talking about how it's our duty to remember Dale Hunter. To honor our fallen hero by remembering him in our hearts.

Listening to the minister's speech about the duty we all have to remember the dead is what does it. Suddenly I *know* where to find Rachel Clark. Where she will surely go sometime today. On this anniversary of Dale Hunter's death. Since her letter to Boyce shows she clearly remembers Dale Hunter. But before I can check out my idea, I have a lunch date. With my own destiny.

\* \* \*

"So where do you want to meet?"

"Island Park.'"

"Um—it's awful *cold* out today, Janet."

"That's okay."

"You want me to pick up sandwiches?"

"Not for me. I'm not hungry."

"You want me to pick you up?"

"No. I'll drive myself. Listen, I gotta go. I'll meet you in the parking lot there at 12:05."

I stop by Zingerman's and pick up a complex sandwich. Even though I doubt I'll have any appetite either. Because I can *feel* what's coming.

When Janet pulls up next to my car at Island Park, she's smoking. She rolls down her window. Flips the cigarette butt out into the parking lot. Then reaches across and opens the passenger door. Invites me to hop in. Which I do. We sit side by side. In bucket seats. Looking sideways at each other. Across the wide console in the middle.

Janet is wearing loose, shapeless slacks. And a loose-fitting business jacket. No provocative glimpses of those lithe little thighs or those delicious big breasts today.

And there is trouble in Janet's eyes. They are flat and uninviting. Cold.

"I'm not cut out for this." Janet's voice is flat, too. No emotion at all.

Janet's unblinking eyes look straight into mine.

I wince. Cock my head at her. To indicate I need a little more explanation.

"I can't see you anymore," Janet says.

"John's orders?"

"No—he doesn't know about you."

"But you said—the other night—he—"

"John was just shooting in the dark. He doesn't know anything."

"Well, if John doesn't know, why do we have to stop seeing each other?"

"I can't do it anymore."

"Why not? Did I do something wrong Saturday?"

(I'm always a glutton for punishment.)

"No," Janet says. "You were very nice to be with."

"You, too. You're *always* nice to be with. Not just at the condo. And the hotel. You're also nice to shoot pool with. Talk to at the bar. Hang out with here in the park. Whatever. It doesn't matter where we are, it's always great to be with you."

Janet says nothing. But she doesn't look away, either. It's almost like a stare-down. She seems determined to show me she's not afraid to look me in the eye. As she blows me off.

"If I rushed you into making love too soon," I say, "I'm sorry. Really I am."

"You didn't rush me. You were very nice about it. Not insisting. Letting me make up my own mind. I was the one who decided it was time."

"So what are you saying?" I press. "You must be saying I disappointed you. As a lover."

"Not at all."

"What other conclusion can I draw? We've had so many great times. Wonderful romance. And passion. The way your chest heaves when we kiss. The way you touch me. The way you kiss me. So at last we do what our bodies were screaming at us to do. But after doing that just twice, you say you never want to see me again? Obviously I must have been a lousy lay."

Okay. I'm fishing for compliments. But only because I figure compliments might build some momentum here. To get past this little crisis of conscience. Or whatever Janet's having.

"You were not a 'lousy lay,'" Janet says.

"You did *sound* like you were having a great time. Unless you were faking it."

"I wasn't faking anything."

"Then don't pull the plug on us, Janet," I plead. "You *deserve* this. *I* deserve this."

Janet shakes her head in the negative. But says nothing.

"Why would you give up on us now?"

"I can't love two men at once."

"You never said you *loved* John. You just said you're afraid of him."

"I'm not afraid of John."

"Yes, you are. You're afraid of how he'll react if he finds out about us. You're afraid of how he'll react if you file for a divorce."

"John would never lay a finger on me. I *know* him. John might go after *you*. He might hurt *himself*. But he would never hurt *me*."

"Well, I'm not afraid of Big Bad John, either. Don't worry about me. I can take care of myself. But if he doesn't know anything, then we're still a long way from that kind of problem. Why not keep having fun the way we're having fun? Let the future take care of itself."

"Because I can see where this is heading. I feel way too much for you. And you for me, too. That's the part that *really* bothers me."

"It bothers you I feel so much for you? It bothers you I care about you? What? You'd rather I just treat you like a notch in my belt? Is *that* what you want?"

"No, of course not."

"Then I don't get it. How's the depth of my feeling for you being used against me here?"

"Because I don't want to be a *home wrecker*. I really don't mind if I end up divorcing John. He's not a very nice person. If I had more self-esteem, I would have done it years ago."

"So do it now. Now that you have a reason."

"It's not that easy. In a strange way, I do love him. We have a lot of history together."

"So because he's mistreated you for so many years, he's entitled to mistreat you into the indefinite future, too?"

Janet doesn't answer that one. Can't say I blame her.

"Look, Janet." I take her hand. Which is ice cold. And not at all responsive. But I take it anyway. Thread my fingers through her fingers. *Insinuating* myself into her touch. "You've reawakened all the best things in me. Things that have been buried alive for at least a decade. And I think I've done the same for you. You can't tell me you haven't been enjoying yourself."

"No, I can't say that."

"Because we open up for each other the possibility of different lives than the ones we're leading. *Better* lives. This was never about just jumping in the sack together. Don't get me wrong. You've got the hottest little body I've ever put my hands on. And you are really great in bed. But what I want from you isn't just the sex. If you want to go slower on that, it's okay with me. But please don't walk away from the passion. And the romance."

"That's *exactly* what I have to walk away from."

"Why?"

"Because I don't want to be a *home wrecker*. I don't know Elaine. I don't care about her. But I care about Rachel and Sara."

"You've never met Rachel and Sara."

"Through you, I have. Through your pictures. It's written all over those pictures. How important those girls are in your life."

"They are important to me," I concede.

"*Very* important," Janet corrects me. "There's that picture of you playing Monopoly with them. Or the one of you with that big cast on your leg, reading to them. It's in their eyes. The way those girls look at you. The way you look at them."

"Elaine does take good pictures."

"What chance would I ever have with those girls, if I was the home wrecker who broke up their happy home? They'd hate me the rest of their lives."

"No, they wouldn't," I say. "Why blame you? They'd be too busy blaming me."

"I'd be guilty by association."

"Maybe at first," I concede. "But they're strong girls. They'd move on. They're old enough to handle this. And in the end, that strong bond you sense from the pictures would keep us all together. They'd learn to like you because they'd see you were part of me."

Janet still looks straight into my eyes. But looks utterly unconvinced.

Frankly, I haven't even convinced myself.

"I was a teenage girl. I know how much better off I would have ended up if I'd had a father like you. I don't want to be the reason those girls of yours get into trouble."

"Rachel and Sara are not going to get into 'trouble.' I don't know what happened in *your* home growing up. But these girls of mine do not have self-esteem issues."

"*All* teenage girls have self-esteem issues. It's the hardest time for a girl."

"My girls will be fine. I've lived seventeen years with their best interests in mind. I'm not going to stop now. I've got enough money to take care of them. *And* their mother. So they'll never say I left their mom high and dry. And they'll never know I met you before the divorce."

"You know too many people in this town. We'd never get away with it."

I debate confessing that I don't actually live in Ann Arbor. But confessing to such a fundamental lie would just be a weird distraction at this point. And extremely unlikely to help my sinking cause. At this desperate hour.

"We could be more discreet," I say. "Or even take some time away from each other. While we got our mutual divorces."

"You don't know me well enough to throw away your family for me. And I don't know you that well, either."

"So let's go slow. Just be drinking buddies. *Passionate* drinking buddies. If you want to hold off on sex awhile, fine. But don't give up on the best romance you or I will ever find."

Janet keeps gazing at me. But I can read it in her dry eyes.

She's made up her mind. And she isn't going to reconsider.

There's no way to talk a woman out of dumping you, is there? If you protest, you just sound weak. And that's the last thing she wants. Even if a woman *claims* she wants sensitivity—and Janet never made *that* claim—she doesn't mean it. What she really wants—what attracted her to you in the first place—is that you looked self-possessed. Capable of killing the cave bear.

But when you're begging for your life with a 115-pound package of cold-hearted indifference, you definitely do *not* seem capable of killing the cave bear. And I *am* begging. Because I'm devastated. Janet's torn my guts out. Thrown them on the ground in front of me. And now she's grinding them under the toe of her elegant shoe. Like one of her discarded cigarette butts. Which is what's happening here. *My* butt's being discarded.

Janet hands me a CD. "I made another tape for you."

"Thank you."

"I don't think you'll like these songs as well as you liked the others."

Is this a warning? It sounds more like a *taunt*.

So I stare at the CD awhile in silence. Struggling to control my emotions. But as we know, I don't do silent well. "You know, Janet, this whole thing seems backward. It's the married *man* who's supposed to hit and run. While the woman begs him to stay. And wonders if any of it was real. Or if he was just lying, from beginning to end, just to get laid."

Janet keeps gazing at me. Never wavers. But she doesn't respond to the implicit accusation, either. So I make it more direct.

"Was *any* of it real?" I ask. "Or was this all just a *game* for you?"

"Oh, it was real. It was so real I didn't know how I was going to be able to give you up."

"So don't! Don't quit on me. Don't quit on yourself."

Janet keeps gazing at me. Unwavering. And *unmerciful*, too. Truly, the coldest chamber of the human heart is a woman's. When she's bent on rejecting you.

"Because this way," I continue, "it sure feels like hit-and-run. Like you just used me for a little fun on the side. And to get your husband's attention. To warn him. 'Pay more attention to me, big man, or I'll go find someone else.' Which is what *really* happened here, isn't it?"

"No."

"Then *explain it to me*, Janet. There's no way you're pulling the plug just for the sake of my two kids you never met. So what is it? Give it to me right between the eyes. I can take it. If you weren't playing a game, then it has to be something *I* did that's driving you away so soon. We're just two weeks into the best romance of our lives. We've only scratched the surface of what we can be together."

"You barely got to kick the tires," Janet murmurs. Flatly. Again, almost like a *taunt*.

"I know! *That's* what's driving me crazy. You give me a little taste of how sweet your love can be. But then just when I start running full speed, you yank your love away. Like Lucy yanking that football away from Charlie Brown."

Janet struggles to suppress a grin.

"And unfortunately, *I'm* Charlie Brown. Falling flat on my ass. With no idea why."

I stare at Janet a long time. Trying to will her to give me a reason.

But Janet sits silent as the Sphinx. While I cast aimlessly for solutions to her riddle.

"Did I scare you off with the wild talk about New Orleans and living in Europe?"

"No."

"Did I scare you off by plunking down money for the condo?"

"No."

"Is this all because of that dumb little crack I made about my 'weapon?'"

"No."

"That *bothered* you though, didn't it?"

"No. Well—yes. I didn't like it. But this isn't about one word or comment. I'm sure I've said plenty of dumb things, too."

"Not really, Janet. Not until today. You're way more fun than any woman I've ever met. And I know you've had fun talking to me, too."

"Yes, I have. You've got more personality than any *three* men I've ever known."

"So why—"

"I only need one man in my life, David. Right now, that's John."

"So . . . sometime *later*, if things with John don't work out . . . we might get back together?"

"I wouldn't count on it. If I were you."

Ouch. Janet's eyes never flinch. She should get a job firing people. She'd be damn good at that.

"You mean, even if you get divorced, you won't come looking for me?"

Long pause. Still no flinching. "I don't know, David. I don't think so."

"Was I too wild on Saturday? Too demanding? Too controlling? *What's wrong with me?*"

"There's nothing at all wrong with you, David. I'm sure most women would say I'm *crazy* to let you go. There are plenty of women who would jump at the chance to be with you."

"I don't want *plenty* of women. I want *you*."

Sara says she's only seen me cry three times. Once when she closed a car door on my thumb. Once when my dad died. And once when she won a state championship. Elaine knows I've cried a few more times than that. When Sara was too young to remember. But I don't cry much. Frankly I wish I could cry more. It would release emotions. Which I keep locked up inside.

But today, in Janet's car, *Janet's* eyes are the only dry ones. In the end she turns out to be a hard little minx. I wonder if I'm really Janet's first extra-marital conquest. Or her last.

Perhaps that's unfair. But Janet's so hard and business-like about it. Offering no credible explanation. Just making the tough decision. Cutting her losses. And moving on. Like a CEO closing down an unproductive plant. Or a banker foreclosing on a bad loan risk. Like someone who's done it before. And expects to do it again.

While I'm like a lawyer who knows he's losing with the jury. I know if I leave the podium—step out of Janet's bucket seat—the verdict will come in against me. So I just keep talking. Desperately recalling each sweet moment we've had together. Quoting each past positive comment Janet made about me. And trying a wide variety of persuasive tactics. Cajoling Janet to *join me* in remembering. Insisting she admit we're great together. Importuning her not to give all that up. Then switching to more aggressive techniques. Accusing her of chickening out on herself. Predicting she's making the biggest mistake of her mistake-ridden life. And warning that she'll hate herself the rest of her life if she doesn't find out how great we can be together.

Nothing works. Finally the time comes for Janet to go back to work. She grants the condemned man his last request. For one last kiss. I put my *whole soul* into that kiss. Trying to *will* her to come back to me. But Janet's already gone. Even before she says goodbye.

* * *

It's a short drive from Island Park to Forest Hills Cemetery. No time to wallow in the mire. As Jim Morrison would have said. Except he's dead.

Dale Hunter's dead, too. It's a short walk back to his grave. In the back corner.

And there she is. Sitting hunched on a gravestone across from Dale Hunter's grave. With her back to me. A woman with a head of short gray hair. And a ratty checkered scarf around her neck.

Silently I steal upon her. Like a thief in the night. Flip on a tape recorder in my pocket. When I'm almost at her elbow, I speak. Paraphrase the end of a

Wallace Stevens poem. "Peter Quince at the Clavier." Actually, I mangle the poem pretty badly. Twisting the words to suit this occasion. Which finds me together at last with Wallace Stevens's most notorious fan.

> Dale Hunter's story touched the bawdy strings
> Of one reporter but, escaping,
> Left only Death's ironic scraping.

> Now in its immortality it plays
> On the clear violin of your memory
> And makes a constant sacrament of praise.

She doesn't turn to look at me. So I'll never know if my parody elicited even a faint smile.

"Hello, Mr. Fisher." Still she doesn't turn to look at me.

"Hello, Rachel. Please call me David."

Two squirrels chase each other through the dead leaves around Dale Hunter's grave.

"You're not surprised to see me?" I ask.

"I've been expecting you to find me." Still doesn't turn her head. "What took you so long?"

Fair question. But I feel too *raw* from lunch with Janet to answer. For two weeks I felt Rachel Clark was surreal. While Janet was totally real. Now it feels the other way around.

"Tell me about the pennies," I murmur.

She stands up. Turns sideways, so her sad, tired eyes can see me. She looks just as blank and gray and nondescript as she did that first night I saw her outside Davis & Nyman.

"Where are the cops?" she asks. Her tone is curious. And a little suspicious.

"I didn't bring any. I just want to talk to you. Then you can run away again."

"I'm through running."

"Okay. So tell me about the pennies."

She looks back at Dale Hunter's tombstone. Stands a long time in silence. Beyond the grave the trees still flaunt many bright, colorful leaves, even in the weak autumn sun. But beneath each tree are strewn far more dead leaves—the drab harbingers of winter—that lie there random as the dirt they are fast on their way to becoming.

Somewhere close by, blue jays scuffle in the bushes. Farther off, beyond the cemetery fence, children's voices call to each other at play. And farther still, the early afternoon traffic out on Geddes Avenue is barely audible—a distant and almost indistinct hum.

"It was a simple plan." She sits back down on the gravestone. But faces me now. "Paul was sick of talk. He yearned for action. But we'd learned in Chicago to mistrust *mass* action."

"You mean because the Days of Rage was such a bust?" I sit down on a gravestone too. Facing her.

"Yes. We went there all excited. New Weathermen recruits."

"Whaddya mean, 'new?' You had a Weatherman tattoo in the *summer* of '69, right?"

"You talked to my parents?"

"You *know* I did. You were there last night, weren't you? Eating dinner?"

"How do you know that?" Emotion fills her voice. She reaches out and grasps my forearm. Then quickly withdraws her hand. But the touch is as electric as the first time Janet Fickel touched me. At Dominick's. It reminds me Rachel Clark is a real person. Flesh. And warm blood. Not just the abstract archetype of the Fugitive Radical she's been in my mind all these years.

"I don't know. Too many dishes in the sink. I could *feel* you there. Like when I saw you the first time. In that motorcycle helmet. I knew I was looking at Rachel Clark. Don't ask me *how*. I just *knew* it. What were you doing in Centreville yesterday, anyway?"

"I never got to say goodbye to my parents. I hadn't seen them in thirty-five years."

I blink. At the enormity of that idea.

"You won't tell anyone about my parents, will you?"

"Of course not. They're nice people. A little short. But nice people."

Rachel Clark smiles.

"So why'd you have a Weatherman tattoo in the summer if you didn't join 'til the fall?"

"Paul and Al and I decided to join in the summer. But Weather took their sweet time. They were elitists. Melanie hates it when I say that. But it's the truth. Finally they got around to accepting us in September. Just a couple of weeks before the Days of Rage."

"You and Paul and Al Brown joined—and *Melanie McGeetchy, too*, right?"

"I won't name names," Rachel Clark says. "Never have. Never will."

"Fair enough. So you joined. Went to Chicago. And were—disappointed?"

"Weather's leaders thought they were so smart. Days of Rage was supposed to be different from the '68 Democratic Convention. This was supposed to be *organized* violence. Like a military action. Only for peace. They recruited for *months* for Days of Rage. In high schools and colleges all across America. We were told there would be *twenty thousand* people there. So we could march, unarmed. Because there would be no point in shooting us. Even pigs couldn't kill *twenty thousand* people. And couldn't stop us from seizing the Army Induction Center."

"But in the end, only about five hundred kids actually came to Days of Rage?"

"Five hundred suburban white kids. We marched anyway. From Grant Park to the Army Center. Yelling the war yodel from the movie *The Battle of Algiers*. Mr. Fisher—David—you have no idea. We felt so strong. So free. On the way, we threw bricks at rich people's houses. And people eating in restaurants. We felt invincible. But when we got near the Army Center, the pigs were waiting. In lines. Standing. Then kneeling. And then—shooting."

"No one died there though, did they?"

"No. Some kids went down, shot but not killed. Most just freaked and ran. The few of us who kept marching got busted."

"Including you and Paul and Al?"

"Booked. Photographed. Fingerprinted. Charged with rioting. And criminal mischief. Given a court date in November. Then released on our own recognizance."

"And you all drove back to Ann Arbor together?"

"A long ride home. We were all so disillusioned with the Weather leaders. We'd waited so long to be accepted. And then they'd turned out to be no better than the SDS."

"So your cell developed the 'simple plan?'"

"It was *Paul's* plan. He wanted something symbolic. Like burning down the Law School. And he wanted to get Pembroke Watkins. The law professor."

I laugh. "I hated Watkins myself. For different reasons. Why did *Paul* hate him?"

"Watkins was a class criminal. The leader of the counter-revolution on campus, and chairman of a key faculty committee. He drafted fascist disciplinary rules to oppress campus dissidents. It may not sound like much in 2004. But in 1969, *everyone* was upset about Watkins's new rules. The Regents were going to vote on them at their November meeting, to reverse the tide of activism on campus. Paul felt it was really important not to take those rules lying down."

"Did you protest at the Regents' meeting?"

"That's what *SDS* did. But Paul said that type of protest was a joke. Just talk. He said the time for talk was over. It was time for action. And if you were committed to the Revolution, Paul said, then you had to be willing to make the hard choice. The choice to use violence."

"Did you agree with him?"

"I think so. I wanted to be a true revolutionary. I wanted to make a difference. I came to Ann Arbor from Centreville in 1968. A wild child. But all unfocused. In high school, I was the nervy girl. The one who dared to do what no one else would do. One time I stole a car. Mr. McDonald's Skylark. On Main Street. Broad daylight. Saturday afternoon. He'd parked it in front of the drug store. Left the keys in the ignition. My friends dared me to take it. So I did. I drove it around the block, and parked it back in the same spot before Mr. McDonald finished shopping. I laughed in my friends' faces. Like, I can do *any fucking thing* I want. But David, I remember my hands trembling. Five minutes later, in spite of all the laughing, they were *still* trembling."

"So you wondered if you were brave enough to be a revolutionary?"

"You never know what you're really capable of until you're tested under fire. I came to Ann Arbor feeling like I was way ahead of most kids on campus. In high school, I'd already had so much *experience*. Sex. Drugs. And many misdemeanors. Shoplifting. Joy-riding. Vandalism. But none of it had any *purpose*. Then I met Paul Zimmerman."

"Lots of people in the '60s *talked* about violence," I say. "But very few actually crossed the line and took violent action."

"That's right. And I was afraid I was gonna turn out to be just another big talker. Because I felt so strongly drawn to the *non*-violent philosophies. Gandhi. And Martin Luther King."

"What did Paul say about Gandhi?"

"Paul said Gandhi never had to deal with Hitler. Or corporate America." Rachel laughs. "Non-violent protest depends on shame. Gandhi *shamed* the Brits into withdrawing from India. Martin Luther King *shamed* regular Americans into outlawing segregation. But corporate America knows no shame. Paul said the peaceniks were delusional. To think you could shame the Establishment into leaving Vietnam. Because corporations are faceless. They know no shame."

"Did you agree with Paul?"

"I was nineteen. Paul was twenty-seven. We met at a party, smoked some weed, then made love upstairs a half hour after we met. I loved Paul so much. But it was not an equal partnership. Like Melanie told you. When I disagreed with Paul, I kept my opinions to myself."

"I'm not asking if you *debated* him. I'm just asking if, in your heart of hearts, you agreed with Paul Zimmerman that non-violent protest was inadequate to get the job done?"

"*Which* job? It all depended on how you saw your mission. Pembroke Watkins had no trouble stopping non-violent protest. Behind the scenes. He got two campus dissidents kicked out of school for nothing but seizing a microphone at a meeting. Rumor was, he was about to get two more kicked out, for nothing but giving fiery speeches on the Diag. Because Watkins was a law professor. Words were his game. He gave the Regents justifications. Excuses. For acting like fascists. When a huge group of peace-loving professors and students staged the first American 'teach-in' to protest the War, you know what Watkins did? He got his law student lackeys to recruit several *thousand* Michigan students. Jocks and preppies. They all signed a *thirty-foot* telegram to President Johnson. Expressing support for American involvement in Vietnam."

"So Paul said Watkins had to go?"

"That's *exactly* what Paul said! We were sitting at Dominick's. The bar across from the Law School. Revolution was always in the air there."

"I know Dominick's well," I say. Ruefully. For even while listening to Rachel Clark, I cannot stop my errant brain from recalling images of Janet at Dominick's. Cannot stop hearing, like a discordant voice-over, Janet telling me an hour ago that *the* love affair of my life is over.

"*When* did Paul first say Watkins had to go?"

"Three days before the action. A Friday night at Dominick's. We were sitting at a table in front. Looking right across the grass at Pembroke Watkins's office."

"How'd you know which office was Watkins's?"

"Because I went inside the Law School that afternoon to find it. Boy was *that* weird. Back in 1969, law students were almost all male. And totally out of touch with the Peace Movement. Here I come, bopping into their male preserve, their corporate bastion, in my miniskirt, with my long red hair and my Peace headband. I stood out like a sore thumb. You could read it on their drooling pig faces. '*Hot little hippie chick. Man, would I like to fuck that.*'"

"Not exactly an inconspicuous reconnaissance?"

Rachel laughs. "Not at all. But I ducked my head, and avoided their eyes, and dodged them all. Found the directory. Ran upstairs into the stacks. Found Watkins's office—but boy was that hard! The inside of the Law School is like a maze. You have no idea."

"Actually, I do."

"Oh, that's right. I heard you're a lawyer. Did you go to Michigan?"

"Yeah. I was back there just twelve days ago. Trying to find Raven LaGrow's office." I shift my butt to a more comfortable position on my gravestone. "So eventually you found Watkins's office. Which you could see from Dominick's. Then what happened?"

"Al Brown said killing Watkins would be easy. Watkins went home every night at 6:30. Like a clock. Brown said he'd hide in the bushes near the lot where Watkins parked. Pick a night when no one was around. And hit Watkins on the head with a tire iron. But Paul said no."

"Why? I thought you said Paul advocated violence."

"He did. But Paul said a street assault would send no message. He said Watkins had to die *in his office*. The locus of his oppressive actions. So then Brown offered to kill Watkins in his office. Which would have been easy. Because even though *the ground floor* was packed with all those law students leering at me when I went in, *the third floor* was deserted."

"But Paul said no to murdering Watkins in his office, too?"

"Paul said it was too risky. For Brown to go in and kill the man at his desk. With other professors so close. Someone might hear the noise of the attack. Or might just blunder along by accident. And Al would be trapped in a small space. Too much risk he might not get out. Plus Paul wanted us all to be equally responsible. Our whole cell. Paul and Al Brown and me."

"Equally responsible?"

"Like the Three Musketeers. All for one. And one for all. So if any one of us got caught, there'd be no point in trying to rat out the others. We'd all be in it up to our eyeballs."

"And so Paul proposed firebombing the office?"

"Yes. Then Paul and Al Brown worked out the details, like a military maneuver. The timing and all. I sat there with them. The hot little hippie chick, along for the ride. You know what I was thinking about, there at Dominick's, on Friday night, while they made the plan?"

I shrug.

"You should know. You guessed it this afternoon. Wallace Stevens. We'd been studying this poem. In English 232. '*The Idea of Order at Key West*.' The professor made us memorize it. And sitting there at Dominick's, when I should have been thinking about the plan and contributing my own ideas, instead all I could think about was that poem. They have these lights in the ceiling above the front porch at Dominick's. You probably never noticed them."

"Actually I have." Again I am awash in images of Janet Fickel. My hand running up her lovely thighs in those cinnamon stockings. While we drank cold beers from Dominick's mason jars. And drank hot love from each other's eyes.

"There are twenty-one lights there. Three rows. Like the 'glassy lights in the fishing boats at anchor there.' In *The Idea of Order at Key West*.' The lights that 'arrange, and deepen, and enchant the night.' The lights that create *order*. In my mind, those lights at Dominick's were creating order that night. Because it all seemed so *surreal*. That we were gonna kill a man in three days. But those lights were so *real*. So *orderly*. I'm probably not making any sense to you."

"Actually you make perfect sense to me. I've looked at those twenty-one lights myself. And I know that poem. And I think I can imagine that if I were just nineteen and the person I loved most in the world was telling me we were gonna murder someone for a good cause, and he was planning it out to the last detail, I would need an anchor, too. To hold on to my sanity."

"And *my* anchor was that poem. I can't remember how it ends anymore. But—"

I can never help myself. Showing off my poetry memorization skills. So I quote the end to her:

> Oh! Blessed rage for order, pale Ramon,
> The maker's rage to order words of the sea,
> Words of the fragrant portals, dimly-starred,
> And of ourselves, and of our origins,
> In ghostlier demarcations, keener sounds.

Rachel Clark looks at me as if she were looking at a ghost. Here in the graveyard.

"That's it! Back then I knew it, too. Word for word. That little back door at the Law School? With the ivy all around it? In my mind, it was the 'fragrant portal.' And that night, sitting at Dominick's, the fragrant portal was 'dimly-starred.' Before that night, poetry never meant much to me. But it just seemed to all come *together* that night. I felt Paul's 'rage for order.' How he wanted to knock the Law School down and create a *new* order. And I think I also knew, way down deep—where you know the things you don't even know you know—I think I knew the whole plan was going to end up teaching me a lot about my 'self.' And my 'origins.'"

"What exactly was Paul's plan? Blow by blow."

"We'd wait 'til daylight savings ended. That weekend. Pick the first school night. Monday, October 27. Thirty-five years ago today. I'd drive Paul's van over to Monroe Street. Arrive at 5:40. We knew there'd be no problem getting a parking place then. Even if there was, we could always park for a few minutes in front of the loading dock there. But we built in an extra five minutes. Just to be sure. To give us time to get the best parking place possible."

"'Best' meaning—?"

"Closest to the sidewalk beneath Watkins's office. The last space in the line. With a clear shot at two escape routes: west on Monroe Street, or south on Oakland Street."

"Did you get that spot?"

"Yeah. No problem."

"And then?"

"Then we waited five minutes. Because Paul had it all timed out. At 5:45 I was to exit the van. Return in five minutes. At 5:50 Paul and Al would exit. Return in two minutes."

"Like soldiers?"

"Yeah. Soldiers fighting for peace. But aping the military we hated so much. Because Paul saw the Law School as a military target. With a perimeter. Two hundred yards by two hundred yards. The southeast corner is the Achilles heel, because Monroe and Tappan are such quiet streets. And because the pedestrian traffic at the Law School is mostly in the big open quad on the north. And because the two little back doors on the southeast side there gave us options."

"*Two* doors? There's the one you called 'the fragrant portal.' And—?"

"—the metal door up on the loading dock. Brings you in on the second floor, instead of the first floor. It's a maze inside there. But Paul said it's always good to have two ways out."

"So what were you supposed to do at 5:45? When you exited the van."

"I thought you knew this part, David."

"The pennies?"

"The pennies. My job was to drive the van and park it. With Paul and Al in back. With two satchels full of pre-prepared Molotov cocktails. Firebombs. Mason jars filled with gasoline. With rags stuffed in the top for wicks. Then, after parking the van, I was supposed to go inside the Law School. And penny Pembroke Watkins in his office."

"Wasn't Paul afraid Watkins would just break the glass in his office door and get out?"

"Watkins's door was *solid wood*. One of the few solid wood doors up there. That was one of the things I'd observed on my reconnaissance of the Law School three days earlier."

"Why did Paul want *you* to be the one to penny Watkins in? If your appearance attracted so much attention among the males at the Law School? Why not Zimmerman or Brown?"

"I couldn't throw a Molotov cocktail up to a third floor window. Not with accuracy. Since we all had to be equally responsible, I got the job of jamming the pennies under Watkins's door."

"To trap him inside his office. So he would die in the firebombing."

"Like Paul said: Watkins had to die."

"And did you attract attention going into the Law School?"

"Not on Monday night. It was dusk. I wore jeans. And a denim jacket."

"And a motorcycle helmet with the Weather rainbow?"

"Yes."

"But didn't that *helmet* attract attention?"

"A little. But it also kept people from seeing my face clearly. And Paul said people would remember the rainbow and the lightning bolt. So we all wore helmets. Paul wanted people to know it was the Weather Underground who blew up the Law School and killed Watkins."

"So you walked up to the third floor?"

"And stood outside Pembroke Watkins's office. With two stacks of pennies in my hand. I'd spent the weekend practicing pennying someone into a room. In *my* freshman dorm, we didn't penny people into their rooms. But it wasn't hard to learn."

"No, it's pretty easy to do. Any college freshman can do it. In about three seconds."

"Well, I had five minutes. To exit the van. Walk the stairs up to the loading dock. Go in the metal door there. Walk down the hall. Walk up the stairs. Dodge anyone walking around up in the stacks. Get to his third-floor office. Penny him in. Get back out. Return to the van."

"How'd you know the metal door would be unlocked?"

"I'd propped it open with a stick an hour earlier. On my way home from class. I'd also propped the window next to it open. And, if all else failed, I knew I could always go in the 'fragrant portal.' Which they never locked except after midnight. But as it turned out, my stick was still in the loading dock door. So I walked right in."

"How'd you know Watkins would be in his office?"

"We could see him up there. His office lights were shining bright at dusk."

"What were you going to do if other people were around? Or if Watkins's door was open?"

"We'd just come back the next night. If it had been raining, we would have waited. If I'd run into anyone, we'd have waited. And if Watkins was away from his desk, or chatting in the hall, or if his door was open, or anything like that—

we'd just wait. And try again. Another night. But on Monday, October 27, 1969, the sky was clear. Watkins was in his office. His door was closed. And there was no one walking around the third floor stacks at 5:47—except me."

"And then?"

"And then, David, I faced my moment of truth. When I would find out if I was a true, committed revolutionary. Or not."

"And?"

"I stood there in that hallway for an eternity. Probably, in real time, it was only seconds. But to me it was an eternity of seconds. A sliver of light was glowing beneath Watkins's door. I heard a bump from inside. He was definitely in there. I fingered those pennies in my pockets. But I couldn't do it. So I set them down in the hall. And ran back out."

"Why'd you set them down in the hall?"

"I didn't want Paul to hear the pennies still in my pocket, when I lied to him about it."

"How did you think you would be able to get away with that lie?"

"Well, if Watkins died, Paul would never ask any questions. If Watkins lived, Paul would have no way of finding out *how* Watkins escaped. I would insist I put the pennies in place. Paul would assume either I did a bad job of it, or Watkins somehow got help to get out in time. Or maybe that the fire burned down the door and Watkins got out before the smoke overcame him."

"So, why couldn't you put the pennies under the door, Rachel?"

Long pause. "Because of my 'origins.'" She stares at me a moment. "In Centreville, we leave the big decisions in God's hands. Like who should live and who should die."

"You knew Paul and Al Brown were going to throw bombs at Watkins's office?"

"Yes. I totally supported firebombing the Law School. And I understood that people inside the Law School might die. I was okay with that. There was a war going on. People die in wars. People were dying in Vietnam. Each and every day. Some of the people who die in wars are innocents. And those people in the Law School did not seem like innocents to me. Not then. They were part of the System. The oppressors. Especially Pembroke Watkins."

"But you felt that the pennies were—?"

"Too deliberate. Too premeditated. Too sinister. I preferred to let God decide whether Pembroke Watkins should live or die."

I blink. I'm dizzy. We've been sitting a long time. In front of Dale Hunter's grave. And Rachel Clark's moral compass is disorienting me. Vaguely I realize that the surreptitious tape recording I'm making of this interview would not cast her in the prettiest light. My own sanitized fantasy of her innocence was much sweeter. The peace-loving hippie chick. Dragged along by her overbearing boyfriend. Who finds her conscience at the last minute. And refuses to go along with the plan. Not the fairly unrepentant hard-core radical I'm talking to now. Who admits in all candor she would not have minded if people died in that Law School "action." So long as no one did anything as "deliberate" and "sinister" as jamming pennies under Pembroke Watkins's door.

Vaguely I recognize that my disillusionment is following an all-too familiar pattern. I did the same thing with my Janet Fickel fantasy. Wanting to put a sweet spin on what was happening. To believe in fairy-tale love. Even in the midst of a tawdry, illicit affair. Between two married people who should know better. A sweet fantasy that was every bit as silly as believing that a hard-core sixties radical who's been on the run for thirty-five years is really sweet and innocent.

"Why didn't you wear *gloves* when you went into the Law School?"

"No need. I wasn't handling gas jars like Paul and Al."

"Weren't you afraid of leaving fingerprints?"

"No. Remember, I was supposed to put the pennies under a door that was about to be burnt to the ground." She runs a veiny hand over her weary forehead. "I admit, it wasn't very bright to leave those pennies in the hall with my fingerprints on 'em. But I wasn't thinking clearly then. Truth is, I was disgusted with myself. I'd just been weighed in the balances—and found wanting. Lacking true revolutionary commitment. Fingerprints were the last thing on my mind."

"What happened after you stacked the pennies in the hallway?"

"I scooted my butt out of there. Went out the loading dock door. My stick was on the ground. Without really thinking, I put the stick back in the door. No reason. Just a reflex. But it turned out to be very lucky for me. Then I got back in the van."

"Behind the wheel?"

"Yes. Paul asked if I had any problems. I said no. He asked if Watkins was in his office. I said yes. He asked if I thought Watkins heard me put the pennies in. I said no. Then Paul and Al went out the back. Walked up the sidewalk. Very nonchalant. Wearing their helmets."

"They were carrying firebombs? Was anyone out on the street? Or at Dominick's?"

"There were a few people out on the street. And several on the porch at Dominick's. But the firebombs were concealed in their satchels. It all looked so ordinary. The only sound was the loudspeaker across the street at Dominick's, announcing someone's pizza was ready. And the birds way up in the eaves of the Law School, gathered there for their evening feast. But those Law School eaves are eight floors up. So the birds were just a distant background noise, like grasshoppers at dusk in the summer. Really loud—but so steady, you hardly noticed them."

"And you just sat and watched, right? You didn't start the engine or anything?"

"I did not start the engine." She catches my eye for a second, then looks away. But I'm pretty sure from that look on her face—and from the way the question didn't surprise her at all—that she's already heard the question from Sheila/Melanie.

"And then trouble came?" I gesture at Dale Hunter's grave. In front of us.

"Yeah. Paul and Al threw the bricks. And then there was Dale Hunter. Out of nowhere. Cruising down *Monroe Street*. Of all the fucking times. Dale pulled his cruiser right up next to me. Scared the shit out of me. Though I doubt he even saw me. He swerved right in front of me. Went up on the curb. But there was a metal pylon in the sidewalk. So he couldn't drive any further up the sidewalk. Paul and Al were still forty feet away. Dale parked his cruiser right in front of me. Blocking me in. Pointing right at Paul and Al."

"Then what happened?"

"I'm not sure. Though I've replayed it in my head a thousand times. Probably I was in shock. Or just scared shitless. Not the true revolutionary I'd longed to be. Not at all."

"What do you remember?"

"Dale jerked open his door. Yelled 'freeze.' Al whirled and pulled his gun and fired. Dale went down in the street beside his car. I couldn't see him. I heard more shots. From Dale, I assume, on the ground, returning the fire. A *lot* of shots. Al went down. Paul, too. Then all was quiet again. *Too* quiet. For an eternity."

"You exited the van again?"

"I ran out screaming. Hurled myself on top of Paul. He was all twisted like a horse I saw fall once on our farm. I could see Paul's gun, still in his coat. I put my hand beneath Paul's limp neck. It had no strength in it. I put my lips against his lips. No whisper of life. He was already gone."

"And Brown?"

"I crawled over to Al. He was also dead. I looked back down the sidewalk at Dale. Though I didn't know his name then. Dale wasn't moving, either. I remember thinking he looked even younger than Paul and Al. We were *all* so young."

"With all the noise and the shooting, people must have started coming to the scene?"

"Yes. What I remember most was a stupid voice. From up in the Law School. Pembroke Watkins, peering down through his broken window. Into the twilight. '*Hey, you!*' he yelled. '*What the Sam Hill is going on down there?*' I'll always remember that. My father used that expression, too. If he'd ever had the chance to talk to me about the Law School action, I'm sure my father would have said, '*What the Sam Hill did you think you were doing there, girlie?*'"

I notice tears on Rachel Clark's cheeks. I'm not sure when they started.

"I ignored Watkins. An idiot voice, in the wind. But like you said, people were beginning to materialize. So I jumped up, ran a couple of steps back toward the van, and then stopped in my tracks—because the police cruiser had Paul's van pinned. It would have taken several back-and-forths to get the van out. And nearby I could hear sirens. More cops, closing in. So I abandoned the van. I didn't want a high-speed chase. Paul's old van was no race car—and I was no Parnelli Jones. Better to take my chances on foot. The way I used to do in Centreville, whenever the shit hit the fan."

"What made you run back into the Law School?"

"I don't know. I felt hemmed in. People were coming from every direction. Except *not* from the metal door on the loading dock. So I reached in Paul's coat pocket. I grabbed his gun. I scrambled through the ivy along the base of the Law School, and jumped onto the loading dock—just ahead of the cops."

"Greg Hunter shot at you?"

"Cops yelled for me to stop. I skittered across the loading dock and lunged for the door. The one I'd left propped open with the stick. A shot rang out. I felt a blow to the right side of my head. My neck jerked up, and to the left. But my Days of Rage helmet saved me. The bullet bounced off the helmet."

"Must have been strange for you when that helmet showed up two weeks ago in your boss's conference room."

"Stranger than you can imagine. To see that bullet crease. I remember that after I ran inside, I reached up and felt that bullet crease. In the helmet. And then I saw my hands were shaking. Much worse than when I stole Mr. McDonald's car. And my eyes were tearing. Much worse than today. And my heart was about to burst. But I had to survive. So I went for the steam tunnel."

"How'd you know where the steam tunnel was?"

"I'd stumbled across it by accident the Friday before, on my reconnaissance. When I got lost. I told you, it's a maze inside that Law School. Somehow that day I ended up two stories underground, trying to find my way out after locating Watkins's office. I came to a door that was really warm. Opened it. Hot air on the other side. I remembered kids in my freshman dorm saying the entire university is connected by steam tunnels. That you could walk from one end of campus to the other, underground. So on Monday, with the cops chasing me, it seemed like my best bet. I prayed like hell those kids were right. I raced down the hallway, found the stairs, went down two flights to the warm underground door I'd found before—and ran. As fast and as far as my feet would take me. Turned out those kids in my dorm were right. The steam tunnel led me all the way to the other end of campus. To open air. To freedom."

"How'd Lane Davis find out you escaped through that steam tunnel?"

"He musta heard about it from someone I told."

"How many people did you tell about the steam tunnel?"

"Two."

"Who?"

"I don't name names."

"But I already know about Melanie and Amy."

"Then you don't need me to name names you already know."

"Okay. So you ran out the steam tunnel. To a lifetime on the lam. As the fugitive radical."

"Yes. But I'm through running, David."

"So you're going to turn yourself in?"

"No. I don't want to go to prison. I just want you to keep quiet."

I cock my head. Janet Fickel style.

"You got your interview. Go ahead, print it. Win some journalist award. Just don't tell anyone where I'm hiding. Leave Naomi Williams out of it."

"You don't have to go to prison. You withdrew from the conspiracy. When you disobeyed Paul's orders. About the pennies. Any lawyer worth his salt could get you off. Though you might need some coaching on your testimony. So you wouldn't sound so unrepentant."

"What makes you think I'm 'unrepentant?'"

"The way you talked about how people might die in the bombing. How it was a war. And innocent people die. In wars."

"That's how I felt *back then*. I've had a lot of time to think about it since then. Haven't you ever changed your mind about anything in your life?"

"Yes," I admit.

"Me, too. One of the reasons I hitched a ride back to Ann Arbor in 1989 with Lane Davis was to try to make amends. To Boyce—the kid whose father I helped take away."

"Did Lane know you were Rachel Clark when he gave you that ride?"

"Absolutely not. He still doesn't know. Though I suppose he may have *guessed* by now."

"But Lane must have noticed you used a passport with a different name at the borders?"

"Yes, he did. I told him Sanne ter Spiegel was a Dutch citizen and *persona non grata* in the US because of political activism. So I needed to use Teresa's passport. Lane believed me."

"How'd you get a dead nun's passport?"

"Luck. When Teresa died, I was the one who packed up her things. I saw the passport. Teresa looked a lot like me. So I pocketed it. Then a few months later Lane came through, from Ann Arbor. When I told him I missed Ann Arbor, he offered me a ride."

"Did you have a love affair with Lane Davis?"

She hangs fire a long time. Then shrugs. "Yes."

"When did it end?"

"Almost as soon as it began. Lane told me he was marrying Camille. I said I didn't care, I just wanted him to make love to me. So he did. For a short time. But then real life called."

I nod ruefully. Since real life is calling *me*, too. No more Janet Fickel fantasies. I re-focus. I know there are other questions I should ask.

"Were you pregnant with Sarah on the date of the Law School action?"

"Yes. But I didn't know it."

"Where'd you go after you fled through the steam tunnel?"

"Took a friend's van. Lived in it. But in the winter, it was too damn cold. So I drove south. Got a job in rural Virginia. Found a midwife to deliver my baby. And a plastic surgeon."

"Plastic surgeons are crazy expensive. Where'd you get the money?"

She looks me square in the eye. "A friend helped me. But I told you—I won't name names you don't already know."

I meet her stare awhile. "I bet it was *your parents* who paid for your surgery."

She continues to meet my stare. Poker face. No response.

So I move on. "How'd your baby end up being named Sarah Pierce?"

"I couldn't keep her, living on the run like that. So Amy drove down to Virginia. Took Sarah back to the commune. At first Amy said she was adopting an abandoned child. But then the commune's landlord started making trouble. He wanted to be convinced Sarah was legally there. Amy tried calling my parents to get them to sign papers. That was a big mistake."

"Because Ray and Ruth refused?"

"Yeah. And then the FBI found out about it. So then they knew I had a child."

"How'd Amy get around the landlord?"

"She told him it was really her kid. Claimed she'd been too embarrassed to admit it at first. Amy got a fake birth certificate to satisfy the landlord that Sarah was really her child."

"But the FBI found out from Ray and Ruth about the child?"

"Right. So then the FBI started sitting on Amy and the commune. They figured sooner or later I'd come back. So I couldn't see Sarah the first six years of her life. And Amy had to stop getting arrested, because she didn't want to have Sarah taken away."

"When did you go to Europe, and why?"

"Travel was risky. But I figured once I got there, I'd feel safer. By 1972 I'd saved enough money. I found a boat to work on. And I went to Spain. Lived there 'til 1976."

"Until Amy moved to Amsterdam with Sarah?"

"Right. Then I decided to risk joining up with them."

"You lived with Amy and Sarah until the 1980 arrest?"

"Yes. Four wonderful years. With my little girl and my best friend. But when I got arrested, I had to go. Amy was very angry about my getting arrested. And Sarah—when she found out I was leaving without her—well, that was the worst day of my life."

"Even worse than October 27, 1969?"

"Even worse. You have children, David. Imagine telling them you're leaving them behind. Nothing in life is worse than that."

I wince at the thought. "Let's get back to Boyce Hunter—the reason you returned to Ann Arbor. What was in the envelopes you've been giving Boyce at the homeless shelter?"

"Money."

"Why?"

"Guilt."

"Did you know Boyce attacked your daughter on Monday?"

"It was a misunderstanding."

"Sarah gave you a letter from your parents. Then you gave a letter to Boyce from Rachel Clark. And Boyce thought it was the same letter?"

"Yes."

"Don't you see, though, they'll come ask you where you got that letter. If *I* could figure out that Naomi Williams is Rachel Clark, don't you think the cops'll figure it out, too?"

"Maybe. But I don't think they're as smart as you. So let's wait and see if they figure it out."

"Oh, great idea, Rachel. And while we wait, I'll probably be committing a felony."

"How?" She sounds suddenly anxious—and a little hurt by my sarcasm.

"By not telling them who Naomi Williams really is. That's probably aiding and abetting a fugitive. Same thing Lane Davis is charged with. No thank you."

"I thought you told Melanie you'd be my lawyer."

"I will. I consider myself retained. By you."

"Good. So we have attorney-client privilege."

"Right."

"So then you don't have to nark on me."

"Wrong. See, I was assuming you'd run. So I could honestly say 'I don't know where my client is.' But if you stay put, and I know Naomi Williams is really Rachel Clark, well—the law may require me to tell them what I know. Especially when they ask me in court tomorrow."

"But you said you think I'm innocent."

"I do."

"So if you think I'm innocent, how could you live with yourself? Turning an innocent woman over to a lynch mob?"

"If you know Lane Davis is innocent, how can you live with *your*self? Leaving an innocent man to twist in the wind with that same 'lynch mob?'"

"They have no case against Lane. He'll be fine."

"Well, they have *me* under subpoena. Who knows what they're going to ask me. But whatever they ask, my lawyer says I have to answer all their questions tomorrow. Because it's a felony case."

She sighs, and looks a little exasperated with me. "Well then, answer all their questions. Just don't *volunteer* anything you don't have to, okay?"

"I risked enough by not bringing the cops here, Rachel. So I'm not promising anything more. You still have time to run."

"No, I don't, David. I'm all through running. You have no idea. It's a relief to tell you all this. After so many years of silence. If they figure out who Naomi Williams is, then I'll be able to stop pretending I'm someone else. I'll even be able to talk to my daughter."

"I thought you talked to Sarah at the shelter. When she gave you the letter."

"I did. But I didn't tell Sarah who I was. She thinks I'm a *friend* of her mom's. She has no idea I'm actually her mom."

"Why didn't you tell her?"

"Because I'm still a fugitive. And Sarah's still a junkie. You don't give junkies information they can sell—not even if the junkie is your only child that you haven't talked to in twenty-five years."

# CHAPTER SEVENTEEN

# CINDERELLA'S SLIPPER

## Thursday 28 October 2004

The Washtenaw County courthouse opens at 8:00. At 8:05, the large "show" courtroom is packed. Even though the show won't start 'til 9:00.

Twelve reporters from mainstream dailies grab the best seats. The twelve seats in the jury box. Along the wall the photographers gather. Including my friends, the Germans. But not me this time. I'm under subpoena. Which means they'll want me "sequestered" outside the courtroom 'til I'm called. To prevent me from hearing the other witnesses' testimony.

The problem is, I don't want to be sequestered. I *want* to hear the other witnesses' testimony. So I'm hiding in the back corner of the spectators' pews. Crushed in the corner. Because a hundred and fifty people are crammed like sardines onto benches designed for a hundred.

I'm sitting next to Frank Winters. From the *Globe*. And behind Alex Timmons. From the *Sun*. Normally the worst seat in the house. Obstructed view. Because Frank and Alex together weigh almost as much as your car. These are big lads. Frank smells of egg salad. Even at eight in the morning. Alex smells of whiskey. At all hours. Both tend to fall asleep. And snore.

At the Yankee stripper trial, Frank got to snoring so soundly he actually fell off the spectators' bench. Into the aisle. Still snoring. During Raven LaGrow's testimony. Unbelievable.

So Frank is sitting nowhere near the aisle. If he falls asleep here, it'll be on my shoulder.

But you can see why this is a good spot for me today. At 9:00, when they call the case, Bruce Stuart will ask the judge to "sequester the witnesses." Most of the witnesses will already be out in the hall. They'll look briefly around the courtroom. For stragglers. But they'll miss me. Because I'm invisible back here. Wedged behind half-ton Alex and next to half-ton Frank.

Now we've got an hour to kill. Crammed in our seats. No one dares go to the bathroom. Because there's a crowd in the hall. Dying to get in. The Davis PX is big news in my hometown.

Frank farts. This was to be expected. But man! You cannot imagine. I take shallow breaths for five minutes. Breathing through my shirt sleeve. And still I nearly die.

To distract myself, I crane my neck around Frank and Alex to study the crowd. I divide the 150 members of the audience into four groups. First, Lane Davis supporters. I count sixty-seven. Second, prosecution supporters (off-duty cops, assistant prosecutors sucking up to their boss by watching his rare courtroom appearance, etc.). I get twenty-two. Third, the media. I see twenty-seven. Fourth, miscellaneous (lawyers, court clerks, drunks getting warm, etc.). Thirty-four of these. Including Ray and Ruth Clark, two rows up, on the aisle. They haven't noticed me.

No sign of Sarah Pierce. No sign of Boyce Hunter.

The Davis supporters are wired. They were first in line this morning. Grabbed the best seats in the spectator benches. Up front. All the usual suspects are here. Camille. Sheila. Raven. The Davis & Nyman associates, George and Emily. And Naomi, aka Rachel Clark—sitting just two rows in front of her parents, on the aisle.

Debbie the receptionist is missing. But Sue Webber is here. And—*oh, shit!*—Janet Fickel.

When I see Janet, my heart skips a beat. Acid dread fills my stomach. And waves of emotion engulf me. *Fear*. Because if Janet stays, she'll find out who I really work for. And where I really live. *Sadness*. Because I know I can't talk to her. *Hope*. Because I'll always think, to the day I die, that maybe I can find some way to win her back. *Lust*. Because Janet's by far the sexiest woman in the courtroom. And *pain*. Wrenching my heart. Because every time I glimpse that auburn hair, falling softly on Janet's soft shoulders, I feel the deep pain of knowing that never again will I run my fingers through that hair. Never again will I squeeze those soft shoulders. Never again will I have the chance to rise above my meager little life and feel as exhilaratingly alive as I felt in those all too fleeting days when Janet loved me.

Frank farts again. Or is it Alex? Who knows. In real novels, the climactic courtroom scene is elevated. Dramatic. Noble. In my life, however, the climactic courtroom scene is viewed from an obstructed-vision seat. Through a miasmal cloud of human methane gas. With occasional uplifting glimpses of an auburn-haired beauty who, unfortunately, has just dumped me.

At last the judge arrives. Patrick Flynn again. Even though he said he wouldn't be here. No surprise, though. I'm guessing the regular district judges didn't want any part of this case. Whereas Patrick always had the guts to step up to the hard fight. Even back in high school.

"Ladies and Gentlemen," Judge Flynn says. "This is a public courtroom, and you are all welcome. However, we do not usually hold proceedings in such crowded quarters. The participants in this important case need to be able to hear everything. So, if there is any outburst, you will *all* be removed. I'm warning you now. I want you to be here. But I also want the participants to have a fair proceeding. This is not a football game. If you try to influence the outcome by cheering or booing, or even just talking—you'll *all* be removed. That includes the media. Sue me if you like. But by the time you drive up to the Court of Appeals in Lansing, *this* hearing will be over."

Well. After *that*, you could hear a pin drop. Even Frank and Alex feel compelled to confine their farting to the "silent but deadly" variety. Thank you, Judge Flynn.

Bruce Stuart gets up. One Brow. Asks that witnesses be sequestered.

Prosecutor Barnett cranes his neck. Looks all around the courtroom. But Barnett doesn't see me behind Alex. So he tells the judge none of his witnesses are in the courtroom. And of course, none of my colleagues has any idea I'm under subpoena. So they don't nark on me.

What's the worst that can happen when I get called to the stand? Stuart may pitch a fit. About me hearing the other witnesses. But if so, I'll just claim I didn't hear that witnesses were being sequestered. And even if Judge Flynn gets mad and won't let me testify, well heck, that's exactly what I *want*. To avoid embarrassing myself in my hometown. And in front of Janet Fickel.

Prosecutor Barnett calls his first witness. "Greg Hunter."

Greg Hunter takes the witness stand. Wearing a rumpled corduroy sport coat. A ten dollar J.C. Penney tie. And a ratty-looking pair of slacks. I hate to admit it. But I'm beginning to like Hunter. No pretenses. What you see is what you get. One ugly bulldog. Who never lets go.

Hunter testifies that he's an Ann Arbor police detective. And the younger brother of Dale Hunter. Who died thirty-five years ago. At the Law School. "The Ann Arbor Police Department, and especially myself," Hunter testifies, "have been searching for Rachel Clark for thirty-five years."

"So Rachel Clark is a fugitive from justice?" Prosecutor Barnett asks.

"Yes."

"Wanted for her role in the conspiracy to firebomb the Law School thirty-five years ago?"

"Yes."

"There's been a warrant out for her arrest continuously for thirty-five years?"

"Yes."

"And Rachel Clark's status as a fugitive has been widely reported in the local media?"

"Yes."

"So no one in Ann Arbor could have any doubt that helping Rachel Clark remain at liberty would be a violation of the law?"

"Objection, Your Honor," Bruce Stuart says.

"Sustained."

Barnett looks annoyed. But moves on. Asks Hunter to summarize his recent investigation.

"The current investigation began," Hunter testifies, "four weeks ago. When we learned that a man originally from Ann Arbor named Jim Lacy had a motorcycle helmet."

Barnett holds up Rachel Clark's motorcycle helmet. "Is this the helmet?"

"Yes. The bullet crease on the back is from my gun. Thirty-five years ago."

The helmet is marked Exhibit One. Offered into evidence. No objection. Admitted.

"Who was Mr. Lacy?"

"A former associate of Rachel Clark's. From the 1960s."

"How'd you obtain the helmet?"

"I posed as a U of M history professor. A collector of sixties memorabilia. I bought it from Mr. Lacy out in California four weeks ago."

"What'd you do with the helmet after you bought it?"

"I gave it to an actress. Norma Lee. Asked her to present it to Lane Davis. As a gift."

*Now* we know why no one wanted to arrest Norma Lee! She's their stool pigeon!

"Why'd you do that?"

"To see what would happen."

"And what happened?"

"Ms. Lee gave the helmet to Mr. Davis on October 12. I have a tape recording of what transpired."

"How'd you get a tape recording of what transpired?"

"Ms. Lee wore a microphone. Concealed in her bra."

A mild titter sweeps the audience. At the thought of a lonely little microphone lost in the enormous expanse of Norma Lee's bra. But Judge Flynn glares. Quiet prevails. Immediately.

Hunter plays a tape recording of the conversation that I, too, have on tape. The one set forth at pages 17-20 of this novel. If you need to refresh your memory.

Hunter identifies the speakers. Which I could do now, too. The first "unknown woman" is Camille. The second "unknown woman" is Sheila. And the third is Naomi.

"No one there admitted to knowing how to contact Rachel Clark?"

"Correct."

"What condition was the helmet in when you had Norma Lee give it to Lane Davis on the evening of October 12, 2004?"

"Except for some cracking caused by the old bullet crease, the helmet had no marks. And no fingerprints. I wiped it clean myself. And told Norma Lee to handle it only with gloves."

"What time was that tape recording made?"

"Approximately 5:30 p.m., the evening of October 12, 2004."

"What happened next?"

"At 6:15 that same night, David Fisher came to Police Headquarters. Carrying Exhibit One."

Luckily Judge Flynn doesn't see the ripple of interest in the back of the courtroom. As my tabloid colleagues turn to stare at me. Even Frank and Alex. Uncharacteristically, still awake.

"Who is David Fisher?"

"A newspaper reporter. He is also a former high school basketball teammate of a colleague of mine." Hunter looks at Judge Flynn. "Cliff Bryant, Your Honor."

"Did you or Cliff *ask* Mr. Fisher to bring the motorcycle helmet to you?"

"Definitely not. We were not planning to retrieve the helmet at all. We wanted to see what Mr. Davis would do with it. Mr. Fisher was the proverbial wild card. The fly in the ointment."

"What did Fisher want?"

"He asked Cliff to have the helmet inspected for fingerprints."

"And?"

"We figured since Fisher'd brought it in to us, we might as well inspect it. Turned out we found two sets of fresh fingerprints on the helmet: Lane Davis's—and Rachel Clark's."

The crowd murmurs. Judge Flynn raps his gavel. *Instant* quiet. We all look at our toes. Fearing we're about to get the boot. But it turns out, Judge Flynn's bark is worse than his bite.

"How'd you know they were Rachel Clark's fingerprints?"

"She was fingerprinted in Chicago in 1969. And she left fingerprints at the Law School in 1969, too. They match the fresh fingerprints on the motorcycle helmet perfectly."

"Are you an expert in fingerprints?"

"No. But the computer made the match. And we sent the prints up to the State Police laboratory in Lansing. Last week they confirmed beyond any doubt that the fresh fingerprints on the helmet match the fingerprints of Rachel Clark from Chicago and from the Law School."

"How many women had the opportunity to touch Exhibit One between 5:30 p.m. and 6:15 p.m. on October 12, 2004?"

"At least thirty-three. Mr. Davis had a fundraiser that evening to capitalize on Ms. Lee's star power. Twenty-six females attended. Add the four females you heard on the recording Ms. Lee made, plus three other female employees at Davis's firm, and we have thirty-three suspects. Not counting any women who may have touched the helmet *after* Mr. Fisher obtained it."

Wow! I'm losing respect for Hunter. How did he fail to find out that the fundraiser ended at 4:30? If he knew *that*, he'd have one suspect now instead of thirty. What an idiot.

"How did you identify Lane Davis's fingerprints?"

"Mr. Davis was a prosecutor here in the 1970s. His prints are on file."

"Your Honor," Stuart says, "we'll stipulate that the prints on the helmet are my client's."

"Thank you," Judge Flynn says. "Anything else from this witness?"

"Yes, Your Honor." Next Barnett offers the 1989 immigration records from Galveston, Texas. No objection. Admitted into evidence. Barnett asks Hunter to summarize the records.

"In 1989," Hunter testifies, "Mr. Davis transported medical supplies to Nicaragua. In a moving van. These records show that on July 7, 1989, Mr. Davis crossed the border into Mexico alone. But on July 29, 1989, when Mr. Davis re-entered the United States, he was accompanied by an adult female. Using an American passport. In the name of Teresa Rodriguez Lomas."

"Who was Teresa Rodriguez Lomas?" Prosecutor Barnett asks.

"Teresa Rodriguez Lomas was a Catholic nun who worked at a mission in Nicaragua. But the woman traveling with Mr. Davis on July 29, 1989, could not have been Sister Teresa."

"Why not?"

"Sister Teresa Rodriguez Lomas was murdered on April 20, 1989."

"Did you ask Mr. Davis who it was he brought into the United States on July 29, 1989, using Sister Teresa's passport?"

"I did. Just this past weekend. But Mr. Davis said he would never 'name names.'"

"Do you have any other reason to believe the person traveling with Mr. Davis on July 29, 1989, was Rachel Clark?"

Stuart gets up. "Objection. To the word '*other*.' We haven't heard *any* reason yet to believe that Mr. Davis was traveling with Rachel Clark on the date in question, or on any other date. So it can't be a proper question to say 'do you have any *other* reason.' It's argumentative. It's misleading. It assumes facts not in evidence. And it's just plain wrong."

Judge Flynn smiles. But overrules the objection. Tells Hunter he can answer.

"A confidential informant supplied information indicating Rachel Clark was living in Nicaragua in 1989."

Stuart is on his feet again. "Objection! Hearsay! If they have a confidential informant, they need to call the informant. Not put on the informant's testimony through Detective Hunter."

"Objection sustained. The testimony about Rachel Clark's purported 1989 domicile is stricken."

Prosecutor Barnett looks like he'd expected this. He moves on.

"One last thing, Detective. How did Rachel Clark escape on October 27, 1969?"

"She ran into the Law School. Preventing police on the scene from shooting at her. Then she made her way out of the Law School. To other parts of campus. And disappeared."

"Has the Ann Arbor Police Department or the FBI ever made public the exact route Rachel Clark followed to escape out of the Law School building?"

"No."

"Was the escape route ever put into a report?"

"No. It was deliberately left out of all reports."

"Why?"

"The University of Michigan asked us to keep the escape route highly confidential. Which we did. We put it in no reports. We did not disclose it to witnesses. Except for Rachel Clark, a very small group of Ann Arbor Police Department personnel and FBI agents were the only people who knew, until today, that Rachel Clark escaped through a university steam tunnel."

"No further questions, Your Honor."

"Mr. Stuart?"

Bruce Stuart drapes himself over the podium. I see his face in three-quarters profile. Even from my obstructed-vision seat, I see that single bushy eyebrow sticking out half an inch from his forehead. Jumping up and down dramatically with each question and answer. That crazed eyebrow is so fascinating, I can barely concentrate on the substance of his questions.

"Good morning, Detective Hunter. You and I have never met, have we?"

"No sir."

"You are the brother of Dale Hunter?"

"Yes sir."

"The policeman who was shot in 1969 during the attack on the Law School?"

"Yes sir."

"You have a strong personal interest in seeing Rachel Clark brought to justice?"

"Yes sir."

"You are yourself a thirty-seven-year veteran of the Ann Arbor Police Department?"

"Yes sir."

"And for thirty-five years, you have been unable to capture Rachel Clark?"

"Not just me. Nobody has been able to find her."

"And you feel bad about that?"

"Yes sir."

"You would do pretty much anything in your power to capture Rachel Clark?"

"Anything *lawful*," Hunter says.

"And if push came to shove, and the only way to catch Rachel Clark was to do something *un*lawful, well, you'd consider that too, wouldn't you?"

Hunter hangs fire. But the look on his face leaves no doubt he would indeed do *anything* to catch Rachel Clark. "I'm sworn to uphold the law, Mr. Stuart. I'd never break my oath."

"But if someone dangled in front of you the possibility of finding Rachel Clark, you would certainly push as hard as you possibly could to catch her?"

"Yes sir. Within the limits of the law. Sir."

"You said Rachel Clark's steam tunnel escape was known only to"—Stuart checks his notes—"'a very small group of Ann Arbor Police Department personnel and FBI agents,' right?"

"And to Rachel Clark."

"But no one else?"

"No one else."

"Just Rachel Clark, and a 'small group of AAPD and FBI personnel?'"

"Right."

"How big was this 'small group of AAPD and FBI personnel?'"

"About eight or ten guys."

"Who?"

"Oh, I can't say, really."

"What? You're unwilling to 'name names?'"

The audience chuckles. Until Judge Flynn pounds his gavel. And glares at us.

"If you want me to, I'm willing to name 'em," Hunter says. "It's just been so long. I can't be sure I'll remember all the names."

"Try," Stuart suggests.

"Gene Hensley. Al Smith. Mark Boim. David Taddio. Doug Hirsch. Jack Hornung. Alex Birchfield. Me. That's all I remember."

"How about the police chief back then?"

"Yeah, he knew."

"How about the assistant chief and the first lieutenant?"

"Yeah, they knew."

"How about the prosecutor at the time—Bill Delhey?"

"Yeah, he knew, too."

"Mr. Delhey wasn't in the Ann Arbor Police Department or the FBI, was he?"

"No."

"But Mr. Delhey knew?"

"Yeah."

"How many people did Mr. Delhey tell about the steam tunnel escape?"

"Objection," the prosecutor says. "Detective Hunter can't possibly know that."

"Exactly," Stuart says. "You really have no idea how many people got a hold of this big secret about the steam tunnel escape, do you?"

"It was a very small group." Hunter says, stubbornly sticking by his guns.

"What about at the university? How many people *there* were privy to your investigation?"

"No one at the university was involved in our investigation," Hunter says.

"Well, who asked you to keep the steam tunnel escape quiet?" Stuart presses.

"The Law School dean asked us to keep it quiet."

"So *the dean* knew Rachel Clark escaped through a steam tunnel?"

"Yes."

"And you don't know how many people the dean told, do you?"

"Well, he wanted it kept quiet, so I doubt he told anyone."

"But you don't *know* how many people the dean told, do you?"

"No."

"Did you know Lane Davis was a Michigan Law Student in the early 1970s?"

"Yes."

"Did you know Mr. Davis also worked in Mr. Delhey's office in the 1970s?"

"Yes."

"Now, Detective. Mr. Davis didn't hide that motorcycle helmet from you, did he?"

"No sir."

"When you went to see him last Friday, it was sitting in plain view on his credenza?"

"Yes sir."

"And when you asked him what it was, he told you without any hesitation that it was Rachel Clark's Days of Rage motorcycle helmet?"

"Yes sir."

"Detective Hunter, let's go back to 1969. You found two radicals lying dead next to eight Molotov cocktails, directly under the office windows of Professor Pembroke Watkins?"

"That's right."

"You presume they were about to throw the Molotov cocktails into Watkins's office, when your brother stopped them?"

"They'd already broken Watkins's windows with bricks. His office was clearly their target."

"And investigators also found *two stacks of pennies* on the third floor of the Law School, very close to Watkins's office door, yes?"

Hunter looks sick. "Yes."

"Two stacks of pennies. Sixteen pennies per stack. *Neatly* stacked. With *Rachel Clark's fingerprints* on each stack, yes?"

"Yes."

"A janitor said those pennies were *not there* in the early afternoon of October 27, 1969?"

"Correct."

"How far was it from the floor to the bottom of Pembroke Watkins's office door?"

Hunter hangs fire. "I never measured it. But I've been told it's three-quarters of an inch."

"What's the height of sixteen pennies?"

"I've never measured that, either. But I've been told it's three-quarters of an inch."

The prosecutor's up. "Your Honor. I can't see the relevance of this line of questioning."

"But *you* can see the relevance, can't you, Detective Hunter?" Stuart smoothly ignores the objection. "What's the *only* plausible explanation you've ever heard for those pennies being on the third floor of the Law School by Pembroke Watkins's office on October 27, 1969?"

Hunter sets his jaw, like the stubborn bulldog he is. "I do not know why they were there. No one knows why they were there. Except Rachel Clark."

"Oh really?" Stuart is having fun. With material Sheila must have given him. But will *I* get credit for this? Not likely. "You know Rachel Clark went into the Law School just five minutes before her co-conspirators, Zimmerman and Brown, threw those bricks at Watkins's windows?"

"Yes. But no one saw what she did in there."

"You know she went in empty-handed, and came out empty-handed?"

"That's what all the witnesses said."

"And the only evidence of what in the heck Rachel Clark was up to inside the Law School that day is those two stacks of pennies just down the hall from Watkins's office?"

"Well—her fingerprints were in the steam tunnel, too."

"But those she left *after* the attack, right? As she was escaping?"

Hunter grudgingly nods. "Most likely, yes."

"And when she was escaping, your colleagues were very close on her heels?"

"Correct."

"So she didn't have time to run up to the third floor, stack those pennies—*neatly*—and then run back down to the basement to escape undetected through the steam tunnel, did she?"

Hunter looks down at the floor. "No."

"And would you agree, that *if* she'd wanted to, Rachel Clark could have wedged those two stacks of pennies under Pembroke Watkins's office door? Because they *fit exactly*!"

The bulldog sets his jaw again. "I don't really know that."

Stuart is ready for this. He's got pennies. He makes two stacks. On the witness stand.

"How many pennies we got there in each stack, Detective?"

Hunter looks up and sideways at Judge Flynn, pantomiming a request for relief from the question. But Judge Flynn shakes his head, and motions for Hunter to count the pennies.

So Hunter counts them. "Sixteen in each stack," Hunter reports.

Stuart hands Hunter a ruler. "How high is each stack?"

Hunter measures. "Three-fourths of an inch."

"Now, Detective Hunter. Assume for a moment that I can prove the height from the floor to the bottom of Professor Watkins's door was three-quarters of an inch—and you know I *can* prove that, if you make me—what would have happened if Rachel Clark had wedged two three-quarter-inch stacks of pennies like this under the three-quarter-inch gap beneath Watkins's door?"

"He would not have been able to open the door."

"He'd have been *trapped in there*, while Rachel Clark's friends poured fire-bombs in through the windows, until he *burned to death*, isn't that right, Detective?"

The prosecutor's on his feet again. "Objection. Speculation."

"Overruled." Judge Flynn turns to Hunter. "Answer the question."

"In the college dormitories, pennies under the door generally work to trap the occupant in his room. I imagine the same would happen with a law professor's office."

"But in truth, Rachel Clark did *not* wedge those pennies under Watkins's door, did she?"

"No."

"Rachel Clark fired no bullets at your brother, did she?"

"No. Her boyfriend's buddy did."

"Which is why the warrant for her arrest is only based on *felony* murder charges, right?"

"Yes."

"The only basis for charging Rachel Clark with a criminal act is the conspiracy she was part of, which left your brother dead?"

"Yes."

"But if she *withdrew* from the conspiracy before your brother was shot, there'd be no basis to charge her, would there? And if there was no basis to charge *her*, then there'd be no basis to charge my client with aiding and abetting her, right?"

"Objection!" Prosecutor Barnett is livid. "Calls for a legal conclusion."

"Sustained," Judge Flynn says, very quietly. He looks at Stuart. And nods. Judge Flynn is clearly impressed. "I got it. I see where you're going with this." He turns to Hunter. "Does anyone *know* why Rachel Clark set those pennies down in that hall that day?"

"Only Rachel Clark knows that, Your Honor."

"Anything further from this witness, Mr. Stuart?"

"Nothing further, Your Honor."

Prosecutor Barnett stands up. "Call David Fisher to the stand."

The prosecutor's assistant starts out toward the hall to look for me. But all my mates in the back rows have turned to gape at me. So I stand up and identify myself.

Stuart pitches a fit. Moves the judge to bar me from testifying. A motion I *pray* the judge will grant. No such luck. Judge Flynn scolds the prosecutor a little. Tells him to be sure there aren't any *other* prosecution witnesses lurking in the back rows. Asks me if I didn't hear the order sequestering witnesses. I play dumb. Finally get myself situated in the box.

I remind myself to avoid eye contact with Lane Davis. And *all* his supporters.

"Your address, Mr. Fisher?"

I can't help myself. I look straight into Janet Fickel's big brown eyes.

"1621 Hill Street, Ann Arbor, Michigan. I also maintain a residence in Florida. 806 Pensacola Way, Lantana, Florida."

"Your occupation?"

"I'm an editor at *The National Spy*."

"What is *The National Spy*?"

"A weekly news magazine."

My mates in the back row titter quietly. The judge pretends he didn't hear them.

"Is *The National Spy* commonly referred to as a tabloid?"

"It is."

"Do you know Lane Davis?"

"I do."

"How?"

"I hired him as my attorney. Two weeks ago."

"Did you meet with Mr. Davis on October 13, 2004?"

"I did."

"What, if anything, did Mr. Davis tell you about Rachel Clark that day?"

"Lane showed me Rachel Clark's motorcycle helmet. I asked him if he knew where Rachel Clark is now. Lane said absolutely not."

"What *else* did Mr. Davis tell you about Rachel Clark, Mr. Fisher?"

"Lane said as far as he knows, *no one* knows where Rachel Clark is now. Ever since she escaped through that Law School steam tunnel, he said everything about her is just rumor."

"Had you said anything about the steam tunnel before Mr. Davis mentioned it?"

"No sir. That was the first I ever heard that she escaped through a steam tunnel."

"You're quite certain Mr. Davis specified a steam tunnel?"

"Absolutely. I never heard of a steam tunnel escape before. So it stuck in my mind."

"Now Mr. Fisher, I'm going to show you what's been marked as Prosecution Exhibit One. The motorcycle helmet with Rachel Clark's fingerprints on it. You recognize this?"

"I do."

"You are the person who gave it to Detective Hunter?"

"I am."

"Last night you signed an immunity agreement with my office, did you not?"

"I did."

"You were represented by your counsel, Mr. Jonathan Lowe, who is present here today?"

I look up. There he is. The old rat-lover. "Yes, he's right there. Behind Detective Hunter."

"And we agreed in writing that my office will not prosecute you for any crimes connected to the method by which you obtained this helmet?"

"That's correct."

The prosecutor hands a copy of the immunity agreement to Bruce Stuart. While Stuart reads it, I look blankly at the podium. To avoid the glares of the Davis supporters.

"Where did you find this helmet?" the prosecutor asks.

"In the conference room at Davis & Nyman."

"What did you do with the helmet?"

"I knew it was important. So I took it to Cliff Bryant. For testing. Then I put it back where I got it. The next day Cliff and Detective Hunter told me they found fresh fingerprints on it. Lane Davis's. And Rachel Clark's."

"And did you tell Detective Hunter *where* you had found the helmet?"

"No."

"Why not?"

"I believed I had a right, as a journalist, not to give up that information. But this week my company's lawyer, Jonathan Lowe, advised me otherwise. So then

I told you yesterday. Where I'd found the helmet. Right after we signed the immunity agreement."

"No further questions."

Stuart is up at the podium before the prosecutor sits down. "Why did you need an *immunity agreement*, Mr. Fisher, before you'd say where you found the helmet?"

"Because I was a non-consensual visitor at Davis & Nyman when I found the helmet."

"A '*non-consensual visitor*?' What the heck is *that*? Are you a *lawyer*, Mr. Fisher?"

"I am."

"I figured. No one else talks like that. In plain English, you were a trespasser?"

"I was."

"You were in Davis & Nyman's offices when—at night?"

"Early evening, yes."

"Anyone else there?"

"No."

"And how did you *enter* the offices?"

"I picked the backdoor lock."

"You're a lawyer and a *second-story man*, too?"

"The backdoor at Davis & Nyman is on the ground floor. Sir."

This guy Stuart is very good. Doesn't even crack a smile at my little joke.

"Did you take anything else from Davis & Nyman? Besides the helmet?"

"No."

"But your legal training allows you to understand that you committed burglary?"

"I don't actually remember the strict technical definition of burglary, Mr. Stuart. I admit I broke and entered illegally. Without the owners' consent. I admit I asported the motorcycle helmet for forty minutes. Without the owners' consent. I don't know if that's burglary. But it's definitely illegal."

Stuart's eyebrow goes crazy at my use of the archaic legal term 'asported.' But Stuart himself stays on track. "Yet you want this court to take your word— the word of a lawyer who admits to an illegal B&E, and a theft—that you're telling the truth about where you found this helmet? And about what Lane Davis supposedly told you about the steam tunnel escape?"

"I don't actually care if the court believes me or not, Mr. Stuart. I was compelled to come here by subpoena. I asked my lawyer to fight it. He said there's no basis to fight the subpoena. So I'm here. All I can do is tell the truth. Embarrassing though it is."

Stuart throws up his hands. Theatrically. "Oh, *the truth*. You didn't tell the truth when you first met Mr. Davis, did you?"

"No."

"You didn't tell Mr. Davis that you'd already broken into his offices to take the helmet?"

"No, I didn't tell him that."

"And you didn't tell Mr. Davis that you worked for a tabloid, did you?"

"No."

"That's the same meeting where you claim Mr. Davis told you about the steam tunnel?"

"Yes."

"Were you the author of the story that ran in this week's *National Spy* about Mr. Davis?"

"Yes."

"Even though the author is listed as 'Sandy Hill,' it was really written by David Fisher?"

"Yes. 'Sandy Hill' is my pen name."

"And did you take the photographs for that story?"

"Yes."

"Did you break into any *other* places besides Davis & Nyman to get those photographs?"

"No," I lie. Under oath. In court. *Not* a good idea. But what choice do I have? I don't have any immunity for breaking into Raven's house. So all I can do is lie. Or take the Fifth.

I hold my breath. Praying Stuart won't ask me how exactly I *did* get the photo of Lane Davis canoodling with Raven. Luckily, Stuart lets it drop. With another theatrical gesture.

"No further questions for this witness, Your Honor."

The tone Stuart uses for "this witness" is the same tone he would use for "this piece of skunk scrotum." But I deserve it. Hell, I'm lucky to get out of here. With relatively light injuries.

Prosecutor Barnett calls his next witness. Sarah Pierce. Barnett's assistant walks in front of me to get Sarah from out in the hall. Where she's been sequestered.

On my way back to the spectators' seats, I avoid eye contact with the Davis supporters.

Except Naomi Williams. Who's sitting right on the aisle.

Naomi looks deeply distraught. Even though I didn't come close to exposing her. I wonder if Naomi sees the writing on the wall—for Davis.

Sarah Pierce shuffles into the courtroom. Staring at the floor. Biting her lip. Sarah looks worse than her mom. She passes me in the aisle. But doesn't register I'm her hospital visitor.

Even in the witness box, Sarah stares at the floor. She makes eye contact with no one.

Sarah gives her address as the DeLonis Center. The homeless shelter.

"Ms. Pierce," Judge Flynn says, "you'll have to speak louder."

Sarah nods. But doesn't look at him.

"Ms. Pierce," Barnett says, "please tell Judge Flynn who your mother was?"

"I was raised by Amy Pierce. But my birth mother was Rachel Clark."

The crowd murmurs. Judge Flynn pounds his gavel. "Last warning, folks. The participants will not be able to hear this soft-spoken witness if you make noise. So if there's another sound of any kind, the bailiff will clear the courtroom. I mean it. Please control yourselves."

"When was the last time you saw your mother?" Barnett asks. "Your *birth* mother?"

"When I was ten."

"Have you heard from her since then?"

"Yes."

"I'm going to show you what we've marked as Exhibit Three." Prosecutor Barnett hands a letter to Sarah Pierce. And hands a copy to Bruce Stuart. "Can you identify this document?"

"It's a letter my mother sent me."

"What's the date on the letter?"

"July 21, 1989."

"Where were you when you received this letter?"

"Paris, France. My mother mailed it to me in Amsterdam. But I wasn't living there anymore. Amy Pierce forwarded the letter on to some friends of mine in Paris. That's how I got it."

"Do you know where your mother was when she sent this letter on July 21, 1989?"

"Nicaragua."

"How do you know that?"

"The envelope had a Nicaragua postmark on it. And in the letter she says she's there."

"How did you know this letter was really from your mother?"

"She signed it. And I recognized the handwriting. And she—said some things in the letter. Personal things. That—well, only my mother knew those things."

"Could you read the second paragraph out loud to the court, please?"

Sarah blinks. Peers at the letter. "Okay. '*I'm leaving Nicaragua tomorrow. I'm hitching a ride with a lawyer from Ann Arbor named Lane Davis. He's going to take me back there. You may think I'm crazy to risk it. But it's been twenty years now. And I don't look anything like I did in those days. I'm going to start a new life there. With a new name. Darling Sarah, I know you are angry with me. Because I could not bring you to Nicaragua the past nine years. But—.*'"

"That's enough, Ms. Pierce. Thank you." Barnett looks at Judge Flynn. "The People offer Exhibit Three into evidence, under the state-of-mind exception to the Hearsay Rule—and the co-conspirator admission exception."

Stuart takes a minute to read the whole letter. While he reads, I chastise myself for failing to find out about this letter during my two-hour interview of Sarah Pierce at Dominick's. Score one for Greg Hunter. The old bulldog proved to be a better interviewer than me.

Stuart engages in a whispered conference with Lane Davis. Then stands. "No objection to Exhibit Three. And no questions for this witness, Your Honor."

Barnett stands. "The People rest, Your Honor."

Sarah Pierce shuffles out of the witness box. Passes the bar between participants and spectators. Naomi Williams makes a place for her on the aisle. Sarah sits down beside Naomi.

"Do you have any witnesses you wish to call, Mr. Stuart?" Judge Flynn asks.

"Your Honor, I don't believe that's necessary. The prosecution has failed to establish probable cause that my client committed the crime charged. We ask you to dismiss the charges. The pennies on the third floor of the Law School demonstrate that Rachel Clark withdrew from the conspiracy before Dale Hunter was shot. Which means she was not guilty of felony murder. Therefore *my client* also cannot be guilty. You can't 'aid and abet' an innocent person."

"Mr. Stuart," Judge Flynn says. "I understand your argument. But I must disagree. I understand the inference you want me to make. From the discovery of those pennies on the third floor. And I can see that those pennies may pose a very big problem for the prosecution at trial. But right now, absent testimony from Rachel Clark herself, no one knows for sure why she put those pennies up on the third floor. This is only a preliminary examination. Where the standard for binding over the defendant for trial is merely probable cause. Therefore, I must find—"

"Excuse me, Your Honor," Stuart says. "I sincerely apologize for interrupting the court. I remember in law school they taught us that's generally a very bad thing to do. But in light of your comments, and before you make any actual findings, I *would* like to call a witness. *Before* you rule."

"Of course," Judge Flynn says. "Who's your witness? Mr. Davis?"

"While my client is indeed very eager to testify, Your Honor, first I call Naomi Williams."

Naomi walks forward. Pats Lane Davis on the shoulder as she passes.

Davis looks stunned. And fearful.

Naomi raises her right hand. Swears and affirms to tell the truth, the whole truth, and nothing but the truth.

Prosecutor Barnett rises. "Your Honor, for the record, this witness was not sequestered."

"Are you objecting?" Judge Flynn asks.

"No. Just wanted to point this out." Barnett sits back down.

This brief colloquy about sequestration occupies everyone's attention for a few seconds. And affords Naomi Williams a chance to do something quite unusual on her way to the witness chair. As she walks by the clerk's desk, without breaking stride, Naomi scoops Exhibit One up off the clerk's desk. The motorcycle helmet. And in one smooth motion she puts it on her head.

A perfect fit. Like Cinderella's slipper.

Witnesses do not normally handle exhibits. But it happens so quickly, no one stops her.

"Your name?" Stuart asks Naomi as she sits down, wearing the helmet.

"Rachel Clark."

Lane Davis gasps. As do all the spectators. And the press. Cameras click madly.

And a groan comes out of me. As I realize my story is no longer an exclusive.

Judge Flynn hits his gavel at least a dozen times, trying to restore order. Things are noisy and chaotic enough I decide to risk standing up. So I can get a clear view of Sarah Pierce's reaction. Sarah looks completely stunned. And she's blinking back tears, I think.

When the noise finally begins to subside under the constant hammering of Judge Flynn's gavel, I sit back down. Judge Flynn turns to the witness. "Do you wish to have me appoint legal counsel for you, ma'am?"

"No, thank you," Rachel Clark says. "I've already consulted with my conscience. I understand what I'm doing."

Judge Flynn nods. But still looks somewhat at a loss. Unsure what to do.

"Were you part of a conspiracy to bomb the Michigan Law School in 1969?" Stuart asks.

"In the beginning, I was, yes."

"And what was your role in the beginning of the conspiracy?"

"I drove Paul Zimmerman and Al Brown to the Law School. Then I was supposed to enter the Law School. Wedge two piles of pennies under Pembroke Watkins's door. And come back outside. So that when Paul and Al threw fire-bombs into Watkins's office, Watkins would die. And then I was supposed to drive Paul and Al away."

"And did you, in fact, follow your orders?"

"No. I did not wedge the pennies under the door. And I did not drive them away."

"Why didn't you carry out your assignments?"

"I decided it was wrong. So I stacked the pennies in the hall. Like Detective Hunter said. Then I went back out. And lied to Paul. I said I put the pennies under the door. When really I did not."

"After you disobeyed Paul, did you do anything else to help the conspiracy?"

"No."

"After the gunfire that day in 1969, did you escape through a steam tunnel?"

"Yes."

"Did Lane Davis play any role in assisting your escape?"

"No."

"Where'd you go?"

"All over. Mostly the eastern United States."

"Did Lane Davis assist you in any way during that time?"

"No. I did not even know Mr. Davis then."

"Did you eventually leave the United States?"

"Yes. I went to Europe."

"Did Lane Davis play any role in assisting your exit from the United States?"

"No."

"When did you first meet Mr. Davis?"

"In 1989. In Nicaragua."

"What name were you using at that time?"

"Sanne ter Spiegel."

"Did you tell Mr. Davis your real name was Rachel Clark?"

"No."

"Did Mr. Davis in any way indicate he *knew* you were a fugitive from justice?"

"No. He didn't have any idea."

"Did Mr. Davis bring you back to Ann Arbor?"

"Yes."

"And did you go to work for Mr. Davis at his law firm?"

"Yes."

"What name did you use there?"

"Naomi Williams."

"Why didn't you just stick with Sanne ter Spiegel?"

"I'd been using that name nine years. That's a dangerously long time for a fugitive to use one name. Many of my friends in America knew that name. In Nicaragua, it was safe enough. But I felt if I was going to come back to America, then I needed a fresh start. A new name. To reduce the chances that Detective Hunter would come knocking at my door one day."

"Did you explain to Mr. Davis the real reason why you wanted to be called Naomi Williams instead of Sanne ter Spiegel?"

"No. I told Lane that if I was going to live in the US, I'd have to change my name. Because Sanne ter Spiegel was a Dutch citizen who'd been involved in college protests. And I was worried the US might not grant an extended visa to Sanne ter Spiegel. So I told Mr. Davis I wanted to call myself Naomi Williams. And just act as if I were already an American citizen."

"Did Mr. Davis agree to go along with that?"

"Yes. But he didn't do *anything* to help me with it. Except call me Naomi."

"Did Mr. Davis indicate he had any idea the true reason for the name change?"

"No."

"Up until your testimony a few moments ago, did Lane Davis ever have any idea you were really Rachel Clark, the Fugitive Radical?"

The prosecutor tries to get up to object, but before he can, the witness has answered.

"Absolutely not. I only told *you* last night. And I made you promise not to tell Lane."

Lane Davis still looks stunned. And fearful. Even as Bruce Stuart turns to the judge.

"Your Honor, we ask that the charges against Mr. Davis be dismissed."

The judge looks at the prosecutor. Who rolls his eyes. But then nods his agreement.

A big cheer goes up from the Davis supporters. But then almost immediately dies back down. As the sheriff's deputies approach the lonely figure in the witness box. With handcuffs.

We spectators stand. One and all. And watch in silence. As the deputies wait for Rachel Clark to remove the bullet-creased motorcycle helmet from her head.

Except for two people. Who walk up to the bar. Ray and Ruth Clark.

"Your Honor," Ruth Clark says. "I'm Rachel's mother. May I—?"

Judge Flynn nods. Ruth and Ray *run* forward to the witness box. They're surprisingly speedy. For old people. Rachel steps out of the witness box. And hugs them.

Cameras click madly. And even the hard-ass tabloid guys like me are wiping away tears.

After a minute, the deputies intercede. Lock the handcuffs on Rachel Clark.

"Hasn't she suffered enough?" Ruth Clark asks the judge.

"Even Richard Nixon got a pardon!" Ray Clark adds.

Judge Flynn opens his palms. "It's not up to me right now."

Rachel looks past her mom and dad. Picks out a lonely figure standing in the spectators' aisle. Smiles. Raises her handcuffed hands. And flashes Sarah Pierce the peace sign.

Then she goes quietly with the deputies. Back behind the judge's bench. Into lock-up.

As the door closes behind her, the Davis supporters chant. "Let her go! Let her go! Let her go!"

The prosecutor, escorted by Hunter and Bryant, walks through the gauntlet of chanting Davis supporters. The crowd follows, still chanting. Outside, the crowd continues to follow the prosecutor and his police escort a few yards down the sidewalk, before letting them go. The crowd turns back to the courthouse plaza. Where Lane Davis is holding court again. With his hand-held microphone.

"I consider myself very lucky to live in the greatest country in the world. With the fairest system of justice. In many other countries, the government can get away with ruining a man's life with false charges. Not here. Not with someone as able as Judge Flynn to call it like it is.

"I told you Monday these charges were baseless. And you saw for yourself how utterly non-existent the prosecutor's case was. So now, ladies and gentlemen of the media, it's up to you. To report accurately that the prosecutor's irresponsible rush to bring charges was exposed by my very able attorney, Bruce Stuart, as nothing but a political ploy. An attempt to take the election away from the voters. Please tell your audience, the voters, that the prosecutor's effort failed. That I have been completely exonerated on all charges! As I promised I would be."

A roar goes up from the Davis supporters.

When the roar subsides, an *Ann Arbor News* reporter pipes up. "Were you surprised to learn that Rachel Clark has been secretly working as your paralegal the past fifteen years?"

"I was shocked," Davis says. "Of course. I had no idea."

"What do you think should happen to her? Should she be prosecuted? Or set free?"

"She should be set free. I would hope the prosecutor listened carefully to the evidence concerning the pennies—which proves her innocence, beyond any reasonable doubt."

Another reporter pipes up. "Jeff Sloan, *Detroit Free Press*. Mr. Davis, would you comment on the tabloid story that appeared this week, accusing you of marital infidelity?"

Davis turns red with anger. Spits into the microphone. "Yellow journalism at its worst. This afternoon, Professor Raven LaGrow and I will be filing a lawsuit for libel and invasion of privacy against *The National Spy*. And against reporter David Fisher, aka Sandy Hill."

"Does that mean you deny the charges made by *The National Spy*?" Sloan presses.

"I won't try that case in the media. Our lawsuit will speak for itself. And frankly, Mr. Sloan, you have much more important matters to report on. The most important election in this country's history is just five days away. Here in Ann Arbor, it's time to focus again on the issues. Judge Flynn has ruled. This election in Ann Arbor will be decided by the voters. Not by the prosecutor. Not by the police. And certainly not by the tabloids! So let's talk about the issues."

Davis launches into a campaign speech. Adroitly ducks all further questions about his "alleged affair" with Raven LaGrow. And all questions about Rachel Clark, too. No one even asks the one question they *should* ask. How exactly *did* Davis learn of the steam tunnel escape?

But there's no point in *my* asking the question. I'm being shunned by one and all. Dirty looks cascade my way like rain. From Camille. Sheila. Raven. And worst of all, from Janet.

Even my tabloid mates are shunning me. Like I'm a leper. On their faces I see amazement. Pity. And fear. *Amazement* that a tabloid hack could be forced to be a witness in a felony case. *Pity* that I've been forced to disclose some of the more unsavory methods of our work. And *fear* that I've become too dangerous a person to hang out with anymore.

All except the Germans. Who come over to stand beside me. In my hour of need.

At first I think it's ironic. The guys I've spent the past two weeks ducking. Taunting. And harassing. And here they are. Turning out to be my only pals.

But then the Germans hand me a brown envelope. And suggest I look inside.

Large glossy pix. 8x10s. Janet Fickel and me. Kissing at Dominick's. Wrapped in each other's arms in the doorway at the Law School. And wearing very little clothing at the Sheraton. (These last shots must have been taken through the window whose blind I evidently neglected to close.)

The Germans grin at me. But not in a friendly way. "We thought you'd want first chance to buy these lovely photos," one of the Germans says. In an Ah-nold Schwarzenegger accent.

"You guys aren't trying to blackmail me, are you? Right here in front of the courthouse?"

The Germans put on a look of mock horror. "Oh, no," one says. With broad sarcasm. "We would never do *that*," the other one chimes in. "That would be *illegal*."

"Good. I wouldn't want to have to report you guys to my new friend, Prosecutor Barnett. Tell you what, though. Why don't I keep these"—I take the envelope and stuff it in my briefcase—"and by way of payment, I'll buy you both several drinks at the nearest open bar we can find?"

The Germans exchange glances with each other.

"Deal," one says.

"But of course, we'll still have to discuss the *negatives*," the other one says.

"No we won't," I say.

"Why not?"

"Because you're going to give me the negatives, too. Free of charge."

"Why the fuck would we do that?"

"Professional courtesy."

# EPILOGUE
# PERISH THE THOUGHT

## Friday 1 September 2005

Ernest Hemingway once said: "All true stories end in death."

I'm not sure I buy that. I think all true stories end with messy loose ends. Cuz that's life.

Here, no one has died (so far). And only a few of the loose ends have been resolved.

The same day Lane Davis was exonerated, the Germans *did* give me the negatives. Not that they turned out to be good guys. But you don't blackmail future customers. I persuaded the Germans they'd make more money selling future celebrity pix to the *Spy* than blackmailing me.

That same day, Raven and Lane filed their lawsuit. As threatened. Graham hired Jonathan Lowe. Who worked out a settlement the day after the election. I'm not allowed to say how much we paid. But it was less than we paid Lowe for the two hours it took him to write up the settlement papers. Turns out Raven and Lane didn't want money. Just *cover*. So they could tell people "the whole story was a lie, we sued them, and they paid us to make it go away."

Jonathan Lowe also worked out a deal on the assault charges the Déjà Vu bouncers brought against me. I got "pre-trial diversion." Meaning if I keep my nose clean through all of 2005, the charges will be dropped. Eight months in, I'm beginning to think I might make it.

I got to know Jonathan Lowe. What with all the cases I brought him. Turns out the giant rat on his wall is only cuz he went to Ann Arbor Huron High. Lowe's an old River Rat. Like me.

Lane Davis lost the election. The Democratic incumbent was re-elected mayor.

Prosecutor Barnett was also re-elected. He took some hits for charging Davis on thin evidence. But Barnett's defenders scored points for him by noting that the Davis prosecution flushed out a notorious fugitive who'd been wanted for thirty-five years.

After the election, Prosecutor Barnett declined to bring charges against that notorious fugitive. Because of the pennies. No one questioned the decision. Not even Greg Hunter.

Rachel Clark gave no interviews. So my interview remained an exclusive. We ran it in the *Spy*. Even though it really wasn't a tabloid story. I won a prize. Not a Pulitzer. But a Newspaper Association of America prize. Not bad. Those prizes almost *never* go to tabloid hacks.

With no charges against Rachel Clark, even Greg Hunter saw no point in trying to figure out which of the old radicals had been aiding and abetting her. I considered doing a follow-up story. On the "secret radical underground." But decided I'd brought enough misery into their lives. So I left this loose end untied. Obviously Naomi's roommate helped her escape from my stakeout that Tuesday morning. But I never told anyone about the roommate, and I don't even know for sure if she knew who Naomi really was or why she needed to get away from me. My best guess is Sheila and Amy—and Ray and Ruth—were always helping Rachel. Best guess is Camille and Raven were not. As for Lane Davis, who knows? Not me.

Turned out there was one other person helping Rachel Clark. Inadvertently. Norma Lee. Norma was the reason Hunter mistakenly thought the fundraiser was still going on at 5:30 when Norma Lee was secretly taping the conference room unveiling of the helmet. Norma was rushing to the airport when she gave Hunter the tape recording Wednesday morning. Her account to Hunter of the Wednesday press conference, the Tuesday fundraiser, and the unveiling of the helmet came out as one garbled whole. Hunter came away believing Norma was there for the Tuesday fundraiser as well as the Wednesday press conference. Norma is such a wonderful ditz!

The one good deed I did in 2004 was the reward money. Rachel Clark couldn't claim it for turning herself in. But I persuaded Greg Hunter that *I* should get the money. Since I really found her. And forced her to turn herself in. Rachel Clark backed me up on this.

So Hunter gave the money to me. But only after we signed papers (drafted by Sheila Nyman) with my written promise to place the entire $200,000 into a trust fund. With just two beneficiaries. Boyce Hunter. And Sarah Pierce. The remaining victims. Then I delegated my trustee powers back to Hunter. To administer the trust in the best interests of Boyce and Sarah.

I'd love to report that, aided by the trust money, Boyce and Sarah have both kicked their drug problems. But life ain't so simple. They're trying. With the help of the reward money. And they'll probably spend the rest of what's left of their drug-shortened lives trying.

Why would I trust Hunter to do right by Sarah Pierce? Because Sarah won Hunter's heart, when she agreed not to press criminal or civil charges against Boyce—a decision Sarah reached with good counsel from Sheila, and her mother, and me. And because Hunter turned out to be a much better guy than I ever would have guessed. He abandoned his vigilante vow from 1969 to make Rachel Clark pay with her life for Dale's death—and put reconstructing the lives of Sarah and Boyce ahead of avenging Dale's death. In my book, that makes him a good guy.

The credit card bill from the Sheraton turned out to be no problem. I told Graham I put Sarah Pierce up for a night. When I thought she was a key witness. Graham wasn't born yesterday. His eyes told me he wasn't fooled. His eyes also said, "if you're this desperate to get me to pay a $150 hotel bill, I'll pay it." Graham's a pretty damn good boss.

The $2,500 personal check I wrote for the Barclay condo turned out to be more of a problem. Not to mention my signature on a one-year, $12,000 lease. But Brian the gay realtor turned out to be a good guy. Brian worked with me on it. Found another tenant four weeks later. No easy feat, in the slow season. Meanwhile, I told Elaine the condo was a place I needed for a stakeout. Told her Graham would reimburse us. Then, when Brian sent me $1,500 back from my $2,500 check, I acted like we'd be getting the rest from Graham soon.

Elaine wasn't born yesterday. Her eyes told me she wasn't fooled. Her eyes also said, "if you're this desperate to act like $1,500 from some guy in Ann Arbor is really Graham approving a $2,500 expense, I'm not asking any more questions." Elaine's a pretty damn good wife.

So I let the lie ride. For about a day. And then I couldn't stand it. So I confessed. The whole story. The one you just read. Soup to nuts. (With me in the soup. As the nuttiest of nuts.)

I told Elaine it was up to her. Whether to divorce me. Or to forgive me.

Elaine pointed out that this was classic David Fisher. Not making the hard choice myself. Getting *someone else* to impose the choice on me. Like Michigan Law School did, when they made me grow up. Like the *Enquirer* did, when they fired me. Like Janet did. When *she* fired me.

I pled guilty. To this—and all other—charges.

We had several rough weeks. Elaine asked me many times if I still loved Janet Fickel.

What could I say? I lied each time she asked. Said no, I don't love Janet Fickel anymore.

In the end, Elaine forgave me. Who knows why?

But I thank my stars she did. And I'm awful damn glad I still get to live with my kids.

It's taken longer to get our marriage back on the old footing. But Elaine and I are "working" at it. And gradually, the trust and easy loving is coming back.

Though I'm sure there will always be a scar. A very deep scar.

Loving Elaine is definitely easier than loving Janet. Because Elaine, like Janet, is one of the few women with whom I've ever managed to share both halves of Love's bitter mystery. The great romance. *And* the great sex. But unlike Janet, Elaine does not have this huge undifferentiated anger toward the male race. With Elaine, I never have to worry that somehow I've become a surrogate for other men whose crimes were committed without my complicity.

But you probably want to know: did I *learn* anything from my adventures in Ann Arbor?

I'd love to report that I am now a sadder and a wiser man. Chastened into wisdom. By failing so miserably at my quixotic attempt to lead two lives at the same time. Chastened back into fidelity. By failing so miserably at my quixotic attempt to love two women at the same time.

Anne Tyler once said, "if I weren't a writer, I'd be six times divorced, and schizophrenic. Because I've never really accepted the reality that I only get one life to live."

So I guess in 2004 I learned the wisdom of Anne Tyler's insight. That it's safer, by far, to lead one's alternate lives *vicariously*. By writing fiction. Rather than actually trying to lead two lives at once. Or trying to love two women at once.

And yet.

There's still a part of me that wonders. Did I fail with Janet only because I'm too timid? Wouldn't a *real romantic* keep on trying? Didn't Pierre Abelard stand outside Heloise's convent in the rain until they dragged him away? Shouldn't I besiege Janet with flowers and love letters and bad poems until finally her hard heart melts and we can ride off into the sunset?

Actually I've had lunch with Janet twice since the Davis case ended. She's not mad about me lying about my job. Or my Florida residency. But she's also not the least bit interested in me anymore, either. She wore shapeless slacks and baggy sweaters to both lunches. You've never seen someone dial down the heat so fast. From blazing passion to frosty ice. In four days.

And to this day Janet's never really explained why. And she never calls, either.

Of course, I've been in love with Beyonce for years, too. And Beyonce also never calls. But it hurts a whole lot more that Janet never calls. In fact, it drives me crazy. I just keep beating myself up. Like I did in that humiliating car break-up scene. Where I kept asking Janet, "what's wrong with me?"

Sure, my rational mind can see that Janet has her own faults. Which contributed at least as much to the failure of our romance as *my* deficiencies. Janet is the living embodiment of the old Groucho Marx self-esteem joke that Woody Allen used so well in *Annie Hall*: "I would never want to belong to any club that would have me as a member." Janet was flattered at first when I showered her with attention—but after a few weeks her self-doubt drove her to conclude, in classic self-defeating fashion, that anyone who could fall in love with her must be either crazy or worthless (or both). And so she cut and run. Her lifetime M.O.

But this rationalization doesn't make the rejection hurt any less. My irrational mind—the little voice of self-doubt we all have in the back of our heads—keeps muttering "Janet rejected you because you're still just the same old Number Zero you were back in high school." I try not to listen to that little voice. But no matter how hard I try, sooner or later, I get out the pix of Janet the Germans gave me, and beat myself up all over again.

The Germans weren't the only ones who provided me pix of my failed romance. Late last year the Main Street photographer sent me the proofs. Of my lunchtime shoot with Janet. So I ordered a few. To keep in a box. Along with the Germans' pix. And Janet's Sweetest Day Card. And her compilation CDs.

Actually, I listen to Janet's second compilation CD a lot. The one she gave me at Island Park. The day she blew me off. It's much more country/western than the first one. And instead of breathy female vocalists professing their undying lust for me, this CD is packed with bittersweet break-up songs by the likes of SheDaisy and the Dixie Chicks ("Funny how the girls get burned/Honey as far as I'm concerned/The tables have turned.") But painful though Janet intended the songs to be for me, I can't stop listening to them. Because those songs are the last link I have to Janet. To the love I felt was so right.

Of course, Happily Married Reader, you may feel there was *nothing right* about my illicit love for Janet Fickel. I won't argue the moral issue with you. Morally I'm bankrupt anyway.

But to paraphrase Dr. Laura Kipsis: Do we really believe people should be required, for the sake of marital fidelity, to cut off romance and sexual attraction to all other people? Isn't that as crazy as voluntarily amputating a healthy limb?

And even if we do it, for the sake of our marriages, whom are we kidding? Don't we still feel the phantom pain of the love we deny ourselves?

On the other hand, I can hardly recommend my Ann Arbor adventures as a blueprint for happiness. Trying to love two women simultaneously, I only ended up as confused as Rachel Clark. When she was finally freed of the need to be both Naomi Williams and Rachel Clark.

Rachel Clark spent some time this past winter in Centreville with Ray and Ruth. And Sarah. I'd love to report that they enjoyed a happy reconciliation. But life ain't so simple. They tried. Yet old tensions soon surfaced. In the end they concluded they were better off living apart. Ray and Ruth in Centreville. Sarah in drug rehab in Ann Arbor. And Rachel in California.

Officially Rachel's on "sabbatical" from Davis & Nyman. But no one expects her to come back. Ever. In fact, no one knows where the heck in California she is. Or even what name she's using. Sheila Nyman says Rachel was so used to being "Naomi" she couldn't adjust to living in Naomi's house and working Naomi's job while being known as Rachel Clark. Probably right. I also think Rachel got so used to living obscurely and anonymously for thirty-five years that she couldn't come to grips with all the notoriety and attention she got after the Davis prosecution. So she checked out to California. To start over again. With at least her fifth identity. In fifty-four years.

I feel there's a lesson in Rachel Clark's story that could help me.

If only I were smart enough to know what that lesson is.

Maybe the lesson is just, *"the grass isn't really any greener on the other side."*

Or maybe it's, *"be careful what you wish for, because you just might get it."*

But I think it's probably closer to Philip Dick's wry claim that *"insanity is sometimes an appropriate response to reality."*

Because it can drive you crazy. How the best moments in life are so fleeting.

One day there was Rachel Clark. In the prime of life. Nineteen and sexy as hell. Passionately interested in politics and poetry. Yet in ten minutes, it was all gone. No more boyfriend. No more college. No more Rachel Clark. Disowned by her parents. Forced into giving up her daughter. Forced into exile from her home. Forced into exile *from herself.*

And then thirty-five years later, when her harsh sentence was finally commuted, what did Rachel Clark find? The saddest truth of all. Her "real" life as Rachel Clark was even less appealing than her "fake" life as a fugitive with borrowed names. And borrowed lives.

And one day there was David Fisher. Not exactly in the prime of *his* life. Forty-eight and not especially sexy anymore. A tabloid hack for a third-rate tabloid. But then one day this aging tabloid hack was awakened from his mid-life slumbers. By a lively legal secretary. With a foxy strut. A wicked mouth. And a gift for romance she herself doesn't even know she has. Awakened to find himself still passionately interested in romance and poetry. Still capable of learning new things about Love's bitter mystery. And yet, in two weeks, it was all gone. Snatched away like Charlie Brown's football. No more Janet Fickel fantasies. No more fantasies about a new identity. Forced back into "real" life.

The hardest things in life are failure and aging. Failure, like aging, reminds us that Death is just around the corner. Waiting. And Death's a hard guy. Who accepts no excuses. Grants no adjournments.

Which is why no failure hurts like Love lost. Because Love is the one chance we get to shake our fist at Death. To say, *Fuck you buddy, life is so great right now, you can't hurt me.* But then, when you fail at Love, all you can do is admit, Death's gonna get you after all. And probably fairly soon.

In the meantime, I get up each day. Go to work. Love my kids. And love Elaine, too.

And I truly *do* love Elaine. All the more for her amazing capacity to forgive a schmuck like me.

So I play my part each day. The good husband. The good father.

But I still wake up wondering, was any of it with Janet real? Was any of it true?

Did I miss out on another life—the life I was truly meant to live?

Perish the thought.

Eventually, I will die. Elaine will die. And Janet will die, too.

And then, at last, I guess ours will be a true story.

# ACKNOWLEDGEMENTS

The narrator of *A Question of Identity* is a copycat. A serial imitator. And a rip-off artist.

In his meager defense, the narrator does expressly acknowledge most of his sources in the text of the novel. Thus at various places the narrator expressly credits:

(1) Composers Bob Dylan, Bob Marley, Bob Seger, Jim Morrison, Stevie Forbert, Stevie Nicks, Alfred Schnittke, Fountains of Wayne, SheDaisy and the Dixie Chicks.

(2) Poets William Shakespeare, W.B. Yeats, Wallace Stevens, Delmore Schwartz, Theodore Roethke and Maurice Sagoff;

(3) Novelists William Faulkner, Ernest Hemingway, Ralph Ellison, J.D. Salinger, James Baldwin, Philip Dick, Anne Tyler, Neil Gordon and Dan Brown;

(4) Humorists Yogi Berra, Dennis Miller, Groucho Marx, Woody Allen, Bill Murray, Jimmy Carter, George W. Bush, the editors of *World Weekly News* and the editors of the internet service called the "Darwin Awards";

(5) Philosophers John Stuart Mills, Emil Bergson, Alfred Kinsey and Laura Kipsis; and

(6) The screenwriters of *The Maltese Falcon, To Have And Have Not, From Here To Eternity, Splendor In The Grass, The Battle of Algiers, La Dolce Vita, Last Tango In Paris, Colombo, Body Heat, Fletch, Beverly Hills Cop, Les Miserables, Saturday Night Live!* and *Love Actually.*

But other sources deserve credit, too. Some of these unacknowledged sources are published authors; some are obscure friends of the author; some are both. Since none of them *asked* for credit, please understand: *only* credit should go to them. If you didn't like the way their ideas ended up being expressed in *A Question of Identity*, then blame *me*, not them.

First, major credit goes to Dr. Laura Kipsis, author of the marvelous polemic *Against Love*. Dr. Kipsis is a journalism professor at Northwestern. Who is ten-times funnier than Jay Leno—and ten-times more insightful about sex and adultery than Dr. Kinsey. If you read *Against Love*, you'll laugh out loud a hundred times. And you'll approach long-term romance with far more wisdom than you do now. Who knows how many ideas and phrases my narrator aped from Dr. Kipsis? Certainly not me. But it's a lot. Thank you, Dr. Kipsis.

Second, full credit goes to my friends David Gewanter and Craig Ross. David (author of *In the Belly* and *The Sleep of Reason*) and Craig (author of *The Obscene Diaries of a Michigan Fan*) persuaded me to try the comic narrative voice and the short staccato sentence fragments. Thus David and Craig deserve full credit for the fact that this novel scores out, on my computer's "readability" measure, as being written at the fourth grade level. But don't blame David or Craig for the sex and profanity. That's all my fault.

Third, extra credit goes to my friends Barry Kowalski, Bert Hornback, Barbara Babcock, Jonathan Shames and Sidney Gewanter. Barry inspired the comic anecdotes, "not guilty, not guilty" and "*if* that really is your name." Bert told me the stories of David Garrick, Branwell Bronte, and J.M.W. Turner. Barbara originated the "inadequate personality" anecdote. Jonathan told me about Schnittke's tombstone. And Sidney first coined the new verb tense, the "future evasive," to describe the tortuous syntax his nephew David and I used to avoid answering questions about what we planned to do if we ever grew up.

Fourth, special credit goes to my official editors, Sarah Hart and Ryan Schrauben, for their many great ideas, as well as my unofficial editors, Justin Adams, Joanne Barron, Joan Boonin, Hon. Timothy P. Connors, David Diephuis, Prof. David Gewanter, Gideon Hoffer, Angela Jackson, Susan Kessler, Hon. Melinda Morris, Craig Ross, Anne Rowe, Paul Saginaw, Prof. Theodore Trost, and Bruce Wallace, each of whom improved the manuscript with thoughtful suggestions.

Last, eternal credit goes to the four ladies of my family, Susan Kessler, Rachel Rowe, Kyla Rowe and Anne Rowe. In spite of the admonitions contained in the *Reader Advisory*, many readers will assume that David Fisher's family in *A Question of Identity* is, in truth, my own family, thinly disguised. This is not true. But I do acknowledge that Susan, Rachel, Kyla and Anne all contributed snippets of dialogue that make my persistent denials all the less convincing.

If anyone *else* should have been credited, please drop me a line. I won't deny ripping you off. But I will get you into the acknowledgments in the second edition. *If* there is a second edition.

# ABOUT THE AUTHOR

Jonathan Rowe was voted "Least Likely To Grow Up" by his high school class in Ann Arbor. In college his hero was "Zonker" from *Doonesbury*. Like Zonker, Mr. Rowe prolonged his student daze beyond belief, by piling up various interim degrees and low-paying writing awards—first at the University of Michigan, and later at Stanford University. Mr. Rowe's despairing relatives even invented a new verb tense—the "future evasive"—to describe his rare gift for switching programs just in time to avoid graduating from anything with actual job potential. Until one dark day in 1982, when a clerk at the Registrar's office informed Mr. Rowe that he'd accidentally graduated from the Stanford Law School.

Jonathan Rowe was then sentenced to a lifetime of hard labor as an attorney. He served twenty-three years—first as a federal prosecutor in Washington, DC, prosecuting criminal civil rights cases, and later in private practice in Ann Arbor, specializing in media litigation. Fortunately, Mr. Rowe's harsh sentence was recently commuted. He now writes fiction full-time.

Jonathan Rowe holds the Guinness world record for "Longest Continuous Mid-Life Crisis." And still shows no sign of growing up. He lives in Ann Arbor with his lovely and long-suffering wife, Susan Kessler, their joyously lippy teenage daughters, Rachel and Kyla, and their paranoid schizophrenic dog, Kafka. There is absolutely no truth to the vicious rumor that Mr. Rowe secretly writes for the tabloids under a *nom de plume*.